MURDER
AT
MIDNIGHT

MURDER
AT
MIDNIGHT

A LILY ADLER
MYSTERY

Katharine Schellman

CROOKED
LANE

NEW YORK

Copyright © 2023 by Katharine Schellman Paljug

Published in the United States by Crooked Lane Books, an imprint of The Quick Brown Fox & Company LLC.

Crooked Lane Books and its logo are trademarks of The Quick Brown Fox & Company LLC.

Library of Congress Catalog-in-Publication data available upon request.

ISBN (hardcover): 978-1-63910-432-1
ISBN (ebook): 978-1-63910-433-8

Cover design by Nicole Lecht

Printed in the United States.

www.crookedlanebooks.com

Crooked Lane Books
34 West 27th St., 10th Floor
New York, NY 10001

First Edition: September 2023

10 9 8 7 6 5 4 3 2 1

For the Paljugs.
I am so lucky to have you in my life.

And for Brian.
You're pretty great too.

CHAPTER 1

Hertfordshire, 1816

The snow began to fall just as the guests were arriving.

It was nothing more than a light dusting. But after a year with such uncommon weather, everyone glanced at the sky as they emerged from their carriages in their winter finery, swathed in yards of wool and fur to ward off the chill of the evening. The torches lining the drive of the country house, whipped into a frenzy by the bitter wind, illuminated the tumbling snowflakes briefly before they disappeared into the flames.

But after an uneasy glance upward, the guests turned their faces toward the glowing doors and windows ahead of them, lit from within by dozens of candles and hung with the cheerful splendor of holiday greenery. Laughter filled the air, and strains of music could be heard every time the front door opened to admit another guest.

Lily Adler, normally the sort of woman to take in every inch of her surroundings with a critical eye, barely noticed. Instead, even as she accepted her brother-in-law's hand and let him help her down from the carriage, her attention was fixed on the vehicle arriving just behind theirs and the two people emerging from it.

The first, a plump, stylish woman whose age was north of fifty but otherwise undisclosed, was laughing heartily as she alighted from her carriage. The second was the man making her laugh, tall and handsome, with one sleeve of his stylish driving coat pinned up over the spot where his arm was missing below the elbow.

"I ought to have told you Mother was inviting him for the week."

The comment made Lily start and drew her attention back to the man at her elbow. "I am amazed you kept the secret, John," she replied, giving her late husband's brother a wry look. Sir John Adler looked a great deal as his younger brother had, and it always gave Lily a wistful pang of memory to meet his eyes. But the resemblance between them was almost entirely physical. Freddy had been of a more cheerful nature than Lily, but his personality had been equally determined and driven. Sir John, on the other hand, was easygoing, a little absent-minded, and always eager to please the person with whom he was currently in conversation.

"It was not so much kept as forgot," he admitted, looking embarrassed as they waited for his mother, the dowager Lady Adler, and her guest to join them. "I kept meaning to write you, but . . ."

"There are many demands on your time, I am sure," Lily replied, her voice low.

"She means . . ." John hesitated. "That is, she wishes . . ."

"Your mother is hoping Mr. Spencer and I will make a match," Lily said, saving him the awkwardness of having to be the one who said it out loud. The sideways look she gave him was not entirely without humor.

"How did you know that?"

Lily patted John's hand. "She is not subtle in her designs. And she thinks I am far too young to stay a widow."

"Well, you are only . . ." He cleared his throat. "That is to say, we all wish—"

"And your wishes are well meant, I am sure, but they have no bearing on mine. Or Mr. Spencer's, for that matter." Lily's rebuke was delivered kindly, but there was a firmness to her voice, almost a sharpness, that her brother-in-law did not miss. It was hard to tell in the dim light of the torches, but Lily thought he blushed.

"Well, what *are* your—"

"Lady Adler," Lily interrupted him, fixing a smile on her face as the other two joined them, having navigated the slippery, frozen ground of the drive. She liked Sir John very much, but there were some questions of his she had no intention of answering. Particularly not when she wasn't sure what the answer was, or what she wished it to be. "Mr. Spencer. Shall we make our way inside to greet our hostess for the evening?"

"Indeed yes." Lady Adler smiled kindly.

She was always kind, always interested in what she thought was best for those that she considered her responsibility. Lily, whose own mother had died when she was an infant, could forgive Lady Adler a great deal because of that kindness. Lady Adler would have felt it her duty to help a daughter of her own, widowed at such a young age, to find a second happy marriage. And so she took it as understood that she would do the same for Lily. It did not seem to occur to her to ask whether Lily wanted such assistance.

"John, dearest, give me your arm, if you please. My eyes are not what they were in my younger years. My, did you see Mrs. Hammersmith entering with her daughters? Five of them, would you believe! And such pretty, accomplished girls. But I am sure I do not know any prettier or more accomplished other than our own dear Lily." Lady Adler cast a smile back over her shoulder. "Mr. Spencer, do give her your arm and step lively. Dear me, the snow is picking up . . ."

Matthew Spencer, the gentleman from Lady Adler's carriage, did as he was ordered. There was a dusting of snow on the shoulders of his driving coat, and in the torchlight, the brim of his hat cast shadows that were almost mysterious across his face. But even in that dim light, his smile was a force to be reckoned with, a mix of pure charm and genuine attention set in a distractingly handsome face. Lily had once teased him that he could probably get away with murder with the help of his smile.

Now, as he offered her his arm, there was a wry edge to that expression. He, too, was under no illusions as to why he had been invited to join the Adler family for the Christmas season. But they had not discussed it, for which Lily was grateful. They enjoyed each other's company. And she had spent far too long, after her husband's death, wondering whether she would ever enjoy any-thing again. For her, for now, it was enough.

"It has been some years since I have been to a Christmas ball," Matthew murmured as they climbed the steps behind Lady Adler and her son. "Our vicar does not approve, nor did his predecessor, of too much celebrating around the Christmas season." He pulled a face. "Too Catholic—and too pagan—for him."

"Let us hope that your children do not betray your secret once you return home," Lily teased. "Shall you have to bribe them?"

Matthew laughed. "There is no bribe can ensure a child will hold their tongue in such a case. They are guaranteed to speak as soon as it would be most embarrassing for their parent. Has Mrs. Grantham always hosted a Christmas ball for the neighborhood?"

"Since I have known the Adlers, yes," Lily replied. "It began as a small affair, the sort of party you often see this time of year, with dinner and music for friends. But apparently one year there was dancing, and then the next year there was more dancing, and now . . ."

Lily glanced around as they entered the house, reaching up to unclasp the neck of her cloak and letting it fall into the hands of the waiting footman. There were candles everywhere, blazing with light that was reflected from sconces and mirrors. Boughs of holly hung above the doors and windows, and ivy spilled out of pitchers on every surface. Everything sparkled, polished to gleaming, and the servants were all clad in new livery for the occasion. Down the expanse of carpeted hall, the doors to the ballroom stood open, and the strains of a pretty Highland tune drifted out.

"I think the pleasure of the evening will be worth the risk of my vicar's disapproval," Matthew murmured, once they had greeted their hostess and were following Lady Adler toward the ballroom. He looked down at Lily and smiled. "And of course, Mrs. Adler, I am always glad to be by your side."

Lily smiled, feeling no need to pretend that she was not pleased by the compliment. But she did not know if Lady Adler was close enough to hear their conversation, so she changed the subject.

"You were not too uncomfortable, I hope, having to leave your children the very first night you arrived?"

Matthew shook his head. "When I visited the nursery, they were already becoming fast friends with Sir John and the young Lady Adler's own children. I heard Eloisa declaring as I left that she would be the leader of their expedition to South America, as she is the oldest and best at reading maps. They practically pushed me out the door so they could return to their preparations."

"As far as South America? My goodness."

"They are most adventurous." His pleasure in his children was evident in his voice, but the sideways glance he sent her direction caught Lily off guard. "I promise, though, that I will not speak of my children all evening. I've no wish to try your patience."

"You need not worry on that score. I've grown quite fond of your children," Lily said, giving his arm a pat. Though she had no children of her own—and since Freddy's death, had come to think she likely never would—Matthew's care for his son and daughter was something she admired. Her own father had been a distant and disapproving parent, almost Matthew's exact opposite, and the comparison was always striking to her. It was one of the first parts of Matthew's character that she had truly appreciated.

As she had come to know him better, she had appreciated more about him, of course. His kindness carried into every aspect of his life, including his work with members of Parliament. They had grown easy in each other's company, and had even, the year before, begun a sporadic affair, spending nights and an occasional afternoon together when they found themselves in the same place. Lady Adler's obvious motives in inviting him and his family to Hertfordshire had made their reunion after so many months a trifle awkward. But Lily hoped Matthew would know her well enough to believe she had taken no part in such designs.

He gave her another glance that was almost relieved. "I am glad to hear it. They have enjoyed your company as well, I hope you know." He took a deep breath. "In fact, there is something I wished—"

He was interrupted that moment as the music broke off, the gentle background tune falling into a momentary jangle, then silence, before swelling into the strains of the evening's first dance. A murmur of delight went through the room as gentlemen found the partners they had solicited earlier in the evening and young ladies who had arrived more recently looked about hopefully for someone to request the pleasure of their company. With so many families in the country for the Christmas season and the Adlers not the only ones who had brought guests, the room was a busy, cheerful bustle as the dance began.

"You were saying?" Lily asked politely.

But Matthew merely shook his head. "What I ought to have been saying was that we must find you a partner. You mustn't sit out the first dance of the night on my account."

Matthew, who had lost one arm below the elbow to a wartime injury some years before, could manage many dances with no more trouble than a few adjustments. But the Scottish reel just beginning required the use of both hands, and he would not be able to complete the figures.

Lily was still curious to know what he had been about to say. "I am happy not to dance."

"Nonsense." Matthew smiled, giving a little shrug. "You're a lovely dancer, Mrs. Adler, and just because I cannot join in is no reason you should miss out on the pleasure. Besides." His gaze fixed on something over her shoulder. "I believe a partner has just arrived for you. And I can guess who is accompanying him, though I hope you will make the introduction."

Lily turned to see where he was looking. She was not a woman who put her emotions on display for all to see, especially not in a place so public as a ballroom. But she could not stop herself from smiling in welcome at the two people who were approaching, and to those who knew her, the delight in her expression was clear.

"Mrs. Hartley." Lily took the older woman's hand, dipping into a quick bow of greeting. "What a pleasure to see you."

"Lily." Mrs. Hartley's voice was low and musical, suited to the statuesque way that she moved and held herself. Her thick hair was piled on top of her head like a crown, jewels sparkling in the black locks, and everything about her dress was the height of fashion.

There were many who found her an intimidating woman, always so elegant that the reserve with which she surveyed the world could occasionally come across as disapproval. But Lily, who had met Mrs. Hartley shortly before her own marriage, had at once recognized in her a kindred spirit, a woman who had learned early on in life that it was not wise or safe to put her whole self on display. For Lily, that lesson had come at the knee of her father. Mrs. Hartley had learned it when she came to England more than three decades before, a young Indian bride forced to brave the sly glances and cutting whispers of her new peers to build a life with the British officer she had married.

But the Hartleys had been a fixture in the country village so long now that the glances and whispers were mostly memory. And having known Freddy Adler his whole life, Mrs. Hartley had welcomed Lily into her circle of intimates with no hesitation, for which Lily had always been grateful.

They shook hands warmly, Mrs. Hartley asking briefly after Lily's father and about her travels for the winter. "And will you introduce your friend?" she asked, turning a curious glance toward Matthew. Lily suspected by the lift of her eyebrows that Lady Adler had already informed her neighbor of exactly what manner of guest she was inviting.

Lily made the introduction while Matthew bowed, then turned to the man whose arm Mrs. Hartley was holding. "Captain." Her smile grew; though her friend was a faithful correspondent, they had not met in person for nearly half the year. "It is good to see you again."

Jack Hartley returned her smile. "And you, Mrs. Adler." The sincerity in his voice warmed her, in spite of the chill in the air. There were not many people Lily considered true friends. But Jack, who had been the boyhood companion of her husband and had become her own trusted confidant, was one of them.

A bit of a scoundrel by nature, he had his mother's good looks but little of her reserve. And he never lost an opportunity to tease Lily or make her laugh. So she was surprised when he offered no other comment or greeting, merely turning to Matthew and asking, "And how do you do, Mr. Spencer?"

"Well, thank you, Captain." Matthew glanced at Lily, a small frown gathering between his eyes, as though he could sense something was amiss between them. "How are you enjoying your return to Hertfordshire for the Christmas season?"

"It is good to be with my family again." Jack looked at his mother and around the ballroom for a quick moment before turning back to them.

"And we are as glad to have him with us," Mrs. Hartley agreed. "I, in particular, am delighted by his decision, as I am sure you can imagine, Mrs. Adler."

Jack had written nothing out of the ordinary in his last letter to Lily, but his mother was smiling as though confident that whatever her son's news might be, his friend would surely have heard it. Lily didn't bother to hide her curiosity. "I am sure I will be delighted as well, should he see fit to share this decision with us. Or is it a secret?" she asked, turning to Jack.

Whatever she might have expected him to say, Lily was unprepared for what came next. Looking far more serious than she was accustomed to him being, Jack replied, "I am resigning my commission in His Majesty's navy, just after the new year."

Had he announced that he was moving to the Arctic, Lily would not have been more stunned. He had mentioned once or twice over the last year that he had thought of giving up his commission, but he had never seemed serious about the idea, and Lily had never expected anything to come of it. Jack had been a navy man since he was a mere boy; to picture him permanently on land was almost impossible. She stared at him, unable to think of anything to say, equally stunned by the news as by the fact that she was only just now learning it.

"I do not know if congratulations are precisely in order," Matthew said, covering the surprised silence with admirable quickness.

"But I can say welcome to that particular fraternity, Hartley, of those who have left His Majesty's service and must now scramble for ways to occupy our time."

Jack laughed. "You seem to have busied yourself admirably, Spencer. I, however, lack political skill, and I've no children to demand my attention."

"Perhaps you might think about remedying that, dear one," his mother put in with a sly smile. "I'd be ever so pleased with more grandchildren. Shall I find you a dance partner once you've taken a turn with Mrs. Adler?"

"Oh, are we to dance, Captain?" Lily said, a little more archly than she intended.

Jack gave her a crooked grin. "I was coming to ask you, but if you and Mr. Spencer—"

"No need to worry about usurping my place for this one," Matthew said easily. He smiled down at Lily. "Though I hope you will rejoin me not too much later in the evening?"

"Were you not about to tell me something?" Lily asked, a frown gathering between her eyes.

He shook his head. "It can wait."

He looked as though he wanted to say more, and Lily wanted to ask what he was keeping from her, but she was too conscious of the other eyes on them. In the end, she gave a polite nod and turned to Jack. "Very well. I shall accept your kind invitation, Captain, even though you have not precisely issued one."

"How good it feels to be put in my place once again," Jack said cheerfully, making his mother laugh. But he looked more serious as he glanced at Mrs. Hartley. "Will you be with my sister when I return?"

Some of her mirth faded; she gave him a quick, tight smile and a nod. "Indeed. Enjoy yourself, my dear. No need to worry about me."

Matthew gave Lily's hand, which was still tucked into the crook of his elbow, a squeeze with his arm. "Enjoy your dance, Mrs. Adler," he said as he released her, and she took the hand Jack held out toward her.

"And I, meanwhile, shall have the pleasure of enjoying a very handsome man's company," Mrs. Hartley said, holding out her hand to Matthew with a regal air, though she smiled as she did so. "You may tell me about yourself, and in return I shall make sure you know all the best local gossip . . ."

"For heaven's sake, Jack," Lily said as he led her toward the dance floor. Some of the guests—the local ones—glanced at them as they made their way through the throng, their eyes lingering on Jack in particular. Lily was puzzled by the assessing glances they seemed to give him and wondered if news of his departure from the navy had already begun to spread. "Why did you write nothing of this to me?"

"Would you believe I hoped to surprise you?" he replied, smiling wryly. "I have so few opportunities to do so. And . . ." He hesitated, then shrugged. "I wanted to be confident in my decision before I announced it to anyone."

"And are you?" Lily asked as they took their places among the other couples.

The dance separated them for a moment, and Lily had to attend to the other dancers so she would not miss any steps. But when she and Jack took hands again, he nodded. "I am. It will be a change, certainly, but . . ."

He trailed off as the steps took them apart again. "Have you heard from Lady Carroway since you came to Hertfordshire?" he asked when they were rejoined.

It was a deliberate change of subject, but Lily did not protest. "There was a letter from her waiting when I arrived. She and Sir Edward are firmly settled in Somerset for the winter, but she sends her greetings."

"Good of her to think of us in her married bliss," Jack said, though his chuckle sounded a little forced. "I hope you will send her mine in return, when next you write."

Lily smiled as they parted once more. When they had first met, Jack and her young friend Ofelia, now Lady Carroway, had barely tolerated being in the same room with each other. But the three of them had survived more than one intrigue in the time since Lily had moved to London, and Ofelia had written of her impatience to see her friends together again when Jack was next ashore.

That thought made Lily glance at Jack again as she wove through the figures back to his side. He still looked uncommonly serious.

"Captain," Lily said, catching his arm just long enough to shake it a little as they passed by each other. Her tone was teasing. "For Captain you always will be to me. I would have expected you to take more pleasure in my company after such a long absence. Did you not miss me? Or has someone else taken over my responsibility to keep you in line?"

Jack did not rise to her bait. "I did miss you," he said quietly before they separated again. He glanced around the ballroom, as though looking for someone.

Lily's expression remained serene as they took hands with the other couples for the next figure, but she was growing nervous. Something had happened to upset him, she was sure. She watched him glance around the room once more, his eyes fixing on a small group of people in the far corner, before his attention returned to the dance.

"Jack." As the song ended and the dancers bowed, accompanied by the polite applause of the rest of the guests, he offered his arm. Lily took it, but instead of letting him lead her back to their party, she pulled him a little way away from the crowd.

The ballroom's tall windows were set back in alcoves, their curtains pulled against the chill that seeped through the glass. Glancing around to make sure no one was too close by, Lily stepped back into one alcove. They were not alone, nor were they completely out of sight. But they were shielded from the view of many of the guests, and the heavy fabric of the curtains would muffle the sound of their conversation, affording them some privacy as long as they kept their voices low. In the gap between the curtains, Lily could see the snow still falling, thick and heavy against the darkness.

She glanced around to make sure no one was close enough to overhear them before fixing her gaze on Jack. "What has you so distracted tonight?" When he hesitated, she asked quietly, "It has something to do with your sister, does it not?"

Jack had been born in the middle of his family, with one brother his elder and two sisters after him. One of those sisters was married and living to the north with her husband and children. The other, the youngest of the four siblings, stood just at her mother's elbow while they talked with Lady Adler and Mr. Spencer. Amelia Noor Hartley, according to her older brother, had been quiet, studious, and occasionally a little spoiled while growing up. Now she was a cheerful young lady who, though she might have inherited some of her mother's reserve, seemed to be doing nothing more than having a lovely time at a Christmas ball.

But Lily had seen the way Jack kept glancing toward his sister, as though determined to keep an eye on her. And even Mrs. Hartley, normally enigmatic, looked tense every time her youngest child joined in the conversation.

Jack lifted his hand as though to run his fingers nervously through his hair before he recalled the time it must have taken his father's valet to style it. He dropped his hand and smiled wryly. "I ought to have guessed you would see through us. My mother has charged me not to say anything of it tonight, but . . . as you have guessed, it is weighing on me."

"What is?" Lily asked softly.

"That is the trouble." Jack blew out a frustrated breath. "I do not know."

Lily frowned. "Explain, please."

Jack grimaced. "I discovered when I arrived home this week that my sister is involved in some sort of . . . well, there has been gossip. Speculation. And there are enough versions of the story being tossed about that it is hard to see how her reputation can escape undamaged."

Lily glanced toward where Amelia stood, chatting calmly with Mr. Spencer, looking nothing like a young lady whose public standing hovered at the edge of disaster. "What does your sister say of it?"

"That is one of the most troubling parts of the whole business. Amelia seems determined to pretend that there is no scandal at all. And she has steadfastly refused to tell any of us what truly happened."

CHAPTER 2

"Has she told you anything at all?" Lily murmured, trying to peer out of the alcove without attracting attention.

She wasn't looking at Amelia this time, but at the party guests surrounding her. Now that she knew what to look for, she could see the glances—sly or curious or scornful—directed toward the youngest Hartley. Neither Amelia nor her mother acknowledged the onlookers, but they were unquestionably there. And if the whispers hadn't yet begun to follow the glances that evening, it was only a matter of time before they did.

Lily thought of the quick, tense exchange between Jack and his mother, of the considering looks that many of the other guests had given him as they made their way to the dance floor.

It wasn't just Amelia whose reputation was at risk. Her whole family could suffer by association. But she—young, unmarried, and a child of mixed heritage—had the most to lose from a scandal. She stood the greatest chance of becoming a pariah in her own home.

"Nothing." Jack followed Lily's gaze, his brows drawn together in a worried frown as he watched his sister. "We know the man's name, and that whatever it was happened at a dance the vicar and his wife were giving for the young people of the neighborhood. What kind of fellow gets up to something nefarious at a vicarage?" he added, looking disgusted.

"You do not know for sure that it was nefarious," Lily pointed out. "Given the lack of detail available."

"Whatever the truth of the matter, it was nefarious enough," Jack said. "Before we left that evening, there were rumors spreading that Amelia had been seen with him, alone, in the garden. And within a very few days, the speculation about what they might have been seen doing was . . ." His mouth twisted in a humorless smile. "Creative."

"People do tend to be at their most creative when they are finding ways to judge the behavior of young women."

Jack sighed, slumping against the wall, then straightening abruptly. They were still in full view of the ballroom, after all, and a family that was the subject of so much speculation could not afford for its members to appear distraught. "I thought if anyone could persuade Amelia to say what truly happened, it would be me. She always seemed to look up to me. But she has been resolute in her silence. To talk to her, you would think nothing untoward happened at all."

"Perhaps nothing did happen," Lily suggested.

Jack shook his head. "She would have said so. But she has refused to discuss the matter at all, which tells me *something* passed between them." He sent a scowl in his sister's direction. "She has never kept secrets from me before," he muttered.

"That you know of," Lily pointed out, earning a scowl of her own. "But that is beside the point." She looked up at his worried face and asked simply, "How can I help?"

The smile Jack gave her was pure gratitude, though it was still tense with worry. "That's the fellow right there," he said, gesturing for Lily to join him in peering around the corner of the alcove. "In the burgundy coat, with the striped waistcoat beneath, just going down the line now."

"A very handsome young man," Lily said thoughtfully. "If Amelia did choose him for some illicit rendezvous, she has good taste. If one judges by appearances alone, that is."

"Lily," Jack said sternly.

"Which I never do," she continued, giving his arm a reassuring pat. "Is he not Mr. Edison's son? What is his given name?"

"Gregory," Jack supplied. "Yes, he's Edison's son. The oldest of the bunch. He has been away a great deal these last few years, first at school and then with his godparents either in Bath or London, depending on their mood. My mother says that since his return last spring, he has become the local charmer."

Lily nodded. "And what are your plans for young Mr. Edison?"

Jack sighed. "I considered beating an admission out of him, but that might reflect poorly on Amelia."

"Likely." Lily gave him a sympathetic look. Jack was a born protector; it had to pain him to see his sister in difficulty and be unable to help. "I think the best we can do tonight is pay attention. Is the rest of his family here?"

Jack shook his head. "One of his brothers, likely. My mother says they are often in each other's company. But his parents do not socialize much, and the other children are still too young for such gatherings."

"Do you know who began the rumors?"

Jack grimaced. "Perhaps Amelia does. But once again, she refuses to reveal anything. And she and young Mr. Edison are staying far away from each other."

"Wise of them, under the circumstances." Lily nodded firmly. "Well, if we keep our ears open—"

"And what are the two of you up to so secretly?"

The unexpected voice made Lily start, though she hid the motion as she turned to see who had joined them. Her mind reeled for a moment at being suddenly pulled out of such a serious conversation, and she worried about what might have been overheard. Out of the corner of her eye, she saw Jack tense.

She stepped between him and the newcomer to give him time to compose himself. And her smile, as she held out her hands, was genuine. "Peter," she said warmly. "It has been too long."

"Lily." He bowed over her hands. He was a quiet, unassuming man, around Jack's age, with sandy hair and a weak chin that was not helped by his fashionably tall shirt-points. But he had been good friends with Freddy Adler when he was still alive, and Lily was fond of him. He and his mother had been regular visitors in the two years after Freddy's death when she was still living with the Adlers.

He smiled good-naturedly at her. "How have you been? Still gallivanting about London, I hear? I was not sure we would see you before the end of the year."

"Hardly gallivanting, though I do enjoy London very much," Lily said, scrambling a little to gather her thoughts. "But I am happy to spend some time with the Adlers. And your mother, is she here as well?"

"I spotted Mrs. Coleridge holding court in the cardroom a short while ago," Jack put in. "Coleridge, how do you do?"

Peter laughed, but Lily noticed a hint of a grimace in his expression. "Mother always does find herself an audience to command," he said, shaking his head. "I'm well, Hartley, thank you. I hear you will finally rejoin those of us on land. Are congratulations in order? Or perhaps commiseration?"

Peter shook Jack's hand as he spoke. They did not know each other well. But Freddy Adler had been the sort of man who wanted his friends to be friends with each other, so they had become at least acquainted in the times that Jack was back on land and visiting his family.

"My answer varies on the hour," Jack replied.

Peter glanced briefly in the direction Jack and Lily had been watching. "And how is Miss Amelia?" he asked, lowering his voice.

"You know about these rumors, then?" Lily asked, her attention sharpening on Peter. He wasn't the sort of man who engaged in frequent gossip, and he was more likely to miss social undercurrents than to participate in them. If he had heard rumors about Amelia, then the news had spread to a startling degree.

Peter looked apologetically at Jack. "Nothing definite, of course. And no doubt it will all be put to rest soon." His smile was downright encouraging as he added, "A quick marriage, I imagine, whether to the fellow involved or someone else? Has your family discussed potential matches?"

"What?" Lily asked, caught off guard. Jack hadn't said anything about a marriage—and glancing at him, she thought he was as taken aback as she was.

"Well, naturally." Peter looked surprised, as though they were foolish not to be thinking the same thing. "As my mother said when she heard, a wedding is the surest way to still the wag of gossiping tongues. I've no doubt, Hartley, your parents are thinking the same."

"If they are, they have not informed me or my sister of it," Jack said, his voice and his back equally stiff. "Amelia is young yet to think of such things."

Peter seemed to realize he had misspoken and flushed with embarrassment. He had always embarrassed easily, Lily remembered. "Of course, of course. To be sure. Well." He cleared his throat. "Well, whatever is being said, it will blow over soon. And in the meantime, I can assure you I do not believe a word of it."

"Good of you," Jack said, a trifle shortly, but Lily couldn't blame him for that. "Your opinion carries some weight in the village these days, after all."

Peter cleared his throat again. "Well, yes, as to that, I am sure I deserve it no more than the next fellow."

"Why, Peter, what does that mean?" Lily asked, motivated as much by genuine curiosity as by a desire to introduce a new subject to the conversation. "What have you been getting up to since my departure?"

"Nothing, really, I can assure you. It's not something I like to—"

"He is being delicate because it involves talk of money," Jack interrupted. "Coleridge has been making himself rich, and half the neighborhood along with him. At least, those with sufficient ability to invest in his Irish properties."

"It's called the Irish Consolidated Banking Concern," Peter explained, looking apologetic at having to talk about himself while his blush grew under Lily's scrutiny. "You know my family holds a number of financial concerns there. They have been doing so well,

I began taking on other investors last year, and I hope to do very well by my neighbors through it."

"Quite the popular fellow, as a result," Jack said.

"The initial returns have been well received," Peter said modestly. He hesitated, then added, "I do not wish to presume, Lily, but I know managing one's broader finances is a task that women are rarely prepared for. Should you need any advice when it comes to—"

"You are good to think of me," Lily said, polite but firm. "But I could never do business with a friend."

He was not entirely wrong. No one had ever taught her to manage her own income and investments, assuming that she would never need to understand more than pin money as a child and household accounts as a wife. And Peter, in spite of having six elder sisters, had long been accustomed to managing the finances of his whole family as his sisters married and moved away one by one. But Lily couldn't help resenting the implication that, three years after her husband's death, she might have been content to remain ignorant.

"I've no wish to risk any awkwardness that might affect our goodwill down the road. Besides," she added, a little playfully so that Peter wouldn't be offended, "the gentleman Sir John arranged to advise me in such matters would be most put out if I made any changes without consulting him. He looks like a grandfather, but I have heard him roar like a lion."

Peter nodded, looking somehow both disappointed and relieved. "I am glad to hear you have advisers you can trust. Though I am sure the Adlers would have allowed nothing else—"

"Coleridge!" a gentleman bellowed cheerfully, making them all start. Lily didn't recognize him, but she could guess from the slight sway to his step that he had already sampled deeply from Mrs. Grantham's sherry and port. "Good to see you, man, good to see you. Can I persuade you to a game of vingt-et-un?"

"Shortly," Peter said with an amiable smile. "If my companions will excuse me?"

"By all means," Lily said. "Do not let us keep you from your entertainments."

"Oh, by the by," the gentleman said, slinging a friendly, drunken arm about Peter's shoulders as he towed him away. "The elder Edison was looking for you; did he ever pin you down? No doubt he wants to talk about joining your little arrangement . . ."

"I ought give my mother a respite and take my turn at Amelia's side," Jack said, once they were alone again.

"Is it as bad as all that?" Lily asked, turning to look at Amelia. Jack's sister was still making polite conversation with her mother and a number of other women, but she was starting to look around the room a little restlessly.

"Not yet," said Jack, looking grim. "But I'll not allow it to become worse."

With that grim thought hanging over them, they made their way back. Both Mrs. Hartley and Amelia greeted them with evident relief.

"Raffi, you've brought Mrs. Adler to see me at last," Amelia said, curtsying prettily. Lily had always found their custom of calling each other by their middle names—the names chosen by their mother, rather than their father—to be deeply endearing. The first time she had asked Jack about it, he had told her all four of his siblings did so, though his parents might call their children by either or both of their given names, depending on how stern they were feeling.

Lily smiled, bowing in return. "It is good to see you again, Miss Hartley."

"Do you mind if I take a turn about the room, dear ones?" Mrs. Hartley asked. Lily did not miss the slight flick of her eyes toward her daughter. "Mrs. Robertson and I need to discuss the new teacher at the parish school."

"Not at all," Jack said, nodding gravely.

Lily watched the whole exchange, then glanced at Amelia. The girl's lips were pursed slightly as she followed the interplay between Jack and her mother. But whether she was amused, annoyed, or simply resigned, Lily could not tell.

"Hmm," Amelia said, briefly and cryptically, once they were alone.

"What does that mean?" Jack demanded.

Amelia gave him a condescending look, then turned back to Lily. "How are you enjoying your family visit, ma'am? It has been some time since you were last with us in Hertfordshire."

"Too long," Lily replied warmly. "I have missed the Adlers."

"And they you," Amelia said. She had followed Lily's line of sight and now was watching Lady Adler thoughtfully. "I think they still see you very much as a member of the family, as their connection to dear Freddy." She glanced at her brother. "The same for you, Raffi. Lady Adler looks for news of you almost as often as Mama and I do."

"Then it is good I am such an excellent correspondent," Jack said with a chuckle.

Lily smiled with them, but she could tell Jack's merriment had a forced edge to it. He had taken up a position next to his sister that was almost guardlike, and he sent more than one scowling look into the crowd.

"You and Raffi made a lovely couple out there on the dance floor," Amelia added. "Though I saw that you entered the ballroom with a gentleman who is far handsomer than my brother. I applaud your taste."

"Mr. Spencer is a good friend, to be sure," Lily said, unable to stop herself from putting an extra emphasis on the word *friend*. "Did Lady Adler have a chance to introduce you?"

"He is not more handsome than I," Jack interrupted indignantly.

"*Far* more handsome," Amelia said with a younger sister's smugness. "And yes, she did. He was charming, and—" She broke off, her amused expression dimming as a pair of young ladies walked past, both of them cutting their eyes in Amelia's direction before turning to whisper behind their hands in a way that was clearly meant to be noticed. Amelia lifted her chin. "And it was so pleasant to speak with someone new for a change. Someone with things to say that were actually interesting." Her voice rose on the last few words, and the young ladies scooted away as if they were being chased, though their whispers did not abate.

Jack watched them depart with his jaw clenched. "Do you wish to dance, Noor? I would be happy to find a partner for you."

"No need," she said, looking unconcerned. Up close, Lily thought that air of indifference might be costing Amelia a great deal to maintain, but if she had not been looking carefully, she would not have noticed. "In fact, I must beg you to excuse me for a moment."

"What? No, indeed not," Jack said, affronted. "How you could think of going off by yourself, at a time like . . . Wherever you need to go, I shall accompany you."

"You needn't stick to me like a burr on a horse," Amelia said, her exasperation plain. "How much trouble do you think I shall get up to?"

"I don't know, Noor, how much will it be this time?" Jack asked, glaring at her. "You managed to surprise us all before."

Amelia sighed, accepting her fate with a shrug. "Well, you cannot accompany me where I must go next, as only ladies are permitted."

Jack gritted his teeth. "Are you being deliberately provoking?"

"No." Amelia laughed at his expression. "But I did have rather a large glass of punch when we first arrived. Shall we go find our mother, then?"

"No need," Lily interjected. "If your brother will allow me to play chaperone?"

Jack nodded gratefully. "I shall wait here." He fixed Amelia with a stern look. "We are only trying to look out for you, you know."

"I know," she said, looking serious at last. "I just wish you would not worry. I wish you did not *need* to worry."

"It will blow over soon," Jack said, giving her arm a squeeze. "Keep your chin up and pay no mind to what anyone says."

"Will you follow that advice too?"

"No," Jack grimaced. "And if I hear too many more things that I mind, I might have to start knocking some heads together."

"That will quash the rumors for certain," Lily said dryly. "Come along, Miss Hartley."

"From what I hear, Mrs. Adler, you get up to plenty of trouble on your own," Amelia said as they made their way to the retiring room set aside for the party's female guests. "Though I suppose it is of a different variety."

"I like to think I help solve problems rather than create them," Lily said.

"Well, I recently heard a rumor that you helped to solve the problem of a missing set of emerald earrings," Amelia said, giving Lily a sly look as they paused in front of the doorway. "That cannot be true, can it?"

"How on earth did you hear of that?" Lily asked, not sure whether to be flattered or worried that news of her assorted investigations had made it as far as Hertfordshire.

"From my brother, of course," Amelia said. "Did you really? Had someone stolen them?"

"The owner's son," Lily admitted. "Young people often do unwise things when they would be better off simply talking to their parents about the trouble they are in."

Amelia gave her a sideways look, her mouth thinning for a moment before she shrugged. "I suppose that is meant as a lesson for me," she said with forced lightness as she turned away. "I hope you will not be too disappointed if I do not follow it."

"I will be unsurprised, at least," Lily replied, shaking her head.

That made Amelia laugh as she pushed open the door of the retiring room. Lily followed her inside. She waited in the comfortable room, where a few women clustered around the toilette table, while Amelia excused herself into the adjoining chamber that had been set up as a washroom. When she emerged, a mother had just ushered her daughter into the room and was asking if there was something on hand with which to mend a tear in her dress that stretched nearly to one knee, leaving an unseemly portion of the young lady's leg on display.

There were brief murmurs of "Let me see" from the women present. Amelia, who had her reticule in hand, spoke up.

"I've a paper of straight pins. Will that do, Miss Rutledge? They should tide you over for the evening." Smiling in a friendly fashion, she held them out to the girl.

The girl was reaching out to take them, beginning to offer her thanks, when her mother laid a hand on her arm. "You're very kind, I'm sure, Miss Hartley, but we've no need."

Amelia's jaw tightened, but her voice stayed calm as she replied, "Mrs. Rutledge, I just heard you ask—"

"Thank you for your offer of assistance, Miss Hartley," the woman said, a little more loudly, as she gave her daughter's arm a tug, forcing her to step away from Amelia. "But as I said, we've no need."

Amelia's lips parted as though she was about to reply, and Lily could see the snap of temper in her eyes. The other two women in the room were deathly silent, watching the miniature drama unfold with undisguised interest. But Amelia merely closed her mouth on a thin smile, inclining her head as politely as if the woman had just paid her a compliment. "Mrs. Rutledge. Miss Rutledge. Do enjoy the rest of your evening."

She stalked out of the room, her shoulders tense but her head held high. Lily did not follow immediately.

"Really?" she said, fixing Mrs. Rutledge with an icy stare. "You could not accept the loan of a pin?"

The woman's mouth tightened peevishly, her cheeks pink with embarrassment. "I'll thank you not to judge—"

"That is a rich request from a woman clearly full to the brim with judgments," Lily said, not bothering to keep the scorn out of her voice. "And you've hurt your own daughter in the bargain, who is now stuck with ten inches of torn skirt and no means of repairing it."

"Madam, I do not know who—"

"Virtue is not passed through the loan of a pin," Lily said coldly. "And if it were, you would have done better to accept, as the only virtue I have seen on display here was the offer of aid to someone so clearly undeserving of it."

"Mama, what are we to do about my dress?" Miss Rutledge whispered, tugging at her mother's sleeve.

"A very good question." Lily gave Mrs. Rutledge one more scornful look. "Do enjoy answering it," she said as she swept out of the room after Amelia.

Whom she found waiting in the hallway. "I do not need anyone coming to my defense, you know," the girl said, a little crossly. Then she sighed. "But I am grateful for it."

"Whoever she is, she is a spiteful cow," Lily said, her temper still high as she followed Amelia back toward the ballroom.

"I feel sorry for Miss Rutledge, at least," Amelia said. "It is a shame for such a pretty dress to be ruined. And she must have been mortified when it ripped. She is only sixteen, you know."

Lily gave her a sideways glance. "You are very calm about it."

Amelia shrugged. "As you pointed out, her own daughter was the most injured by her behavior. I emerged unscathed. Such opinions have no power to wound me."

Lily hesitated. She admired Amelia's sentiments, but they were true only to a certain point. Past that, if the gossip became more vicious, Mrs. Rutledge's behavior would look mild in comparison. Amelia could find herself snubbed and scorned everywhere she went.

Just as she was debating whether or not to argue—was it worth pointing out something that Amelia surely already knew, even if she was determined to put on an air of unconcern?—they were interrupted by two women, gossiping furiously on their way to the retiring room.

"She would have done better to wear her pearls with a gown like that."

"Didn't you hear? They went missing after that dinner they gave."

"Really? Mr. Robertson said his sapphire cravat pin disappeared as well, after that party the Hounslows gave in the fall."

"Do you think there is a thief in the village?"

"Surely not—" The woman broke off, eyeing them in surprise. "Lily Adler. How surprising to see you this evening. And in company with our dear Miss Hartley." She smiled, and it was not a kind expression. "How is your evening, Miss Hartley?"

"Perfectly pleasant, Mrs. Taylor," Amelia said with no hesitation. "And yours?"

Lily had known Caroline Taylor a while back when she was Caroline Reed, during her first marriage. Their paths had not crossed often, and other than being vaguely aware of Caroline's second marriage, Lily did not know much about her.

"I am surprised you've not been dancing this evening," Mrs. Taylor continued, pursing her lips with false thoughtfulness. "Was it not just a few weeks ago that your company was so sought after by the young men of the neighborhood? Strange," she added, smiling once more. "Surely there is no reason you might wish to avoid being seen in such *close* quarters with a gentleman?"

"I am sure you know a great deal of such matters," Amelia said calmly. "Were you not quite *close* with my brother for some time after the death of your first husband?"

Lily's eyes widened, though she managed to keep any other signs of surprise from her face. She had forgotten that Jack had once had an affair with Mrs. Taylor. It had been a short-lived thing, in any case, when he was home on shore leave for the summer, and Mrs. Adler had written of it with great and scandalous relish. Lily had found it amusing at the time, though that had been before she knew Jack so well as she did now. The woman in front of her was certainly beautiful, and she was said to be engaging and clever in her manner. But Lily could only hope that her character had grown worse in recent years, rather than Jack's judgment having been so poor once upon a time.

Mrs. Taylor's jaw clenched, while her friend tittered. But she inclined her head as though in grudging respect for Amelia's rejoinder. "True enough, my dear. But remember, I had the good judgment to avoid such situations until I would not become a pariah as a result."

"I see no pariahs here," Lily pointed out. "Only four women who were all invited to the same Christmas party."

Mrs. Taylor laughed a little. "Well said, Mrs. Adler. And what a pleasure it is to see you returned to the neighborhood. And wearing colors?" She gave Lily a look up and down, taking in the deep blue of her gown, a far more vibrant shade than the hues of half mourning that Lily had still been wearing when she left Hertfordshire. "I always approve of a woman moving on with her life. One cannot stay tied to a dead man."

"We are always tied to those we love," Amelia said, before Lily, stunned, could think of how to reply. "At least, those of us who live our lives with deep affection. Though perhaps that does not include everyone here."

Mrs. Taylor's smile grew thin as her friend tittered again. "A bit of advice, dear Miss Hartley. I would be wary of talking too broadly about my propensity for *deep affection*, were I you. There are those who might make assumptions. Come along, Mary," she added briskly, giving a tug on her friend's arm. "We mustn't stand here all evening."

"I've always thought a hasty departure to be a cheap way of ensuring that one has the last word in an argument," Lily said, watching them disappear down the hall.

Amelia let out a snort of laughter. "Please call her cheap in front of my brother. I should love to see the look on his face." She watched Mrs. Taylor go, then wiggled her shoulders, as though shaking off an unpleasant sensation. "I am glad he does not show any inclination of taking up with her again," she added.

"He wouldn't, not with a married woman," Lily said, a little more sharply than she intended. But there was no chance of Jack's doing something so dishonorable—his character was unimpeachable, even if she couldn't, at the moment, say the same of his judgment.

"No, he would not," Amelia agreed. She glanced sideways at Lily. "You know, there is at least one way in which I have found myself in less trouble than you, Mrs. Adler."

"And what way is that?" Lily asked.

"I have not found myself embroiled in any kind of murder."

That, at last, made Lily turn to stare at her. "Your brother told you of that too?" she asked, horrified.

"He tells me nearly everything," Amelia said, smirking a little in an expression that was disconcertingly reminiscent of Jack.

"A shame you do not extend him the same courtesy," Lily pointed out softly.

Amelia's face fell, but she shrugged once more. "Yes, well. As the saying goes, least said, soonest mended. Shall we return to the ballroom before my parents send out a search party?"

CHAPTER 3

Amelia's mother did not bother to disguise her relief when they rejoined her. But however worried she had been, she still greeted them warmly. "There you are, dear one. Are you enjoying yourself this evening?"

"As much as I can, though I've not had the pleasure of a dance yet," Amelia said, sliding her arm around her mother's waist and giving her an affectionate peck on the cheek. Mrs. Hartley held her tightly for just a moment before releasing her almost reluctantly, a protective gesture that brought a lump to Lily's throat. Whatever Amelia might be facing, she was fortunate to have her family so firmly on her side.

The Adlers, Lily was pleased to see, were offering their support as well. Lady Adler's stately presence dared anyone to offer an off-color comment in her presence. And at Amelia's words, Sir John stepped forward.

"Would you do me the honor of joining me for the next one, Miss Amelia?" he asked.

Sir John was pleasant and an excellent dancer, qualities that would make him a desirable partner, even though he had known Amelia since she was born and was already happily married. But more importantly, he was respected by his neighbors and a baronet—two factors that would go a long way toward counteracting any gossip or rancor directed toward the youngest Hartley. In a small village like theirs, something as simple as whether or not men were willing to dance with Amelia could do a great deal of either repair or damage to her reputation. Lily felt a burst of pride for her brother-in-law, and she saw his mother and Mrs. Hartley nod in approval.

"With the greatest pleasure, Sir John," Amelia said, the gravity of her response a clear indication that she understood exactly what his gesture meant. As she took his offered arm and let him lead her to the dance floor, Lily heard her murmur more quietly, "You, sir, are an extraordinarily kind man."

The musicians were beginning the opening bars of a waltz, a dance that just a few years before would have been deemed too *risqué* to be played at a country ball. There were a few titters around the room, and one or two disapproving looks. But for the most part, the guests seemed pleased at the prospect, and many couples were beginning to turn about the room.

Matthew Spencer held out his arm to Lily. "Mrs. Adler, may I have the honor?"

He had to hold her closer than he might otherwise have done in public, his right hand clasping hers and the elbow of his left arm resting gently against her side, just under her shoulder, to guide her through the turns. The first time they had waltzed together, he had waited for a particularly slow song to ask her, wanting her to have time to adjust to how he had relearned to lead. But they had waltzed together enough now that they could turn about the room easily, enjoying the cheerful sweep of the music, which was underlaid with the tune of a traditional wassail carol.

The pace of the dance was quick enough that it did not leave much breath for talking, and when it ended, Lily found that Matthew had steered them to the opposite end of the ballroom from where her friends waited. When she gave him a curious glance, he smiled a little slyly.

"Will you sneak away with me for a moment?" he murmured, his head by her ear.

Lily considered for a moment. As Mrs. Taylor had pointed out, cruelly but truthfully, the actions of a widow were given far different weight that those of an unmarried young woman. Besides which, she had missed Matthew. And she had a suspicion of what he was going to suggest.

"Very well," she murmured in response. "As it seems no one is watching us just now. Perhaps we can find somewhere private for a moment or two?" Matthew offered her his arm, and moving sedately so as not to attract attention, they left the ballroom.

The corridor he had chosen led toward the cardroom, where Lily remembered Peter's mother was said to be holding court. But halfway down the hallway another passage opened up, and they were able to slip down there when no one was looking.

It led them to a series of rooms, one of which proved to be a small study. They could still hear the music from the ballroom, even after Matthew closed the door behind them. For a moment, the room was dark except for a banked fire, so Lily crossed to the window and pulled the curtains open while Matthew bent to light a branch of candles.

The open curtains let in more light than she had been expecting. It was coming off the ground, she realized, where a thick layer of snow had fallen and was reflecting the moonlight, even as the clouds gathered overhead. Enchanted, Lily opened the window, which was tall enough to be practically a door, and stepped out onto the narrow terrace, barely more than a ledge.

There was enough of an overhang above her that the snow was not deep just outside the window; the heels of her shoes made a soft crunch on the fresh powder. Beyond the terrace, though, she could see many inches of snow had already gathered on the ground, and more was still falling, heavier and thicker by the moment. She was stunned by its loveliness, enough to make her forget for the moment that goose bumps were springing up all over her body. She had never seen so much snow before in her life.

"How beautiful," Matthew murmured, stepping up behind her. "And how very romantic."

Lily's lips curved into a smile as she felt his arm around her waist. "In spite of the chill?" she asked.

"So long as we do not linger," he said, chuckling a little.

"Mmm." Lily murmured in agreement, turning her head so she could look up at him. His face was in enough shadow that his eyes looked black in the moonlight, and she could not tell what expression they held. "Why did you wish to sneak away, Matthew?" she asked, a little teasingly. She did not wait for an answer but turned so that she could slide her arms around him and lift her face for a kiss.

She saw the smile that crept over his face before her eyes closed, and a moment later she felt it against her mouth. When she shivered, he pulled her closer against him, and she slid her hands under his coat, sinking against the heat of his body.

When he finally eased back, she was surprised by his rueful smile. "While I do not object at all to your idea—far from it—that was not actually why I wanted to steal you away this evening."

"Really?" Lily asked, laughing a little in embarrassment at her eagerness. "Then what was it?"

"Well . . ." He hesitated, and through the arm that was still around her waist, she could feel him take a deep breath. His hand slid away, traveling up to cup her jaw. "I wished to ask you something."

Lily suddenly felt as though she were frozen.

"Mrs. Adler." His voice grew softer. "Lily. I hope you know in how many ways I have come to admire you. How I have enjoyed every moment of our time together. How very much I have come to care for you."

She had thought he was going to suggest that they resume their affair, cut short earlier that year by distance and the competing demands of their separate lives. But that was not what was about to happen at all.

"And I hope—I very much wish—that you will do me the honor of becoming my wife."

CHAPTER 4

There was snow gathering in Matthew's hair, a light dusting that sparkled in the moonlight before melting. For a moment, it felt as though time had stopped. Lily was suddenly conscious of every goose bump that prickled her arms and legs, of the heat on her cheek where his hand still rested, of the cold that was beginning to seep in through the soles of her shoes.

Matthew smiled. "I think this is the first time I have ever managed to truly surprise you."

"Not so," Lily said, finding her voice at last. "I was surprised when you persuaded your cousin to help us investigate the Wyatts." She cleared her throat. "I thought you were going to suggest that we begin spending time together once again, at least while we are both in Hertfordshire."

"Well, I'd not object to that either," he said with a quickness that would have made her laugh only moments before. "But I hope it will be as something more than a simple affair."

"I do not know what to say," Lily admitted. After Freddy's death, she had been certain that she had no wish to marry again. The loss of her husband, after a brief two years of marriage, had been devastating. And it had taken all the determination she possessed to chart a new path.

She liked the life she had built, and until that moment, she had not considered that she might marry again.

But Matthew . . . their affair had brought back to life a part of her that had lain dormant since Freddy fell ill. Matthew was everything admirable in a man. It wasn't just that he was handsome. He was also charming and kind, devoted to his children, determined to use what influence he possessed to improve the lives of those less fortunate than himself. He was that rare sort of person who, despite his past misfortunes, was content with his life: a like feeling that they both recognized in each other. And she had come to care for him very much.

"Then say nothing for the moment," he suggested, his thumb stroking her cheek. "I have never yet known you to make a hasty decision, and I see no reason why you must do so now. We shall be in Hertfordshire for some time. Indeed, I should be happier in your acceptance if I know that it comes after your very exacting mind has sorted through every consideration."

"I am not entirely sure that is a compliment," Lily said, laughing in spite of the conflicting emotions that were knotting together in her chest.

It was too dark to read his eyes, but she could see enough to know that he was smiling at her. "I assure you it is."

Though he sounded confident, he had not spoken as though her answer was a foregone conclusion, for which Lily was grateful. She did not yet know her own mind—a situation that did not often arise and left her more unsettled than she liked. If he had acted as though *he* knew her decision when she did not, she would have been tempted to refuse him on the spot. And she was not ready to do that. Not yet.

A gust of wind rose around them, making her shiver, and the sudden swirl of snow that accompanied it had them both turning their heads toward the sky.

"It is growing even heavier," Matthew said. "I should not keep you out in the cold any longer."

"And we ought to return inside before anyone notices our absence," Lily added as he held out his hand to assist her back over the threshold of the window.

"The roads will be growing treacherous soon," Matthew said as she closed the casement once more. In the candlelight, Lily could see the worried frown creasing his forehead. "Perhaps . . ."

He trailed off, but she could guess what he was thinking. "We can find the Adlers," she said. "I am sure they would not object to leaving early. No doubt they will wish to outrun the weather as well."

The hallway was still deserted when they emerged from the study, and they made their way with calm but brisk steps back toward the ballroom, not wanting to attract any attention. Widowed though they both were, and granted certain leeway as a result, neither wanted to deal with the speculation or whispers that would come if the wrong person discovered them alone together.

Halfway back, though, a sudden rise of voices made them pause, both of them giving the other a nervous look.

But the voices weren't in the hallway itself. The door ahead of them was ajar, and they could hear two men arguing on the other side.

The first voice Lily did not know, and the man spoke too quickly for her to pick up exactly what he was saying. But the angry, anxious tone of voice was unmistakable.

"It is a debt of honor," a calmer man replied. To her surprise, she recognized Peter Coleridge's voice. "And as gentlemen, we both know those must be repaid. It is not a question. Though of course—" His voice grew thoughtful. "A gentleman might also offer a friend the time he needs to gather his funds."

"Damn it, man," the first man said, his voice cracking, making Lily wonder exactly how old he was. "Will you make me humble myself? I have need of the money . . ."

Lily felt herself blushing with secondhand embarrassment for the unknown man. Peter was an easygoing man, but even he would expect a debt of honor to be paid in a timely manner. How dreadful it would be to be the man who must ask to be excused from such an obligation to his neighbor because he could not afford to repay what he owed. She was not surprised to see Matthew looking uncomfortable, and he urged her past the room quickly so they would not overhear anymore.

"Did you recognize who it was?" she asked, once they were far enough from the room that their voices wouldn't carry.

Matthew grimaced. "I think it was the younger Edison brother. Clearly, he's not yet learned never to gamble with what you cannot repay."

"Poor fellow," Lily murmured as they left the hall. "Young men can be so rash."

The heat of the crowded ballroom hit like an unexpected wave after the chill of being outside. Lily was relieved that no one seemed to have noticed their absence. But her relief was short-lived. The musicians had fallen silent, and their hostess had clearly just finished speaking; she was stepping down from the dais at the side of the ballroom.

"What do you think happened?" Matthew murmured, glancing around uneasily.

Lily cocked an ear toward the nearest group of people. "I believe it is the weather," she whispered back. "We lingered outside too long."

Guests were beginning to cluster and break away, many heading toward the doors, as Lily and Matthew made their way toward where the Adlers were gathered.

"Oh, Lily, Mr. Spencer, there you are!" Lady Adler was fanning herself, looking around anxiously. "We ought to depart at once—the drive back is not a short one, and if we are to stay ahead of this wretched snow—"

"I am afraid I must advise you against that, Lady Adler." Mrs. Grantham, their hostess, said as she joined them. Mr. and Mrs. Hartley were with her, trailed by their children, all of them wearing equally uneasy expressions.

Jack had a thick layer of snow in his hair, which was quickly melting in the heat of the ballroom, giving him a disheveled appearance at odds with his elegant evening attire. "I was one of those out investigating the roads, along with Mrs. Grantham's footmen," he said. "The snow is growing worse, and the roads are becoming impassable."

"But . . ." Lady Adler fanned herself more briskly. "But what does that mean for us?"

"The guests who live close by will be safe returning home," Mrs. Grantham said. "But I hope that you, and all those whose homes are at a greater distance, will remain here until conditions improve."

"Surely it is not as bad as all that?" Matthew demanded. "Not so quickly?"

"It is growing rapidly worse. And I could not dream of allowing you to return home in such weather," Mrs. Grantham said. "You would never make it. Excuse me, please, I must tell the others before they attempt to depart as well."

"But my children—" Matthew broke off, blowing out a frustrated breath as he watched their hostess hurry away. Lily, her hand still on his elbow, gave him a sympathetic squeeze. "There is no help for it, I suppose?" he asked, turning to Jack.

Who shook his head. "I think we would go twenty minutes down the road and find ourselves in serious trouble," Jack said. There was sympathy in his voice, but it was firm.

"And Charlotte is there to care for the children," Sir John put in, referring to his wife, the younger Lady Adler, who had not come with them that evening. "She will ensure all is well."

Matthew sighed again. "And I certainly would not want to ask you to put your own driver and horses at risk," he said, nodding to Sir John.

"No doubt we will be able to leave in the morning," Mr. Hartley added. He was a solid, handsome country squire, with the roguish good looks that his son had inherited, though they had grown softer as he aged and were now set off by a pair of shining silver spectacles. "But I think it best that we all avail ourselves of Mrs. Grantham's hospitality for the night."

Amelia had drifted away from the group as they continued discussing the logistics of the evening and when they might be able to return to their respective homes. Lily went to join her by the window, where she had pulled aside one of the heavy draperies and was peering out.

"Can you see anything?" Lily asked. Already the icy swirl was heavier than it had been when she and Matthew had been outside.

"Just snow," Amelia replied, letting the fabric fall. "I do not think we will be leaving tomorrow." She turned to glance back at the ballroom and sighed. "This will be an interesting group to become housebound with."

Lily followed her eyes. Most of the guests had departed, flooding the front hall and carriage drive in their hurry to get home before the weather grew even worse. Only the ones whose homes were too far away remained in the ballroom, many of them still talking and laughing as they sipped drinks and glanced around at their fellows. Peter Coleridge and his stately, silver-haired mother had joined the Adlers. A pretty, well-dressed woman about Lily's own age was just returning to the room and moved to join Mrs. Taylor and her husband, who were talking with a pair of tall young men.

"I see Mr. Gregory Edison will remain tonight," Lily said quietly. "And the gentleman who looks so much like him must be—"

"His brother, William," Amelia said as she turned away. "As I said, not the party I would like to be snowed in with. But there's no help for it."

"Who is that speaking with the Taylors?" Lily asked. "I do not know her."

"A Mrs. Crewe," Amelia said, shrugging. "She moved here earlier this year from London, and she always wears the most magnificent hats, but beyond that, I cannot claim to know anything about her." Amelia glanced around. "Mr. and Mrs. Hounslow will remain as well, I see. Stay away from them if you can. He pinches bottoms, and she loves to gossip. Though their son and daughter are pleasant enough—or at least they can be, when they wish it. I knew them better as a child than I do now."

"I did not know that about Hounslow." Jack joined them just in time to hear his sister's final comment, and he scowled in the silver-haired man's direction. "Why have you never said anything?"

"You mean during the nearly two decades of my life that you have been at sea, Raffi?" Amelia asked, brows rising in an expression that Lily had seen on Jack's face many times.

He grimaced. "Well, I am here now. And you can tell me anything, you know."

She met his gaze with a long stare that gave nothing away. "Perhaps," she said cryptically, turning away. "We ought to rejoin the others."

Jack caught Lily's arm as she was about to follow Amelia. "What were you and Mr. Spencer doing outside?" he asked quietly.

"What makes you think we were outside?"

His gloved fingers brushed over the twisted-up curls of her hair, the gesture quick enough that anyone else would miss it unless they had been watching the pair of them closely. "It has dried now, but it was damp when I first saw you. What have you been up to, Lily?"

She thought about telling him what Matthew had asked. But Amelia was right; Mrs. Grantham was gathering her remaining guests. And Lily was not yet sure she wanted to share the question she was pondering. Not even with Jack. "Merely looking at the weather. The snow is beautiful, even if it is less than convenient."

"Keeping secrets from me, Lily?" he murmured.

She gave him a sideways glance. "I see Mrs. Taylor is watching us," she commented, amused to see his ears grow red.

"Looking for gossip, no doubt," he said, clearing his throat. "She always did like to know everything that passed in the neighborhood."

His embarrassed tone made Lily purse her lips against a smile. She couldn't help asking, "Has she propositioned you since you returned?"

Jack scowled at her. "I shall tell you that when you tell me the truth about why you and Mr. Spencer sneaked away this evening."

"Keeping secrets from me, Jack?" she said, repeating his own words back to him. They eyed each other, neither one of them giving ground, until their hostess's voice called their attention back to the small crowd of guests.

"And if you would be so good as to follow," Mrs. Grantham was saying as they rejoined the group, "I have made arrangements for each of you for the night. I apologize that some of our preparations have been a bit hasty, but I will do my best to ensure that everyone is comfortable."

"No need to fret, dear ma'am," Lady Adler said, patting her arm comfortingly, while the other guests hastened to agree. "You are exceedingly kind to take us all in, and I am sure any discomforts are all in your own mind."

"Indeed, indeed," Peter Coleridge put in. "Your hospitality has always been greatly admired for a reason, Mrs. Grantham."

"That is good of you," Mrs. Grantham said, beaming around at the assembled group. "Now, if you will all come this way to the hall, my housekeeper has arranged for each of you to be shown to your quarters for the night . . ."

The murmur of conversation continued as they followed her out of the ballroom.

"Still can't believe this weather—"

"Did I see you dance with her twice?"

"After such a summer—"

"Miss Claret's dress tonight had ten rows of flounces, at the least—"

"Let us hope she put Miss Hartley far away from the young gentlemen."

The snide whisper carried through the small crowd, as it was surely meant to. In front of her, Lily saw Mr. and Mrs. Hartley freeze for the barest second, both of them drawing closer to their daughter, who walked between them. Lily might have thought Amelia hadn't heard the comment were it not for the sudden, tense lift to her chin.

Lily glanced sideways at Jack, who was still beside her. He was looking around, trying to spot who had spoken, but the guests were beginning to disperse to follow various servants to their rooms. There were a few titters, but no one who remained would meet his eyes other than Peter, who grimaced sympathetically. Jack's jaw clenched, and for a moment Lily was afraid he would say something. She laid a hand on his arm, and when he glanced down, she shook her head in a slight warning. A muscle jumped in his jaw, but he nodded without a word, turning to follow his family.

Behind her, Lily saw Gregory Edison, who, as a man, had easily escaped the rumors and insinuations that now dogged Amelia, grimace as his younger brother jostled his elbow. The brother, whose name Lily could not remember, was grinning as he whispered something. But Gregory shrugged him off and stalked after the servant who was waiting to lead them. His brother rolled his eyes but followed without any further comment.

"Poor fellow," Peter said, pausing beside Lily. She turned to him in some surprise, her mind still on Gregory Edison, but saw that Peter was looking after Jack. "I suppose it's a hard thing to be an elder brother." His round, friendly face was drawn into an expression of sympathy.

"Not something you and I know a great deal about," Lily said. She had no siblings, and Peter, as the youngest of seven children, had never been able to hide his relief as his sisters married and moved away. "But I imagine for someone as protective as the captain, it can be a trial at times."

"Do you think he'll do anything about it?" Peter asked as they climbed the stairs.

Outside, the wind was rising in a low, moaning undercurrent. It made Lily shiver, and she was grateful that she was not traveling home. "He is not that foolish," she said quietly, hoping it was true.

Lady Adler was waiting for her at the top of the stairs. "Our rooms are next to each other, Lily," she said. "Peter, will you tell your mother I shall look in on her in a few minutes to see that all is well? I am sure Mrs. Grantham will furnish us with what we need for the night, but dear Mrs. Coleridge is, well—"

"Not as hearty as she once was," Peter agreed. "I am sure she will be grateful for your attentions, Lady Adler. I bid you both a good night."

"Things are a bit helter-skelter, no shame to Mrs. Grantham for it," Lady Adler said as they headed down the opposite hallway from Peter, who was being shown to a room in the wing on the other side of the stairs. "Your room is next to mine, I understand, and across the hall from Sir John and Mr. Spencer. They have tried to put us in family groups."

"I am surprised you would include Mr. Spencer in that assessment." Lily knew she should have kept the thought to herself, but the words were out before she could stop them.

Lady Adler gave her a pointed look, making Lily think of a pert, plump mother bird. "Family is what we make of it, my dear," she said. "And I hope you know that no matter what comes next in your life, you will always be family to me."

Lily felt an unexpected lump of emotion in her chest, and she had to clear her throat before she could respond. "You seem to think I am about to make some drastic change."

Lady Adler drew to a halt between the two doors that had been assigned to them. "Life is nothing but change," she said, gently and a little sadly. "One change after another, whether we wish for them or not. All I know for certain is that you are a young woman yet, with a great deal of life ahead of you." She gave Lily's cheek a pat. "Good night, my dear."

As the door closed behind Lady Adler, Lily turned back toward her own room just in time to see Matthew pausing outside his door, just across the hallway. She wondered how much of the conversation he had overheard, but before she could decide whether or not to ask, he gave her a smile and a bow. His eyes, as they locked on hers, were deep with emotion, holding none of the gentleness of his smile. "Good night, Mrs. Adler," he said, his voice just carrying across the wood paneling and carpeting between them.

"Good night," Lily managed to reply.

Inside her room, the fire had been built high, crackling and dancing to warm the room, which had the chill of a chamber that had just been opened. Candles on the nightstand flickered against the darkness, and a basin of steaming water waited on the wash-stand. A nightgown and wrapper, which must have once belonged to Mrs. Grantham or her grown and married daughter, waited on the bed.

The maids and footmen would be going from room to room to assist the guests who needed it. Though Lily was accustomed to having a servant help her dress and undress, she could man-age without assistance. Shivering, trying not to listen to the rising moan of the wind, she undressed and laid her ball gown over a chair. The steaming water was welcome on her chilled fingers and face, but a sudden wave of fatigue overtook her, and that was all the washing she had energy for. Sliding the pins out of her hair, she brushed and braided it, her fingers trembling in the cold that still filled the room, and she dressed as quickly as she could before bundling herself under the counterpane. There was a warming pan under the covers, and her toes stretched greedily toward it as she sat up just enough to blow out the stand of candles.

One of the curtains wasn't quite closed, and without the flick-ering light of the candles, the snow-swirling darkness seemed to press more closely against the window. Now that she was still, Lily couldn't ignore the wind, which rose and fell like a living voice. A sudden crack, loud as a gunshot, made her start nearly upright, and it wasn't until it was followed by two more that she realized what it was: tree branches cracking, from either the wind or the cold. Lily shivered, wrapping her arms around herself, glad they had not tried to brave the storm.

The heat from the warming pan joined the heat of her body, creeping through the covers until her chilled limbs relaxed. The wind continued to moan and call outside, and every so often she thought she heard the crack and shot of another tree branch breaking. But, cozy in the banked firelight, Lily was at last able to sleep.

She woke slowly with the sense that something was missing, and it took her a moment to realize it was the wind. It had died down in the night, and through the half-open curtain, she could see the dawn just beginning to creep over the world, reflected eerily by the glittering white of the snow that continued to fall. The room was cool again, but it was warm under the bedspread, and the maids would be along soon to light the fires. Lily burrowed more deeply into the covers, closing her eyes once more.

She had just started to drift off again when she heard the scream.

CHAPTER 5

Lily sat bolt upright. Where had the sound come from? It hadn't been loud . . . another part of the house? For a moment, in the pressing silence, she wondered if she had drifted back to sleep without realizing it and imagined the whole thing.

But a moment later, the sounds of a commotion rose just outside her window. Lily dashed to the window, throwing it open with some effort and peering out into the swirl of snow and early-morning light.

The guest room she had been given was one of the smaller ones—the better to quickly heat rooms that hadn't been prepared in advance—and as was typical for such rooms, it lacked a pretty view. Hers looked over what she realized after a moment must be the poultry yard. Darkly clad figures who she could guess were servants stumbled through the thick layer of snow that had fallen, trying to reach the two people in the middle of the yard.

One Lily could see from her vantage only as a still, upright figure, hand outstretched and pointing toward the second person, who lay sprawled on the ground. The one on the ground was half covered by the ice and snow, unmoving.

Lily grabbed the dressing gown from the chair, pulled on her shoes, and ran from the room. In the hallway, a few guests were poking their heads out of their doors, hair tousled and faces creased with sleep, inquiring grumpily if anyone had heard an odd noise.

Lily didn't stop to consider propriety or worry about what anyone else might think before she yelled "Jack!" as loudly as she could.

She didn't know which room he had been given, but a moment later, a door past the stairs was flung open and the navy captain's head appeared.

"What is it?" he demanded. He was already dressed and wearing his driving coat over his clothing. That was odd at such an early hour, but Lily didn't have time to be surprised.

"Downstairs." In spite of the months they had spent apart, Lily knew she could depend on him to understand and act quickly. "Something happened. We have to help."

And in spite of those months apart, he didn't stop to ask questions. More guests were emerging, summoned by Lily's shout, and questions were beginning to fly back and forth as she dashed down the stairs, Jack on her heels.

They didn't need to wonder where to go; on the floor below, Mrs. Grantham was following a stately-looking woman who might have been the housekeeper or another upper servant. Their pace was just barely too dignified to be a run, but they couldn't hide their worry as they disappeared down the steps to the kitchen. Lily and Jack hurried after them.

The servants' staircase was narrow and cold. At the bottom, servants clustered in the kitchen, talking in shrill, anxious voices as the cook tried to keep some order. The underservants glanced uneasily at Lily and Jack as they came into the kitchen, but no one seemed to know what to do or say. The door to the yard had been left wide open, and the wind blew in gusts of snow and icy morning light. Outside, more servants were gathered, though they parted like a wave as the housekeeper led Mrs. Grantham out to see what had happened.

As Lily and Jack tried to follow, they were stopped by the frail but determined body of the butler, who interposed himself between them and the open door. "Madam, sir, perhaps you would care to return to your rooms? Breakfast will be ready shortly."

Jack drew himself up, clearly prepared to use his rank to push his way past the aging servant. Before he could say anything, though, and before Lily could think how to reply, Mrs. Grantham turned sharply.

"What is . . ." She trailed off, eyeing Lily and Jack with trepidation. She looked ready to send them on their way with some commonplace assurance. But half a dozen emotions chased their way across her face in that moment, and she instead asked, "Mrs. Adler, how many of the rumors about you are true?"

"That depends on the rumors," Lily replied calmly, though her heart was pounding. Behind Mrs. Grantham, she could see the limbs of the eerie, still figure sticking out of the snowbank. "Though if you refer only to the ones that are most relevant at this moment . . ." She turned her gaze pointedly toward the body in the snow. "There is indeed some truth to them."

Mrs. Grantham hesitated, then seemed to make up her mind in a rush. She stepped aside, pulling the confused housekeeper with her. There were boots for the servants lined up next to the door, crusted with mud from repeated use. Lily pulled off her delicate evening slippers, slid her bare feet into the pair that looked closest to her size, and followed as she and Jack were ushered into the yard, their eyes fixed on what awaited them there.

A man dressed in borrowed clothes, his skin white with cold, his hair thick with clumps of ice and snow. He could have fallen, hit his head, been caught in the storm and frozen. He could still be alive, in need of help. He could have had an innocent reason for being out in the storm.

He could have. But this close, Lily could see the snow that had been kicked aside and trampled by half a dozen feet in the servants' frantic attempts to clear it away. The icy powder was too thick on the ground for her to see the mud of the yard. But it was still stained with red and brown from where the man's life had leaked away in the night.

The once-snowy linen of his shirt was stained the same color, jagged and torn from the bullet that had ended his life. The gun that had fired it had been unearthed beside him, as snow-logged as his own body. The man's frozen eyes and mouth were wide open, as though he had not believed until the last moment that whoever had faced him in that yard could be capable of the shot that had ended his life.

Lily glanced around the courtyard. The snow was trampled around the body and leading toward the kitchen door, but it was pristine in the rest of the yard, unmarred by any telltale footprints. She turned to the cluster of servants who had drawn back as she surveyed the scene. "Who found him?"

A wide-eyed scullery maid stepped forward, her mouth trembling. "Me, mum."

"When you came outside, was there any sign that someone had walked here? Any indication of which way someone might have gone?"

The scullery maid shook her head. "No, mum. Just blank snow was all. I was going to see if there was any eggs in the coops when I saw . . ." She glanced at the body, then looked away quickly. "I screamed," she added in a whisper.

Lily nodded. She had expected as much, though she had hoped otherwise. But whatever traces might have been left behind, the snow had hidden them thoroughly. She turned back to Jack, who was still staring at the body. His jaw was clenched so tightly he looked as though he would vibrate with the effort of keeping still. Mrs. Grantham, wringing her hands and clearly uncertain what to do next, eyed him uneasily.

"Someone ought to fetch Sir John Adler," Lily said, briskly taking charge of the situation. "We cannot bring a coroner here, not with all the snow, but we at least have our magistrate."

While Mrs. Grantham gave orders to her servants, Lily laid a hand on Jack's arm. "It's going to look very bad for Amelia," she said softly.

Jack nodded, a quick jerk of his chin, though he didn't seem able to speak.

He didn't need to. They both knew exactly what rumors would begin flying as soon as the rest of the guests heard what had happened.

The man lying dead in the snow was Gregory Edison.

Chapter 6

It didn't take long for word to spread. Amelia Hartley, roused by her frantic mother and dragged to the breakfast room in a show of cool defiance, felt more afraid with each passing moment.

By the time the guests were gathering at the table, the undercurrent of whispers rustled through the room like a wind, murmuring just beneath the valiant attempts at normal conversation. Amelia eyed the group over the edge of her teacup. It was an odd-looking assembly. There was a noticeable chill in the air, in spite of the fires that had been built high in the room, and no one wanted to wear their evening clothes. Those who were similar in size to Mrs. Grantham, her absent son and daughter, or her late husband had been given clothes to borrow. The others had to make do with the sorts of garments that collected in family homes: old but still in good repair, pulled from the chests and wardrobes where they had been waiting for their fabric to be turned into something else or for the entire garment to be passed on to someone in need in the parish. The result looked almost like a costume party, with at least three decades of styles represented, and would have been entertaining in other circumstances.

But no one seemed amused. Everyone had appeared at the breakfast table that morning, even those who, like Lady Adler or her own parents, would have been otherwise likely to take their coffee and tea and toast in their rooms. At the moment, only Sir John and Gregory's younger brother William were missing.

Amelia hadn't thought there was any real harm in Gregory, but she should have known better than to trust him, even if he was handsome and entertaining. With his death, horrible though it was, there was suddenly a real chance that everything he knew, everything he could have revealed about her, would stay secret.

Unless he had told his brother.

She had hoped to catch William before anyone else did, to find out how much he knew. But Sir John had found William first, and she had no idea what they might be discussing while she sat, silent and anxious, at the breakfast table. And Gregory . . .

Amelia felt her stomach turn over, and she set down her fork and knife, unable to take a bite of food. She had thought, naïvely, that when she presented him with her request, it would stay between the two of them. But the whole thing had been a mistake, start to finish. It had been bad enough when her neighbors—even those she had once thought of as friends—had looked at her with scandal in their minds and gossip on their lips.

Now it was so much worse than she could have ever imagined. No one seemed willing to voice a guess as to what had happened to Gregory. They either avoided her eyes or stared straight at her, unspeaking. But she could sense what thought was in everyone's minds.

Could she have been the one to do it?

Amelia wanted to run away, to seek refuge in her borrowed room until the snow had stopped and she could convince her parents to let her run away even farther. But she couldn't do that. For the moment, centuries of polite conventions were on her side. If she stayed with the rest of the guests, they would exchange shocked and meaningful glances, but they wouldn't say anything out loud. Not yet.

They would have to become either much more certain or much more fearful before that happened.

She needed to talk to William. She had time. Now all she had to do was use it wisely—more wisely than she had used her time with Gregory Edison.

In the meantime, she was trapped with her family at one end of the table. They had drawn protectively around her, and her brother staring down everyone who glanced his way. Dear Raffi, always a man of action. She had always been a bit in awe of her second brother, godlike and unknowable in his absence, though his rare visits were always playful, joyful occasions. When Raffi had sent word that he intended to leave his naval life behind, she had hoped she would finally have the chance to impress him, as he had always impressed her. She wasn't sure, now, whether that would ever be possible.

But perhaps she still could, if she could hold off the whispers a little longer and keep the situation from becoming any worse. He seemed to have grown more thoughtful in the last few years, and she suspected that the woman seated next to her mother was responsible.

Amelia had known Freddy Adler her whole life, and even after Raffi left for the navy, Freddy had still been a frequent visitor to the Hartley household. They had all been curious about the woman he had brought home as his wife, but Mrs. Adler, polite and reserved, had not been the easiest person to get to know. And then Freddy had fallen ill. While the Hartleys had rallied to support Freddy's family during such a terrible time, his widow had drawn even more into herself, first focused on caring for her dying husband and then hemmed in by the expectations and needs of mourning.

But in Raffi's letters, Amelia had come to see a new side of Mrs. Adler. Raffi had clearly grown to respect and even admire her. And then there had been those other parts of his letters: the danger, the intrigue, the mysteries he and Mrs. Adler had faced.

What did Freddy's wife make of Gregory Edison's death? Of Amelia herself? She and Lady Adler sat on either side of the Hartleys, bolstering them with unspoken but clear support in the face of the other guests' suspicion. The gentleman who was their guest would have sat with them had he not been waylaid by Mrs. Grantham just as he was carrying his breakfast to the table. But Amelia could see him casting occasional glances in their direction.

Lady Adler was talking in a deliberately normal voice. Mrs. Adler, by contrast, said very little. Instead, her eyes made a slow, thoughtful circuit of the room while she stirred her tea. Amelia, wondering what she saw, did the same.

The other guests were arrayed on the other sides of the table, none of them quite willing to sit next to the Hartleys or engage them in conversation. Though some of them tried to be less obvious about it, Amelia could easily see the whispers and glances being sent her way. Even Mrs. Grantham, attempting to have something like a normal conversation from the head of the table, had not brought herself to speak directly to them. Amelia's mother was impassive in the face of their neighbors' scrutiny, but Amelia could see her brother's tightly clenched jaw and her father's obvious unhappiness.

"Right there, Peter, if you'd be so good."

Preoccupied with her observations, Amelia nearly jumped in her seat when a plate was set next to Mrs. Adler. She turned, unable to hide her surprise as Peter Coleridge helped his mother into a chair, then took the seat on her other side.

"Good morning, Miss Hartley, Mrs. Hartley, Mr. Hartley," he said with polite gravity as he nodded at all of them. "Lady Adler. Mrs. Adler. Captain."

The others in the dining room had fallen silent to watch the Coleridges, and Amelia felt a rush of gratitude for their support, chased immediately by the specter of guilt. She was the reason her family needed such support. It was a wonder they did not hate her for it.

"Good morning," Mrs. Coleridge added, leaning over to look at Lady Adler. She had grown silver haired in recent years, with a slight stoop to her shoulders, and she had been leaning heavily on her cane as she approached the table. But she spoke with the crisp voice of a woman who had spent her whole life being listened to with great attention and clearly expected that those around her would continue to do so now. She was not wrong; Amelia had been terrified of her since childhood. "Agnes, that is a handsome brooch you are wearing. Very pretty."

"Thank you, Mrs. Coleridge," Lady Adler replied, giving her a sunny, pointed smile before seeming to remember that a sober mien would be more appropriate that morning. She adjusted her expression and nodded politely. "It was a gift from the late baronet, dear man."

"Was there not a bracelet to match, last night?"

Lady Adler's calm expression faltered. "I seem to have misplaced it in the bustle of preparing for bed."

There was a small commotion at the head of the table, Mr. Spencer exclaiming in surprise as Mrs. Grantham knocked over her tea. Startled and on edge, half the guests jumped, then tittered nervously, as a footman arrived immediately to begin cleaning up, and Mr. Spencer gallantly went to fetch their hostess another cup.

Looking a little flustered, Lady Adler tried to return to the conversation. "Spending the time to search for it did not seem pressing in light of . . ." She hesitated, her mouth thinning, and she had to look down at her plate for a moment. "I shall look for it after breakfast," she finished, lifting her head once more.

"Hmm," Mrs. Coleridge said cryptically.

"And how are you this morning?" Lady Adler continued, polite but with a hint of what might be condescension in her voice. "You seem not entirely yourself."

"Well enough, well enough. Are any of us ourselves today?" Mrs. Coleridge said with a sigh before turning to the head of the table. "Mrs. Grantham, I thank you for accommodating all of us at such short notice."

"Oh—oh yes." Mrs. Grantham said. "Think nothing of it. It was my pleasure to . . ." She floundered a little. "Well, that is to say, I of course would not have done otherwise."

"Has anyone been out to check the state of the roads?" Peter asked diffidently, buttering his toast.

"I have," Raffi replied. All the heads around the table swiveled toward him.

Amelia was unsurprised: her brother was not the sort to leave a task half-done, and he likely had wanted to be of some service to their hostess by checking to see if the way home was passable.

But that was before . . . well. Amelia bit her lip. It might not have been the wisest thing for Raffi to admit that he had been out and about at, or even before, first light. Many of the other guests watched him hopefully as they waited for him to continue. But some of those who turned in his direction could not, or would not, hide their suspicion. Mrs. Crewe, the neighborhood's newcomer, glanced rapidly between Amelia and her brother, her expression wary. Peter looked concerned, even nervous, before he fixed his gaze on his toast once more. Even Mrs. Grantham seemed apprehensive as she looked at the Hartleys, then around at the rest of the table, before turning back to Raffi.

"And how were things?" she asked, a little hesitantly.

Raffi grimaced. "I could barely get past the gate. It seems we are thoroughly snowed in. And more is still falling, so there is no saying when the situation will improve."

A heavy, anxious silence followed his statement as the guests exchanged glances.

Mrs. Grantham cleared her throat. "Well, I shall do my best to make sure everyone is as comfortable as possible. And in any case . . ." She looked apologetic. "I am afraid Sir John said that even once the roads are passable, he may still need to ask everyone to remain."

"But why on earth would we do that?" Mrs. Taylor demanded. "To impose on you in such a manner! And no doubt poor William is anxious to reach his parents. Would it not be better if we all returned home as soon as we are able?"

"It would be better for one person, certainly."

They all jumped a little as Sir John strode into the dining room, his shoulders and hair wet with melting snow. His normal expression was one of cheerful good humor; now his face was drawn and tight. Amelia had not seen him look so serious since his brother's death three years before. Sir John, always a friend to everyone he met, had been the local magistrate for nearly a decade and had never had to deal with crimes more severe than poaching or a disputed property boundary. Now, suddenly faced with investigating the murder of one of his neighbors, he gazed around the room with poorly concealed discomfort.

Nearly every face had turned toward him when he entered. But Amelia saw Mrs. Adler, instead of watching Freddy's brother, glance around the table once more. Some of the guests were watching the magistrate, but a few still looked toward Amelia, their eyes narrowed and faces drawn. The Hartleys and Lady Adler were watching Sir John, except for Raffi, who, like his friend, was watching the other guests. He caught Amelia watching him as well, and he tried to give her an encouraging smile. But his usual wry humor was missing, and the expression faltered as he looked away.

Amelia felt as though the bottom had dropped out of her stomach. If Raffi believed she was in trouble . . .

She took a deep breath, wondering which was better: to remain impassive in the face of obvious suspicion, or to look upset and worried like the rest of them. Would they think she was upset about Gregory's death or something else?

There was no right answer. She turned sharply away, deciding to keep her own eyes on Sir John and nothing more.

"Unfortunately," Sir John continued, "Mrs. Grantham is correct. Until I can account for everyone's whereabouts in the night, I cannot permit anyone to depart. Even if the snow stops."

A murmur ran around the table, echoing with varying degrees of shock and unhappiness. Mrs. Grantham watched her guests anxiously, as though worried that one of them might lead a charge for the door in spite of the weather and the magistrate's orders.

"What d'you mean, better for one person?" Mr. Hounslow demanded. He was a fox of a gentleman, his full head of silver hair styled with all the care of a dandy out on the town, even without the benefit of a valet to assist him, his features sharp and patrician though he was growing a little portly around the midsection as he entered his middle years.

"Yes, what are you implying, Sir John?" Mr. Hounslow's wife piped up. She was rail thin and anxious, as elegant as her husband even in a borrowed dress two decades out of fashion, with the bearing of a woman who had once been taught to sit, stand, and walk with a book balanced on her head and had never lost the knack.

Sir John hesitated. Amelia suspected he was trying to think of the most delicate way to phrase the matter so as not to upset his neighbors further. She could have slapped him when his eyes darted toward her before quickly looking away again.

Instead, she decided to be blunt. "He is clearly implying, ma'am, that it would be better for poor Mr. Edison's murderer if we were all to depart." Every head turned in shock to Amelia as she spoke, a gasp going through the room as she uttered the word *murderer*. Amelia's breath came a little faster in the face of their sudden attention, and she spoke more quietly than she meant to. But she still managed to sound calm, as though explaining nothing more exciting than the breakfast menu. "Which is something neither he nor we can allow."

"Well!" Mrs. Hounslow drew herself up, affronted. "If I were you right now, Miss Hartley, I should show far less certainty in my proclamations."

Raffi made as if to rise from his seat, his expression hot with fury, before their mother laid a hand on his arm. He sank back into his chair, but he did not bother to conceal his anger.

"And why is that?" Amelia asked, raising her voice a little so that it carried over the growing whispers of the guests. Her heart was pounding. "Do you not agree that this killer must be apprehended, Mrs. Hounslow?"

"Sir John, do you suspect one of us gathered here?" Mrs. Taylor broke in.

"Who else could it have been, ninnyhead?" Mrs. Coleridge sniffed. "No one was walking through the storm last night, that is for certain."

Mrs. Taylor's cheeks grew red with embarrassment. "Well, in that case," she bit off, turning toward Amelia. "I believe we all know where blame is likely to—"

"I thank you for sharing your thoughts, Mrs. Taylor," Sir John said loudly, cutting off not only Mrs. Taylor but the other exclamations being tossed about the room. "If any of you have anything other than speculation to share, you will have the opportunity. I have already spoken with Mr. Edison's brother, who has returned to his room to collect himself, and I beg you will not pain him with gossip when he reappears. In the meantime . . ." He drew himself up, looking determined and resigned and a little bit terrified all at the same time. "In the meantime, I must ask that you all remain here, in each other's company, as I begin my work."

"What, are we supposed to sit calmly and continue our breakfast with a murderer among us?" Miss Hounslow exclaimed.

There was silence in the room at her words, all of the guests glancing around the table at each other. Amelia could see a mix of fear, nervousness, and disbelief reflected on the faces around her. Many of them dropped their gaze as soon as they met anyone's eyes.

"I am afraid we do not have any other option," Sir John said gently. "Mrs. Grantham, might I prevail on you for the use of your library?"

"Of course," she said, starting a little at being addressed directly before rising from her chair. She looked around at her guests, her voice painfully earnest. "I am sure you will discover this was nothing more than an accident, or that it truly was someone from outside our party. We do not, after all, know what exactly happened, or even when it occurred. But you shall of course have whatever you require."

"Perhaps the rest of us might wait in the drawing room instead?" Peter asked, glancing at his elderly mother. "It would be more comfortable than remaining at the table."

"Very well," Sir John agreed. "Mrs. Grantham, would you show everyone where they need to go? And perhaps a servant or two might be made available to accompany anyone who needs to leave the drawing room for . . ." He cleared his throat, clearly not wanting to mention a visit to the washroom in mixed company. "Well, for any personal needs."

The room was still for a moment as everyone exchanged glances, and Amelia could see the moment when each person realized what he meant. The magistrate did not want them to venture anywhere alone, for their own safety or . . .

Lady Adler stood. "Come along, everyone. Let us leave the magistrate to his work. Mrs. Grantham, if you would lead the way?"

Amelia tried not to notice the darting glances being sent her way. Sir John had said William was in his room. If there was any sort of confusion or bustle, she might be able to slip away to find him . . .

Her mother leaned close, her murmur for Amelia's ears alone. "Do not be afraid, my love. We can weather this together if you do exactly as is expected of you."

"I did not do anything wrong," Amelia insisted, though she couldn't stop her voice from breaking as she said it. It sounded like a lie, even to her ears. She swallowed.

Her mother laid a hand on her cheek briefly. "Then do not be foolish enough to start now. Be wary and careful, and all will be well. Come." She pushed back her chair. Everyone was filing out of the room. "It's best that we stay with the others."

CHAPTER 7

Lily hung back in the breakfast room, watching the other guests leave. Of all of them, Mrs. Crewe seemed the most inclined to keep to herself, but Mrs. Taylor, her husband following closely on her heels, caught the newcomer by the arm and began whispering furiously. Jack stayed close to his sister and mother, though Lady Adler allowed Mr. Hartley to offer his arm. Mrs. Coleridge stomped from the room, her head held high even as she leaned on her cane. Peter, after a moment's hesitation, held back from following her immediately, instead falling in step with Mr. Hounslow. Mrs. Hounslow shepherded their children from the room, her expression stony while they both whispered furiously.

"What do you see?"

Lily had been half expecting the low murmur in her ear, and she turned without surprise to find Matthew watching her. "They are an odd assortment," she replied, her voice equally low. "And I suspect that no few of them are keeping some sort of secret."

"What makes you say that?"

Lily lifted her shoulders. "It is a house party, is it not?"

"An unconventional one. And I do not only mean the death of one of its members."

"Even so, I have never yet been a guest at one where everyone was on their best behavior . . . in private, if not in public." Lily took Matthew's arm as he offered it to her, the two of them trailing far behind the other guests. Her expression grew grim. "Though murder is far beyond the flirtations and jealousies I am accustomed to encountering at such a gathering."

"Do you suspect everyone here?" There was an edge to Matthew's words that went beyond simple curiosity. She could feel the tension in his arm where her hand rested.

"I don't know that I strictly suspect anyone yet," Lily said, pausing and staring out a window. It was beautiful outside, the entire world glittering and white, the still-falling snow blowing in eddies across the frozen ground. And it was oppressive: they were trapped, with no one able to get in or out, until the snow began to melt. Lily shivered, suddenly feeling the chill that crept through the house, undefeated by the fires burning in each hearth. "I know someone must have done it. But I've no idea who that might be. Not yet."

"Will you suspect me at all, in the course of your ruminations?" Matthew asked. The question was mildly asked, and it made Lily smile a little, in spite of the tension she felt.

"I think you, of everyone here, have the least cause to turn murderer. You do not live in the neighborhood and never have. Before last night, you did not know Gregory Edison from Adam. Besides." Lily gave him an impertinent look. "If you had murdered someone, you would stand up at the breakfast table and confess the crime."

That made him chuckle. "Do you think me that foolish?"

"I think you that honorable," Lily said softly. "You would never allow someone else to take the blame for a crime which was your own."

"I agree."

They both jumped, caught off guard to find Sir John watching them from the doorway of the library, just a few feet down the hall from where they stood. Lily hadn't realized they had fallen so far behind the rest of the party. She started to reply, but before she could, Sir John held up one hand.

"Inside, if you please, both of you. I want to speak with you, if you will permit it?"

Lily exchanged a glance with Matthew, who nodded. "Certainly, brother," she said. "If we can be of assistance in some way."

"I believe so," John said. He hesitated, then nodded swiftly, standing aside in the doorway to allow them into the library. But he didn't follow them in.

Lily was not nervous precisely—she had nothing to hide, and she did not for one moment believe he suspected her of anything nefarious. But it was disconcerting to see her brother-in-law so serious. And it was even more disconcerting to know that he was tasked with uncovering who, of the people in the house, was responsible for a murder.

"What is it, John?" she asked.

He let out a loud breath. "Wait for me here, please. There is something I must do first."

★   ★   ★

Shaken and unnerved, Amelia meant to do as she was told. But she saw him before she reached the drawing room.

William had not returned to his room after all. He was almost, but not quite, hidden, standing in a shadowed alcove beneath the staircase. She wouldn't have noticed him at all—it seemed no one else had, or if they had, they were respectful enough of his grief to give him wide berth—had he not taken a step forward, his eyes fixed on her, and beckoned.

Amelia slowed her steps just enough that she fell behind. Nearly everyone else was in the drawing room already. And Lady Adler had just claimed her mother's attention as they went in, leaving Amelia, for the moment, unobserved. She drew her shawl around her and took a deep breath as she went to join William.

"Amelia." He spoke quietly, clearly no more anxious to be overheard than she was. "I probably should not be speaking with you. Not after . . ." He trailed off, looking sick. He'd always had a weak chin, Amelia though, feeling bad for him. Now it trembled like a child's.

"I know." Amelia glanced around. For the moment, they were alone. "But I am glad you waited for me. I am so sorry about Gregory. Truly."

"Are you?" William's gaze sharpened, so much that she almost took a step back. "Even after everything that happened?"

Amelia swallowed. "So you do know about it?"

"Of course." William looked affronted. "He and I told each other nearly everything."

"Yes. Well." Amelia sighed. "That answers the question I wanted to ask. You must promise me, William, that you'll not breathe a word. Not to anyone." A sudden thought occurred to her, and she grabbed his hand. "You didn't tell Sir John, did you?" When William shook his head, she breathed a sigh of relief. "Thank God." Seizing his other hand in a tight grip, she demanded, "And you won't, will you? Not a word to him or anyone else?"

"Well . . . that depends on you." William gave her a nervous smile. She could see the sweat standing out on his brow, even though the hall was chilled. "That depends on how quickly you can get me fifty pounds."

"Fifty pounds?" Amelia gasped, forgetting, for the moment, to keep her voice low. Dropping his hands, she took a step back, staring at him.

As surprised as she had been by Gregory's demands, she hadn't been surprised that he'd turned out to be the sort of person who could make them. William, though . . . she had thought William was the more honorable of the brothers, or at least too timid to be truly dishonorable.

Her opinion of him had not been high, but clearly it had none-theless been too generous. "You greedy bastard."

"I need the money," he said, though he at least had the decency to look ashamed of himself as he said it.

"Even your brother never asked for more than five pounds at a time," she said. Her chest felt so tight she wondered if she would stop breathing entirely, but she refused to let him see how afraid she was.

"Well, the circumstances were rather different," William pointed out, drawing himself up. His voice was a whispered hiss. "There was no murder involved. And while Gregory had only one secret to keep for you . . . well, I have two. So the price has gone up."

"You haven't any proof," she whispered. As close as the brothers were, she didn't think William could have gotten his hands on Gregory's private letters. Not yet, in any case. It was a stab in the dark—there was proof out there, as she well knew—but it paid off as she saw William flinch, though he quickly tried to hide it with a show of bravado.

"You do not know that. And in any case," he added, his voice growing more confident, "do you really think it will matter? They all suspect you already. Whatever I might tell them would only confirm what they're already thinking."

Amelia's jaw clenched, but he was right, and they both knew it. "Your brother was killed last night," she said, starting to feel desperate. "Can you not take a moment to grieve before embarking on blackmail?"

"I can do both, it seems," William said. His chin trembled, and he clenched his jaw to hold it steady. "And really, I think Gregory would have approved. Fifty pounds."

"Do you think I can conjure fifty pounds out of thin air?" she demanded. "None of us can leave here until the snow subsides."

"So you do have it, then."

"Of course I do not!" she snapped, her voice rising before she caught herself. Nervously, she glanced over her shoulder, dropping it to a whisper once more. "I am saying that even if I did—"

"Then you had best acquire it somehow," William advised. "Or I will tell the magistrate everything I know."

"You know nothing," Amelia protested, hating the way her voice cracked on the last word. She hated William's shrug even more.

"I doubt you want to put that to the test, Amelia," he said. "You have two days."

"*William.*"

He made to push past her, and she, not thinking, grabbed his arm and tried to pull him to a stop. "William!"

He hadn't expected it. Caught off guard, he lost his footing, stumbling into an ornamental table full of knickknacks and vases. He tried to catch himself and succeeded only in sending it all tumbling to the ground. The crash of porcelain and the cracking of spindly wood rang through the hallway. William yelled in pain, and Amelia shrank back.

"Are you hurt?" she cried, wringing her hands and looking around to see if anyone had heard the commotion.

They had. There was a sudden burst of noise from the drawing room as the other guests pushed their way back into the hall, many of them drawing to a surprised halt as they surveyed the scene in front of them.

"What happened?"

"Mr. Edison!"

"What are you two doing here?"

"What did she do?"

Amelia looked back at William, who was clutching one arm against his chest and wincing in pain, a large cut visible on his hand. Before she had time to wonder how he would explain their secretive conversation—surely he was not about to admit to blackmailing her?—he scrambled away from her, pulling himself to his feet.

"She attacked me!" he declared, fumbling for a handkerchief to wrap around his hand.

Amelia's lips fell apart in shock. "I did no such—!"

"Miss Hartley."

Amelia froze, then turned slowly toward the voice.

Sir John Adler was striding down the hall toward them, his face grave and stern. He stopped only a few paces away. "Is there a reason you are not with the others in the drawing room?"

Amelia glanced toward the doorway, where their audience had spilled into the hall. She could see her parents staring at her. Her mother looked furious, her father slightly desperate. She couldn't see Raffi in the crowd. She swallowed as she turned back to Sir John. "I . . . I stopped to speak to Mr. Edison."

"About what?"

She knew she couldn't tell him what William was trying to do without telling him why. That, she thought bitterly, was the whole point of blackmail. She tried to smile as she met the magistrate's eyes, hoping he would see her as the girl he had danced with last night when he was being kind. "I wanted to express my condolences."

"Generally, one does not shout at the recipient of condolences," Sir John said.

Had she really been speaking so loudly? "I . . . I don't believe I was shouting."

"We all heard you raise your voice," Kitty Hounslow said. She was half-hidden behind her mother, but when Amelia glanced over, the other girl's glare was plain to see. "What were you shouting about?"

"And what was your . . ." Sir John glanced at the wreckage of the table and decorations, at the blood that was slowly seeping through William's handkerchief. "Your altercation about?"

"There was no altercation," Amelia said. There was something in the way Sir John was looking at her that made her chest feel tight, as though something were closing in around her and she could not get away. And all those eyes, staring at her, so filled with suspicion . . . Amelia could feel sweat starting to trickle down her back.

But she couldn't tell them what had happened, not with Gregory or with William. No matter how suspicious they were, they had no real proof. If she told them nothing, they would have to move on. If she told them the truth, they could use it against her—now and perhaps for the rest of her life.

She couldn't risk that.

Amelia lifted her chin. "It was an accident, nothing more."

But her voice shook as she said it. When Sir John's brow lowered, she knew he didn't believe her.

"Miss Hartley." His voice was quiet, but there was iron behind it. Iron and regret. "Much as it pains me, I must do my duty, as entrusted to me by the law and the people of this county. I had already decided that until I get to the bottom of your relationship with Mr. Gregory Edison—"

"We had no relationship," Amelia insisted, starting to feel a little desperate. She could hear muttering from the drawing room door, but she kept her eyes fixed on Sir John.

He pressed on. "—and now, with Mr. William Edison as well, I am even more determined that it is the right course of action."

"What are you saying, Sir John?" Amelia's father demanded, his voice rising as he pushed to the front of the crowd. "What are you doing to our daughter?"

"I must insist that Miss Hartley remain confined to her room until I can ascertain what role, if any, she played in Mr. Edison's death."

The gasp that echoed through the hall came from more than a dozen throats. It was followed by silence.

Amelia stared at Sir John, hardly able to believe he was the same man she had known all her life. It was a struggle to find her voice, but when she did, she was pleased that it came out firm. "But I played no role at all."

"Then you will not scruple to tell me why you sought out Mr. William Edison, and why you were shouting at him," Sir John said. When Amelia was silent, he sighed and turned to their hostess, who was watching with wide eyes. "Mrs. Grantham, I will need you to provide me with the keys to Miss Hartley's room. And if there are any duplicates, I require those as well."

As Mrs. Grantham went to ring for the housekeeper, Amelia saw her mother push forward, only to be held back by the firm hands of Lady Adler. "Sir John, you cannot be serious!" Saba Hartley exclaimed. "You cannot mean to . . . to *arrest* Amelia."

"I must do as my conscience, my duty, and my own mind prompt me," he said, his voice heavy.

"You cannot mean it," Amelia insisted, while her parents protested and the whispers from the others grew in volume. "I would never have done anything to harm Gregory."

"If that is the case," the magistrate said, raising his voice to be heard above the noise. "Then you have nothing to fear. In the meantime, you will come with me."

"Sir John—" Mrs. Hartley begged, staring at him with a mix of desperation and disbelief.

But he held up his hand to forestall her as the housekeeper arrived with a jangling ring of keys, a broad-shouldered footman in tow. "I am sorry, madam, but I must do what is prudent. For the sake of everyone in this house. Miss Hartley, if you please?"

Amelia stared around the hall, shrinking back as she saw so many faces turned toward her with fear and scorn. She felt a bubble of laughter rise in her throat. None of it felt real, least of all the idea that they might need someone so sturdy and muscular to protect themselves from her. But she clamped her lips shut. The last thing she wanted was to seem hysterical.

Sir John glanced over his shoulder. "The rest of you, return to the drawing room." He cleared his throat. "At once. Miss Hartley." Sir John gestured toward the stairs. "If you please."

Amelia couldn't bring herself to look at her parents—at anyone. She could feel the eyes of everyone following her. William, she saw when she glanced behind her, had disappeared as soon as the attention of the other guests was off him.

But the magistrate had not accused her of anything specific—had not even said what he suspected her of. Which meant that all she had to do was wait. Even William had as good as admitted that he had no proof. Not yet.

Amelia took a deep breath as the door closed behind her. The sound of the key turning in the lock made her shudder. But she told herself it was only temporary.

With no proof, their suspicions could not touch her.

The fire in the hearth was still burning, chasing away the chill of the room. Amelia had just turned toward it when a sharp knock sounded at the door.

"It's me," her brother's voice said quietly. "The rest of them have gone."

She pressed her cheek against the wood. "Going to break me out, Raffi?" she asked, amazed by the lightness of her own voice. If she hadn't been able to see inside her own mind, she would have thought the girl speaking did not have a care in the world.

There was a pause from the other side of the door. "You do not have to keep pretending, little sister," he said quietly. "And you've no need to worry, either. You did nothing wrong, and so nothing will come of it."

"I know that," she said, closing her eyes.

She could hear his sigh through the wood. "Get some rest. I'll be back when I can. And in the meantime . . ."

"Yes?" she asked, when he paused too long.

"If there was something between you and Mr. Edison, best to tell the magistrate the truth. All will be well if you do, I am sure of it." He did not wait for her answer; she could hear him striding away almost as soon as he had finished speaking.

Amelia slumped against the door, suddenly weary in spite of the early hour. If she was stuck, she might as well do as her brother suggested and get some rest. And if she did not think about the locked door, she could pretend she was there only because she wanted to be.

She took her time, unpinning her hair, brushing it out, and winding it into a thick braid that hung over one shoulder and nearly to her waist. She wrapped an extra shawl around her shoulders and went to kneel in front of the fire. Then she pulled the letter out of her stays.

Gregory had slipped it into her hand as they brushed past each other during the ball, a cheeky grin flirting around the corners of his mouth, though he would not look directly at her. Her heart had skipped a beat, stuttering with anger, but that was Gregory: he had thought of it, it would serve him well, and so he did it. Amelia had clutched the note in the folds of her dress, able to read it only when she was away from Mrs. Adler in the washroom, her cheeks burning with frustration and regret. Then she had slipped it into her stays, where it had remained when she and the others had become snowed in for the night. And while Gregory . . .

She had wanted him to leave her be, but she had not wanted him to die, the stupid boy. Amelia scowled down at the letter, then tossed it onto the fire, stabbing at it with the poker until it was well and truly alight. She watched the edges curl and blacken until finally the whole thing went up in a burst of flame.

She let out a breath of relief that no one had thought to search her person before locking her in the room. Now all she had to do was deal with William.

Perhaps Raffi could help her, after all. She couldn't tell her parents, but Raffi was the sort of man who was caught up in scrapes and adventures all the time. Surely he would see that this was no different? If only she could bring herself to admit what she had done.

CHAPTER 8

Lily had spent the time waiting for her brother-in-law pacing around the library.

"Are you cold or anxious?" Matthew asked from his place by the window, where he was staring out at the snow.

"Both," Lily replied, going to stand by his side. "What are you thinking of?"

"My children," he said quietly, not looking down at her. "I hope they are not too worried that I've not yet returned."

Lily leaned her head against his shoulder, trying to think of something to say that wouldn't sound trite or dismissive. "Charlotte will keep their spirits up," she settled on at last. "And at least you know they are in good and very mischievous company."

The smile he gave her was strained but grateful. "How much longer do you think—"

He broke off as the door opened. They stepped apart quickly and turned to see Sir John entering. He stopped in the doorway, eyeing them both and looking uncertain.

"John." Lily frowned at her brother-in-law. "What is it? What happened?"

He hesitated. "I will tell you shortly," he said. "For now, please, sit down. There is something delicate I must ask you."

Lily and Matthew exchanged a glance before taking seats by the fire, though they left a good deal of room between them. Lily studied her brother-in-law. He paced from one end of the mantelpiece to the other before taking a seat opposite them, his brows drawn into a frown and his hands clasped in his lap.

He did not mince words once he was seated. "The two of you disappeared from the ballroom for some time yesterday. I must ask: Is there an understanding between you?"

Lily glanced at Matthew, who inclined his head slightly, gesturing for her to speak. "We are not engaged," she said. Little though she wanted to discuss the subject—especially not with John—it was not the time to withhold information. "But Mr. Spencer has proposed, and I am considering my answer. Is that relevant?"

"Not strictly," John admitted. "But I must be blunt, and it would have been easier to do so with you, Lily, were you engaged once more. As you are not . . ." He stood, pacing around the room again as though gathering his courage. When he spoke, he did not look either of them in the eye. "Did one of you visit the other's rooms last night?"

If it wasn't precisely the last question Lily had expected him to ask, it was certainly at the bottom of the list. She stared at him too long, not sure how to answer and unwilling to look to Matthew to see how he felt about such a line of inquiry. John waited, staring past her shoulder, his face scarlet but his expression stoic.

"We did not," Lily responded at last, her voice calm as ever, though she felt her own cheeks heating. "Were you hoping we could provide some confirmation of each other's whereabouts?"

"No, not that." John grimaced, fiddling with the knickknacks on the mantelpiece. He was always fidgety indoors, preferring movement and outdoor activities to occupy his time. "I do not believe either of you could be responsible. But I was hoping one of you might have seen or heard something in the night."

Lily shook her head, irrationally irritated with herself. There was no way she could have known that a murder was taking place, no reason for her to have paid attention to the movements of her fellow guests, and yet . . . "I was in my room all night," she said. "Listening to the wind and the branches cracking in the storm.

Though I suppose . . ." She shivered, pulling her borrowed shawl closer around her shoulders. "I suppose one of them must have been no breaking branch, but a pistol shot."

"I heard footsteps," Matthew said slowly.

John perked up. "When was this?"

"The storm woke me at one point," Matthew said. "I don't know how long I had been asleep. I think it might have been . . ." He made a frustrated face. "Between midnight and three o'clock in the morning? It is hard to say for certain."

"What kind of footsteps were they?" Lily asked before she thought better of the question. "Fast? Slow? Someone in a hurry or being careful?"

"Lily," John said, sounding a little put out. "If you would allow me to do my duty?"

She sighed. "My apologies, brother."

"But . . ." John cleared his throat. "If you would please answer her question."

Matthew looked as though he might be trying not to smile, though it took only a moment for his expression to grow serious once more. "Slow," he said. "And I noticed because they halted in front of my room. I thought I was imagining things until they began moving once again, so I went to look out the door."

"And?" John prompted eagerly. Lily leaned forward, not bothering to hide her interest.

"It was very dark," Matthew said apologetically. "All I could see was a woman at the end of the hall. I cannot say with any certainty what she looked like or who it might have been."

"Which end of the hall?" John asked.

"The one closest to the stairs, right where it branches into the other wing. It was there that she was joined by someone else."

"Who?" Lily asked, before she could stop herself.

Matthew shook his head. "It was too dark. But I believe it was a man. So I closed my door quickly and did not look anymore." He laughed shortly, a humorless sound. "I did not want to risk seeing anything untoward."

Lily glanced at her brother-in-law, wondering what he might make of such news. It was entirely possible that the two figures in the hall had something to do with Mr. Edison's murder. It was also possible that they were simply engaged in an illicit affair of their own. There had been so many worried and guilty looks around the breakfast table that morning. An affair might be the least of what her fellow guests were hoping to keep hidden from each other.

John scratched his chin. "That puts an interesting light on—"

A sudden knock at the door made him break off, and all three of them turned in surprise to discover who had interrupted them.

Jack stood in the doorway, his hair wild and his expression determined. But he spoke in a calm, measured voice. "I apologize for the intrusion, but I decided it was best not to wait to talk to you."

John had stood, and to Lily's irritation, he moved to block the door, his expression nervous. "For heaven's sake, John," she said, trying not to sound sharp. "The captain is hardly going to make a scene just now. Stand aside and let him speak his piece."

"I do not need you to tell me what to do," John grumbled, but he stood aside anyway, gesturing for Jack to close the door. "Come in, then, Hartley, if you must. But I was going to get to it eventually."

"I've no doubt of your thoroughness, Sir John," Jack said. To Lily's ear, he was leaning heavily on formality, an oddity between him and someone who had frequently trounced him at ninepins when they were boys and whist when they were grown. Clearly, he wanted to be as persuasive as possible. Then he glanced at her, and she climbed to her feet without thinking, pulled by the intensity in his gaze. "He's not told you yet, has he?"

"Told me what?" Lily frowned, turning on her brother-in-law. "Told us what, John? What happened while you were gone?"

He sighed heavily. "I wanted to talk to you first," he said through gritted teeth.

"The magistrate has arrested my sister," Jack said, biting off each word.

"What?" Lily exclaimed. "How could you not tell me—"

"I did not *arrest* her," John insisted, scowling.

"She is confined to her room," Jack said. Lily had never before seen him so tense, nor holding himself under such tight control. "Locked in until our magistrate can . . . what was the phrase you used? Determine what role, if any, she played in Mr. Edison's death."

"Which it is my responsibility to do," John said, drawing himself up, though he was still several inches shorter than Jack. "For each of you, I might add."

"And yet it is Amelia who is locked up."

"And it is Amelia whose name has been connected to Gregory Edison's so recently—to her great detriment, I might add, but not his—and Amelia who only minutes ago was heard shouting at his younger brother." He glared at Jack. "And who, unless I am grossly mistaken, failed to tell the truth when I asked her why."

A muscle jumped in Jack's jaw. "My sister is not a murderer," he said quietly, his eyes never leaving the magistrate.

John sighed. "Were it anyone but your sister, Hartley, you would say I acted prudently."

"Captain." Lily stepped forward, laying her hand on Jack's arm. "Arguing will not help her."

He let out a slow breath. "I know. I did not come to argue."

John's eyebrows rose. "Then why? Have you something of note to share?" He leaned forward eagerly. "Did you also see someone abroad in the night?"

Jack frowned. "Who . . . ?"

"I did," Matthew said quietly. He too had risen from his seat, but as he glanced between the three of them, Lily could not guess what he was thinking. "Though I cannot say who it might have been."

Jack hesitated, then shook his head firmly. "I wish I had. Alas, I slept soundly until I rose to check the roads this morning. And I went out the front door, so I did not see anything that might have happened in the direction of the yard."

Lily wondered about that beat of hesitation, but she didn't draw attention to it.

Sir John gave Jack a hard look. "So you say. Then why are you here?"

"To persuade you, I hope." Jack smiled grimly, taking a seat. After a moment, the rest of them did too. Jack leaned forward. "You can understand, I am sure, why I want this matter cleared up as quickly as possible. Which is why I think you ought to accept assistance in your investigation."

Lily tried to catch Jack's eye, but he was watching the magistrate—who, at the moment, was looking offended.

"See here, Hartley, I know I've not much worldly experience compared to someone who has sailed half the globe. But I know my neighbors, which I think counts for rather more in a situation like this. And I'm hardly a stupid fellow."

"I would never dream of saying that you are," Jack said, quiet and earnest. "But these sorts of things are too much for any one person to handle alone. And everyone here will be on their guard around you. They know you're going to unearth whatever secrets and petty problems they are hiding, and they will do their best to prevent that from happening."

Sir John had grimaced when Jack mentioned *these sorts of things*. He might not know details, but Lily kept up a regular correspondence with the Adlers—he had to know that Jack knew more about investigating the intricacies of murder than he did. But he still shook his head.

"Hartley, you must understand why I cannot allow you to assist me," he said, more gently than Lily would have expected. "It is your sister who . . . That is to say, you are too close to the situation for me to accept your help."

"I was not proposing that I be the one to assist you," Jack interrupted. Lily sat up a little straighter.

John frowned. "Then who?"

Jack cast a wry look in Lily's direction. "Mrs. Adler, of course."

There was silence in the room as Sir John stared at Jack for a moment, then turned to Lily. "I hadn't . . . that is . . ." He trailed off.

Lily sighed. "Are you going to protest that my sensibilities are too delicate for such a task?" she asked. Beside her, she heard Matthew let out a quiet huff of laughter.

"God forbid." John shook his head. "I know you better than *that*. But I had thought . . ." She saw him glance at Matthew, who drew back a little, glancing uncomfortably between them. Lily's mouth tightened angrily.

"Accept my assistance or do not, brother, as you wish. But do so on the merits of what I may offer, not on the basis of any permission you have imagined I require," she said tartly. "I am my own woman, am I not?"

Jack was staring at all of them, a frown gathering between his brows. She hoped that he wouldn't ask her any questions she wasn't ready to answer—not in front of Matthew—and was relieved when he cleared his throat and added, "She has a great deal more experience than either of us in such matters, as you know, and as well, she has seen some of the new methods of the Bow Street investigators up close."

"You may as well let me," Lily said. "Since no doubt I will end up poking around regardless. It is what I do, it seems."

She heard another quiet laugh from Matthew, and for a moment she felt his leg press against hers—a small gesture of support that wouldn't draw the attention of the others. But she didn't look away from her brother-in-law.

John drummed his fingers against the mantelpiece, studying her. "And what sort of things do you think your 'poking around' might unearth?"

"Do you wish a demonstration?" Lily asked, folding her hands in her lap in a show of demureness that she knew wouldn't fool any of the men in the room for a moment.

John raised his brows. "I do."

For a moment, Lily didn't respond, her eyes fixed on him. With that challenging, skeptical expression on his face, he reminded her so much of Freddy, and the sudden memory of that loss made her chest tighten. That didn't happen often anymore, and it took her a moment to gather her thoughts once again. The sensation lasted only a heartbeat, but it still left her flustered. Taking a deep breath, she drew her knee away from Matthew's and stood.

"What I have observed," she said, buying herself a moment more as she walked toward the window. The snow was falling more heavily again, and the morning light had grown dimmer. The solid weight of the sky looked low enough to reach out and touch. There could be no leaving that day—and perhaps not the next one either.

Lily lifted her chin and turned back to her small audience, unsurprised to find all three watching her. "Mrs. Grantham is afraid of her guests," she began. "That could be because she is hiding something and fears discovery. It could also be because she fears they will blame her for what happened, or for their own inability now to escape, even though the weather is hardly her fault. I cannot say yet which it is."

John nodded slowly, his expression growing thoughtful while one hand turned a candlestick in absent circles on the mantel. "Anything else?"

Lily smiled with grim humor. "Oh yes. I believe Miss Hounslow was in love with Mr. Edison—her eyes have been red, clearly from weeping, and her mother has been whispering and scolding her all morning."

"She might not be the only one in the neighborhood to harbor a *tendre* for him," Jack said. "From my mother's letters, I have gathered he was quite a popular fellow."

"But it seems she was the only one in this house to feel such sentiments," Lily said.

"Unless the captain's sister is to be counted among his admirers," John put in quietly.

Jack's expression turned stony. "I do not believe she is."

There was a moment of tense silence in the room, and Lily hurried to fill it. "Peter Coleridge wants something from Mr. Hounslow. They have been often in conversation, quite earnestly but carefully, from my observation."

"Are you sure it's not the other way around?" John interrupted. "From what I've heard, Hounslow isn't yet invested in Coleridge's fund, and he's the sort of man who will never pass up an opportunity to line his pockets."

"As expensive as his wife looks to be, I am not surprised," Lily said. "Perhaps you are correct, though I thought Mr. Coleridge was the one to initiate their conferences." Recalling Peter's departure from their conversation the night before, she added, "I also overheard that Mr. Edison was looking for Mr. Coleridge last night, though to what purpose, I could not say. You may wish to ask Peter about that. Of the others, Mrs. Crewe keeps to herself, though there seems to be some friendship forming with Mrs. Taylor. And finally, the younger Mr. Edison is in severe financial distress—the sort that prevents him from repaying his debts of honor."

John, who had been nodding absently along, gave her a sharp look. "What makes you say that?" he asked, seeming more interested than he had been in any other insight she had shared.

Lily gave Matthew a sideways glance. "Unfortunately—or perhaps fortunately, given the circumstances—Mr. Spencer and I overheard him say so." Briskly, she recounted what they had heard the night before.

"Was that your interpretation of the conversation as well, Mr. Spencer?"

Matthew nodded. "It was. I am sure, given the circumstances, that Mr. Coleridge would confirm it for you."

John looked uneasy, pacing with fidgety agitation in front of the fireplace. "I've not had much to do with murder, as you know, but I can imagine money would be a powerful motivator. Gregory Edison was known for spending frivolously and widely—a trait which is often to the detriment of a younger sibling's financial prospects. With him now gone . . ."

"That is certainly worth considering," Lily agreed. "Though we do not know how his family's finances stand, or whether the death of the elder Mr. Edison provides any sort of immediate remedy for the troubles of the younger."

"Then we shall have to ask him about it."

Lily could not help a small, satisfied smile. "We?"

He gave her an exasperated look. "You needn't look so smug, Lily. Though I suppose I would as well, were I in your place. I admit I could use your help. Does that satisfy you?"

Her expression grew more serious. "I shall be satisfied if we discover the truth, with as little damage as possible to those who have the misfortune to be swept along as we do."

"If they are innocent, they have nothing to fear," Sir John said stoutly.

Lily shook her head. "No one's life is entirely an open book, John, and usually for good reason. There may be those here who, while having nothing to do with Mr. Edison's death, have every reason to fear what might be brought to light in the days to come." Seeing her brother-in-law look a little terrified at the thought, Lily tried to smile. "We shall do our best, which is all we can do. What steps shall we take first?"

John, his confidence clearly shaken, cleared his throat. "Well, I have already admitted to needing your help. What do you advise? Talking to our fellow guests?"

"Perhaps the servants first," Lily suggested. "They often know a great deal more about our affairs than they let on."

He blew out a breath. "True enough. Gentlemen." He turned to Matthew and Jack. "I must ask that you rejoin the other guests in the drawing room. And I hope I need not say it, but you are to discuss nothing you have overheard in this room—including Mrs. Adler's involvement."

"Of course," Jack said, bowing.

"Of course," Matthew echoed him, rising. "We shall await your instructions with everyone else." When he turned to Lily, he held out his hand, his expression warm and encouraging. But it was not hard to see the worry in his blue-black eyes as she placed her palm in his. "Mrs. Adler, I hope you know that you may call on me for anything you need."

She smiled back, trying to look more confident than she felt. "Thank you, my friend. I will join you shortly, I am sure."

Jack had looked away as they spoke, but Lily could not help feeling that each gesture was on display, from Matthew's concern to the way his fingers lingered on hers before he released her hand. She felt her face heat and hoped she was not blushing too severely.

Jack followed as Matthew left the room but paused in the doorway and cleared his throat. "Mrs. Adler, might I have a word with you in the hallway? It will not take long."

There were only two things he might want to talk about. "As you wish, Captain."

When they were alone in the hallway, Matthew having gone ahead, Jack closed the library door, cutting them off from Sir John's view. Lily raised her brows. "Do you wish to discuss your sister or Mr. Spencer?"

"The latter." Jack took a deep breath. "I asked you last night what took you away from the ballroom in his company. Tell me," he said, quiet but insistent. "Please. This is not the time for secrets, not among friends. There are already too many of those in this house."

Lily hesitated. Jack and Freddy had been boyhood friends, almost as close as brothers, even after Jack left for the navy. Her friendship with him had grown out of their mutual, lingering grief and Jack's desire to serve as protector in Freddy's absence. It had become a partnership of equals, and Jack had been as pleased as anyone to see Lily lay off her mourning clothes at last and fully reenter the world. But Lily could not shake the worry that he might feel she was betraying her husband's memory in considering someone else's proposal.

But he was trusting her with his sister's safety. To offer him anything less than her honesty, after all they had been through, would be its own kind of betrayal.

"Mr. Spencer asked me to marry him," she said quietly. "I have not yet given him an answer."

Jack was very still for a moment, then nodded slowly. "Do you love him?"

Lily was not ready to answer that question. "I have not yet given him an answer," she repeated. "And for the moment, I think the question itself must wait. There are more pressing matters at hand."

"Perhaps," Jack said. He glanced behind him, where Matthew still lingered at the spot where the hallway turned toward the drawing room, clearly watching them. "Murder and intrigue might come first, for necessary reasons. But I don't think either of you have put it from your minds."

He spoke carefully, giving away nothing. Lily wanted to ask what he thought; she wanted the insight of a friend who knew her so well. But that felt selfish—he already had enough on his mind, enough to worry about. His focus was, and should be, on his sister.

Her own questions would keep.

At last, Jack turned back to her, a wry smile on his face. "I can tell you what Sir John thinks of the matter, at least."

Lily bristled, remembering her brother-in-law's behavior. "Why do you suspect he knows anything about it?"

"Because it is clear that, in his mind, you have already been handed over to a new lord and protector. Besides." Jack snorted at her expression of instant distaste. "He had to have suspected already. Why else would Mr. Spencer have been invited here?"

"I'm not a parcel to be passed from one family to another," Lily said indignantly.

"I know you are not," Jack said, his voice uncommonly gentle. "Just as I can guess that you have decided not to let yourself dwell on it until you have dealt with the task at hand. For which . . ." He paused, clearing his throat, and his expression grew more serious. "For which I am more grateful than I can say. I am glad Sir John accepted your help, Lily. He needs it. And if I cannot be the one responsible for protecting my sister, there is no one I trust more than you." He bowed, giving her a crooked, hopeful smile. "Good luck."

Lily watched him head toward the drawing room to rejoin the others, feeling a guilty weight settle in her chest. She had not told him that she was not so immediately convinced as he of his sister's innocence. Whatever had passed between Amelia and Mr. Edison had clearly threatened her somehow—at least her reputation, and perhaps even her person. Lily couldn't picture the girl being guilty of planning a murder. But lashing out in a moment of fear or some other strong emotion? That, Lily could imagine.

A draft snaked down the hall, making her shiver, and she pulled her shawl more tightly around her shoulders. And here was Jack, forced to step aside when he no doubt longed to be charging into the fray, relying on her to discover the truth.

She hoped that his faith in her abilities was not misplaced.

CHAPTER 9

The housekeeper looked nervous as she entered the library. Lily couldn't blame her for that, though she kept her feelings off her face.

It was Mrs. Reynaud who had gone to fetch Mrs. Grantham that morning when the dead man was discovered. She was a woman of African ancestry, striking even in the plain garb of a servant. Delicate lines fanned out from the corners of her eyes, and her black hair was pinned firmly back under a starched white cap. Her wary eyes took in every inch of the room as Sir John showed her in.

"You may take a seat, Mrs. Reynaud," he said gravely, though he did not follow his own advice and instead took up his position at one end of the mantel.

"Thank you, sir, but I'll remain standing," the housekeeper said. Her glance lingered on Lily, who was seated near the fireplace.

"You need not worry of being accused of any impertinence in behavior," John said, every inch the magnanimous country squire.

"I hope a woman of my position never need fear being accused of impertinence, as though I were a child or a common scullery maid," Mrs. Reynaud replied, her tone never losing its polite cadence.

Lily had to purse her lips against a smile. The housekeeper was a formidable figure.

John cleared his throat, looking flustered. "Yes, well. Indeed not. But we may be talking for some time. And it is cold away from the fire. This weather is a damnable thing."

Mrs. Reynaud seemed to consider his words, then, very deliberately, took a seat across from Lily. "How may I be of service?"

"I am attempting to form a picture of what happened last night," John said gravely. "I understand that you went to fetch Mrs. Grantham after Mr. Edison's . . ." He cleared his throat again. "After Mr. Edison was discovered?"

"Indeed."

When she offered nothing else, John frowned. "Mrs. Reynaud, you must be aware that, as magistrate, I am duty bound to discover what happened last night. When you withhold information, you are hindering my work."

"How's it withholding to answer the question you asked me, sir?" the housekeeper said, still soft and polite.

He scowled at her. "Tell me what happened."

She considered for a moment. "Constance, the scullery maid, is generally the one to check the poultry in the morning. We're early risers belowstairs, and even earlier than usual today, with a houseful of unexpected guests. I was up and about, seeing to the arrangements for clothing and linens, when I heard Connie scream. We all did, and half the staff came rushing into the kitchen in time to see her run in, sobbing about a gentleman in the snow. Mr. Lambton and me—"

"Lambton is the butler?" Sir John interrupted.

"Yes, sir. He was tending to the silver—he didn't have it all prepared, being as hosting happened so suddenly—so he arrived as quick as I did. There was already a fair crowd heading into the yard, but we were able to clear them out enough to see—" Mrs. Reynaud's cool demeanor wavered a little, and a shiver chased its way across her shoulders. She let out a deep breath. "It was clear quick enough that there was nothing to be done for him. Mr. Lambton did his best to keep everyone back in the kitchen, and I went for Mrs. Grantham."

"And did you notice anything odd?"

She gave him an impatient look. "The gentleman being dead was fairly odd."

"Other than that," John said, with somewhat exaggerated patience. "We may take it for granted that murders do not happen here regularly. Did anything else catch your eye? Were any of the staff behaving oddly? Anyone who might have been out of their room in the night?"

"The staff's all in shock," Mrs. Reynaud said. But she regarded the magistrate with a grim almost-smile as she spoke. "You want to know if I think any of them might've done it."

"Someone had to," John pointed out. "I do not for a moment believe anyone was trudging here and back through that storm."

"Well, it wasn't any of the staff." Mrs. Reynaud spoke with absolute certainty as she fished a chain out from under the neckline of her black gown. Hanging from it was a heavy key. "There's a door past the kitchen, between the servants' quarters and the rest of the house. Anytime we have guests, I keep it locked at night."

"Do you worry about theft?"

Mrs. Reynaud met his eyes. "I worry about the gentleman guests bothering the female staff."

"Oh." John cleared his throat and glanced at Lily. If he expected her to be flustered by such a pronouncement, he was mistaken; her only response was to give the housekeeper an approving nod. Lily didn't know a single woman with any degree of awareness who would have argued that the housekeeper was taking unnecessary precautions.

John nodded slowly, not arguing the point, as he drummed his fingers on the mantel. "Is there any chance someone would have been able to retrieve the key and unlock the door?"

"There's a chance any little thing might happen," Mrs. Reynaud allowed, pursing her lips. "But that doesn't mean it's likely. I sleep with the key around my neck to ensure no one can sneak about in the other direction either. Anyone who wanted to retrieve it would have to do so without waking me. And that," she finished firmly, "is hard to do."

Lily could well believe it.

"What if a guest requires something in the night?" John asked, looking curious.

"The bells are just outside my room. If one of them rings, I can wake the appropriate servant and unlock the door for them."

"And did you have to do so last night?"

She met his eyes steadily. "I heard no bells last night."

"And do you know of any interest among the servants in Mr. Edison or his affairs?"

Mrs. Reynaud considered the question. "Nothing that comes to mind. He'd never stayed here before. Mrs. Grantham knew him well enough to invite him to a large party, but I don't think he'd ever been to one of her smaller ones. She's more in his parents' set."

"One of the maids might have crossed his path. Had an affair, the sort of thing girls like that get up to."

"And what do you know of girls like that?" the housekeeper asked. Lily could see a muscle clenching in her jaw, though her voice was still even.

Sir John was undaunted. "I know that girls of any class who aren't being watched by their parents can get caught up in all sorts of mischief."

Lily thought of Amelia and wondered if he was doing the same. She still could hardly believe that he had arrested Jack's sister. She clasped her hands in her lap to keep them still, her face impassive as she watched the housekeeper.

"They may be out from under their parents' eyes while they're in service, but they aren't out from under mine," Mrs. Reynaud said, stiff and dignified. "Mrs. Grantham insists on a certain standard of behavior in the staff, as do I. And as I said, the door was locked all night."

John nodded again. "Very well, Mrs. Reynaud. Thank you."

She gave him a hard look but did not stand in response to the obvious dismissal. Instead, she turned to Lily, who had sat, watchful and silent, throughout the conversation. "And what questions do you have for me, madam?"

Lily gave the housekeeper an assessing glance. "What makes you think I am here for any purpose other than to provide a chaperone?"

"Two reasons, madam, which you know well enough. And I'm no fool, so I know them too," Mrs. Reynaud said. She had not once raised her voice, even when she was clearly offended. And she did not hesitate to look directly at Lily as she spoke. "First, because no one worries about providing a chaperone for servants, and certainly not for the housekeeper."

"You're rather young and pretty for a housekeeper," Lily pointed out. "I imagine you might benefit from that locked door as much as any of the maids."

Mrs. Reynaud shook her head. "Soon as a servant pops the word *missus* in front of her name, there's no gentleman giving her a second glance. Wouldn't you agree, sir?" she added, glancing at John.

Who blushed bright red. "I am a happily married man, Mrs. Reynaud," he said firmly. "I don't give a second glance to any woman, in service or otherwise."

"Then you're an uncommon sort," the housekeeper said, polite but pointed.

"Was there ever a Mr. Reynaud?" Lily asked curiously.

The housekeeper hesitated, then shook her head. "There wasn't." Sir John made an involuntary movement at the admission, his gaze growing sharper, and she glanced at him, looking a little defensive for the first time. "I don't claim the title as any sort of deception. It's custom for a housekeeper to be called *missus*, whether or not she's ever been married."

"Of course," John rumbled, but he still looked thoughtful. Lily didn't blame him. In such a case, anyone who was pretending, in even a small way, to be someone they were not would prompt his suspicion.

"What was the second reason?" Lily asked, drawing the housekeeper's attention back to herself. At Mrs. Reynaud's puzzled frown, she added, "You said not needing a chaperone was your first reason. May I ask the second?"

The housekeeper narrowed her eyes. "The second reason is that I was there this morning. Mrs. Grantham didn't let you look at that body for nothing, and I'm guessing the squire here didn't let you stay for nothing either. So. I expect you have other questions for me."

Sir John blustered and protested, but Lily nodded slowly. "It is a rare thing for a woman of your age to have risen to the position of housekeeper in a household this large. You must be very good at your work."

"Is there a question in there, madam?" the housekeeper asked stiffly.

"Indeed. To be an excellent housekeeper, one must see a great deal, to anticipate the needs of both employer and guests, to know the strengths and weaknesses of each person who sits in the servants' hall. To almost predict what is going to happen before it happens. So." Lily's voice grew sharp, though it stayed as soft as the house-keeper's own had been. "What have you seen, Mrs. Reynaud?"

"Nothing," the housekeeper said firmly.

Lily waited, letting the silence draw around them, her eyes fixed on the other woman. Mrs. Reynaud shifted a little in her seat, then glanced at Sir John. At last, she sighed. "Nothing about the staff. And I don't like to gossip about Mrs. Grantham's guests."

"It is hardly gossip if a magistrate is asking you about it," John pointed out.

Mrs. Reynaud pursed her lips, still looking uncomfortable, but she nodded. "Mr. Edison was, I believe, having financial difficulties."

Sir John exchanged a glance with Lily. "Mr. William Edison?"

"No." The housekeeper shook her head. "Well, that is, not just him. The elder brother, who died, was in difficulties as well."

"How do you know?" Lily asked, sitting forward.

Mrs. Reynaud sighed again. "We all had to help get the guests settled last night. It was busy, with the whole staff hurrying to see all was comfortable. While I was setting new candles in the elder Mr. Edison's room, his brother came rushing in, all in a lather. I wasn't intending to eavesdrop, you understand," she added, looking a little nervous for the first time. "It's a point of pride that I never do. But they weren't exactly being careful with their words."

"Which were?" John prompted.

"Mr. William wanted to borrow money from his brother, I think. He might have complained about their funds being unequal, with him being the younger brother. I was trying not to listen. And the elder Mr. Edison said something about Mr. Dawson the carriage-maker hounding him for payment. For his phaeton, I believe. I know he said, 'I'm as hard up as you right now and can't advance a penny until next month.' I left as quick as I could, so I didn't hear much more than that." She sniffed. "Young men of his class are often unwise with money. Begging your pardon, sir," she added, almost as an afterthought.

"You shan't hear any argument from me on that score," the magistrate said, shaking his head. "Thank you, Mrs. Reynaud."

"And you have nothing else you can tell us?" Lily asked. "Anything else you saw in the night?"

"I saw nothing in the night," Mrs. Reynaud said, quickly and firmly. She glanced down at her hands, which were folded demurely in her lap. "After all, I was on the other side of that locked door, same as every other servant."

Lily waited a moment, then nodded. "Very well. I thank you for your honesty, even if it was a bit uncomfortable."

Mrs. Reynaud stood at last. "Is that all? Can I have anything sent up for you? Tea?"

"No, you may continue with your work for the day," John said.

"Very good, sir. Madam." Mrs. Reynaud gave the barest drop of a curtsy before leaving.

As soon as the door was closed behind her, John let out a loud sigh. "What did you make of that?" he asked, resuming his pacing. "Do you think she was telling the truth about everything? The bit about William and Gregory squares well enough with what you heard."

"It does," Lily said slowly. "I believe she was telling the truth about that much, at least. As for the rest . . ." She glanced up at her brother-in-law as he took a place on the settee across from her. "She was lying, you know. She would not meet my eyes at the end there."

"What do you think she was concealing?"

Lily turned over the housekeeper's words in her mind. "I wonder if she is hiding her own whereabouts. The locked door would prevent any of the servants from going upstairs, as she said. But she kept the key on her person. There was nothing to stop her from using it."

John looked unhappy. "Do you think that means she turned murderer? Or . . ." He trailed off, looking a little hesitant to say what he was thinking.

"Or, as we discussed, she is young and pretty, particularly for a housekeeper?" Lily suggested. When he nodded, she couldn't help adding, "I was a married woman, John, as you well know. You needn't be so delicate with me."

"Yes, but you were married to my brother," he grumbled. "There are some things a man does not care to think about in relation to his own family."

"Well, thank God you never had any sisters, then," Lily said. "I should hate to see how squeamish you would be about them."

"Very squeamish," he said with a small chuckle, looking relieved to have something to laugh about. A moment later, though, his expression grew more sober. "You look as though you are thinking about something."

"Always," Lily said, her eyes fixed on the crackling fire. "Was there anything found with Mr. Edison?"

"The gun," replied John, his fingers tapping restlessly against the arm of the settee. "Mrs. Grantham thought it was one from her gun cabinet, but she was not sure—they are taken out regularly to be cleaned, but not used much since her husband's death."

"Did you check?"

He nodded. "There was a pistol missing, so it seems she was right. But no one can recollect when the cabinet was last opened or who would have been responsible for locking it after. It seems perfectly possible that it was left unlocked at some point, which means anyone could have gotten in easily."

"Wise of our killer to leave it with the body," Lily said thoughtfully. "If they had taken it back into the house and hidden it in their room, it might have been found. And if they had attempted to conceal it somewhere else instead, they would have risked being seen in the act."

"Would be easier if he—"

"Or she," Lily interrupted.

"Or she," John acknowledged. "Lord knows the female sex can be deadly when they wish it. It would have made things easier for us if he or she had been stupider."

"Alas," Lily said. She didn't like to admire a murderer, but she had found it was better to acknowledge her quarry's strengths than otherwise. Someone who would kill was not someone she wanted to underestimate. "Was there nothing else with him?"

"A candle in a holder, which we unearthed from the snow as well. It was the same style as the one in my chamber, so I imagine he brought it with him when he left his room. A piece of paper in his pocket that looked like it had once been written on, but the ink was blurred from the wet. And a string clutched in his fist."

"A string?" Lily propped up her elbows, resting her chin on her clasped hands. "You mean like a bit of twine?"

"No." John shook his head. "I think it was a necklace. It was very short, but it had part of a clasp still at one end. And the other end was knotted before it frayed." He gave her a bit of a smile. "I have purchased enough jewelry for my wife to know what sort of necklace would be knotted like that."

"Pearls," Lily said slowly. "Why would he be holding a broken bit of a pearl necklace?"

"He wouldn't," John suggested.

"No, he wouldn't," Lily agreed. "He would be holding the whole necklace. Whoever needed to remove it from his hand would have been the one to break it."

"And the knots would mean they wouldn't lose more than one or two of the pearls."

"Indeed. So somewhere in this house is a broken pearl necklace that we need to find." Lily frowned. "But what does it mean?"

"You mean, why would the necklace itself have been important?" John shook his head. "Your guess is as good as mine."

Lily stood, feeling fidgety. She paced toward the window, her hands clasped together in front of her lips and her fingers tapping together. "Why do I recollect something about pearls?"

"Do you?' John asked, surprised. "Was one of the ladies wearing them last night?"

"No," Lily said, shaking her head. "None of the ladies who remained here, at least. Not that I can recall . . ." The memory was at the edge of her thoughts, but she could not quite capture it. "Perhaps it will come to me in time," she said, grimacing in frustration.

"I hope so," John said fervently. Lily felt a pang of sympathy for her brother-in-law, always so straightforward, constitutionally incapable of entertaining dark thoughts about anyone he met.

Sir John was magistrate through default of his elevated rank in the county, but there were few people less suited to the task. In the past, the poachers and petty thieves he had been required to deal with had been let off with small fines and admonishments to change their ways, and he was more likely to give those arrested for vagrancy a hot meal and a shilling than he was to have them run out of town. Since most of the criminals who had previously crossed his path were equally straightforward, guilty of little more than having fallen on hard times or of quarreling with the neighbors they had wronged, his good-natured leniency and impulse toward forgiveness had been all that was required to maintain order and keep the peace.

A murder, however, was an entirely different matter. And poor John was clearly feeling out of his depth.

"I suppose I need to speak with the other guests," he said, sighing as he stood up.

"Perhaps all at once?" Lily suggested. "If you share a bit of information or ask a question of the whole company, no one person will feel singled out by your attention. They may be more likely to reveal something by accident, either in manner or expression."

"A good idea, that," he said, nodding. He rubbed his hands together briskly. "You are rather good at this, you know."

Lily smiled a little. "Indeed I am. But I do appreciate you noticing."

CHAPTER 10

Mrs. Grantham had clearly been trying to keep everything feeling as much like a typical house party as she could. Someone had brought in tea, though few of the guests were partaking, and around the room various groups sat talking, reading, or playing cards. Mrs. Taylor practiced at the pianoforte, tactfully playing a quiet tune that was neither too cheerful nor so melancholy that it became oppressive. Mrs. Hounslow and her daughter were even writing letters, though that pursuit seemed particularly desperate. They all knew no letters were going in or out, any more than they themselves were. Still, Lily couldn't blame the women for wanting to preserve some sense that all was normal.

No one looked toward the windows, where the snow was still falling.

Lily entered alone, and at the sound of the door closing behind her, nearly every head turned toward her. She met the other guests' eyes—some curious, many worried, a few impossible to read—as calmly as possible, nodding to Mrs. Coleridge and Mrs. Grantham in response to their murmured greetings.

Lady Adler was playing cards with Matthew and Mrs. Crewe, and Lily went to join them, intending to take a seat facing the room where she could keep an eye on everyone. But her path took her past where Mr. Hartley was reading an old newspaper and Mrs. Hartley was working on a piece of embroidery. Neither of them looked up or made eye contact with their neighbors.

Jack was nowhere to be seen.

Lily's eyes darted around the room, wondering if she had somehow missed him. But no, Jack was not there. She closed her eyes briefly, wishing she could go find him just to shake him and tell him he was being an idiot. For him to slip away just then . . . she could guess where he had gone, but he had to know how it would look. When Mrs. Hartley met her eyes, her tense, humorless smile said she knew it too.

Lily bit the inside of her cheek and turned away, not wanting to say anything and draw attention to his absence. Instead, she took a seat at the card table, though she shook her head when Lady Adler offered to deal her in.

"Any news?" Mr. Spencer murmured as he considered his cards.

Before she could answer, though, a more strident demand echoed his query. "Mrs. Adler, did I see the magistrate pull you aside when we left the breakfast room?" Mrs. Hounslow asked, laying aside her pen. "You were gone some time. What did he say? What did he ask you? Are we all to remain penned in here for the rest of the day?"

"Penned in the house, certainly," Peter said, glancing out the window as he delivered a cup of tea to his mother. "At this rate, the light will barely last the afternoon."

"Not to worry, sir, we've plenty of candles and firewood laid in," Mrs. Grantham said reassuringly. She was seated with Mrs. Coleridge and Mr. Taylor, and she reached out to give Peter's hand a pat where it lay on the back of the settee. "And it cannot snow forever."

"I was not talking about the weather," Mrs. Hounslow said impatiently, fidgeting with her writing things and glancing about the room as she spoke. "If he already has Miss Hartley arrested, why keep us here? We can all guess what happened easily enough."

Beside her, Lily saw Miss Hounslow try to wipe away her tears before they fell, but they splashed on her paper anyway. She crumpled up her ruined letter with sudden, surprising vehemence, before taking a deep breath and drawing another sheet from the pile to begin again. On the table next to her were two or three more crumpled attempts.

Without looking at his daughter, Mr. Hounslow, who was reading the paper at the same table, passed her a handkerchief. Her brother slouched in his chair with the rest of his family, flipping a coin over and over, looking bored.

"I am afraid I am not privy to his thoughts, Mrs. Hounslow," Lily replied, trying to sound as demure as possible while she lied with a straight face. They would all be less on their guard around her if they did not know she was assisting the magistrate, and that meant they would be more likely to reveal something important without realizing it. "He spoke to me only as a brother, dear man. He is always concerned about the delicate feelings of women."

That earned her a sharp look from Lady Adler, who knew full well that Lily had few delicate feelings for anyone to be concerned about, let alone her son. But it was delivered from behind a hand of cards, and Lily hoped she was the only one who noticed.

"Not so dear right now," Mrs. Hounslow grumbled. "Did he say what he will do next?"

"I believe he is planning to speak with us soon," Lily said, speaking slowly and a little uncertainly. "Though what he intends after that, I could not say."

"Does anyone know what he thinks happened?" Mrs. Crewe asked quietly. She did not look up as she spoke, her eyes on the cards she was playing as she laid three on the table, but Lily could see her fingers trembling as she did so. Without gloves on, the tips of them were reddened and rough, as though she were suffering from the uncommonly cold weather.

"Well, we all know what happened," Mr. Hounslow said, still not looking up from his paper. "Edison was always a stupid boy, and apparently he was stupid enough to get himself—"

"Albert!" his wife snapped. Mr. Hounslow shrugged and shook his paper to straighten the pages. But the warning in his wife's voice was enough to make him fall silent.

"We *do* know what happened, though," Miss Hounslow said, her voice shaking. She looked around the room, as though seeking approval. And it seemed she found it from at least one person— Lily tilted her head, trying to see who—because her voice grew stronger. "There is one person here who had reason to harm Mr. Edison, and she is—"

"If you have some proof of who harmed Mr. Edison, I look forward to hearing it."

The sound of the heavy drawing room door opening echoed through the room, and half the company jumped at Sir John's sudden speech. Miss Hounslow flushed bright red, sinking back in her seat, while her brother chuckled and gave her a pat on the shoulder.

"But you locked Miss Hartley up, sir," Mrs. Hounslow insisted shrilly. "And we all heard her altercation with William Edison not an hour past. What more do you need?"

"A great deal more, I am afraid," John said, stiff with dignity. "Suspicion is not the same as proof, however likely we may think an outcome to be."

"Then do you think my daughter—" Mr. Hartley had leaned forward in his chair, but he stumbled over his words a little, looking uncertain. "That is, you are not convinced that she—"

"I am convinced of nothing yet, whatever my suspicions may be," John said. Mr. Hartley sank back in his chair, closing his eyes as he let out a slow, shaking breath. "Which is why I have asked you all to gather and remain here. The less we are each alone right now, the more room I have to learn what I must. And . . ." He hesitated. "And the safer you will all be."

A shiver went through the room at his words. Some, like Mrs. Grantham, looked down unhappily, clearly unsurprised by the magistrate's words. Others, like Mrs. Hounslow, looked stunned by the reminder that the danger might not be past.

"I've no doubt I will speak to some of you individually," John continued, surveying the room. "But having talked with some of the servants, I have decided that my first questions are best asked of everyone. I know this is a difficult situation—"

"To say the least," Mrs. Coleridge interjected sharply, thumping her cane.

"Indeed." John cleared his throat, scowling a little at the interruption. "A difficult situation, and I've no wish to keep you in more suspense than I can avoid."

Lily watched the company out of the corner of her eye, taking in their reactions. Mrs. Coleridge lifted her chin imperiously, though it was impossible to tell whether she approved or disapproved. Mrs. Grantham fiddled with her teacup, turning it in anxious circles on its saucer. Mrs. Crewe let out a slow breath, as though she had been holding it in suspense and was suddenly relieved. The younger Mr. Hounslow merely looked bored.

The rest of the guests kept their eyes fixed on Sir John, who was still speaking.

"What I am going to share with you now is . . . well. It has come to my attention that some number of guests may have left their rooms in the night."

A murmur went through the room. Lily saw Mrs. Taylor and her husband exchange a pointed glance as she joined him on the settee. Mrs. Crewe made a sudden movement that knocked her cards from the table, and she had to bend to retrieve them.

"I must ask that, if anyone saw anything suspicious, you tell me so—privately, if you wish—as soon as you can," John continued. "On my honor as a gentleman, I promise not to reveal whatever you will be forced to tell me about your own . . ." He cleared his throat. "Nighttime activities."

A nervous titter went through the room as some of the guests glanced at each other, wondering who Sir John might be speaking of. Lily ignored it, focusing instead on those who remained silent. Mrs. Grantham's eyes were fixed on the magistrate, her hands clasped around the arms of her chair so tightly that they trembled. Her face had gone painfully pale at Sir John's words, then just as swiftly deep scarlet.

She certainly had been out of her room in the night. Or perhaps had been visited by someone who was. But who?

Lily looked around the room, her gaze settling on the senior Mr. Hounslow. He looked the type to engage in a clandestine affair. But looks could be deceiving.

"It is vital, in such a matter as this, that we all work together and be as honest as possible," John said, speaking a little more loudly over the whispers darting through the room. "However painful or embarrassing certain revelations might be. Which is why I must also ask that if anyone knows of any financial difficulties that Mr. Edison—the elder, I mean—might have been experiencing, you speak with me about that as well."

Another murmur went through the room, this one equally divided between curiosity and affront that such things were being discussed openly.

"Well, if he was in difficulties, there was a simple solution for that," Mrs. Coleridge said in a loud whisper, poking Mrs. Taylor in the side as though sharing a confidence. The other women gave a pained smile and scooted an inch farther away. "Should have invested in Peter's Irish fund. Silly boy. Has Mr. Taylor done so yet?"

"Mother," Peter said, looking embarrassed as a chuckle went through the room, breaking the tension that had gripped them all. "This is hardly the time—"

"Well, I, for one, know nothing of any of these matters," Mrs. Crewe said, more loudly than was necessary. She glanced around the room, her chin lifted, then turned back to Sir John. "I did not leave my room the entire night and know nothing of any comings or goings. And I would never dream of prying into my neighbors' finances. What a horrid thought."

"No, nor do we know anything," Mrs. Hounslow agreed. "Is that not right, my dears?" she added, turning to her family.

"Slept like the dead," her son agreed. An awkward silence fell over the room at his words, and he turned bright red as he realized what he had said. "I mean . . . that is to say . . ."

"Mrs. Taylor, did I not once hear that you suffer sometimes from insomnia?" Peter asked suddenly. Mrs. Hounslow took the opportunity to scoot closer to her son and speak to him in a low, hissing voice. Mrs. Taylor gave Peter an uneasy look. "Perhaps it was you who was spotted in the corridors in the small hours of the morning?"

"No, I am sure it was not I," she said quickly. "That is . . . perhaps? I don't quite remember. Do you recall, my love, whether I needed to take myself for a stroll last night? I know the storm kept me awake for some time."

"I am afraid not," her husband said, giving her a bored look. "I never wake once I go to sleep. As you know." He glanced in Peter's direction. "What about you, Coleridge?"

"Our hostess's accommodations were so comfortable that I, too, slept through the night." Peter gave a small bow in the direction of Mrs. Grantham.

Who nodded several times in a row. "Nor do I have anything helpful to share, I fear. I always sleep soundly."

"And my mother never wakes at night," Peter added, glancing at the imperious Mrs. Coleridge, who nodded a little absentmindedly, as though she had not quite followed the conversation.

"Nor do I."

"Nor I."

"Please, everyone," Matthew said. He spoke quietly, but his voice was pitched to carry—he had a been a soldier once, after all—and the room, which had been buzzing with suggestions and denials, fell silent. "A man has been killed. One person, certainly, has reason to dissemble. But the rest of us have every reason to be honest, and we should do so."

A murmur of embarrassed agreement went through the room, until Mr. Taylor snorted. "Easy for you to say, sir. We barely even know who you are, and you have offered no hint of your own whereabouts. Perhaps you might enlighten us first?"

Lily could see Matthew's jaw clench. "I was in my room all night."

Mr. Taylor laughed. "As we've all said."

John sighed. "I realize these topics are delicate and that everyone is one edge. Which is why I shall invite each of you to join me, one at a time, beginning in a quarter hour. Again, you have my word that I will do my best to keep what you tell me in confidence."

"Does that mean we are all released from this room?" Mr. Hartley asked, glancing around. Lily was used to seeing him as a confident, friendly man. For him to look at his neighbors so nervously was jarring. But under the circumstances, she couldn't blame him.

"Why would we want to leave?" Mrs. Taylor asked, sounding a little shrill. "If the magistrate is correct and a murderer could still be among us, I for one much prefer to be always in the company of others."

"Don't worry, dear," Mrs. Coleridge said, patting the younger woman's hand and chuckling. "No one wants to murder you except your husband."

Bursts of nervous and unkind laughter chased each other through the room, and more than one person began speaking at the same time.

"Mother, under the circumstances—"

"Oh, hush, Peter, I was only teasing. If one cannot make a *joke* at my age—"

"Well, *I* did not find it amusing—"

"In very poor taste—"

"No sense of humor—"

"In a quarter of an hour," John said, raising his voice. "I hope someone will choose to be more forthright once fewer eyes are upon you."

The room buzzed with conversation once he had left. One by one, they fell into small groups, talking quietly and glancing at each other with poorly concealed anxiety. Mrs. Taylor, still clearly offended, returned to the pianoforte, while Mrs. Coleridge, looking bored, thumped her way over to the Hartleys, handing Mrs. Hartley the book that had been resting on her lap.

"My eyes are not what they once were. Saba, you will be good enough to read to me."

It was clearly not a request, but Mrs. Hartley still nodded as graciously as she could under the circumstances. But Lily could see her hands shaking as she flipped to the first page.

"Mrs. Adler?"

Lily's attention was drawn back to the card table by the question from Mrs. Crewe.

"Shall we deal you in for the next round?"

"Oh—no, I thank you."

Matthew stood. "Mrs. Adler, would you care to take a turn about the room?" he asked, offering his arm. When she took it, nodding to the others, he steered her away from the card table. "Shall we join Mrs. Grantham by the tea cart? Or I can find you a novel, I am sure, in the stack they brought up with us."

"I do not think I could read a single word," she said, letting out a shaky laugh.

"Perhaps not," he agreed as he handed her into a chair set a little apart from the others, close to the half-open door. There was indeed a pile of books on the table next to the seat he had chosen; he selected one and handed it to her, bending low to whisper in her ear as he did so. "But you might need to pretend to read while you keep your eye on everyone."

She looked up at him as he took the seat next to her, a book of his own in hand. "Are you afraid?" she asked quietly.

"Damn near terrified," he admitted. "You?"

"Yes," she whispered. "Desperate people are unpredictable. They stop seeing those around them as neighbors and start seeing them as . . ." She let out a slow breath. "As obstacles that need to be removed."

"And everyone here is growing desperate."

"Yes." She did not add that she was afraid of what Jack might do if he became convinced that his sister was in danger. He was already being foolish; she did not want to think about how much more risk he might be willing to take.

But no one had yet noticed his absence—or if they had, they had not commented upon it. Which meant that they might not notice hers either. "I need to find Sir John," she murmured to Matthew, setting her book aside. "If anyone asks where I have gone . . ."

"I shall think of some embarrassing excuse," he said, smiling a little. Lily gave a short laugh, grateful for the attempt at humor. But a moment later, his expression grew more serious. "Or do you want me to come with you?"

"No, I think he would wish it to be just the two of us." She laid a hand on Matthew's arm. "You will be careful, remaining here?"

He caught her fingers and, to her surprise, raised them just long enough to brush a kiss across her knuckles. His back was to the room, mostly shielding the gesture from the view of the others, but still. It was a shockingly intimate moment for such a public space. Lily felt a shiver skate its way up her arm, in spite of her worries.

"Promise me you will be careful too," he murmured, his eyes serious.

"I promise," she replied. "Wish me good hunting?"

★ ★ ★

It did not take her long to find her brother-in-law once she had slipped out of the room. He was pacing the hall between the drawing room and the library with his hands clasped behind his back, his mouth and brows drawn into tight lines that cut across his face. She could recognize the expression; Freddy had often looked the same when he was steeling himself for some unpleasant task. She pushed the memory abruptly aside. "John?"

He looked up, startled, then let out a sharp breath when he saw her. "Lily. Did something happen?"

"Not yet. But it occurs to me . . ." She glanced back toward the drawing room. "They are all buzzing in there, growing more anxious, but they are not leaving. And they have not been back to their rooms since they left this morning, before what happened to Mr. Edison was common knowledge."

He nodded slowly. "You think it is time for a search."

"I do," Lily said, nodding. "Shall we find Mrs. Reynaud again and ask for her help?"

CHAPTER 11

The staff had left the curtains tightly drawn over the windows to keep in as much heat as possible. Amelia, shivering a little, drew one back to peer outside. It was brighter than she expected. The sunlight that trickled through the low, heavy clouds reflected off the icy surface of the snow, and it took her a moment to realize what that meant. The storm had, for the moment at least, stopped. Her heart lifted with the realization. Perhaps . . .

But a moment later it crashed back to its accustomed spot. Even if the snow did not begin again, the roads would not be passable by morning. And even if, by some small chance, it was possible to leave tomorrow, Sir John would not allow it. She wasn't sure whether the delay was good or bad for her. The longer he looked, the more likely the magistrate was to find someone else on which to pin the blame for Gregory's death.

But that sense of being trapped would weigh on everyone, including the magistrate. Eventually, desperate to leave, they might be happy to accept her guilt as the price of their own liberty. Feeling penned in and anxious, Amelia let the curtain fall back into place and turned away from the window.

The tap on the door made her jump. "Who's there?" she called, clutching the shawl tight against her chest.

"Luncheon, miss," a wary, masculine voice called. There was the sound of a key turning in the lock. "Stand back, if you please. I've been told not to let you leave the room."

Amelia was tempted to place herself immediately before the door, defiantly wanting to exercise what little power she had left. But she was hungry, and she was scared, and she didn't have it in her to make more trouble. She retreated toward the fireplace. "Come in."

The sturdy footman was standing there when the door swung open, a covered tray in his hands. And someone else.

"Raffi," Amelia said, taking a step forward before she thought better of it. "What are you doing here? Is there news?"

The hopeful feeling that had risen into her throat plummeted into her stomach when he shook his head. "But I thought you could use a friendly face."

"Are you allowed to be here?" she asked him, glancing at the footman.

The footman snorted as he set down the tray but didn't say anything as he turned to Jack, one hand held out expectantly.

Raffi sighed. "Again?" He turned away from Amelia, but she heard the clink as coins changed hands. The footman nodded, looking satisfied, and stepped out into the hall. He left the door open but turned away so that his body was blocking it.

Raffi let out a noise like a small growl. "It is the best we can hope for, I am afraid," he said quietly. "But it'll do, if we are quiet. Come over here." To her surprise, he grabbed her arm and pulled her toward the window, glancing again at the door. "We do not have much time."

Amelia felt cold all over. "What do you mean?"

"Sir John is wise enough to know that just locking you up here does not actually provide the answers he needs. At some point, he will decide to search all the rooms—and if he does not think of it, Mrs. Adler certainly will. So tell me, quickly." Raffi dropped his voice even further, so she had to strain to hear him. "Is there anything he might find that we do not wish him to find?"

The intensity in his eyes was unnerving. Though it did not hurt where he gripped her arm, she could feel the tension in him, the coiled strength, like a piece of clockwork that had been wound too tightly and might burst forth at any moment.

She had been so young when he went to sea that she didn't remember his leaving. Between the visits he had made when he could and the many letters they had exchanged, she had grown to know and love him. There was no one she admired more in the world, except perhaps her mother. But seeing him in person like this, studying him while he studied her, Amelia was reminded of the many ways they were yet strangers to each other. "Do *Ammi* and Papa know you came?"

"I tried to slip away without anyone noticing."

Stalling for time, not sure what to say or how to say it, she glanced toward where the footman's back filled the doorway. "It will not reflect well on me, or you, should Sir John find out about this."

He growled again. "Answer the question, Noor."

"I cannot."

"Noor—"

"I cannot," she insisted, her whisper growing heated. "Because I do not know. I know there is nothing in here." She almost added *now* before she caught herself, but her eyes still darted to the fire-place in spite of her effort to keep them locked on Jack's face.

He followed her line of sight, going very still. "Were you burning something, little sister?"

She did not answer.

He let out a slow breath, glancing once more toward the door. "You said nothing in here," he muttered. "What about Mr. Edison's room?"

"I don't know," she bit off. "Gregory might have—I don't know."

"He might have what?" Raffi stared at her. "Does that mean something *did* happen between you two?"

"Of course it did," she snapped, fighting to keep her voice to a whisper. She closed her eyes, too afraid to see the disappointment she was sure must be in his. "It should have been nothing. It *was* nothing. But it was a nothing that ended up mattering very much."

"What were you going to say he might have?"

Her whisper was strangled. "Letters."

"What kind of . . ." She opened her eyes as Raffi broke off, dropping her arm so that he could clench his hands into fists. "Please, just tell me what happened."

"To Mr. Edison?" Amelia lifted her hands helplessly. "I've no idea. I was asleep all night." A sudden cold sensation flooded her midsection. "You do believe me, don't you?"

"Of course I believe you. That was not what I meant. What passed between the two of you that night at the vicarage? You can tell me." He reached out to give her braid a tug, something he used to do when she was a child and he was home on shore leave. The gesture brought tears to her eyes. "Leaving Mr. Edison's death aside, what happened to *you* matters to me. I hope you know that."

His voice was low and persuasive, and she wavered. The idea of confessing what had happened, what she had done, made her feel ill. But she knew she needed help. She opened her mouth, about to reply.

"Whatever it was, it is the reason your neighbors are watching you with such suspicion right now," Jack continued. And Amelia suddenly felt cold again.

Your neighbors, he had said. Not *our neighbors*. Because navy or no, he would leave when all of this was done. She would be the one left behind, to bear the disappointment and disgust of the people she loved if they found out what she had done. The cold feeling inside her was swiftly replaced by hot shame. And anger—at Sir John, at Gregory, at the unfairness of it all. And most of all at herself. She had been so, so stupid.

"Noor," Jack said gently. "It is my responsibility to keep you safe."

"As you did all the years you were gone?" she said, the hot feeling making her lash out. "You left your family behind years ago. Why worry about keeping me safe now?"

He flinched at that, and she instantly regretted her words. "I was keeping you safe then too," he said, taking a step back. "I was doing what I could to keep all of you safe."

"I know." Amelia turned away, trying to swallow down her tears. "I know. I should not have said that."

"Noor." He caught her hand, pulling her back to face him. "I am sorry I have not been here all these years. Perhaps if I had been, you would trust me more." There was frustration in his voice, in the way he ran one agitated hand through his hair and shook his head. "But I am here *now*, and you are in trouble *now*. This is real."

"You think I do not know that? Someone I know was *murdered*. By a person in this house. It isn't only me who is in trouble. We all are."

"Then let me do what I can to protect you. The way I could not before." His voice was low and urgent. "What do the letters say?" He must have seen the look of panic in her eyes, because his voice became low and urgent. "Very well, you do not want to tell me. But you *must* at least tell Sir John."

Amelia shook her head, almost frantically. "I cannot."

"*Why*?"

"Because." Amelia met his eyes. "He will think I wanted Gregory dead."

Raffi stared at her, his hand tightening on hers. "Did you?"

"What is going on here?"

The sudden question, and the fury behind it, cracked through the room. Amelia was so startled that she screamed, pulling away from her brother as she spun around toward the door.

Sir John stood in the doorway, Mrs. Adler just a pace behind him. She watched the room with a curious, narrow-eyed expression that gave away nothing that she was thinking. But the magistrate didn't bother to hide his anger as he strode into the room.

"I repeat, what is going on here? You"—he glared at Raffi—"are not supposed to be here."

Her brother crossed his arms, leaning back a little against the windowsill. "I brought my sister her luncheon. Surely you don't mean to say she should not eat?"

"I did not . . . That is not . . ." Sir John made a frustrated sound in the back of his throat. "That is not what I meant, and you know it. What were you talking about?"

"Nothing at all," Jack said calmly.

"Then why did Miss Hartley scream?" the magistrate demanded. "Were you so scared to be overheard?"

"Do I need more reason to be scared than the obvious?" she demanded, drawing closer to her brother without thinking. "There is a *murderer* in this house."

"Let them be, John," Mrs. Adler said suddenly. "The captain is in his protective mood, and you ought to know you'll get nothing sensible from him in such a state. Besides which, you're making poor Hugo here think his employment is at risk."

Sir John turned his glare on the shamefaced footman trying hard to be invisible outside the door. "Hugo, is it?" Sir John demanded. The footman nodded, eyes wide. "I assume he paid you?" A darting glance toward Raffi, and the footman nodded again. "I'll be telling the housekeeper, then. She can decide what's to become of you. You may leave." As the young man scurried away, looking relieved, Sir John let out a loud sigh.

"We came to search, John," Mrs. Adler said, her voice still quiet. But to Amelia's surprise, the magistrate was clearly listening. "We should focus on that."

Sir John nodded. "Very well. You." He rounded on Raffi once more. "Out. And if I hear you've gone anywhere other than straight back to the drawing room, I shall lock you up as well. You know better, Jack."

"She is my sister," Raffi snapped.

"You. Know. Better." Sir John bit off every word, his eyes snapping. "Now go."

Raffi gave Amelia's hand a final squeeze. "It will be all right," he murmured. "I promise, I'll not let anything happen to you."

She watched him leave, her heart thumping painfully fast. She hoped he was right.

"Well, then. Stand over there, if you please, Miss Hartley." Sir John gestured to the corner by the fireplace. Amelia could not help glancing at it as she obeyed, though she looked away quickly. "We've work to do. Is there anything you wish to tell us before we do?"

Amelia shook her head. "No, sir," she whispered, wishing she sounded more confident.

He sighed again. "Very well. Lily, you start over there, and we will both work our way to the middle."

It was almost a relief to watch them look through the few things she had in the room: her evening slippers and bag from the night before, the folds of her dress, the pockets of her borrowed dressing gown. Mrs. Adler pulled back the linens and searched under the bed. Sir John went through all the drawers of the desk in the corner. But it was a quick search, and before long they were both done and standing before Amelia.

Sir John cleared his throat. "Very well. I hope you will understand, Miss Hartley, why it is necessary to conduct a search of your person."

Her heart sped up. "Will . . . will you do so, sir?" she asked, pulling back a bit.

His face flushed bright red. "Good God, no. What do you take me for, Amelia?" he demanded, sounding for a moment more like her cheerful neighbor than the magistrate who had arrested her. "Mrs. Adler shall." He cleared his throat again. "I will wait in the hall. Lily?"

Mrs. Adler gave a small smile. "I am sure it will not take long." When the door closed behind him, she turned to Amelia, giving a little shrug. "No help for it, I am afraid. Shall we get it over with?"

This search did not take long either. As Amelia pulled off each piece of clothing, including her stays, until she was clad only in her chemise, Mrs. Adler examined each item. When there was nothing to be found, Mrs. Adler nodded, looking relieved. "Your brother was the one who suggested I assist Sir John," she said quietly as she helped Amelia dress once more, doing up the row of tiny buttons along the back of the dress. "You know he wants nothing more than to protect you."

Amelia felt her face grow hot as she remembered her cruel words to him—words she had not even meant, not truly. "I know."

Mrs. Adler watched her a moment longer, then nodded slowly. She glanced at the fireplace. "Were you burning something, Miss Hartley?"

Amelia looked down before she could stop herself, checking to see if there was anything still remaining of Gregory's letter in the fireplace. But no, of course there was not. She had watched it burn. There was only ash, of the sort that any fireplace might have. She looked up again, hoping the glance had been short enough to go unnoticed. "No, not at all."

"And is there anything else you wish to tell me?" Mrs. Adler asked softly. She was watching Amelia closely as she spoke, but still her eyes gave away none of her thoughts.

Amelia swallowed. If Mrs. Adler was assisting Sir John, then anything she learned, she would have to take straight to the magistrate. But there was a chance Gregory had not brought the letters with him. Without those, Amelia knew, there was nothing more than gossip to point the finger of blame at her. She could wait out gossip.

"No, Mrs. Adler," she said. Her brother might trust Freddy's widow, but Amelia had trusted too easily before, and look where that had gotten her. She would be more careful this time. She shivered a little and wrapped her arms around herself. "I have nothing at all to tell."

CHAPTER 12

Lily glanced at the sketch Mrs. Reynaud had made for them. It was a stiff, awkward drawing, but it served its purpose, showing the doors in each hallway and where each guest was staying. A number of the rooms were unoccupied; Mrs. Grantham's home was large, and she had deliberately spaced her guests out to give them more privacy the previous night.

"It might have been more helpful had she put us closer together," John commented, pulling a face while they looked at the sketch. "Perhaps then someone would have seen or heard something useful."

"I suspect someone did anyway," Lily replied. "The trick is discovering who."

Mrs. Reynaud had been reluctant to provide the map and had insisted on getting Mrs. Grantham's permission first; during that time, Sir John spoke with a few guests one at a time, as he had originally intended.

Mrs. Grantham had not been pleased at the thought of her guests' minimal privacy being invaded. "He intends to search their rooms?" she had demanded, her voice growing cold while she stared at Lily. "He intends to search *my guests' rooms*. Without their permission."

"That is the intention, yes. And very much the point." Lily was uncowed by the shocked stare being directed her way. "This is not a normal house party. And these are far, far beyond normal circumstances. There is a criminal among your guests, and we are *trapped* here with this person for at least one more night—likely more. Either you wish to see this person found, or . . ." She had shrugged. "Or you explain to the magistrate why you will prevent him from doing his duty."

Mrs. Grantham's mouth had trembled, whether from worry or anger, Lily couldn't say. But at last, she had nodded. "Of course. Of course Sir John shall have whatever assistance he may need."

Mrs. Reynaud had brought the map while Lily was with Amelia. Now Lily and John stood at the stairway between the two wings of bedrooms, consulting the drawing to decide where to go next.

"Perhaps—" Lily began, but she was cut off abruptly when the door closest to them swung open. She took two quick steps back, nearly colliding with her brother-in-law, who caught her arm to steady her.

"Careful now!" he said gently, glancing at the man in front of them. "Mr. Edison. I did not know you were still up here. How are you holding up?"

"Managing," William Edison said, swallowing and yanking the door shut behind him.

Lily didn't blame him, though she did study him. It was the first time she had seen him up close, though she had glimpsed both brothers at the ball the night before. She had noticed the family resemblance between them then. But from what she remembered, Gregory Edison had been uncommonly handsome, while William was merely good-looking—or at least, she could see that he would be on a normal day. At the moment, he was twitchy and anxious, his cheeks pale and his borrowed clothes hanging a little too large on his wiry frame. One hand was wrapped in a bandage; Lily grimaced, remembering what John had told her of the young man's altercation with Amelia and wishing the girl had been more forthcoming.

"There is luncheon in the dining room—cold meats and hot tea, I believe," John said, his voice still kind. "If you feel up to joining the others, of course."

"Yes . . ." William trailed off, blinking rapidly at them and glancing about the hall, as though looking to see whether anyone else was present. "I believe I shall. They are all down there? No one else about here—just you?"

"They are all downstairs," John said. "Or you could ring for someone to bring a meal to your room. You must eat, you know. A man needs his strength to bear up under grief."

"Yes." William nodded. "I shall go down. My thanks for your kindness, sir." He glanced at Lily, inclining his head politely. "Madam." Before they could say anything else, he had hurried toward the stairs, as though he could not wait to get away from them.

"I apologize. I ought to have introduced you," Sir John said, shaking his head. "Clumsy of me. A death is no excuse for bad manners."

"Why was he here?" Lily asked, frowning. "I thought you told everyone to stay downstairs."

"Well, not him, of course," John said, looking puzzled. "His brother just died. I told him he might retreat to his room and take all the time he needed to gather himself for what lay ahead."

"John!" Lily stared at him. "The point of having everyone downstairs was to prevent them from hiding anything or doing anything before you talked to everyone and looked around."

"His brother just died," he insisted. "What else could I have done?"

"And what if it was he who was responsible?" Lily demanded.

John scowled. "He—no. A man could not do such a thing." He shook his head. "I refuse to believe it."

Lily sighed, speaking quietly as she glanced toward the stairs to make sure no one was around to overhear them. "You are entirely too good for this sort of task, John. It does you credit, but you shall have to learn to be more ruthless in your thoughts. William was a young man with strained finances and a handsome, charismatic older brother who was, by all accounts, excellent at spending their parents' funds. Do you think there is no chance that under such circumstances brothers might quarrel—might even come to violence?"

"You have a dark turn of mind sometimes, Lily," John said, but he looked embarrassed as he said it. He sighed loudly and rubbed at his temples. "I suppose I oughtn't to have treated him differently than the others."

"Especially . . ." Lily frowned, consulting the drawing. "Especially since the room that he just left was not his." She glanced up. "It was his brother's."

John went very still, then let out a slow breath. "There are any number of reasons he might have been in there."

"There are," Lily agreed. "But I think this is where we should continue our search."

John nodded, squared his shoulders, and reached past her to open the door.

Lily gasped when they entered the room. Like the rest of them, Gregory Edison had not expected to spend the night after the ball. That meant he hadn't had much with him other than his clothing. But the room still looked as though a storm had swept through it.

Like the rest of them, Mr. Edison had been provided with borrowed clothing, both for the night and the following morning. His formal knee breeches and evening coat were discarded and tossed across the floor, next to the nightclothes that he hadn't had time to don before his death. The bed linens were thrown aside, half the drawers in the desk and tallboy were open, and two of the pillows from the bed were tossed on the floor. Even the artwork hung crooked on the walls, as though it had been pushed aside, or removed and hastily rehung.

John closed the door slowly, as speechless as Lily, and they both stared around the room without saying anything for several long moments.

"Well," Lily managed at last. "Either the elder Mr. Edison was beyond slovenly, to have created such a mess in such a short amount of time, or . . ."

"Or the younger Mr. Edison was searching for something," John said quietly.

"Indeed." Lily stepped forward. "My money is on the latter. But the question is, did he find it?"

"And if he did, is there any use in us looking around?" John asked, turning in a slow circle as he surveyed the chaos.

"Yes," Lily said. "If there is even a chance of finding something, we cannot afford to miss it."

But in the next ten minutes, neither of them discovered anything. They each took half the room, slowly going through the furniture and linens, searching under the seat of the desk chair and the slats of the bed, looking behind each painting as they set the room to rights. Whatever Mr. Edison might have brought with him, it was gone. Only his clothing remained.

They moved on to the next room, which belonged to Mr. and Mrs. Hounslow. There was nothing to be found there either.

"I realize there is no help for it," Sir John said as he replaced the bedclothes. "But going through our neighbors' rooms . . ." He grimaced. "It feels so underhanded. So dishonorable."

"People lie, John," Lily said, a little absently as she examined the dressing table.

There were several papers tucked in the back that she pulled out and leafed through, her lips pursing slightly, before replacing them. It seemed that Mrs. Hounslow had spent part of her evening beginning a letter to her sister, mostly a litany of complaints about other people's children at the ball and praise of her own, mixed in with a very dramatic account of the snowstorm. Had she been writing because she was not yet ready to sleep? Because she was so attached to her sister? Or because her husband was nowhere to be found and she was waiting up for him?

Lily looked up at her brother-in-law. "People lie, but their things do not."

"Shame none of them were planning to stay here, then," John said wryly as he held the door open for her. Lily took one more glance around the room before following him out. "If it were a real house party, we would have a great deal more to discover."

"Too true." Lily waited in the hallway as he closed the door behind them. "Who is next?"

John consulted the map once more. "Peter Coleridge. It says he is just on the other side of the stairs, with a connecting door to his mother's."

"Poor Peter," Lily said with a sympathetic grimace. "Small wonder he has never married."

"Can you imagine bringing a wife home to a mother-in-law like that?" John agreed with a small chuckle.

"Many men do," Lily said, shaking her head. "I think Peter is too kind to wish that fate on anyone."

"Shame he cannot avoid it himself."

Lily shrugged. "I think they are genuinely fond of each other, formidable though she may be. I have never heard him admit to any resentment."

"I suspect it is a task that grows more arduous for him by the month," John said quietly. "Mrs. Coleridge is formidable, certainly, but she seemed . . . frail today. Do you not think so? I think her age may be catching up to her at last. She is a great deal older than my mother, you know."

"Age, and raising seven children," Lily pointed out.

John nodded. "And she does not strike me as a woman to accept frailty with grace."

"In herself or anyone else," Lily agreed. "She often took it upon herself to tell me what was incorrect in my household management when Freddy and I first married."

"I remember," John agreed, smiling a little sadly at the thought of his younger brother. "Lucky for you, it was only telling."

That made Lily smile as well. There was a story in the Adler family of how Mrs. Coleridge, the first time she was ever shown into Lady Adler's drawing room, spent the five minutes she was waiting for her hostess rearranging every bauble and ornament in the room. When Lady Adler had entered and stared around her in astonishment, Mrs. Coleridge had replied that Lady Adler might change it back after the visit, but if she was a clever woman she would keep it thus, as it looked a great deal better. Lady Adler, who had very little ego and a new bride's eagerness to please her neighbors, had merely shrugged and allowed the room to remain as Mrs. Coleridge had arranged it.

"I suspect—" Lily broke off as they came abreast of Peter's door. The hall was empty except for the two of them, so it was easy to hear someone moving about inside the room. She glanced at John, who suddenly looked as wary and alert as she.

All the guests had been instructed to stay downstairs. And none of them was supposed to know the rooms were being searched.

John motioned for Lily to stand back, and she didn't hesitate to obey. There was a time to push herself forward, but there was also a time for practicality. And if there was a thief on the other side of the door, her brother-in-law was far more suited to deal with whatever might happen next.

John nodded to her, then, without any further warning, flung the door open.

CHAPTER 13

"Dear God in heaven!"

Peter Coleridge looked ready to jump out of his skin or pass out from shock. He was standing in front of the washbasin, his cravat dangling loose and his shirt open at the neck. He stared at them, confused and red-faced. "Sir John, what . . . And Mrs. Adler . . ." Hurriedly, he began fastening his shirt once more, sending embarrassed looks in Lily's direction. "What is the meaning of this?"

"I might ask you the same question," John said sternly, while Lily averted her eyes, though she used the opportunity to glance about the room. "Everyone was supposed to remain in the drawing room."

"I was . . . that is . . ." Peter fumbled to knot his cravat into a hasty bow. He gestured to another shirt, tossed carelessly across the bedspread, a brown stain splashed across its front. "I spilled my tea, unfortunately, and came up here to change."

Lily's eye was caught by the fire, banked mostly to coals, as the staff had not expected anyone to be in the room. For a moment she hesitated, unsure whether it was wise to let anyone else know that she was assisting the magistrate.

Peter was frowning at them. "Sir John, are you . . . are you *snooping* in everyone's rooms?" he demanded.

"It don't think it can be called snooping when a magistrate does it," Lily pointed out, taking a few steps into the room. Peter had already seen them together, and he would have already deduced that she was not accompanying Sir John for the exercise. There was no reason to dissemble further. "At that point, it becomes investigating."

The frown did not leave Peter's face. "And what about you?"

"Assisting," Lily said blithely. "Sir John is a gentleman, after all, and far too delicate to be the one to go through the ladies' private things."

"So you *are* going through our things."

"Investigating," Sir John said firmly, drawing himself up in the face of Peter's accusatory tone.

"And what do you expect to find? No one brought anything with them."

"One must be thorough when dealing with this sort of . . . shall we call it an unexpected occurrence?" Sir John said, still cautious.

"It certainly sounds more polite than calling it a murder," Lily said dryly, crossing to the window and pulling aside the curtains as though looking out at the weather. It had begun to snow once more, but she barely noticed it as she scanned the length of the windowsill for anything that had been tucked out of sight. When she turned back around, Peter was glancing uneasily between her and her brother-in-law. She gave him a reassuring smile, noting the way his eyes darted to the fireplace and back, but didn't pause as she crossed the room, heading for the door that connected his chamber to his mother's. Neither Peter nor his imperious mother seemed to have been particularly connected to Mr. Edison, but fairness demanded that they search every room equally. "But you've no need to be squeamish on my account, John."

There was not much furniture in Mrs. Coleridge's room—it had likely been chosen purely because of the connecting door. Lily went to the wardrobe and began going through it slowly. As she had hoped, Peter followed, standing uncomfortably in the doorway between the two rooms. His mouth opened and closed silently while he watched her, as though he wanted to protest but knew he could not. She hoped Sir John was using the opportunity to look through the other room. And more than that, she hoped he had noticed what was smoldering in the banked embers of the fire.

The reluctant magistrate cleared his throat. Lily, glancing over her shoulder, saw that he was hovering in the doorway just behind Peter. She held back a sigh. Poor John. He really was not suited for this sort of thing. She turned back to the wardrobe, which held Mrs. Coleridge's evening things: gown, fan, reticule, stockings—everything that a lady would need for an evening out. She had been regal as ever the night before, and Lily could recall how the gold embroidery and lace of her evening gown had caught the light in the ballroom.

But she had not been wearing a necklace with it. Curious, that. Lily tucked the memory away to be examined at a later time as she knelt next to the bed and pulled aside the heavy counterpane, looking underneath the bed frame for anything odd or out of place.

"You said you were in your room all night, Mr. Coleridge," Sir John said. When Lily glanced over her shoulder, she was relieved to see that he had turned back into Peter's room and was beginning to search through the bedclothes. "Did you hear anything unexpected? Poke your head out the door at all?"

"Nothing unexpected at all," Peter said earnestly. "Not until all the shouting began this morning, that is. Here, now, is that really necessary?" he added.

"Does your mother's mind wander at all, Peter?" Lily asked, to distract him from whatever Sir John might be looking at. She sat back on her heels and looked toward where he was hovering in the doorway, trying to keep an eye on both her and Sir John at the same time. "She seems . . . less commanding, or less in command perhaps, than I remember her."

Peter laughed shortly. "Does she? Well, do not tell her I said so, but she is . . ." He looked like he was considering his words carefully. "Losing her touch, from time to time of late. Age comes for us all, even my mother." He looked around, his face wrinkling up with displeasure. "Is there anything else I may tell you? I do wish to be helpful, however uncomfortable it may feel to have you poking about our rooms."

"It is uncomfortable for us as well," Sir John said.

"Oh, indeed," Lily agreed, polite but not meaning a word of it. Once upon a time she might have felt a pang of guilt at going through her neighbors' things. But murder left little time to indulge in such squeamishness. Lily stood up, patting a little dust off her skirts. "Sir John, have you finished Mr. Coleridge's room yet?"

"Nothing to be found," he said, reappearing in the doorway. Peter didn't bother to hide his sigh of relief. "Shall we move on?"

"Whatever you think best, brother," Lily said politely as they both stepped aside to let her through the connecting door. "Though if you will permit me, I will just take a moment . . ."

Before either of them could move to stop her, she strode toward the fireplace.

"Here now!" She could hear the alarm in Peter's voice, though she didn't turn back around. "What do you think you're—"

"Investigating, as our respected magistrate has said," Lily replied as she knelt once again. The letter in the fireplace looked freshly singed, and half of the paper was burned away. But the banked embers had not been strong enough to set it fully alight, and it had drifted to the side, charred but still retrievable. Lily pulled it out with a single, quick movement, wincing at the heat on her fingers and shaking it back and forth rapidly to cool it. Bits of ash tumbled down from the burned edge, but a great deal of writing remained.

"Unless you object to our reading that, for some reason?" Sir John asked. He had interposed his body between them.

"I should think a gentleman would always object to someone reading his private letters, especially when he clearly intended to destroy them," Peter said with stiff, offended dignity, still trying to get past Sir John.

"An odd choice to destroy it, though," Lily pointed out. "When one sees who it concerns." Holding the paper carefully, she passed it to Sir John.

Who read it, the frown between his eyes quickly growing to a scowl. He looked up, that scowl locked on Peter. "This is a promissory note."

Peter sighed. "Yes."

"Written to you, from the elder Mr. Edison, for an amount of one hundred pounds."

"Yes."

"And you attempted to *burn it*?" Sir John demanded, his voice rising with indignation and disbelief. "After what has happened? Can you offer any explanation for such astonishing behavior?"

When Peter hesitated, Lily said quietly, "It does look very bad, Mr. Coleridge."

"I know." Peter sighed once more. "It was for his brother's sake. After I heard about Gregory Edison's death . . . well, there was no chance of him paying me then, was there? I knew his debts would fall to his parents or brother to discharge, and I had no intention of calling it in. So I just tossed the note on the fire without really thinking it through."

Sir John's scowl had grown less thunderous as Peter spoke. "You mean to say you had no intention of collecting the debt?"

"Well, I intended to before," Peter said, shrugging in discomfort. He looked between them, his hands tapping his thighs in sharp, agitated movements. "But now . . . what am I supposed to do, approach William and demand payment? I could not dream of such a thing, not after his brother has been . . ." Peter hesitated, looking ill. He barely managed to choke out the word "*murdered*."

"And his brother's debt?" Lily asked.

Peter stared at her in confusion. "His brother's debt?"

"Will you forgive Mr. William Edison's debt as well, under the circumstances?"

"What do you . . . I am not sure how . . ."

"I happened to overhear the two of you at the ball," Lily admitted. "I do apologize, but it was rather impossible not to. Do you intend to collect his debt—I do not know how much it is for—or will you forgive it as well?"

"Ah. That. Forgive my confusion; I am not accustomed to thinking my private conversations might be overheard in such a fashion." The look Peter gave her was almost accusatory, but Lily merely shrugged.

"Then you should conduct them with quieter people," she suggested, refusing to feel cowed. "Or at least in a more private place. Mr. William Edison was strident in his denials."

"He is an emotional fellow," Peter admitted, nodding in reluctant agreement.

"I assume you have his promissory note as well?" Sir John put in.

"I . . ." Peter glanced down at the fireplace. "I do not, in point of fact. I burned that one as well." He looked back up at Sir John and gave an apologetic shrug. "I decided William has enough to get on with at the moment."

Lily looked back down at the fire, but only char and ash remained; whatever other letters Peter had burned were gone. "And did you speak with the elder Mr. Edison about his debt at the ball?" Lily asked. When both men glanced at her, looking a little puzzled by the assertion, she added, "You must have intended to, or you would not have brought the promissory note with you to an evening engagement."

Peter looked uncomfortable. "I had planned to but did not have a chance."

"But he was looking for you," Lily pointed out. "Surely you would have taken the opportunity to speak with him on the matter."

Peter laughed a little uncomfortably at that. "That was my intention, yes. But Mr. Edison did not leave me any chance. As you already know about William's debt, I need not scruple to tell you that was what Gregory wanted to discuss." He shook his head. "He would barely let me get a word in edgewise once he found me. I admit, I was impressed by such brotherly devotion. But it left me no opportunity to direct the conversation myself." He shrugged, clearing his throat as though realizing he had begun repeating himself. "Perhaps that was his intention. I've no idea."

Lily nodded, hesitating a little. She did not want to accuse Peter of anything, but she also did not want to be led astray by her own assumptions. If she would have asked the question of someone she knew less well that Peter, then she needed to ask it of him as well.

"Perhaps you were able to address the matter at another time?" she suggested delicately.

Sir John had been nodding and looking mostly satisfied, but Lily's question sharpened his attention. "Later in the night, perhaps?"

"No," Peter said, looking indignant. "I was . . . I did not leave my room last night, if that is what you are implying."

"It's a natural thing for gentlemen to argue over, an unpaid debt of honor," Sir John pointed out, looking unhappy but determined to press on. Lily felt a good deal of admiration watching him; she knew how uncomfortable it had to make him, to be investigating his neighbors and friends. But he squared his shoulders and continued gamely, "And all too easy for an argument to get out of hand."

But Peter only looked bitterly amused. "Perhaps it sounds unbearably conceited, but consider to whom you are speaking, sir. What need have I to kill a man over a hundred pounds? Or even to argue with him about the sum? No." He shook his head. "The Mr. Edisons—both of them—are young, but a gentleman's word must be his bond at any age. I intended only to remind them of their obligations, as a manner of principle. Now that Gregory is . . ." Peter cleared his throat. "Well, I am content to put it behind me. I've no need to collect their debts."

Sir John nodded, acknowledging the point.

"Will that be all?" Peter added, not quite managing a polite tone as he gestured them toward the hall.

Sir John sighed. "That is all for now. Lily, shall we? There are still more ladies' rooms to be checked."

"Of course, brother," Lily said, trying to look demure, though she wasn't sure she did a convincing job of it.

"Perhaps Mr. Edison stumbled on something he should not have," Peter suggested as he followed them into the hall. He shook his head. "I suppose I shall see you downstairs once more when you have finished your poking and prying. Perhaps you might read to my mother, Lily? She is growing restless, and you have such a knack for it."

"Certainly, if she wishes it," Lily agreed politely. "You and she are fortunate, I think, to have slept so soundly last night."

He gave her a sharp look. "What does that mean?"

"Just that," Lily said, not bothering to hide her own surprise at his accusatory tone of voice. "If you had heard something, you might have gone to see what it was, and then who knows what might have happened."

"Ah. Yes. Well, that is very true." Peter shook his head. "Dreadful to contemplate." He blew out a breath, gave them both a terse nod, and made his way toward the stairs.

Sir John watched him go, then turned to Lily. "Shall we?"

She took a deep breath. "Lead on. Let us see what we can discover."

Chapter 14

Nothing. Even hopeful Sir John had to admit, by the time the dinner hour came, that they had discovered nothing of use.

The light faded quickly through the evening, disappearing into the low-hanging clouds, and the snow had begun falling once again as they gathered in the dining room. The conversation around the table was stilted. After spending the entire day trapped in each other's company, the guests were running out of things to say. Lily glanced around the candlelit faces as they rose and made their way to the drawing room for tea and coffee, remembering her quiet talk with Matthew that morning.

Right now, the rituals they were all accustomed to were keeping them calm. But the longer they were trapped, the less that calm would last. Already the cracks were beginning to show in the tense voices, the uncomfortable silences that fell in the middle of conversations, the too-loud rattle of the tea things that made more than one person jump as Mrs. Grantham knocked over the sugar bowl.

"Allow me to assist you," Jack said, sounding very gallant in the silence that followed. Lily saw him give their hostess an encouraging smile as he bent down to help her pick up the silver pots. "Take heart, ma'am," he murmured. "None of us blame you. And the whole situation would be far less bearable without your inestimable skills as a hostess."

She let out a slow sigh, nodding as she reached out to give his cheek a pat. "You're a dear boy, Captain. You always have been."

She lowered her voice—almost too low for Lily, hovering nearby with her tea, to hear. "And I don't believe a word of what they're saying about Miss Amelia, I assure you."

Lily saw Jack's hands clench into fists, but the look he gave Mrs. Grantham was gentle. "You are very good," he said quietly as he straightened.

"Leave off hounding me, you little whelp!" Mr. Hounslow snarled suddenly. When Lily turned—along with everyone else in the room—he was looming over William Edison. "Every time I turn around, there you are, *just reminding* me of a paltry debt."

"If it is so paltry, why have you not yet paid me?" William demanded, knocking into a delicate occasional table in his haste to put some distance between them. He would have sent it tumbling had Matthew not been there to catch it and set it upright again.

"Perhaps because we are stuck here, boy? I do not bring my purse to an evening party, because *gentlemen* trust other gentlemen to repay them."

"I've spent two months trusting you—"

"I beg your pardon?" Mr. Hounslow thundered. "Are you implying that my word of honor is not sufficient assurance for you?"

"How dare you?" Mrs. Hounslow hissed, glaring at William from behind her husband, her hands on her hips. "It is not surprising, though. Only those who cannot be trusted themselves are so suspicious of others."

William drew himself up in outrage. "Are you saying that *I*—"

"Of course she is," Mr. Hounslow snapped. "You're always so desperate for money, you worm. I think you would even kill your own brother for it. Had the magistrate not already arrested Miss Hartley, my first suspicion would fall on *you*."

William made a choked sound, his face going first bright scarlet, then ashen. His mouth worked, as though he were trying to speak but couldn't string his words together. "How dare you?" he managed at last.

"Very easily," Mr. Hounslow said, his face red, the words dripping from his lips. "A paltry younger brother, always in need of more funds? How many of us have witnessed you spending what you cannot afford and constantly begging for more?"

"Mr. Hounslow," Sir John said, stepping forward and looking uneasy. "Throwing around such words is a serious thing indeed."

"He was my *brother*," William choked out, trembling all over. He stuck out his chin. "But then, perhaps you are the sort to whom that does not matter. Perhaps *you* are the one who would kill your own brother for a shilling." He spun around, pushing past the silent, gaping spectators and heading toward the door.

When it slammed behind him, all eyes turned back to Mr. Hounslow, who looked suddenly uncomfortable under such scrutiny. "Well, if he is so damn upset about his brother, why is he bothering me for a few measly pounds?" he demanded, though no one had said a word. "Stupid bas—"

"I think perhaps Mr. Edison had the right idea," Mrs. Grantham said, standing quickly and cutting him off. "An early bedtime seems like the best thing all around, do you not agree? I shall ring for more candles."

No one argued with her. Lily, smothering a yawn as she followed the group toward the staircase, felt so worn down from the day that she could have gone straight to bed and slept for a week. But that was not an option.

As the guests were collecting their candles and leaving the drawing room, she had seen Jack slip away toward the library. And she had plans for the night for which she could use his help.

She had to wait some time for the comings and goings in the hall to die down. Servants brought wash water and clean nightclothes; fires were banked and books supplied. But at last, the house had grown quiet. Lily wrapped a shawl around her shoulders, checked that the coast was clear, and went in search of her friend.

It was eerie walking the halls by candlelight, hoping that no one else was doing the same. She wished Jack had chosen a less out-of-the-way place to brood. But at least this way there was no chance of their conversation being overheard.

He didn't say anything as she entered the library, looking up only briefly before turning his scowl back toward the glass of amber liquid in his hand. Lily blew out her candle—she didn't need it and didn't want to waste it—and went to pour herself a drink.

"He was not pleased that you went to see your sister today," she said quietly.

Jack flashed her a quick grin, though it was more strained than usual. "I've always had a knack for making John displeased with me."

"This is rather different than hiding his shoes or putting jam on his hairbrush when you were seven," Lily said dryly.

That made him chuckle. "Freddy told you about those pranks, did he?"

"Those and a great many more," she said, shaking her head as she sat down across from him and took a sip of her whiskey. "How was she?"

He considered the question. "Scared. And pretending not to be."

Lily snorted. "She and every other person in this house. What else?" She listened in silence as Jack described his whispered, interrupted conversation with his sister. By the end she was leaning forward, her drink forgotten in her hand. "And she said nothing more about the letters or what might be in them?"

"Nothing." Jack shook his head. "I do not know if they are even in the house, and I do not think she does either. She seems to think *least said, soonest mended* is the best path forward."

"She might not be wrong," Lily said, tapping one finger against her lips thoughtfully.

"You do believe her?" Jack asked. It was strange to see her devil-may-care friend so serious. "That she had nothing to do with it?"

Lily did not point out that Amelia hadn't precisely said that. "Do you think she will tell you more, if you ask?"

"I do not know," Jack said, running a hand through his hair in frustration. He set his glass down heavily, standing and striding toward the windows. "All I wish is to help her, as she clearly needs." He met Lily's eyes, then looked away quickly. "She accused me of wishing to swoop in and solve things after having abandoned my family to go to sea."

"Oh," Lily said softly. She could well guess how such an accusation would hurt him, not his pride, but his sense of duty, always torn between family and profession. "You know there is no truth in such words, do you not?"

"Perhaps she thinks there is," he said softly.

"No," Lily said, shaking her head. "She does not. She worships the ground you walk on, Jack; any fool can see that. She just—"

"It is why I have decided to resign my commission, you know," he said abruptly. "I could not have my heart be always torn in two. And after . . ."

He trailed off, but she knew what he could not say. Three years before, he had been away at war when Freddy died, unable to say goodbye to his friend. And last winter, his brother's wife had died in childbirth, the baby following soon after. His brother had been devastated, left a widower with three young children.

There had been happy occasions he had missed as well. Most of Amelia's childhood had passed while he was at sea, as had his other sister's wedding. It had taken three more years before he was able to meet her husband and the two children they'd had in that time. Many families were spread across the country, or even the entire Empire, their lives shared in letters and distant memories. But Jack grieved what he had missed.

"I know," Lily said simply. "And Amelia knows it as well, I promise. You know what she wants, do you not?"

"To act like a stubborn little fool?" he grumbled.

"She wants you to see her as grown-up," Lily said gently. She could well remember how she had felt at that age, with everyone in her life telling her what to do, her own opinions rarely considered or consulted. Amelia had family who loved her, to be sure, and Jack certainly had his sister's best intentions at heart. But even love could feel overbearing, especially for a girl who had lived her whole life sheltered and surrounded by her family. "She wants you to see her as her own person, not just your younger sister."

"Well, I'd see her as grown-up if she'd start bloody acting like it," Jack growled, staring at the fire. "What reason had she to keep secrets from me in the first place?"

Lily was silent for a long moment, thinking of all the things that could have transpired at that vicarage and been labeled *scandal* by someone who stumbled on them. "Any number of reasons," she said, staring at the fire herself. "But browbeating her will never be the way to gain her confidence."

"I know." Jack pulled the curtains aside. It was dark outside, and he had to press his face close to the glass. "Still this damned snow. Are we never to be free?"

It was the most restless and angry she had ever seen him, and it made her heart ache for her friend. Jack had faced any number of enemies at sea. He had never stood down from a challenge or hesitated to throw himself into any adventure or scheme that she might drag him into. But faced with a threat to someone he loved—a threat he could do nothing about—he was like a caged animal, pacing and roaring to no avail.

She stood and crossed to the window as well, laying a hand on his shoulder. Beneath his coat, she could feel the muscles knotted with tension. He wanted a fight, something tangible that he could defeat. Instead, he had to stand aside. She was honored by his trust in her. And she was terrified of failing. Lily wanted to lay her head against his shoulder—as much to seek comfort for herself as to give it to him. But she stayed upright, knowing he needed to believe in her confidence when she told him, "It will be well, Jack. Nothing will happen to her." When he turned to look down at her eyes— tall though she was, he still had a number of inches on her—she lifted her chin. "I shan't allow it."

That made him chuckle. "If anyone else said that . . ." He placed his hand over hers, pressing it against his shoulder.

In spite of how close their friendship had become, they rarely touched, and certainly not skin to skin. His hand was warm against hers, and he squeezed it tightly, holding both against his shoulder as though grasping a lifeline. He held her gaze as he did, and the heat from his hand seemed to spread through her. He was about to speak, she was sure, and she found herself holding her breath as she waited for what he would say.

He closed his eyes briefly, took a deep breath, and stepped away.

"What does Mr. Spencer think of your investigating?" he asked, returning to his seat and retrieving his glass from the side table.

Lily stared at him for a confused moment before she could gather her thoughts. "Mr. Spencer?" she asked at last, following his lead and sitting once again. "He finds it admirable, I believe, though of course it makes him uncomfortable. How could it not?" She laughed, almost in disbelief. "It makes *me* uncomfortable. A man was murdered, after all."

"And we are trapped here with his murderer," Jack agreed, not meeting her eyes.

"Mostly he knows that it is happening, regardless of what he thinks. And that he does not have a say in the matter one way or another."

"Do you want him to?" Jack asked, looking up at last. "Forgive me for asking, Lily. I know I should be thinking of other things—and I am, to be sure—but I cannot help wondering . . ." Jack hesitated. "Are you going to marry him?"

"I don't know," she answered honestly. "I do care for him, and he would make an excellent husband." She thought of saying more but wasn't sure how much she wanted to reveal, or how much Jack had already guessed about her relationship with Matthew. Like Jack, she hesitated, her eyes falling to her glass once more.

"Would he make an excellent husband for you?" Jack pressed.

"I don't know," she said again. "The idea of marrying again at all is so surprising that it is hard for me to . . . It is as though I have to wrap my thoughts around two entirely new ideas at once." Lily looked up to discover that Jack was watching her closely. "What would Freddy say, do you think?"

He did not respond right away, and Lily almost regretted asking the question. Did he think that her marrying again would be a kind of betrayal, though she had been widowed more than three years?

Did she, in her heart, think so too?

But then Jack smiled. "Freddy would wish for you to do whatever would make you happiest," he said gently. "As do I."

Lily leaned back in her chair, shaking her head. "It is hard to know what would make one *happiest* of all the choices out there. Happy, certainly. But happiest? That is a tall order."

"Do you think so?" Jack asked, studying her. "I think it the other way round. Once we know ourselves, we can know in an instant what would make us truly happiest. The trouble is, that choice is so often unattainable, or perhaps simply unavailable, for many reasons. So we must settle and choose between a number of options that are almost, but not quite, as good. And those paths, which will make us happy and unhappy in different degrees, are much harder to choose between."

Lily had sat forward as he spoke, her eyes fixed on her friend. She had never heard him speak so eloquently before, or with such emotion. It left an unexpected, achy feeling lodged in her chest. "And what would make you happiest, Jack?"

"I?" He was silent for a long moment. "What would make me happiest," he began slowly, before he was interrupted by a sudden noise from outside, a thunderous crackle and rumble that made them both leap from their chairs and dash to the window.

They could barely see outside through the thicket of branches that pressed up against the windowpanes. A tree branch had broken under the weight of the ice and snow, large enough to be almost a tree on its own. And more snow had begun to fall again.

Jack cursed with a sailor's flair. Lily, rather than upbraiding him for his language, tucked the obscenities away in the back of her mind for when she might have need of them. "What would make me happiest is getting out of this damned house," Jack said fiercely as he turned away from the window. "Taking my sister somewhere she is safe would make me happiest."

They were silent a moment, and in that silence the clock began chiming the half hour.

"Well, I cannot offer you that," Lily said. She squared her shoulders as though preparing for battle. "But may I suggest a challenge of another sort?"

Jack raised his brows in surprise. "What sort of challenge?"

"Everyone went to their rooms before ten o'clock, and it is nearly midnight now, which means that every reasonable person in this house is asleep."

"We are unreasonable, then?" Jack asked with a trace of his normal humor.

"Very unreasonable," Lily agreed, going to snuff out most of the branches of candles. She left two burning. "But that is not the point. What I want to discover—what Sir John agreed we must learn—is if anyone else is unreasonable as well. And whether they are bold enough to leave their rooms."

"You think that if they leave their rooms tonight, they might have left last night as well."

"Precisely," Lily said, smiling at him as she handed him a candle, keeping one for herself. He had always followed her thoughts with ease, and it was a relief to discover that months apart had not changed that. "And if someone else was wandering the halls last night, they might be able to tell us something useful."

"Do you think they will risk it again tonight?" Jack asked as they made their way into the hall, retracing their steps toward the staircase that led to the bedrooms.

"Perhaps. Most of them seemed to think the mystery had been solved with the blame pinned on your sister, however cautious Sir John might still be." Lily spoke in a hushed voice, as Jack had, the silence of the empty rooms pressing on them. Lily was grateful for the carpeted halls; whenever they had to cross stone or wood floor, she could feel the cold through the soles of her borrowed slippers. "If that's the case, someone might decide to be bold."

"Do you have anyone that you expect to see?" Jack asked, the words barely above a murmur as they climbed the stairs, glancing left and right to make sure no one was yet up and about. Usually, Lily would not expect any clandestine meetings to happen before midnight at a house party. But this was no ordinary gathering, and everyone had retired early. There was no saying at what o'clock a furtive nighttime excursion might begin.

Lily did not reply until they were settled in the hiding spot she had chosen earlier, at the top of the stairs on the third floor. The widely spaced bars of the banister meant they could see downstairs still, but it was dark enough that their own shadowy forms would be difficult to spot from below. They crouched at the edge of a large, decorative cabinet, hoping to blend into its bulk, while Lily felt around for the dark lantern that Sir John had left for her earlier. Jack had already extinguished his candle without needing to be prompted; Lily slid open the lantern's shutter to light the one inside it before hooding it once more and blowing out her own.

With the light hidden completely behind the dark lantern's shutter, they were plunged even further into blackness. But the curtains were open on the second floor, and their eyes slowly adjusted. They had a good vantage of both hallways and would be able to see and hear anyone moving below, especially if they carried a candle.

Finally, Lily answered Jack's question. "Did you find anything odd in the exchange between Mrs. Taylor and her husband this morning, when Sir John asked how everyone spent their night?"

★　★　★

They spotted her sooner than Lily expected.

The flicker of light was easy to see in the dark hall. Jack tapped Lily's hand and silently pointed to where a candle glided along, Mrs. Taylor's face illuminated above it. Lily laid a hand on his arm, silently telling him to wait, and he understood without her needing to speak. They stayed where they were while Mrs. Taylor glanced up and down the halls, then went past the staircase and continued down the second wing. But she did not look up.

Lily lifted the dark, hooded lantern as they slipped in near silence down the stairs. When they reached the bottom, they could see the light of the candle pausing in front of a door. Lily threw open the shutter on the lantern, and the beam of light sped down the hall.

Mrs. Taylor gasped, spinning around toward them, one hand flung up in front of her eyes and her mouth opened to scream.

"It's only me, Caroline," Jack said quickly, his voice pitched low but still loud enough to carry down the hall.

Mrs. Taylor let out a sob of relief. "Good God, Jack, I thought I was about to be murdered here in the dark."

"Then why the hell are you wandering alone in the middle of the night?" he demanded, striding toward her, a fearsome scowl on his face.

She scowled right back. "What do you care?" she hissed.

"Just because I've no wish to begin an affair with a married woman does not mean I want you to be in danger."

"Hmm." She glanced past him as Lily drew near them, sliding the shutter on the lantern halfway closed so the light was not so bright. "And what are the two of you doing so furtively in the dark?" she asked.

"Waiting to see how foolish you would be," Lily said dryly. "Very foolish, it seems." She glanced at the room they were closest to, the one Mrs. Taylor had paused before. "Is it a long-standing affair?"

"Hardly," Mrs. Taylor snorted. "But when one needs comfort, and company, and someone to care what one says on occasion . . . well." She gave them a cold look. "I do not care to discuss it with either of you."

"But perhaps he will care to," Lily said, stepping briskly forward. Before either of them could stop her, she tapped quietly on the door.

Peter Coleridge swung it halfway open, a pleased smile on his face, which fell with almost comical abruptness as he saw Lily standing there. "Lily, what are you . . . That is, you should not be wandering . . . What are you doing here?" he whispered.

"I know, I am not who you were expecting," she replied. "Now—"

"I was not expecting anyone," he interrupted, speaking too quickly. "Why would you think I was expecting anyone?"

Lily took Mrs. Taylor's arm and pulled her into view. "I saw Caroline on her way to meet you and decided to come along. Will you let us in?"

Even in the candlelight, Lily could see Peter's look of surprise. "I . . . I am flattered, Lily, but I would not, that is, I do not think of you in such a manner . . ."

"Oh, for heaven's sake," Lily said rolling her eyes. She disliked lingering in the hallway, certain that at any moment someone would overhear them and emerge from their room to find out what was going on. "Captain, come here."

If Peter had looked surprised before, it was nothing to the flush of embarrassment that flooded his face when Jack stepped forward. Peter's eyes were wide, even a little panicked, as he glanced between the three of them, speaking quickly enough that he stumbled over his words. "I do not know what Caroline has, ah, represented to you, but I—I do not find that my—that is, my interests do not tend toward—"

"Good God, man," Jack growled. "We are trying to catch a murderer, not titillate ourselves. Open the damn door and let us in."

"A murderer?" Peter exclaimed in a whisper, his voice cracking a little. He stepped aside, though, allowing them to hurry into the room and shut the door behind them. Inside, the fire was built high and every candle in the room was lit, giving it a warm, welcoming glow. "But surely—" He broke off, glancing at Jack uneasily.

"Miss Hartley's guilt is far from a settled thing," Lily said.

"I am glad to hear it is so," Peter said quickly.

"And until it is, Sir John has wisely decided that we must pursue all courses of inquiry open to us," Lily continued, crossing to the chair in the corner and seating herself without hesitation. Shuttering the lantern once more and setting it on the floor, she lifted her brows as she examined her small audience. "That, apparently, includes the two of you."

Mrs. Taylor, looking disgruntled, had taken the window seat, her arms crossed defensively before her. Jack stayed near the door, his legs planted wide and his hands clasped behind his back. Peter, hovering awkwardly in the middle of the room, stared from one of them to the other.

"I still do not follow," he said slowly. "Why are you here? What . . ." He glanced at Mrs. Taylor. "How did you discover . . ."

"They saw me in the hallway," she said, glaring at Lily. "Though you were not surprised to see me, Mrs. Adler, which makes me think you had already guessed what was happening."

"I was unsure which gentleman you were visiting," Lily admitted. "I thought it might be Peter, as he had gone to such pains to provide an excuse for your presence in the hall, had anyone chanced to see you. Though there were other possibilities as well. But no, I was not surprised to see you. Your conversation with your husband was revealing, I am afraid."

"He does not care that I am here," Mrs. Taylor said, glancing pointedly at Jack. "He wanted someone to manage his house and his calendar, that is all."

Her voice was resigned, rather than bitter, and Lily was surprised. She had never liked Caroline Taylor, though there was something admirable, she supposed, in a woman who so unapologetically lived her life as she wished. But she was not a kind person, and Lily could not help remembering how cruel she had been to Amelia. Still, the obvious unhappiness underlying her statement made Lily pause. "And what did you want?" she asked out of genuine curiosity.

Mrs. Taylor lifted her chin. "A home. I had no desire to live alone, in rented rooms, on a miniscule income. Another marriage was the only way to remedy that. And if Mr. Taylor does not care where I spend my nights—" Her voice grew sharp. "I do not see what concern it is of yours." She gave Jack a taunting glance. "Unless it bothers you?"

Peter cleared his throat uncomfortably.

Jack's smile was cold. "You may do as you wish, Caroline, as you always do. But Mrs. Adler has some questions for you and Mr. Coleridge first. And if you think to object, I can assure you that she is here at the magistrate's behest."

Mrs. Taylor looked as though she would indeed like to object. But though her mouth tightened into a thin line and she did not uncross her arms, she nodded. Peter sighed and sat on the bed, glum and still red-faced with embarrassment.

"What do you wish to know?" he asked.

"Did you see each other last night?" Lily asked. She assumed they had, based on that uncomfortable exchange between the Taylors that morning. But she would not fail to be sure.

Peter sighed. "We did."

Lily nodded. "A couple was spotted in the hallway last night. Or, if not a couple, a man and a woman together. Is it likely that was you?" She watched them closely as she asked, looking for signs that they might be less than honest.

But they both shook their heads immediately, with no need to look at each other first. "It could not have been," Peter said. "We were never in the hall together."

"Why would we be?" Mrs. Taylor pointed out. "It isn't as though Mr. Coleridge could come to the room Mr. Taylor and I share. I visited here last night, so there was no call for him to leave his room at all."

Lily and Jack exchanged a quick look. It was a believable enough response. And neither of them had shown any hesitation or uneasiness in their answer.

"Very well," Lily said. "Do you remember what time, Mrs. Taylor, you left your room? Or when you returned?"

Mrs. Taylor frowned. "I certainly did not leave my room before midnight. All the other guests departed around eleven, I think, and I waited some time after we were shown to our rooms before I left again. Perhaps around one o'clock?"

"Do you know the time any more precisely?" Lily asked, turning to Peter.

He shook his head. "I do not have a watch with me, and I cannot hear the clock from downstairs in this room. I believe Caroline was here for . . ." He cleared his throat, his face growing redder. "At least an hour."

Lily looked down at her lap to conceal her flash of amusement at his discomfort. If he was telling the truth, Mrs. Taylor might have returned to her room between two and three in the morning. She nodded, looking up once more. "And is there anything else either of you can recall? Since you were both awake for at least a part of the night? Anything out of the ordinary that you saw or heard?"

Peter shook his head again, but Mrs. Taylor's expression grew thoughtful rather than petulant.

"I heard a door open and close," she said slowly. "It was at this end of the hall, I believe. I heard it as I made my way back past the stairs."

"Did you see any sign of who it was?" Jack asked eagerly.

She shook her head, looking horrified by the question. "And risk drawing attention to myself? No indeed," she said. "If I had turned to look, they would have seen the light of the candle I carried, perhaps even seen my face. No, I returned to my room as quickly as possible. Mr. Taylor was asleep," she added. "Snoring like an ox."

"You did not hear it?" Lily asked Peter, hopeful but not really surprised when he shook his head. She stood, sighing, as she retrieved the lantern. "Very well. We shall leave you in peace. Thank you for answering my questions."

"Mrs. Adler." The hesitation in Mrs. Taylor's voice made them both pause at the door. "Captain." When they looked back, she was watching them with a worried look in her eyes. "Can I count on your discretion? Mr. Taylor may not mind my . . ."

"Nighttime entertainments?" Jack suggested dryly. Lily elbowed him in the side, giving him an exasperated look when he glanced at her.

Mrs. Taylor scowled at him. "If you wish," she said, looking like she wanted to snap at them but taking a deep breath instead.

"But he would be less far less tranquil about the matter if it became public. I hope I may count on you not to spread any gossip."

Lily, remembering everything Mrs. Taylor had said to Amelia in the hall outside the retiring room, was tempted to throw the request back in the other woman's face. She gritted her teeth against the impulse. "Certainly, you may count on our discretion," she said. "Though I might wish you had the character to extend the same courtesy to others."

Mrs. Taylor had the decency to look embarrassed at the rebuke.

Lily glanced at Peter. "And I know we may count on your discretion, not to reveal that we've been . . ."

"Working with the magistrate?" Peter laughed shortly. "Certainly. And not just because spreading such a rumor would reveal too much about what I have been up to myself."

Jack smiled crookedly. "There is that." He turned to Lily. "Is that all?"

She was about to say yes when a sudden thought occurred to her. Holding up a hand to forestall Jack from opening the door, she turned to Mrs. Taylor. "What can you tell me that I do not already know about Mrs. Crewe?"

★   ★   ★

Lily and Jack engaged in a very quiet argument as soon as the door was closed behind them. He won and, against her protests, walked her down to her room, which was on the other side of the stairs.

"You are the one who keeps pointing out that a murderer might still be at large," he said in a heated whisper. "Am I now supposed to allow you to wander the halls by yourself?"

"It is only a moment's walk away," Lily hissed. "It is far more likely that someone will see us and create yet another scandal than that you will keep me safe. Besides," she added, scowling as he plucked the dark lantern from her grasp, "I came to the library on my own, and you did not protest then."

"I was *moping* then," he said with great dignity. "I have recovered." He gestured down the hall with his free hand. "If you would care to lead the way?"

Lily sighed but did not argue any further. He could not protect Amelia as he wished. There was no harm in allowing him to be a little extra protective of her if it made him feel better.

They walked quickly but softly, not wanting to create any noise that might bring others into the hall. And Lily was thoughtful as they went.

"It does not speak well of Peter's character," she said at last, "that he would have an affair with a married woman. However her husband might feel—or not feel—about it, it shows a lack of integrity, of honesty, that I would not have thought him capable of. Would you?"

"You have always had a high opinion of him, because Freddy had a high opinion of him," Jack pointed out. "I have not had the opportunity to know him so well."

"Meaning you do not think highly of him?" Lily asked, a little surprised to realize he was right. Freddy had thought the world of Peter—but Freddy, she knew with the benefit of hindsight, had thought the world of everyone he considered a friend. She had always accepted his opinion of Peter. But if Jack knew something else . . . gentleman were often privy to a different side of each other than ladies might be. "Do you have a reason not to?"

"I can hardly have a high opinion of someone I do not know," Jack said firmly. "Equally, I cannot have a low one. I would not have thought him the sort of man to attract Caroline, but . . ." He shrugged. "If it is an arrangement that suits all three, I cannot find fault with it. Even if I did, though . . ." He glanced down at her, and in the dim light, she thought she saw him smiling. "Everyone must make some error in judgment in their lives."

"True," Lily said, a little more archly than she intended, pointedly not mentioning his own affair with Mrs. Taylor. "No one's judgment is perfect all the time."

"Speaking of judgment." Jack paused as they reached her room. His face was in shadow, but she could picture the thoughtful frown on his face. "Did you believe them?"

"That they were not in the hall together? It had a ring of truth to it, especially as they both issued an immediate denial without needing to exchange so much as a glance. But that leads to an interesting question, does it not?"

Jack nodded slowly. "If we assume the man was indeed Mr. Edison . . ."

"Who was the woman he was meeting with?" Lily said quietly. "If it was he, why was he there? And if it was not . . . who is our mystery man, and what was he doing last night?"

CHAPTER 15

Lily woke early, a habit formed from country hours and chilled toes, to the sound of a maid laying the fire in her room. She was tempted to burrow deeper into the covers, tired not only from her late night but from the stress and worry of the past day. If she kept her eyes closed a little longer, she could pretend that it was all a dream, that she was at a normal house party, that lives might not hang on her actions.

But it was not in her nature to pretend for long. Steeling herself, Lily sat up quickly, making the poor maid gasp and drop her fire irons. Lily, embarrassed, apologized and asked for warm water so she could wash.

"It's heating up, ma'am," the girl replied, glancing back at the door furtively. Lowering her voice to a whisper, she added, "Begging your pardon, ma'am, but is it true what they're saying? The magistrate caught Mr. Edison's murderer and has her locked up?"

Lily hesitated, her instinct being to keep her own counsel until she and Sir John were more certain what had happened. But the girl and her fellow servants were trapped in the house as well. They had as much right to know what was happening as anyone else.

"What is your name?" she asked, plucking her shawl from a chair and bundling it around her shoulders.

"Jane, ma'am."

"Well, Jane, you are right that Sir John has locked up Miss Amelia Hartley," Lily said. The words felt surreal, even as she said them, but she pressed on. "Primarily, though, his suspicions are based on some pieces of gossip that have been circling about her and Mrs. Edison over the past weeks."

"Scandalous gossip?" Jane asked with wide eyes.

Under other circumstances, the question would have made Lily smile. Now, though, she grimaced. "Rather scandalous, yes. Which many of the other guests believe might have given her reason to wish harm to him. But the magistrate, whatever he might be thinking with regard to Miss Hartley's guilt or innocence, has determined that with no proof, there is no firm conclusion to be drawn. Miss Hartley insists she had nothing to do with Mr. Edison's death. Whether she is telling the truth or not remains to be . . ."

Lily trailed off as her eyes fell on the maid's roughened, work-reddened hands.

"Ma'am?" Jane asked after a moment, looking worried.

Lily shook her head, jolted out of her thoughts. "My apologies. It still remains to be seen what truly happened the night Mr. Edison died."

Jane's eyes were wide, and for a moment she was silent. A little shiver chased itself visibly across her shoulders. "Thank you for telling me the truth," she said in a quiet voice as she bent to gather up her things. She considered her words, then added, "It's been hard to know, down in the servants' hall, what exactly's been happening. We've all been that anxious, as I'm sure you can guess." She dropped a little curtsy as she stood once more. "I'll see whether the hot water is ready now."

★   ★   ★

The thought struck Lily at the breakfast table, after William Edison had slunk into the room.

The snow was still falling that morning, though less heavily than it had been, and the temperature had dropped even further. The windows were frosted in crackling, icy swirls that would have been beautiful had they not been yet another sign that no one would be leaving the house—that day or perhaps even the next.

"Sir John," Lady Adler said diffidently as she buttered a muffin. "Is there a need for us all to stay absolutely together still, as we did yesterday? There is no chance of leaving yet, of course, but I think perhaps we would all be more comfortable if we were permitted a little more—" She hesitated, her eyes flickering between Mr. Hounslow and William Edison, who had placed themselves at opposite ends of the table. "A little more space," she finished delicately.

John puffed his cheeks and blew out a slow breath, turning his teacup on the table in fidgety circles. "Perhaps not entirely together," he said at last. Mr. Hounslow, who was reading a week-old copy of the *Times* with his breakfast, snorted but did not look up. "But I must ask that no one go off on their own at any point. Please stay to the main rooms—the drawing room, the music room, and such—"

"May we go into our own rooms?" Peter asked, a little sharply. "Or will you be searching them once more?"

Several voices rose in surprise. Most of the guests had not realized, until that moment, that Sir John had been in their rooms. Lily wanted to kick Peter. She could not blame him, not truly. They were all on edge. But the last thing they needed was for everyone to be stirred up against the magistrate.

"Well, better our rooms than our persons," Mrs. Crewe said with soft humor. "Mrs. Coleridge, may I fetch you more tea?"

An uneasy chuckle went around the table, the tension of the moment releasing slightly.

"I imagine it will not present a problem if you wish to return to your own rooms," John said, a little stiffly. "Though again, I suggest no one go off on their own for any great amount of time. There is still . . ." He hesitated. "A great deal we do not know about Mr. Edison's death."

The guests nodded or murmured their assent. But Lily had seen William Edison's hand go to his breast pocket when Mrs. Crewe spoke, almost involuntarily, before he scowled and quickly dropped it.

"It will be good to have a little more liberty, even if we must remain confined to the house," Lady Adler said, patting her mouth delicately with a napkin. "Mrs. Grantham, perhaps we might arrange some entertainment to help pass the time, rather than sitting around staring at each other's noses?"

"What?" Mrs. Grantham started at being addressed. She had been sitting with her eyes fixed on her plate, not really attending to what was passing among her guests. Her hands were clenched tightly around her silverware, though she had not eaten more than a bite.

"A card tournament, or something like it?" Lady Adler suggested. "Or watercolors and billiards, perhaps, if you have them in the house? We shall be at each other's throats if we sit idle much longer."

"Oh. Yes, of course." Mrs. Grantham nodded, standing. "I can arrange all three, but perhaps we can start with cards? Or charades . . ." She trailed off, looking toward the Hartleys, and cleared her throat. "Though perhaps that would not appeal to everyone. But I am sure we can find something."

Still talking uneasily, she led the group from the room. Lily caught her brother-in-law's eye as she stood, and he hung back with her while the others went ahead.

"What is it?" he murmured as they lingered in the hallway, just out of the breakfast room so the servants cleaning it could not hear them.

"William Edison is hiding something," she replied, keeping her eye on him as he trailed after the others, still aloof and apart. It could have been grief—easy enough to understand. But it could also be something else. "I think perhaps he found something in his brother's room yesterday that he did not want anyone else to see."

"But we found nothing when we searched William's room," John pointed out.

"True," Lily said. "But did you notice how uneasy he was when Mrs. Crewe mentioned personal searches? He felt at his breast pocket immediately afterwards, as though he were checking that something was still there. And look." She nodded down the hall. William was holding back. But when he glanced around and saw them watching, he turned quickly, hurrying after the others and disappearing into the music room.

"You think he has whatever it is on him," John said slowly. "And that he is considering sneaking away to hide it." Lily nodded. "Do you think Mr. Hounslow was onto something with his complaints yesterday?"

Lily hesitated. William seemed like a weak, weaselly sort of young man, and it was hard to picture him with enough bravado or passion to shoot anyone, let alone his own brother. But someone had lured Gregory Edison out of his room and into the snowy, empty yard. Who better than a trusted younger brother? "I think young Mr. Edison is worth keeping an eye on," she said at last. "To see what he does."

John let out a gusty breath. "I need to interview the servants today. I cannot afford to wait longer. They might know or have seen something, in spite of that locked door."

Lily gave him a small smile. "Lucky for you to have an assistant, then."

He grimaced. "Very well. You keep your eye on him. Just . . . promise me that you'll not do anything foolish. No going after him on your own or anything like that."

"As you say, brother," Lily murmured, earning herself a skeptical enough look to make her smile in spite of the circumstances. "If you've not returned before Mr. Edison makes his move, I shall be sure to take masculine assistance with me."

"It is not a joke, Lily," he said sternly.

"No, it is not," she agreed. "But we must still lift our spirits where we can." She gave his arm an encouraging pat, but even as she did so, her eye caught several figures making their way down the hall at a rapid pace. One was Mr. Lambton, the wispy butler. The others, wrapped in outdoor clothing, she did not recognize. "What do you think is going on?"

John frowned. "We should go see before we do anything else."

When they came into the library, Mrs. Grantham was speaking with a burly, older man whose red, wind-weathered cheeks and warm layers of clothing proclaimed him a member of the grounds staff. He was accompanied by two footmen wrapped in their own coats and mufflers, who were handing out mismatched layers of outdoor clothing and heavy gloves to several of the younger gentlemen.

"What is this?" John demanded, frowning. "No one is to leave the house. Mrs. Grantham, what has happened?"

"I am afraid it cannot be helped, Sir John," Mrs. Grantham said, wringing her hands and glancing at the grounds keeper. "A tree has come down, it seems, right on the drive from the house. Mr. Humphry says that if we've any hope of leaving in the next few days, it needs to be hauled away now, while the snow is not falling so heavily."

The grounds keeper nodded respectfully, a cap clutched in his callused hands. "Begging your pardon, sir, but it's work that can't wait, and we've need of more hands for't. If we leave it too long, it could become iced over, or sunk in mud if things thaw, and then the road becomes near impassable. We've a short window to pull it out of the way. I've got two boys out there chopping branches off, and we'll bring the horses what are suitable for heavy work. But we need men."

John glanced around the room. Jack, Peter, and the younger Mr. Hounslow were all bundled up now, looking uncomfortably hot as they waited for the magistrate's verdict.

At last, he nodded. "Very well, since it must be done. But no one is to be alone for any part of the process. Everyone must stay together, and if you have to go off at all, do so in groups of no fewer than three. And Mrs. Grantham, no one else is to leave the library until the men return. Do I make myself clear?"

They all murmured their agreement, including the footmen. John gave them one more stern look before turning toward the butler, taking the man's elbow and leading him from the room.

"Mr. Lambton, I will be speaking to the staff today. In the house-keeper's room, perhaps, if Mrs. Reynaud can spare it . . ."

The bundled-up men began to file out, the grounds keeper already issuing instructions as they went. There was a moment of confused bustle as they left and the people in the library shifted, settling into new groups. Matthew appeared at Lily's elbow. But before she could give him her attention, she caught a small, extra movement from the corner of her eye.

She turned, just in time to see William Edison take advantage of the confusion and slip out the door after the other men.

"Mrs. Adler?" Matthew asked, sounding concerned. "What is wrong?"

"William just left," she whispered, sending a quick glance around the room. No one else seemed to have seen him go. But John had already left with the butler. "He might be . . . I need to get the magistrate. Will you follow to see where he goes?" she whispered, taking Matthew's arm and pulling him toward the door. "Just to see. Do not stop him. We need to know what he—"

"Lily, where are you going?" Lady Adler called from the card table, standing. Her question was loud enough to quiet the other conversations in the room for a moment.

"I shall return in a moment," Lily called over her shoulder, hoping no one would follow.

"But Sir John said not to—"

Lily did not stop to argue. She pulled Matthew from the room and nudged the door abruptly shut behind them. They were just in time to see William disappearing down the end of the hall.

"Just watch!" Lily whispered to Matthew, not waiting for his response as she hurried in the other direction, where Sir John and Mr. Lambton were vanishing down the hall toward the servants' stairs. It would have been quicker to call after him, but she couldn't risk William hearing. Instead, she bunched her too-long skirts in her fists and dashed after them.

They turned at the sound of her footsteps, the butler looking alarmed and John frowning. "Lily, what—"

"He sneaked out," Lily said quickly. "I think he is going upstairs. Mr. Spencer is following him."

John understood instantly and turned to follow her. "See to it, please, Mr. Lambton. I shall return in a moment."

Moving as quickly as they could without making a racket, she and John hurried back in the direction they had come. When they passed the library, Lily winced—the door was open again, and several guests were peering out, trying to see where she and Matthew had rushed off to so suddenly.

Lady Adler stepped into the hall when she saw her son. "John, what is—"

"Stay in the library," John barked, not stopping to explain.

They found Matthew around the corner, standing at the foot of the stairs. He didn't speak, just gave a quick upward jerk with his chin, falling in behind them as they hurried up the stairs.

William's room was in the wing of the hall opposite the one his brother had occupied, Lily remembered from their search the day before. The door stood open now; she slowed her steps as they approached, laying a hand on John's arm to indicate that he should do the same. The floor was heavily carpeted for warmth, and the thick rug muffled the sound of their footsteps as they approached.

William was inside, his back to the door. He was just hanging the coat he had worn at the ball in the wardrobe.

"Were you thinking of dressing for luncheon, William?" Lily asked, stepping through the doorway.

He yelped in surprise, spinning around and slamming the door of the wardrobe closed behind him. "What are you doing?" he demanded.

"I might ask you the same, Mr. Edison," John said sternly, stepping into the room. "Did you not hear me instruct everyone to stay in the library while the others were out of the house?"

"I . . . I did . . . I just had a quick . . ." William stammered unconvincingly, looking frantically around the room, anywhere but at the wardrobe he was clearly standing in front of. He drew himself up and attempted to smile. "That is to say, I was merely—"

"Hiding something?" Lily suggested. "Stand aside, sir."

"I will not," William said, looking affronted. "You've no right to order anyone around in this house. Nor to cast aspersions on my behavior."

"She hardly needs to," Matthew pointed out. "Not when you have done such a thorough job of it yourself."

"Stand aside, Mr. Edison," John said quietly, walking toward him. "Or will you question my authority as well?"

William wavered, looking panicked. John did not ask a second time but took him by the arms and moved him bodily from in front of the wardrobe.

William yelped again, stumbling over his own feet as he tried to grab the magistrate. But Matthew was there too quickly, grabbing his arm to stop him. "I do not advise interfering."

John already had the coat in hand; it took but a moment for him to search the pockets and draw out two folded letters. He looked up at William. "I will read them regardless," he said quietly. "But this is your chance to tell me what they are before I do."

William stared at him, his mouth working silently, as though he could not think quickly enough to come up with anything to say. John did not ask again, bending his head to read first one letter, then the other. As he did, his brows, which had been creased with worry, drew down into an expression altogether more thunderous. Lily, still by the door, held her breath as she watched him.

At last he looked up. "Your brother was attempting to blackmail Miss Hartley," he said, so stunned that there was almost no inflection in his voice.

Lily stared at him, then at Matthew, whose astonishment mirrored her own. She had thought they would find evidence that incriminated William, or perhaps shone some light on what Gregory had been doing. But this . . .

If Gregory had been blackmailing Amelia . . . There were few people who would not see that as a reason for her to want him gone. For a moment, the only person Lily could think of was Jack. Was it better or worse that he was not there? What would he say when he returned and discovered what was happening—and that she had not only been unable to stop it but had not even seen it coming? Would he ever forgive her?

"You took these from your brother's room. Did you know what they said when you did?" John asked quietly.

Lily flinched; she had never heard her brother-in-law sound so furious. William hunched his shoulders unhappily, pulling away from Matthew's grip as he nodded.

John's expression grew even darker. "Why?"

"They . . ." William looked down at the ground. "They do not reflect well on my brother, as you can see. I thought . . . I wanted to spare my parents. Protect his memory and all that." He looked up, smiled weakly, but the expression faded in the face of the magistrate's fury.

"They are from Miss Hartley," John said quietly. "Are they not?"

William nodded again, his mouth twitching nervously.

Lily couldn't keep silent any longer. "John, what is it?" she demanded, taking a step forward. An icy knot of dread was curling in her stomach. "What do they say?"

John shoved the paper toward her. "Read them, if you like."

The first, signed only *A.*, was a simple, furtive request to Gregory Edison: to meet in the vicarage garden at midnight during the dance, because she had a proposition that could only be fulfilled by a gentleman like him. Lily winced as she read it. Whatever Amelia had intended, there was only one conclusion anyone would draw from such a missive, and it would brand her a pariah for the remainder of her life.

The second was a messier scrawl, angry and astonished, dripping with vitriol and disbelief. It was a response to a blackmail demand, unsubtle and unhidden. That would have been bad enough on its own. But it was the last paragraph of the letter that was the most damning.

Were I a man, Amelia had written, *this is when I would demand that you meet me with pistols at some early morning hour to answer for this insult. As it is, I will make it my mission to ensure you regret your actions for the rest of your miserable and hopefully very short life.*

Lily looked up. "She is very young," she began.

But John cut her off, shaking his head. "Lily, you know I can only draw one conclusion. And a court will do the same."

"People often say stupid things when they are angry," Lily insisted. "He was blackmailing her."

"Blackmail that threatened the reputation and well-being of not just her but her entire family," John pointed out. "That is how these things work. And in retaliation she threatened his life, *in writing*."

"Well, then she would have to be very stupid to follow through on such a threat," Lily pointed out, starting to feel a little desperate.

"People are as likely to do stupid things as say them," John said quietly. Stepping toward her, he pulled the letters from her grip. "Which you know as well as I. I have no other option, Lily. I must follow the evidence I find." He let out a slow breath, glancing back at William, who nodded in quick agreement. "And right now, that evidence points squarely at Miss Hartley."

Chapter 16

Lily paced around the drawing room, unable to stay still. She had been pacing for what felt like hours.

The others had gone to luncheon not long past, but Lily hadn't been able to bring herself to join them. Some had given in to their curiosity—or perhaps their fear—and followed her and John up the stairs. And though they had not seen the letters, which John had thankfully kept to himself, they had heard enough to know what had happened. To know that, whereas before only suspicion had pointed toward Amelia, now there was evidence.

Lily hadn't wanted to listen to the speculation and gossip.

Matthew had stayed with her, bearing silent company to her restlessness and not asking her to speak when she didn't want to. She was grateful. And at the same time, she wished he would leave her in peace. She wanted to be alone with her thoughts.

Lily glanced at the window. The snow, which had been falling all morning, was tapering off. Though the wind whipped fiercely, echoing under the eaves as it circled the house, she could see the sun shining at last.

Lily shivered. Once the guests could leave, John's investigation would come to an end. She was running out of time to find out what had truly happened to Mr. Edison.

She had, at first, been skeptical of Amelia, suspicious of the girl's obvious secrets. But something was not sitting right. And it was not just that she was afraid of what Jack would do when he found out that she had failed him.

As if her thoughts had summoned him, she heard a bustle of voices out in the hall, Jack's among them. The gentlemen were returned from their task outside.

Matthew turned toward the sound, then glanced back at her. Seeing her hesitate, he stood and went to open the door. "Coming?" he asked.

The gentlemen were trudging down the hall. Lily could see that they were all wet through, their clothes muddied and damp, their cheeks red and hands pale from the cold.

She felt Matthew stop by her shoulder. "He does not yet know, I think," he murmured.

She knew he meant Jack, who was talking with Peter while the young Mr. Hounslow trailed behind them. All their movements were heavy with exhaustion, but Jack had a more satisfied look to him than Lily had seen since their dance at Mrs. Grantham's ball. That didn't surprise her—a sailor since the age of fourteen, Jack was used to activity, to purpose, to using his hands and his wits in pursuit of a tangible goal.

Looking at his relaxed expression, Lily quailed at the prospect of being the one to tell him what had happened to his sister.

Matthew seemed to sense her hesitation as Peter spotted them and called out a polite, if wary, greeting. There could be any number of reasons for that wariness, and another time Lily would have been curious to decide which it was. But she couldn't take her eyes from Jack.

"Shall I do it?" Matthew asked quietly.

Jack was frowning at her now, as though sensing that something was amiss. Lily squared her shoulders. "No," she replied. "I thank you, but it should be me."

Jack was striding toward her, his weariness forgotten or ignored. "What happened?" he asked as soon as he was close enough not to shout. Peter and Mr. Hounslow hovered behind him, looking confused by his sudden change in attitude. "Something is wrong, I can tell by your expression. What is it?"

"Is someone else hurt?" Peter demanded, his voice rising anxiously.

"Captain," Lily tried to begin, her voice creaking a little bit. She swallowed, lifting her chin so she could meet his eyes. She felt the brush of Matthew's hand against the back of her arm, gentle and reassuring, but he did not interrupt. "No one else is hurt. But it . . . something has happened that concerns your sister."

"Tell me."

Lily did, a little haltingly at first, though her voice grew stronger as she continued. She hesitated to describe what had been in the letters, not sure she wanted the others to overhear. But Jack needed to know. Quietly, she told him what Amelia had written.

While Mr. Hounslow exclaimed in surprise, Jack said nothing, and Peter jumped in, his distress evident. "But has she admitted to being the one who . . . Even if he was blackmailing her, it could not have been her, surely. I refuse to believe it."

"As do I," Lily said. But she was barely listening to herself. Instead, her eyes were fixed on Jack, who was staring past her. She could not read his expression. "Captain? Will you say something?"

She was unprepared for the self-recrimination she saw in his face when he turned toward her at last. "This is all my fault."

"No," Lily insisted. "No one could have foreseen—"

"No, Mrs. Adler." Jack drew himself up to his full height, a look of cold determination coming over him. "I am her elder brother. It was my job to protect her, and I have tried to do so. But it was not enough." He looked past her, toward where Matthew stood. "You understand, Spencer, I am sure. Sometimes a man must make things right, no matter the cost."

"Captain, what are you saying?" Lily demanded. But Jack merely bowed and turned abruptly toward the stairs. Lily stared, too surprised for a moment to move, then ran after him.

She didn't catch up to him until they reached the bottom of the stairs, Matthew and the others on her heels as she grabbed Jack's arm and pulled him to a stop. Lily glanced back at Matthew, who looked as confused as she did. "Captain, what are you doing?" she asked.

"Making things right," he said shortly, shaking her hand off and continuing toward the dining room.

"What does that mean?" Lily yelled after him.

But he didn't answer or look back at her. A sick feeling began to settle in the pit of Lily's stomach as she hurried after him. When he came to the dining room, he didn't hesitate before throwing the doors open so heavily that one crashed into the wall.

Several of the ladies shrieked in surprise at his entrance, and more than one guest started to their feet, forks and knives still in their hands.

"Jack!" his father exclaimed. "You've heard?"

"I have," Jack replied, though he did not look at his father as he spoke. Hie gaze was fixed on Sir John.

Who got to his feet slowly, his expression somber. "Hartley, will you sit down?"

"You have evidence against my sister?" Jack asked, ignoring the request.

John nodded, his expression wary. "I have." He cut a glance at Lily, who stood in the door behind Jack. "No doubt Mrs. Adler has apprised you of the circumstances."

"I have heard something of them," Jack said. He did not speak loudly, but his voice rang through the quiet dining room. "Though what they were, it turns out, does not matter. I am sure you had very good reasons, sir, but the fact still remains that you are wrong."

"Hartley—"

Lily realized, too late to stop him, what Jack was about to do. She grabbed his arm anyway, but he shook off her hand and stepped forward. There was dead silence in the room as he spoke.

"It was I who was responsible for Mr. Edison's death."

CHAPTER 17

"I know you are lying."

Lily stared at Jack through the narrow door. Amelia, under suspicion only, had been locked in her bedroom as a precaution. But Jack, now a confessed murderer, had been hauled as far away from everyone else in the house as possible. The attic storerooms had once been servants' quarters, back when a larger Grantham family had been in residence and had required more staff. Now one of the rooms had been pressed into service as a makeshift jail.

Jack, lying on the bed and staring at the ceiling, glanced toward the door. Not at her, but at Sir John, who stood next to her. Lily had demanded to speak to Jack alone. Her brother-in-law had refused to allow it, though whether it was her he did not trust or Jack in this instance, she couldn't have said.

Jack looked back at the ceiling. "I have already explained what happened, Mrs. Adler," he said quietly.

"Of course, that you were outraged by the insult that Mr. Edison inflicted upon your sister's person," Lily said, not bothering to keep the scathing disbelief from her voice. "You retrieved a pistol from Mrs. Grantham's gun cabinet, followed Mr. Edison when he went downstairs, and shot him."

The expression on Jack's face could almost have been considered a smile. "I was defending my sister's honor."

"Liar."

"Enough." Jack swung his feet around and sat up so abruptly that John grasped Lily's arm to haul her back. "I'll not sit here and listen to you insult me."

Lily gaped at him. He sounded nothing like the friend and confidant on whom she had come to depend. There was a hardness to his voice and expression that she did not recognize. "You will confess to murder, but you balk at being called dishonest?"

That almost-smile returned. "A gentleman has his limits."

"He is right," John said quietly. "You may not like what he has revealed, but you cannot change it. He has confessed to murder, and so must be held and brought to trial."

Lily glared at them both. "And you are as witless as he if you think I am going to let such obvious nonsense stand."

John's face darkened at the insult. "There are times you cannot have your way, Lily. Perhaps this is one of them."

Lily took a deep breath. Her brother-in-law was generally the most easygoing of men. She was used to speaking her mind around him and expecting nothing but indulgence, or at the worst pleasant disagreement, in return. But the past few days had put John under a strain that he had never before experienced. And now he had the son of a family he had known his whole life—and the childhood friend of his beloved, deceased brother—under arrest for murder.

She needed to be gentler with him.

Lily took a deep breath. "Please, John," she said quietly. "I need to speak with the captain in some degree of privacy. Would you stand a little way off? Please?"

For a moment she thought he would still refuse. Then he nodded stiffly, striding away until he was down the hall from them, before turning to watch them, his arms crossed over his chest.

"Jack," she whispered. She knew that, were someone he loved truly in danger—physical or otherwise—he would not hesitate to do whatever was necessary to protect them. To save them even from themselves. "Don't do this. Please."

"What are they saying downstairs?" Jack asked instead of answering.

Lily blew out a frustrated breath. "It is nearly an even split, I believe, between those who say you could never do such a thing and those who are amazed no one else guessed your guilt sooner, because of course they were not surprised at all." Lily stepped closer to the door. "But there does seem to be a general agreement that acting in defense of your sister should be grounds for some leniency. You certainly know how to charm a crowd, even when confessing to murder."

He gave her a crooked smile. "You know me. I could never let any harm come to my sister."

It was an answer that could mean too many things. She stared at him, silently willing him to say more. But he looked at Sir John, not quite out of earshot, and shook his head.

"I trust you, Lily," he said for her ears alone. "I know you will always do what you think is right. I hope you believe I will do the same. No matter what it costs me."

★　★　★

"Are you satisfied now?" Sir John asked as he locked the passage door behind them. Once it had separated the halls of the female and male servants. Now it created another barrier between Jack and the rest of the house.

"I would not describe myself as such, no."

He gave her a sideways glance. "You do not believe him still?"

"Do you?" Lily demanded. "You have known him since you were children, John. Do you?"

"If you had asked me three days ago, I would not have believed any of my neighbors capable of taking a life in cold blood. But someone must be guilty." He sighed, rubbing the bridge of his nose with two fingers. "He has confessed. Whether I wish to or not, I must treat him as a criminal and a murderer unless there is compelling evidence for the guilt of another." He gestured broadly. "And meanwhile, I have a houseful of people tired of being kept prisoner themselves and about to mutiny under my nose. What else would you have me do?"

Set my friend free, she wanted to say. He could not, and she knew it, but she opened her mouth to ask anyway. Both Amelia and Jack were now locked up. The least he could do—

She fell still, her lips still parted. "The little swine," she breathed as a piece of William's deception fell into place.

"What?" John took a step back. "Do you mean me?"

But Lily wasn't listening. She had already spun about on her heel, striding toward the stairs, her pace only just short of a run. She could hear John following, but she did not look back or stop until she had reached the dining room, where the rest of the guests still lingered uncomfortably.

She walked straight to William, planting her hands on the table and leaning toward him. He shrank back, looking startled. "What—"

"Mrs. Adler, what is it?" Matthew asked, standing as soon as he saw her, the other gentlemen rising to their feet a moment after him.

Lily didn't look at any of them. Her attention was fixed on William Edison. "You liar. You weren't trying to protect your brother by keeping those letters. You wanted to continue what he started."

William gaped at her, his face going pale, then bright red. "I-I-I don't know what you mean," he stammered. "And I'll thank you not to make insinuations—"

Lily cut him off. "It was not an insinuation, Mr. Edison, it was an accusation. You intended to blackmail Miss Hartley yourself."

"I . . ." William looked away from Lily, only to find every other face in the room turned toward him. "I . . ."

Out of the corner of her eye, Lily saw John watching from the doorway. But she didn't look away from William. "Is that all you have to say for yourself?" she bit off, leaning even closer.

He tried to lean back from her, but there was nowhere to go. "I . . . I needed the money," he mumbled. His shoulders hunched up protectively, and he could not meet anyone else's eyes as his voice shrank to a whine. "And Gregory did it. So why not me? Why should he get away with everything and not me?"

"Considering he ended up murdered, I would not say he got away with much of anything," Matthew said dryly. "Perhaps his were not the best footsteps to follow?"

"So *that* was what you and Amelia were arguing about in the hall," Lily continued, standing straight once more. "*That* was why she was so angry and why she would not say what your conversation was about. What did you threaten her with? Her unwise words from those letters? Or something more?"

William's mutter was too low to be heard. But Lily did not need to hear it. She turned toward her brother-in-law.

"If he believed Miss Hartley had something to do with his brother's death, he would not have withheld those letters from you. He would have shared them the instant he found them. But he did not. Can you truly justify keeping her locked up?"

John let out a sigh that was nearly a groan. "Mr. Hartley, Mrs. Hartley, did your daughter say anything to you of Mr. Edison's blackmail? Give any hint of what had happened?"

Both of Jack and Amelia's parents were standing now. Mr. Hartley glanced at his wife, who shook her head. "No," he said, wrapping a protective arm around her shoulders. "She was unhappy and worried of late. But we thought that was due to—" He glanced around at his neighbors, his expression growing hard. "The gossip she was forced to endure."

"Might she have told her brother about it?" John asked, his voice strained.

Mrs. Hartley made a noise like she was biting back a sob. "She might have," she whispered. "I do not know. Excuse me, I must—" She pulled away from her husband. "I cannot be here. Excuse me, please." She hurried from the room. Mr. Hartley, after a moment's hesitation, followed.

There was silence. "Come, everyone," Lady Adler said abruptly, taking charge of the situation. She met her son's eyes briefly, then turned away. "We must leave the magistrate to his work. Mrs. Grantham, will you lead the way?"

"What?" Mrs. Grantham started at being addressed. "What did . . . Oh, yes, of course. Where shall we . . . ?"

"Perhaps the library, for a change of scenery?" Lady Adler suggested. "Mrs. Crewe, perhaps you would help me fetch the drawing things from the morning room? Peter, some might wish to play cards—yes, thank you. Mr. Spencer, would you give Miss Hounslow your arm? She looks peaked. And you, young man—" She caught William Edison by the shoulder when he looked as though he would try to slink away. "I am not letting you out of my sight. You may read to Mrs. Coleridge. It's about time you do something useful for someone other than yourself." Bullying and cajoling in turns, she managed to empty the room, leaving only Lily and John behind.

He sighed when he saw her watching him. "What do you want me to do now? I cannot arrest William just for being an ass. And we've no proof of anything more than that."

"You can give me the key to Amelia's room," she said. She wanted to yell, but John did not deserve to bear the brunt of her ire. "The least you can do for the Hartleys is release one of their children." When he hesitated, she couldn't stop the sharp, angry breath that escaped her. "If you believe Jack was involved, you have to know that he would keep his sister out of it."

He hesitated a moment more, but at last he nodded, fishing the key out of his waistcoat pocket. "Very well. It is not as though she can leave the house anyway." He grimaced. "None of us can."

"A good thing, that," Lily said sharply as she took the key. "It gives you time to find the person who is truly responsible. Because it is not Jack Hartley."

"Lily—"

But she stalked from the room without waiting to hear what else he might have said.

★　★　★

Amelia, worn out from pacing around the room and trying to decipher the shouting in the hall, was lying on the bed attempting to read but staring at the ceiling. She jumped when the knock came at the door. When the key began to turn in the lock, she felt an intense urge to flee—though whether she wanted to hide or try to make a dash out the door, she couldn't say.

But the person who entered was not who she expected to see.

"Oh, Mrs. Adler. It's you." Amelia sank back onto the pillows, staring unseeing at her book, trying to look unconcerned by her plight and confident in her own innocence. She might have been able to fool herself into thinking she had succeeded had she not seen Mrs. Adler glance at her fingers, which gripped the book so tightly that they were shaking. Amelia made them relax. "Is there something I may do for you?" she asked, gesturing at her surroundings. "Within the scope of this room, of course, as I am not permitted to leave it."

"Yes." Mrs. Adler closed the door behind her and stepped closer. "You can tell me what really happened between you and Mr. Edison to cause so much gossip."

Amelia could feel heat spreading across her cheekbones. "I have already made it clear that I have nothing to say on that matter."

"Well, now you have no choice."

"You are mistaken, ma'am. My circumstances here are not so dire," Amelia said, silently praying that her words were true. "Whatever speculation might be bandied about at the moment, everyone here will soon recall what sort of person William Edison is. They will realize I am far more likely to tell the truth than he. And if all else fails, I can provide a demonstration of my marksmanship, which can generously be described as abysmal. So I do, in fact, have a choice. And once again, I choose silence." She returned her gaze to her book, turning the page with a sharp flick that she knew betrayed her anxiety, however calm she might wish to appear. "Whatever blame they might attach to me now, it will not linger."

"They do not need to attach blame to you anymore," Mrs. Adler snapped, before taking a deep breath. "They can attach it to your brother."

"No." Amelia looked up sharply, certain she had heard wrong. For a moment, she felt nothing but pure fear. Deliberately she shook her head, scowling. There was no way such a thing could be true. "No, they cannot. They have no reason to."

"Amelia." Mrs. Adler took a step forward, her hands twitching as though they wanted to reach out and shake someone. But she clasped them together, pressing them against her lips. Something in her tone made Amelia sit up straighter, her book dropping forgotten onto the counterpane. "He has confessed to Sir John that he was responsible for Mr. Edison's death."

"What?" Amelia started to her feet, stepping forward, then back, her hands rising as though to ward off the news. "No, of course he did not. If you are trying to trick me, it will not work."

"I wish to God I were, truly." As though standing upright suddenly felt like too much work, Mrs. Adler reached out to grip the nearest bedpost, pressing her forehead against the wood. "He was arrested not half an hour ago and locked in one of the attic storerooms."

"Why would he do such a thing?" Amelia demanded, grabbing Mrs. Adler's arm and yanking her upright. Surely Raffi could never be so foolish? "Why would anyone believe him? The idea that he could be—" She pulled away suddenly, unable to stand still. "My brother is the most upright, honorable man. For anyone to accuse him of—or believe that he would—it is laughable." She turned back to Mrs. Adler, pleading. "You know it is laughable."

"I do not for a minute believe his confession was true, but his circumstances are far from laughable," Mrs. Adler said. She gripped Amelia's arm, pulling her to a halt. The expression on her face made Amelia feel cold. "He could hang for this."

"Why would he do such a thing?" Amelia repeated, her voice thick with anguish. "Why would he be so stupid?" She froze. "He thinks I did it."

"No—"

"He thinks I did it," Amelia insisted. She could hear her voice rising. "How could he? How *dare* he? Of all the—"

"Amelia!" This time Mrs. Adler did shake her, and the sharp motion cut off her torrent of outrage and fear. "He does *not* think you did it. He confessed to protect you, the stupid man. William had your letters."

Amelia felt cold all over. She took a step back, losing her balance when her legs bumped against the bed. She sat down hard. "My letters?"

"It seems Gregory carried them with him. For safekeeping, I imagine. Sir John knows he was blackmailing you. And how you responded."

"And that was why Raffi confessed?" Amelia said in a small voice, guilt washing over her in such a fierce wave that she almost could not breathe. She should have been honest from the beginning. She should have known she could not handle things herself. "I wrote some terribly unwise things in them."

"Yes." Mrs. Adler did not bother to deny it or try to comfort her.

Amelia scrunched up her face, trying not to cry. "I should never have written him at all. But I was so closely watched after the . . . the incident at the vicarage. It was the only way I could respond to his demand."

"But in the first letter, it was you making a request of him," Mrs. Adler pointed out. "And the gossip was already spreading about that incident by the time he blackmailed you, so that could not have been what he was threatening to make public."

There was silence in the room. Amelia could feel it pressing on her. She knew that this time she would have to tell the truth. At last, she looked up to meet Mrs. Adler's eyes. "You want to know what happened."

It wasn't a question, but Mrs. Adler nodded anyway. "Yes. Now."

Amelia leaned forward, dropping her head down into her hands, then farther still, until she was pressed against the bed. She said it out loud, once for practice, the counterpane and linens muffling her reply.

"Amelia," Mrs. Adler snapped. "I do not have any patience for melodrama right now."

Amelia nodded and lifted her head just enough that she could meet the other woman's eyes. "He kissed me."

Mrs. Adler stared at her, until Amelia groaned with embarrassment and dropped her face down against the bed linens again. It was not nothing, certainly; an illicit kiss, seen by the wrong person, could do considerable damage to a young lady's reputation, especially in the closed circle of a country village. But Amelia hated how banal it sounded out loud.

"All this over a kiss?" Mrs. Adler demanded. "A *kiss*?"

"Well, he was fairly enthusiastic about it," Amelia muttered into the bedclothes again, remembering the odd sensation of Gregory's hands and mouth, how her lack of interest had seemed like a challenge to him to try harder.

Amelia felt a hesitant hand on her shoulder. "Did you want him to kiss you?"

"No," Amelia muttered. At Mrs. Adler's sharp breath, she sat up quickly. "I mean, I did, I asked him to. But I did not . . . that is . . ." She groaned, then flopped backward onto the pillows. "This is why I did not say anything. I do not know how to explain it."

"Amelia." Mrs. Adler sat down on the edge of the bed. She took a deep breath, and when she spoke again, her voice was almost painfully calm. "I cannot help your brother unless you speak plainly."

Amelia nodded, feeling as if she was going to be sick. "I've made a terrible mess of everything," she said. "And now Raffi is going to . . ."

"*Nothing* is going to happen to him," Mrs. Adler said firmly, but she sounded like she was trying to convince herself as much as Amelia. "I shan't allow it."

Amelia nodded again, but she didn't meet Mrs. Adler's eyes as she sat back up. Her cheeks were so hot she felt like they were on fire, and she had to fix her eyes on a painting on the wall as she spoke. Her words came too quickly, then paused and stumbled over each other at odd moments. "When I made my request . . . he was very hesitant to agree. He had no desire to take such liberties with a gentleman's daughter."

"Wise of him," Mrs. Adler said dryly.

"Self-serving," Amelia said, shaking her head. "Gregory did not care about the morality of the situation; he simply didn't wish to deal with any bother. So I had to . . ." She hesitated. Here was the part that was hard to admit. "I had to reveal some very personal information to convince him to agree. To present it as a challenge, which I knew he would have a harder time resisting. When Gregory met me in the garden, I asked him to kiss me because I'd not been kissed before and because I'd not *wanted* to be kissed before. I've never been interested in any sort of embrace from a man."

"Ah. I see." To Amelia's relief, Mrs. Adler sounded as if she truly did see. "Did you . . . Was there anyone at all who . . ."

Amelia shook her head, glancing over quickly, then looking back at the painting. "No one. Which seemed odd to me. The way other girls go on . . . it seems as if everyone is supposed to want such things. I decided to ask Gregory, since he is—he was—handsome and pleasant and the other girls in town are always falling all over themselves hoping he will dance with them or fetch them punch or anything of that sort. I thought . . . if anyone was going to stir such interest . . . surely he would be able?"

"And you explained this to him?" Mrs. Adler asked.

Amelia nodded. Now that she had begun, it was easier to go on. "He was too proud to decline such a challenge. He did as I asked, and he was . . . thorough about it, given the circumstances. Which is why it was unfortunate that Maria Edwards came upon us. And even though she did not see a great deal . . . she is good friends with Kitty Hounslow."

"Ah."

Amelia nodded. "Ah indeed. We did not discover until the next day that the gossip had spread. Whichever one or both of them it was had been as vague as possible while still making the whole thing sound terribly illicit."

Mrs. Adler sighed. "Leaving the details of a scandal to your neighbors' imaginations will always produce far more interesting gossip than spelling out what actually happened."

"It certainly did," Amelia grumbled. "It worked to my advantage as well, of course, because there was nothing specific for anyone to accuse me of having done. But then it occurred to Gregory that he could make use of such an opportunity. And that was when I received his first blackmail letter."

"So what scared you was the possibility that he would reveal your . . . proclivities. Or lack of proclivities, I suppose. And that is when you wrote the letter?" When Amelia nodded, Mrs. Adler sighed again. "And then William found out, one way or another, and decided to try his own hand at blackmail once his brother was gone."

"You know about that too?"

"He did not manage a very good denial when I confronted him with the possibility, and eventually admitted it," Mrs. Adler said.

"He is a little weasel," Amelia said vehemently.

"In this case, it may be fortunate that he is. By hiding the letters, he made it clear that he did not think you were responsible for his brother's death. Which is why Sir John is releasing you." Mrs. Adler shook her head. "Your choice of words was unfortunate."

"It was a figure of speech!" Amelia protested. "As anyone with half a brain could see. He had been very upset, the night of the party, when I was unmoved by his efforts. I was just . . . the whole situation was very awkward, and it simply was not interesting to me. Which, given the attraction he holds for every other woman within fifty miles, is clearly about me and not him, and I said as much at the time. But he took it quite personally, and I was afraid he would be offended enough to reveal what I had told him."

"I see."

"But doesn't the very fact that I wrote such a letter prove that I could not have been the one who killed him?" Amelia protested.

"Who would commit their plans to paper if they were actually intending to murder someone?"

"Someone who was not planning to, but who perhaps is prone to flights of high emotion," Mrs. Adler said, her voice cool. She was watching Amelia carefully. "The sort of emotion that leads to reckless behavior at a party. And perhaps to striking out at a man who has wronged you when you meet once more in private."

Amelia felt as though the bottom had dropped out of her stomach. She wanted to protest the description, to insist on her innocence, but something in Mrs. Adler's expression stopped her. Amelia met her eyes without speaking.

She *had* behaved recklessly. And she had known it at the time. But she, the indulged youngest child of two doting parents, tired of the protective hovering that had hemmed her in for so long, hadn't cared. She had been convinced that she could handle whatever happened on her own, that she didn't need her family's protection. And when things went from bad to worse, when she found herself in the midst of a scandal that she did not know how to put an end to, she hadn't been able to bear the thought of admitting that she had been so very wrong about herself.

"Is that what you think happened?" Amelia asked at last.

Slowly, Mrs. Adler shook her head. "If you were to kill a man, Amelia, I suspect you would do so only after careful planning, not in a burst of emotion." Amelia could not help the nervous breath of laughter that escaped her, and it made Mrs. Adler smile grimly. "But given everything in that letter, and the gossip surrounding you and Mr. Edison, the other explanation would be easier for most people to believe. And it is an explanation that would have seen you shortly arrested and tried for murder."

"Would have," Amelia said quietly, biting her lip. "But for the fact that my brother has confessed in my place. The stupid man."

"Yes."

"Yes to the confession or to his being a stupid man?"

"Both, at the moment," Mrs. Adler said, standing and pacing toward the fireplace. "Though I understand why he did it, it complicates things terribly. Against an accusation, we could have defended either of you. But a confession leaves very little of either doubt or room for hope."

"Then what can we do?" Amelia asked, feeling, for a moment, overwhelmed with anguish. Raffi had wanted to help her. But she had not decided to trust him until it was too late. And now he had helped her anyway, in the way she could least allow. "For you must know I'll not let him take the blame for me."

"I would prefer that neither of you take any blame that does not belong to you," Mrs. Adler said firmly. "But the snow has stopped. Which means that we have until the roads clear to discover who was truly responsible for Mr. Edison's death."

"And if we do not do it before then?"

"We will. You've been released from your confinement here, now that your brother is locked up. The first thing we ought to do is speak with your parents."

"Dear God, my father must be in a state. And my mother . . ." Amelia stood quickly. "I must go to them immediately."

"What will you tell them?" Mrs. Adler asked, sounding genuinely curious.

Amelia swallowed, feeling as though she were going to be sick. But she straightened her shoulders anyway. "The truth. It is time to tell them the truth."

Chapter 18

"But why did you not tell us?" Mrs. Hartley demanded, leaning forward.

They were in the morning room, which was dim and unwelcoming this time of day, but mercifully solitary. Mr. and Mrs. Hartley had retreated there to be as far away from their neighbors as possible while still unable to leave the house. Now their daughter stood in front of them, hands clasped in front of her like a penitent child before her governess. But she kept her chin up and met their eyes, determined to get through her recitation.

"We could not shield you from gossip if we did not know the cause," Mr. Hartley added, his frustration plain.

"But it was *private*, Papa," Amelia insisted. "It was not the fact of his kissing me—I know that was reckless and foolish. It was everything else. I had already discovered it was terribly unwise to admit that to one person. I did not want to talk about it with anyone else."

"You should at least have told us about the blackmail," her mother said, frowning. "Blackmail thrives on secrecy, my love. If you had told us—"

"I could not," Amelia said quickly. Lily watched her closely as she spoke. Amelia looked past her parents and took a deep breath, as though gathering her strength, before she met their eyes again. "I was too ashamed of what I had done. I did not have the money to pay him. So I stole it from Papa."

"You did what?" Mr. Hartley surged to his feet, shock and anger written all over his face. "How much? How many times?"

Amelia shrank back. Her voice grew very small. "Five pounds. And then another ten." She bit her lip. "And then another five."

"Twenty pounds?" Mrs. Hartley demanded.

Amelia nodded. "I am sorry," she said quietly. "I know you must be very disappointed in me. But—" Her mouth trembled. "You cannot be more disappointed than I am in myself. And if anything happens to Raffi . . ." She looked toward Lily, who was sitting by the window, lending her support but saying nothing. "If anything happens to Raffi, I will never forgive myself. Papa, *Ammi*, I am so sorry."

Lily held her gaze. Everything about Amelia's demeanor made Lily think she was telling the full truth at last. And she had known the girl for years. Occasional bouts of melodrama aside, and that was unavoidable in a girl her age, she was generally cool and rational, more prone to observation than passion. Which fit well, it seemed, with her disinterest in Mr. Edison—or anyone else, as she had admitted.

Mr. Hartley's jaw was clenched, and he strode away abruptly, his brows drawn down. Amelia watched him with unconcealed anxiety as he paced a determined lap around the room before stopping in front of her once more. He took a deep breath.

"I forgive you," he said quietly.

Amelia caught her breath. "You are not angry?"

His wry smile was so much like his son's that Lily felt her heart thump painfully against her chest. "I am very angry," he said. "But I can be angry and still forgive you, because you are my daughter, and I love you."

With a sob, Amelia threw herself into her father's arms.

"It's all right, my girl," he murmured against her hair. "Sometimes life is nothing but mistakes and learning from them. You aren't expected to have everything figured out yet."

Amelia sniffed and looked over his encircling arms. "*Ammi*?" she whispered.

Mrs. Hartley sighed. "Forgiven," she agreed. "If only because children have been lying to their parents since time immemorial. We will discuss a punishment later," she added ominously. "But right now we have more pressing matters to deal with."

"Raffi," Amelia whispered.

Mrs. Hartley sighed. "Raffi," she agreed.

Before she could say anything else, a knock at the door startled them all. A moment later, Peter Coleridge poked his head in. "Mr. Hartley? Mrs. Hartley? I was hoping . . ." His eyes fell on Amelia. "My dear, you've been crying. I apologize—I've no wish to intrude," he said, starting to back out of the room.

"No, please," Mr. Hartley said, gesturing toward a chair and taking a seat himself. Mrs. Hartley did the same. Amelia, looking nervous at the interruption, chose a chair closer to the door. "We were just finishing our discussion. Though I must say, I am surprised you sought us out at such a time." He grimaced. "Under such unusual circumstances, I mean."

"It is precisely that which made me wish to speak to you," Peter said, taking a seat across from Mr. and Mrs. Hartley.

It placed him very near Amelia, and Lily saw him glance toward her several times as he chose his words. Lily herself was still by the window; she didn't know whether Peter had noticed her presence. While under normal circumstances she would have made sure he saw her, at the moment she was content to sit back and see what unfolded for the Hartleys.

"It is terrible, what has happened with the captain," Peter continued. "You have my deepest sympathies. And though I struggle to picture him in the role of murderer, if he was the person responsible, I can hardly blame him for taking such action in defense of his sister's reputation. A truly honorable man, your son."

There was an uncomfortable silence in the room.

"Thank you, Mr. Coleridge," Mrs. Hartley said at last. "It means the world to us to have our friends stand by us."

"But I am sure that, regardless of what happens, the fact of his confession makes no few difficulties for you."

Mr. Hartley smiled without humor. "That is one way to put it."

"Indeed." Peter looked embarrassed. "I apologize; everything I say at the moment feels frightfully banal. I should leave you in peace." He stood, but Mrs. Hartley put up her hand.

"Please, Mr. Coleridge, tell us what you came to say. We are not the best conversationalists just now, as you can see. But we are trying, I assure you."

"No, it is I who . . . That is, it is an awkward thing, what I came to say. But I think it is important. And I think you deserve it." He glanced at Amelia. "Particularly you, Miss Hartley."

Amelia's glance darted toward Lily for the moment, then to her parents, before it settled back on Peter. "I am not sure what that might mean, sir," she said, polite but wary.

"What I wish to say is that, given the long-standing friend-ship between our families, and once the scandal—whatever form it takes—dies down, I wish to make you an offer, Miss Hartley." Peter cleared his throat. "Of marriage."

The surprised silence that followed his declaration was so pro-nounced that Lily could hear the quiet tick of the mantelpiece clock.

Peter glanced around. "I fear I have offended you."

"No," Mr. Hartley said quickly, glancing at his wife. "Merely surprised us. We were not aware that you . . ." He seemed to run out of words.

"What my husband means to say," Mrs. Hartley continued, her cool voice smoothing over the uncomfortable moment, "is that we had no idea you felt such a preference for Amelia."

Peter smiled nervously. "She is an admirable young lady in all ways," he said politely. Lily could see a slight sheen of per-spiration on his brow, but she could hardly blame him for that. It was not every day a man found himself in circumstances that could easily have come from the pages of a novel: proposing marriage to a young lady who had so recently admitted to being blackmailed by the gentleman with whom she had been caught in a compromising position and whose brother was about to be charged in the murder of that same gentleman. She had to admire Peter's determination.

Seeing that both Mr. and Mrs. Hartley were unsure of what to say, Peter continued, a persuasive note coming into his voice. "The generous dowry you have provided for Miss Hartley would, in the normal course of things, make several offers of marriage highly likely. But you must consider whether it will do any good now, given the new circumstances in which you find yourselves. The likelihood of another offer . . ." He shook his head regretfully. "I can imagine what you are thinking, Amelia, and that is that I would not be your first choice for a husband. But I hope you will consider it. I would offer you not only the protection of my name but what I am sure would grow to be a good deal of true affection. We have known each other for many years, after all."

"Indeed," Amelia said. "Many years. Since I was a mere child, in fact."

"Amelia," her mother said quietly, and Amelia bit her lip.

"I apologize, Mr. Coleridge," she said, choosing her words with evident care. "I am honored by your proposals. I hope you will not be offended if I wish for time to hear my parents' thoughts on the matter before I give you an answer?"

"Of course not," Peter said. "A child must always respect the wishes of a parent. And I understand that an answer may take some time, as concerned as you must be with your brother's circumstances." That had the ring of a reminder, Lily thought, and a pointed one at that. "I do believe we would suit well. My mother has a great deal of respect for your family, and I would make sure that you never want for any comforts." He cleared his throat, standing. "I shan't impose on you any further for the moment. But please." He glanced around the room, his nervous smile stopping at Amelia before sliding over to her parents. He nodded to Mr. Hartley. "I hope you will consider my offer."

"Thank you, Mr. Coleridge," Mr. Hartley said, standing and offering his hand to shake. "You and I will certainly find time for further discussion. When all this"—his grimacing gesture took in a good deal more than the room they stood in—"has been settled."

"And I hope you know that we are deeply honored by it, and by your kind motivation," Mrs. Hartley added, her eyes flicking toward her daughter. Her fingers moved in a slight beckoning motion, the sort you noticed only if you were a child accustomed to a parent's silent promptings.

Amelia stood and held out her own hand; Peter, after a moment of surprised hesitation, took it. Her face was unreadable, so set and empty of emotion that it might have been stone. Standing next to him, his offer of marriage hanging in the air about them, Lily thought she seemed very young, hovering just past the edge of childhood.

But no one could remain a child in the face of a murder accusation, or the threat of a beloved brother's death.

"I thank you, Mr. Coleridge," Amelia said, her shoulders straight and tense. "I hope you know that I am grateful, whatever happens."

There was a quick movement in Peter's jaw: the twitch of a muscle, or perhaps he had bitten the inside of his cheek. He was not fully composed—or perhaps he, too, felt the discomfort of the moment, the youthfulness of the girl standing before him. Lily wondered whether the proposal had been his idea or his mother's.

He bowed over Amelia's hand before turning to leave. That was when he caught sight of Lily. His face grew very red. "Lily— Mrs. Adler! I apologize, I did not see you there."

"Oh, no, it is I who must apologize, then," Lily said innocently, lying without hesitation. "If I had known you were unaware of my presence, I would have spoken up sooner."

"I was not . . . that is . . ." Peter's blush crept around his neck and to his ears. "It was a rather personal conversation."

"And I would never dream of repeating a word of it, to be sure," Lily said reassuringly. "Have you any news about the weather, by the by?"

"Oh! Yes, as a matter of fact." Peter turned toward the window, giving Amelia a quick, absent smile as his eyes slid over her. "Before we came in, Mrs. Grantham's grounds keeper said if the snow continues to hold off, they might be able to start clearing the drive tomorrow." He did not bother to hide his relief. "In two days, we could all be going home."

There was silence in the room once he had left. Amelia sat down, her polite mask dropping in an instant, her misery plain. Her father paced nervously in front of the fireplace, looking no less distressed. Her mother remained composed as ever, but she too sought the refuge of distance, walking to the window and staring out. A drizzling rain had begun to fall, bouncing against the glass and leaving pockmarks in the icy crust of the snow. "Two days," she murmured. She did not sound happy about it.

Lily glanced around the room. "Shall I leave?" she asked, standing. The rain outside was a familiar sight, far more than the snow of the past few days, but that did not stop it from making her anxious. If it grew heavier, there was every chance the frozen ground would flood, putting any number of people in danger. But if it stayed light, it would serve to wash away a great deal of the snow—making their departure all the more likely.

"No," Amelia said, shaking her head. "No, because this all comes down to Raffi. And you are going to help him."

"Amelia, we cannot rely on that," her mother said without turning around.

Lily did not sit, her eyes still moving between Mr. and Mrs. Hartley, waiting for their verdict. As distressed as she felt, as painful as it was for her to think about Jack's confession, she knew it was nothing to what his parents must be feeling.

Mrs. Hartley turned around. "But I would value your input nonetheless, Mrs. Adler. My son has written often of his esteem for your judgment and insight, and you know the Coleridges a little better than we do. What do you make of Mr. Coleridge's proposal?"

"I think that question should first be put to Amelia," Lily said.

Amelia raised her head. Her mouth trembled a little before she bit down hard on her lip, taking a deep breath. "I've no wish to marry him," she said quietly. "But I do realize it may be my best option. Especially if . . ." She trailed off, throwing a pleading look in Lily's direction, clearly unwilling to give voice to what might happen to her brother.

"Then it is a good option to have," Lily suggested gently. Mr. and Mrs. Hartley nodded their agreement, though neither of them looked happy about it. Lily wondered if she ought to inform them about Peter's affair with Caroline Taylor but thought better of it. If a marriage to Peter could protect Amelia, she did not want to be the one who took that option away from them. "Though I wonder whether the idea came from Mr. Coleridge or at the prompting of his mother."

"He is, perhaps, more deferential to her than is common," Mr. Hartley agreed. It did not sound as though he meant it as a compliment.

"I hardly think that matters under the circumstances," Amelia said, sighing.

"You might think otherwise if you marry into her household," Lily pointed out, casting a glance at Mrs. Hartley, who nodded in agreement. "But you are right in that it does not change what we must do next."

"Which is?" Amelia prompted, as the sound of the dinner gong reverberated down the hall.

"Dinner, it seems," Mrs. Hartley said, leaving the window and holding out her hand to her husband. He clasped it in both of his, bringing it to his lips in a sincere kiss—there was no romance in the gesture, only two people seeking solace and support in the midst of the unhappy surprises that buffeted them from all sides.

Lily, with no one to clasp her own hand just then, envied them that.

Mr. Hartley tucked his wife's hand against his elbow. "Come, dear ones. We will hold our heads high, no matter what happens."

Amelia nodded, ready to follow her parents out of the room. But Lily caught her arm before she could.

"You and I have another task as well," she murmured while the Hartleys preceded them down the hall to the dining room.

"What?" Amelia asked, glancing around nervously. "I cannot afford to get in any more trouble, Mrs. Adler."

"You needn't," Lily assured her. "Our task is to keep our eyes and ears open at this dinner. Everyone is going to have an opinion on Jack's arrest. Everyone is going to be relieved at the prospect of going home. What we need to watch for . . ." She paused as they crossed paths with the Taylors, who gave them wide berth and cloyingly sympathetic looks as they stood aside to let the Hartleys go first. Lily dropped her voice even further. "Is any sign that one guest feels that relief more acutely than anyone else."

Amelia gave her a startled look. "Am I to hunt a murderer with you, Mrs. Adler?" she whispered.

"Let us be hopeful," Lily murmured as they scanned the table for their seats. "Let us instead say *catch*."

CHAPTER 19

Lily was surprised by the flood of relief she felt at seeing Matthew waiting for her, his hand on the back of her chair to slide it out.

With no luggage, none of the guests had been changing for dinner. Under other circumstances, Lily might have found the informality freeing. Now, though, it was disorienting to live without the rituals that had always demarcated her days. It felt as though everything familiar had been taken away, leaving all of them unsure of how to behave with one another.

When Matthew helped her into her seat, it was a moment of all that was familiar and easy, punctuated by his kind smile, his clear and mutual relief at seeing her.

"How are they?" he asked quietly as he took the seat next to hers, his glance sliding to the Hartleys as they took their own seats.

"As well as can be expected."

"And you?" The look he gave her was measured and sympathetic, but there was an edge to his curiosity that surprised her. "The captain is a dear friend, I know. I can well imagine that this is nearly as shocking for you as it is for them."

"I am angry with him, though unsurprised that he would do anything he could to protect his sister," Lily replied quietly. "But you may guess I have no intention of letting him take the blame for what someone else has done."

"Then you are certain it was not he?"

The question was asked with such careful neutrality that it took Lily a moment to realize what he had said. She stared at Matthew. "Of course I am. He would never do such a thing."

Matthew shrugged a little. "I do not know him as well as you do. But it seems to me not uncommon for a brother to defend the reputation of his sister."

"I hardly think such things are settled with pistols anymore." Lily did not bother to hide the sharpness in her voice, but she did restrict herself to a whisper as the first course was brought in. They were not the only ones having a hushed conversation, she noticed; whispers were humming around the table, along with many curious or pointed glances. But no one seemed willing to broach the subject that had to be on all their minds. "Besides which, he is a rational man who keeps a cool head under pressure. He would not act impulsively."

"He is a naval man," Matthew pointed out, not meeting her eyes as he applied himself to the soup. "And until recently, he has been accustomed to the rigors and trials of war. Impulsive or not, he might be more . . . aggressive in confronting a problem than you or I would be."

Lily took a deep breath, picking up her own silverware. She let it out slowly, reining in her temper. "Some men might. Captain Hartley is not one of them." After a moment she was able to calmly meet Matthew's eyes. "I hope you can trust me on that."

She had to remind herself not to be offended by the way he paused, considering, spoon hovering above his bowl. She was not one to accept the assurances of others without applying her own mind to them; logically, she could not fault him for doing the same. But she had expected Matthew to think more highly of her friend—and of her own judgment.

"Of course I can," he replied at last, giving her another brief, warm smile. "You know how much respect I have for your opinions."

Lily let out a breath. She did not have energy for an argument with Matthew. And she did not *want* an argument. She wanted his help.

"Did you hear the news?" she asked in a more normal voice, one that invited their neighbors at the table into the conversation. She was turned toward Matthew, but she was watching the others out of the corner of her eye to see how they reacted. "Mr. Coleridge says that if the snow does not return, the roads may be safe enough for us to travel the day after tomorrow. As long as the rain does not grow heavier, of course."

"I had heard," Matthew said, letting out a relieved sigh. "I will be glad to return to my children. I do not doubt that Lady Adler has been attending admirably to their care," he added, nodding to Sir John, who sat a few places away from him at the head of the table. "But I'll not be easy until I can see them again."

"Of course you cannot, Mr. Spencer," Lady Adler exclaimed while the servants removed the soup bowls and laid the second course. "And no doubt they are missing you dreadfully, as we are missing dear Charlotte and the little ones in our family."

"And when we leave, Sir John, what will happen to Captain Hartley?"

Mrs. Crewe's question sent a gasp shivering around the table and silenced every voice. They all stared at her.

She shrugged. "I think we've a right to ask, after everything. And no doubt the Hartleys want to know what you have planned for their son."

"Yes." Mr. Hartley's voice wavered a little, but it grew stronger as he spoke. "If you would be so kind as to illuminate us, sir, what will happen when we are finally permitted to leave?"

All the guests turned toward Sir John. Lily, seated toward the middle of the table, took the opportunity to study everyone she could see.

John turned back to his plate, focusing on his dinner rather than meeting the many pairs of curious eyes. "The law will take its course, as it must," he said, his voice carefully neutral. "There will be an inquest, as is customary, at which the captain's confession will be presented. And likely after that, he will go to trial."

"I, for one, do not blame him," Mrs. Coleridge announced. She spoke in her usual authoritative way, her imposing stare fixed on William Edison. "It is an absolute travesty, what your brother attempted to do to poor Miss Hartley. What gentlemen resorts to blackmailing a defenseless young woman? Shameful."

William pushed his chair back, standing so abruptly that the entire table shook, the glasses on it shivering with an eerie, discordant music. "And so you believe he deserved to die?"

"I did not say that," Mrs. Coleridge said, looking offended. "I am sure the captain did not intend his death. And we've no way of knowing, truly, what happened. Perhaps your brother was the one who instigated the violence, eh? Perhaps Captain Hartley was only defending himself. Has no one considered that?"

"It is the sort of thing he would do," Mrs. Taylor added unexpectedly. Her husband, buried in his wineglass, snorted softly, but she took no notice. "He is an honorable man."

"I thought it was considered in poor taste to speak ill of the dead?" William snapped.

"It is also considered poor taste to blackmail someone," Mr. Hartley said coldly, his eyes on his mutton.

"Well, honorable or not, he will still hang for it," William spat out before storming from the room.

There was silence after his departure. Mrs. Hartley pushed her plate away. "I'm afraid I have lost my appetite for dinner."

★　★　★

No one lingered long at the table.

Amelia trailed upstairs behind her parents, knowing it was unwise to be too far from them but stopping for a moment to press her nose against the glass of a window, trying to see outside.

For the first time in weeks, in spite of everything, she had begun to feel like she could take a full breath. Jack's confession hung heavy on her shoulders, but the weight of secrecy had been lifted at last. Though it was too dark to see the rain, she could hear it, a steady, icy drizzle that had been drumming the world all evening.

They had one more day, Mrs. Adler had said. Once everyone left the house . . .

The hallway was mostly deserted as Amelia reached the top of the stairs; the other guests seemed to have moved more quickly than she had after dinner ended.

But someone was just coming out of her room, and it was not her father or mother.

"What are you doing, lurking about here?" Amelia demanded.

Kitty Hounslow stared at her, letting the door swing shut so quickly behind her that the sound of it slamming closed made them both jump. Kitty recovered first, her eyes narrowing as she looked Amelia over head to toe. "Waiting for you, of course."

"Why?" Amelia asked, her patience fraying. "There is no audience here for your gossip and insinuations. So I don't see why you would bother."

"I don't need an audience," Kitty snapped, the color high in her cheeks, her hands shaking so severely that the wax from her candle spilled over her fingers. She winced, hissing a little, but did not pay it any other attention. "But someone needs to make sure you know you shan't get away with it."

"Get away with what?" Amelia demanded. Kitty lifted her chin, not saying anything, her expression so fierce that Amelia found herself taking a step back. "My God, you really believe I had something to do with his death," she said. Kitty's feelings for Gregory Edison hadn't been secret from anyone but Gregory himself, and Amelia had assumed that every sideways look and malicious comment was grief and jealousy, nothing more. But now . . . "How could you accuse me of such a thing?"

They had known each other their whole lives, she and Kitty Hounslow, as their families had long moved in the same circles, offered the same charity, attended the same local picnics and parties and village festivals. They had been friends as children, in the way that friendships often formed simply because two young people were approximately the same size and always thrown into each other's company. But they had grown apart as they grew older, discovering that their personalities did not have much in common after all.

Once, Amelia hadn't thought there was any animosity in that drifting apart. But it seemed she had been wrong.

"You cannot truly suspect me of such a thing, Kitty," she said, shaking with fury and fear. How long had it been since Kitty Hounslow had begun to hate her? "You know me better than that."

"I know Gregory never would have looked at you twice on your own merits," Kitty said. "He never would have *dreamed* of taking liberties with a proper English lady. But you—" Her expression twisted into a vicious smile. "It turns out you are none of those things, are you?"

The sting of the taunt hit Amelia like a living thing, reminding her of every small comment and slight toward her family, ignored for years but so often in the background of her life. It burrowed deep inside her, and her own temper flared in response. "And how you would have *loved* if he had dreamed of taking liberties with you," she said, knowing it was unwise, knowing it was cruel, and saying it anyway. "But he never wanted to, did he? Poor, boring, forgettable Kitty. Tell me, did he even know that you existed?"

Kitty gasped, her face going splotchy red with rage and hurt. "Apologize to me this instant," she said, her voice thick with emotion.

"You first," Amelia snapped, blinking back her own tears.

They stared at each other, neither moving, neither speaking, until the sound of footsteps made them both remember where they were. With a gasp that quickly turned into sobbing, Kitty Hounslow turned and fled down the hall. Amelia glanced toward the footsteps and saw Sir John striding down the hall, his hands clasped behind his back and his brow furrowed in thought. When he spotted her, he paused.

"Miss Hartley," he said gravely, though his politeness did not mask the caution in his tone. "Do you need assistance with something?"

Amelia wondered what she looked like to him, still shaking with rage and holding back tears. She lifted her chin. "No, I thank you, sir. I am perfectly well."

He nodded slowly. "Then I suggest you return to you chamber for the night," he said.

It was clearly not a suggestion. Amelia wanted to argue with him, just on principle, to tell him exactly what she thought about his evidence and his careful politeness. But even she was not that unwise. "As you say, sir."

He bowed. "I will bid you a good night."

He waited to see if she did as he instructed, though, and she could feel his eyes on her back even as she closed the door behind her.

She took her time unpinning her hair, brushing it out, and winding it into a braid. When she peeked her head out the door, Sir John was gone. She wrapped two shawls around her shoulders for extra warmth and retrieved her candle from the nightstand.

"Amelia." Her mother's voice cut through the air. When Amelia turned, Saba Hartley stood in the doorway between their rooms, her frown evident even in the dim light. "You know better than to wander at night. Especially right now."

They both knew the double meaning of the words. *Right now*, when a murderer was somewhere in the house. *Right now*, when their family teetered on the edge of disaster.

"I want to talk to Raffi."

Saba Hartley hesitated. Her jewelry had been removed, but otherwise she hadn't yet begun preparing for bed. She shook her head. "It is unwise."

"*Ammi*, please," Amelia said. "I will go straight there and back, I promise." When her mother still looked unsure, she added, her face falling, "You no longer trust me, do you?"

"It is not a matter of trust, dear one." Her mother sighed. "Do you think I do not wish to go to him as well? But it is not worth the risk of making things worse for him."

"I'll be careful—"

"No." Her mother closed her eyes. "Do not make me regret the freedom we have allowed you."

"I have precious little freedom right now, *Ammi*," Amelia said sadly.

"None of us do. And it could be far less," her mother said, stepping forward to cup her hand around Amelia's cheek. She smelled like tuberose from the oil she dabbed behind her ears each day, and the familiar, comforting scent made Amelia's eyes fill with tears. "It is not only your brother that I must protect."

"I know," Amelia replied quietly. And she did.

"Come." Her mother turned and beckoned her toward the connecting door. "Indulge me and your father tonight in our protectiveness. We have asked the maid to make up a bed for you in here. We will sleep easier if we know at least one of our children is with us and safe."

★   ★   ★

Lily made her way up the stairs, the darkness of the house pressing against the flickering light of the candle she carried, a single key clenched in her hand. John had been more than reluctant to give it to her; he likely would not have if his mother had not interfered.

"What do you think she is going to do?" Lady Adler had demanded, hovering in the doorway of his room while he and Lily argued in heated whispers within. They had both jumped—she had not lost a mother's knack of approaching arguing children unnoticed. "Give her the one to the hall door only, if you are so worried. She cannot do any harm with that."

"Do not encourage her, Mother," John had snapped. "Wandering the halls alone at night is hardly safe."

"Why would it be dangerous?" Lily countered. "I thought you already had your murderer locked up."

John had glared at her. But in the face of pressure from both of them, he had finally thrown up his hands and pulled the key from the ring, grumbling the whole time. But at the door, when he pressed it into her hand, he had held on for a moment. "Tell him I am sorry," he had whispered. "I wish to God I had another choice, but he did not leave me one."

Lily felt her anger toward him soften. "I know," she whispered back. "And he does too."

When she reached the attic storerooms, she fumbled a little with the key, the cold air making her fingers clumsy. The click of the lock echoed too loudly through the darkness, and she closed the door quickly behind her, locking it from the other side. She didn't think anyone had followed her, but she was taking no chances. Pocketing the key once more, she counted the doors, knocking quietly on the sixth one she reached.

"Jack?" she called softly.

There was a creak of bedsprings on the other side of the door, the sound of footsteps. A quiet chuckle. "Come for a jailbreak, Lily?" he asked.

She could hear him settle onto the floor. She did the same, setting the candle down a careful distance away so she could lean her head against the wood of the door. "A daring nighttime escape?" she suggested.

"Only the most daring for the men of His Majesty's navy," Jack agreed with deliberate lightness. "It shall be bold. Swashbuckling, even."

"Alas, I seem to have forgotten my rapier and black cloak," she said. "And Sir John has given me but one key."

Another chuckle. "What are you doing wandering in the night, then?"

"Visiting my friend," she said gently. "I thought perhaps he could use some company."

Jack was silent for a moment. "Your friend is grateful for it," he said at last. "Tell me what has happened downstairs."

She did, describing William's blackmail, Amelia's confession to her parents, Peter Coleridge's proposal. When she mentioned the many people who had come to his defense at dinner, she could hear his derisive snort from the other side of the door.

"Good of them to think it forgivable for me to defend my sister's honor," he said. "What a pity they could not extend that same understanding to the possibility of her defending herself."

"People are rarely reasonable when it comes to young women," Lily said. They were silent for a moment. "Tell me," she said at last. "What does Jem think of you leaving the navy?"

Jack laughed quietly at the mention of the boy who worked as his body servant, a former street urchin of sixteen who had been born and bred in the slums of London before he came to their notice. "He seems to have made peace with it. He took to sea life far more quickly than I expected, and I think he will miss it some. But he was not disappointed when I told him of our return to London."

"Do you think he worries for his mother?" Lily asked. Jem's mother, the only parent he knew, was often sickly, but she had rarely been able to afford a doctor's help until Lily and Jack had begun settling the bills for her.

"Actually, I believe the last time we were ashore, he met a young lady."

"Goodness, is he old enough for a sweetheart?"

"I beg you never to ask him that," Jack said, laughing once more. "He would be mortally embarrassed."

"Well, I hope he is still child enough to enjoy the snow," Lily said, smiling in spite of everything. "However dreadful it may be for us, I do like to picture the young people of the parish out playing in it."

"A nice thought, that," Jack agreed.

Silence fell between them once more. Lily could hear Jack shifting on the other side of the door. She hesitated, then said quietly, "I know you did not do it, Jack."

He was silent for a long moment. "I hope John does not feel too cut up about the whole business," he said at last. "It has to be wretched for him, being forced to lock me up like this."

"Then do not make him," she suggested, her voice cracking as she thought of William Edison's awful words at the dinner table.

"Are you crying over me, Lily Adler?" he said, soft and teasing. "Dear me. This will never do. I thought you far too practical for such flights of emotion."

That made her laugh, which made her glare at the wood of the door, as though he could somehow feel the force of her stare. "Wretched man," she grumbled.

"I heard that," he said. Another pause. "You should get back, you know. It isn't wise to linger up here too long."

"A little longer," she said, tipping her head back to rest it against the door. "You can tell me a story, if you like. A swashbuckling one. Or an embarrassing one. Those are even better."

He chuckled again. "An embarrassing one, certainly, to keep our spirits up. Have I told you of the time that John and my brother Asif had gone swimming, and Freddy and I decided to hide all their clothes . . ."

★ ★ ★

Lily woke with a stiff neck, her fingers and toes feeling half-frozen. The candle, still sitting a few feet from her, had burned down by nearly an hour. She winced, irritated with her carelessness and glad that she had not knocked it over in her sleep.

"Jack?" she called softly.

From the other side of the door, she heard the faint sound of a snore. The sound made her smile a little, in spite of her worries, and she wondered which of them had fallen asleep first. Shivering, she fumbled for the key, glad to find it was still in her lap, before staggering to her feet and collecting the candle once more.

The house was still as she made her way back down two flights of stairs. She was on the third floor, just one more staircase from her room, when she realized she was not alone.

"Good evening, Mrs. Adler."

William Edison had been standing in the shadows by one of the windows; now he stepped forward, the light from her candle catching one side of his face and leaving the other half in shadow.

"What are you doing?" she demanded.

He gave her a long look. "Grieving," he said, biting the word off. "You may recall that it was my brother who was killed, however much the company here seems determined to worry about the sensibilities and well-being of everyone else instead."

"Well, then, I'll not intrude," Lily said, not liking the way he was staring at her.

But he stepped in her path when she tried to head toward the stairs. "Like you," he said, a scowl twisting the half of his face that she could see clearly. "Accusing me of blackmail so coarsely, so cruelly, in front of everyone. No thought for what I have been feeling. And now sneaking upstairs to visit the man who killed my brother?" His voice grew venomous. "What manner of person behaves in such a way?"

"I am sorry for your loss, and for your grief," Lily said, drawing herself up. She refused to let him see that she was unnerved, both by his nearness and his words. "And perhaps my behavior has been unsympathetic. But as you loved your brother, so I love my friends. And I will do anything"—she took a step forward, her eyes fixed on his—"*anything* to protect them."

"Mrs. Adler."

William, about to reply, started, turning quickly around and stepping away from her. Lily looked past him to where Matthew waited on the stairs, his face illuminated by the candle he held aloft. "Mrs. Adler, may I escort you back to your room?"

"Indeed," she said, happy to step past William and join Matthew on the stairs. "Good night, Mr. Edison. My sympathies, once more, for your loss."

They did not speak until they were in front of her room, where Matthew set his candle on a hall table so that he could lay his hand on her arm. "Are you all right?"

"Perfectly," she said, not wanting to admit how unnerved she was. "He was not pleased that I accused him in front of everyone." She frowned at Matthew. "Why were you—"

"Looking for you?" he finished, raising his brows. In the dim light, she could not tell exactly what his expression was. "You had not come back downstairs. I was worried about you."

"You saw me go up?" she asked.

"I did."

She waited for him to say something else, to have some opinion on the matter. She could not tell if he was waiting for the same thing. At last he sighed. "Are you sure you are all right?"

"I am," she said slowly, though she glanced back toward the stairs and shivered. "But I think I will keep my eye on Mr. William Edison."

"If I know you, Lily," Matthew replied, hooking a finger under her chin, "you will keep your eye on everyone." He bent down to brush a quick kiss against her lips. "I am glad you are safe. Will you promise me to stay in your room for the rest of the night?"

Normally, she would have bristled at such a request. But remembering the scowl on William's face, twisted and menacing in the dim light of the candle, she found herself nodding. "I will. And Matthew?" She caught his arm as he started to turn away. "Thank you."

He smiled as he picked up his candle once more. "Good night, Lily." He hesitated a moment, then added, "And please be careful."

CHAPTER 20

The rain had frozen overnight, leaving the world covered in a thin layer of ice. But it had first washed some of the snow away; with no more falling, it was not long before the road from Mrs. Grantham's home would become passable again.

One day. Lily surveyed the other guests over her teacup at breakfast. She had one day—two if she was lucky—to discover what had truly happened to Gregory Edison. She had been distracted by her concern for Amelia and Jack, but that couldn't be her focus anymore.

She needed to know what Gregory Edison had been doing that night. Something had taken him from his bed and out into the storm. But what, or who, had it been?

After breakfast, they all went dutifully in pursuit of the few entertainments available to them. The tensions of the past few days and the strain of being trapped together were beginning to show. William Edison, scowling at everyone that his eye fell on but speaking to no one, went through the connecting door to the second sitting room, pushing roughly past the Hartleys to do so. Mrs. Crewe did her best to make cheerful conversation with Lady Adler and Matthew, suggesting a game of cards that no one else seemed particularly interested in, until Mr. Hounslow told her abruptly to shut up, as he was trying to read.

"You have read that paper three times already since we have been here," Mrs. Taylor snapped, coming to her friend's defense. "If you want quiet so badly, go somewhere else."

"Where do you suggest?" he asked, a nasty edge to his voice. "Into town, perhaps?"

"Out into the snow to freeze, for all I care," she replied, tossing her head. "And good riddance."

"Do not talk to my husband in such a manner, you hussy," Mrs. Hounslow retorted. "Unless you would like us to discuss your own reputation for—"

"If you please!" Lady Adler exclaimed in the tone of voice used by a stern governess to quell fighting children.

They all turned to glare at her. Mr. Hounslow made a rude noise and retreated behind his paper, and Mrs. Taylor flounced off to the pianoforte. Peter, who had been looking carefully elsewhere when Mrs. Taylor's reputation was mentioned, went to attend to his mother, who seemed to have developed a cough.

"Shall I fetch you a blanket, Mrs. Coleridge, if you are feeling unwell?" Mrs. Crewe asked, looking around the room uneasily.

"Oh, thank you, young lady, yes . . ."

Only Mrs. Grantham sat apart, her eyes on a hoop of embroidery, though her hands were still. The tea tray was next to her, steaming and fragrant, in case anyone needed another cup to ward off the morning chill—a comfort that no one seemed inclined to enjoy. Every so often, she looked up, glancing over her guests as though ensuring that they needed nothing from her.

She'd had the same nervous look on her face that first morning, Lily recalled, when Sir John was asking anyone who had been up and about to be honest, in case they had seen anything useful. Distracted by the other accusations, by blackmail and worry for her friend, Lily had not pursued her suspicions about their hostess's nighttime activities. It was time for that to change.

"Lily, dear?" Lady Adler tapped her arm. "Will you be playing with us?"

"No, I thank you." Lily glanced around the room before nodding politely to the three people seated around the table. "I believe I shall go ask Mrs. Grantham for a cup of tea."

Mrs. Crewe nodded and turned to Lady Adler to discuss games that were good for only three players. But Lily could feel Matthew's curious eyes on her as she crossed the room.

Mrs. Grantham didn't notice Lily's approach at first. "Oh, Mrs. Adler!" she exclaimed quietly when Lily took the seat next to her. "My apologies, I did not notice . . . That is, I was thinking . . . May I pour you a cup?"

"If you would be so kind," Lily replied. The rest of the guests were busy, and the music from the pianoforte made it hard to hear anyone else's conversation clearly. Still, she leaned forward and lowered her voice before speaking. "I am sorry such a misfortune has occurred in your home, and after you so generously offered us shelter the night of the ball."

Mrs. Grantham was one of the most hospitable women in the neighborhood. The death of her husband several years before had left her with a comfortable property and even more comfortable widow's jointure, and she hosted dinner parties and dances in all seasons. A woman of middle age, she was high-spirited, pleasant, and known for her sense of humor.

But few of those traits were in evidence as she poured the tea, the shiver that chased over her shoulders making the porcelain cup tremble in its saucer as she passed it to Lily. Her normally rosy cheeks were pale, and if she was trying to summon a polite smile, she was failing miserably.

"It feels like a nightmare," she said in a sudden rush. "Seeing Mr. Edison outside like that . . . Sir John having to treat all his neighbors like criminals, in my house, and I must let him . . . And we are all trapped . . ." She dropped her head into her hands, but before Lily could reach out to comfort her, she gathered herself together once more, sitting up straight and lifting her chin. "I apologize, I did not mean to fall to pieces like that," she said, wiping at the tears that had collected on her lashes.

"You've no need to apologize," Lily said, keeping her eyes on the milk she was pouring into her cup to give Mrs. Grantham time to regain her composure. "I am sure it has been dreadful. But I wanted to ask . . ." She considered her words carefully, looking up at her hostess at last. "You allowed me and the captain to come into the yard that first morning. Why was that?"

Mrs. Grantham gave her a sideways look. "You said the rumors about you are true. Shall I enumerate some of them for you?"

"Please do," Lily said tranquilly, taking a sip of her tea.

Mrs. Grantham blushed, as though embarrassed to be asked to repeat the gossip. "That you have a knack for discovering the bits of truth that others would like to keep concealed. There was a rumor about a family called the Astins this summer and something to do with a duel . . ."

Lily made a small murmur of agreement and took another sip of her tea.

"And I heard that you located some rather valuable jewelry that had gone missing . . ."

"Emeralds," Lily volunteered, nodding. She had been rather proud of that one.

"And I even gathered from something Lady Adler let fall that you had become acquainted with a member of that new Bow Street police force."

"He is a most gentlemanlike man," Lily said politely, looking down at her cup once more so as not to make Mrs. Grantham too nervous. "It seems you have heard rather a lot about me."

"It seems *you* have used the freedom of your widowhood to some purpose," Mrs. Grantham said quietly.

Lily, about to reply, paused, forgetting for the moment what she had been about to say. "I had not thought of it quite like that," she said.

"I have used mine for parties. For entertaining my neighbors. For . . ."

"For adding some joy and merriment to the lives of nearly all around you," Lily pointed out. "That is no small thing."

Mrs. Grantham sighed. "It is kind of you to say so," she said. "Terribly though it has turned out in this instance. In any case, that is why I allowed you to come into the yard. I thought . . ." She shook her head. "I suppose it was unnecessary with the magistrate in the house. I was not thinking clearly. But I hoped you might be able to find out what had happened. If indeed you had some . . . experience with unraveling the mysteries of unnatural deaths."

"Not an unreasonable thought, especially under such trying circumstances," Lily said gently. "And I am flattered by your confidence. Or your desperation, whichever it was. But in that case, I must ask . . ." She took another slow sip of her tea. She could feel Mrs. Grantham's eyes on her, wondering what the question might be. She could hear her hostess shifting, growing more nervous as the silence stretched on. It was a tactic Lily had learned from that gentlemanlike Bow Street officer.

"I must ask," she repeated at last, setting down her teacup. "Why, if you know so much about me, did you think I would not notice what you are trying to conceal?"

The sudden stillness of Mrs. Grantham's body, the wariness on her face, gave her away in an instant. "I conceal nothing, Mrs. Adler," she said a moment later, but it was too late.

"You conceal a great deal, dear ma'am," Lily said, not raising her voice. "I've no wish to shout it for all to hear. But we both know you have kept something back which you should have told the magistrate that first morning."

Mrs. Grantham's expression had fallen further and further as Lily spoke, and now her shoulder drooped. She fidgeted with the tea things, her hands trembling, before glancing nervously around the room. "How have you seen through me so easily?"

"I suspect because dishonestly is not in your nature," Lily replied. "Which made your discomfort quite clear. You are wondering how much to reveal to him. I suggest you start by being honest with me. It will be good practice."

Mrs. Grantham hesitated, biting her lip. Lily stayed silent, not wanting to press so hard that her quarry bolted in fear. But she was certain, from Mrs. Grantham's behavior, that the other woman knew something of who had been out and about in the night, had perhaps even been abroad in the dark herself. She waited.

"Very well," Mrs. Grantham said at last, her voice trembling as much as her hands. "I had not wanted to . . . So many other things seemed so much more pressing, you understand. And I thought, why bother the magistrate with my troubles? But you are right."

Lily felt a moment of triumph. But it was short-lived, replaced by surprise she could barely conceal as Mrs. Grantham looked up at last and spoke.

"I have a garnet-and-gold parure that belonged to my mother and grandmother. Necklace, earrings, and brooch—not a large set, but valuable. Or I should say, I had. Because two mornings ago, when I woke and went to my dressing room, I discovered it was missing."

Lily stared. "Do you mean to say we have a jewel thief in the house as well as a murderer?" she whispered.

"Yes." Mrs. Grantham let out a shaky breath. "It seems we have."

★ ★ ★

"Are you certain?"

Sir John, when he had first heard Mrs. Grantham's news, had regarded her with something like panic in his eyes.

Mrs. Grantham nodded, looking miserable as she stared around her dressing room with him. Lily, having sent a message to John to meet them upstairs, stayed in the doorway, where she could remain unobtrusive. "I am afraid so. I checked with my maid immediately when I discovered they were gone; she has not moved them or taken them for cleaning." She gestured to the silk-lined jewel case, which lay open on her dressing table. There were dips and impressions in the silk underneath the tiny hooks that should have held each piece of matched jewelry that made up the parure. "They were there the night of the ball. But in the morning . . . gone."

John bent to examine the case. "Do you always check them morning and evening? Could they have been missing for longer than a night?"

Mrs. Grantham shook her head. "They are one of the few things I have left from my mother, so I always keep them on my dressing table. My maid has always told me that it was unwise." Her mouth quivered. "It seems she was correct."

"And was there a particular reason you opened the case that morning?" John pressed. "Was something else disturbed that made you wish to check on your jewels?"

"No, nothing was disturbed." Mrs. Grantham blushed a little, looking embarrassed. "It is a ritual of mine, you see, to open it and touch them. I spend a moment thinking on my mother and imagine how she would have handled the challenges of each day. And that morning . . ." She bit her lips. "Once I returned from finding poor Mr. Edison, I knew I would be facing a great many challenges. I opened the case . . ." She sniffed, clearly holding back tears. "And my mother's jewels were gone."

"So, sometime in the night . . ." John trailed off, examining the dressing table and empty jewel case. He turned back to his hostess. "As we are alone, I must ask: Did you leave your room at all that night? Did you see or hear anything unusual?"

Mrs. Grantham's cheeks grew pink, and she glanced in Lily's direction. "We are hardly alone, sir."

"I am happy to leave, if you wish," Lily suggested. "But I assure you, whatever you say, you may count on my discretion."

"Well, I suppose in any case, it does not matter." Mrs. Grantham looked at each of them in turn. "I did not leave my room until Mrs. Reynaud came to fetch me that morning."

Lily tried to hide her surprise. Mrs. Grantham had spoken firmly and met their eyes without hesitation. She acted like someone who was telling the simple truth. But then why had she blushed so quickly when asked for her whereabouts in the night?

John nodded, then beckoned Lily to join him. She came, a little reluctant to assist him so clearly in front of Mrs. Grantham but unwilling to forgo the chance to get a closer look.

"But I don't see how the theft was possible," Mrs. Grantham insisted, peering over their shoulders anxiously. "No one could have . . . That is, I am sure I should have woken if someone came into the room."

"Perhaps the sounds of the storm covered the sounds of the thief?" Lily suggested, a little absently. "It was fearsome that night."

Nothing looked out of place on the dressing table, which was neatly organized, the wood polished and the mirror shined to brightness. The jewel case didn't lock, and it held a place of prominence on the table. Easy enough, Lily thought, tracing a finger over the depressions in the silk, for someone to slip in, spot it immediately, and leave with the jewels in a matter of seconds.

"Your mother could not find her bracelet that morning, Sir John," Lily said thoughtfully. "Perhaps Mrs. Grantham was not the only one who was robbed of her . . ." Lily trailed off in the middle of her sentence, the memory she had been searching for at last floating to the top of her mind. "*Pearls*, John. I overheard Mrs. Taylor and another woman at the ball that night, discussing someone whose pearls had gone missing after a party. And apparently that was not the only time something like that has happened recently." She looked back and forth between the magistrate and Mrs. Grantham. "There *is* a thief in our midst, and there has been for some time."

Mrs. Grantham's cheeks had grown pale as she listened to them. "That cannot be," she insisted. "It is distressing enough to know that a . . . a *murder* has taken place. But a crime of passion is one thing. To accept that one of my guests—one of our neighbors!—could rob us again and again, in such a fashion? Someone we know? Someone we see in our everyday lives? It is impossible."

"Clearly not impossible," Lily pointed out, a little more sharply than she intended. She had no patience for denial. All denial would accomplish was to allow someone to get away with what they had done. "Since it has happened."

Mrs. Grantham looked a little ashamed, and she opened her mouth as though to protest again. But a moment later she pulled her lips into a tight line and nodded.

Lily turned to John. "I am sure Mrs. Grantham will be only too ready to provide whatever assistance you need."

He grimaced. "What do you think of the matter?"

Lily tapped the tips of her fingers together, thinking the matter through. "We did not find Mr. Edison's letters during our first search, because his brother had them concealed on his person. It was only once he was able to return to his room that he hid them."

"Ah." John nodded. "You think we did not find Mrs. Grantham's jewels then for the same reason."

"But our thief has had plenty of time to return to his or her room since then and hide them more thoroughly. Or perhaps not so thoroughly, if we are lucky and they believe all searches to be done. Which means we will need to search again."

"But Sir John, you've already told everyone they need not stay confined downstairs," Mrs. Grantham pointed out. "Most of them seemed settled downstairs, but they might wander up to their rooms at any moment."

"Then we will need to search quickly," Lily said. "Mrs. Grantham, perhaps you can keep as many of the guests as possible in the drawing rooms while we do? And perhaps, John, we ought to acquire a few extra hands."

★　★　★

"What are you thinking?" Lily asked as they made their way downstairs. Mrs. Grantham had already gone ahead of them.

"Murder and theft," John said, grimacing. "It seems a great coincidence to think they are connected. And an equal coincidence to think they are not."

"But they must be," Lily pointed out. "Because we know that someone is missing a pearl necklace. And Mr. Edison was holding the clasp of one in his hand when he died."

John nodded slowly. "Which the murderer attempted to remove with only some success. But was Mr. Edison involved in the theft? Was he a victim? Or did he simply stumble on the thief in action?"

"And why, in any of those cases, did he end up dead in the poultry yard, of all places?" Lily pointed out. "Something about it does not add up. Not yet."

"If only Mrs. Grantham had spoken sooner," John muttered. "Why did she not?"

Lily glanced back toward their hostess's room. "I suspect because she has something yet that she is hiding, though what it is, I could not say. Something happened that night which she did not want us knowing about."

"Do you think it is connected?"

"I could not say without knowing more."

"And you believe a search will be successful now, though it failed before?"

"Well, either our thief intended to commit their thefts during Mrs. Grantham's ball, then leave at the end of the night, or the idea came about because of the storm and our unexpected stay here."

"And in both cases, they would not have brought some means of hiding the jewelry and would have had to make do with what was available in their room," John finished for her, nodding.

"Unless, of course, the thief was someone who lived here," Lily added.

John frowned at her, clearly taken aback. "You suspect our hostess?"

"I suspect everyone," Lily said quietly. "And no one. Not until we learn more." As they reached the bottom of the stairs, she looked around. "All right, you find our helpers. I'm going to see whether Caroline Taylor is willing to gossip."

★   ★   ★

Mrs. Taylor, as it turned out, was quite willing to gossip, though she was surprised that Lily had sought her out for that purpose. But the name she shared jogged another memory in Lily's mind, of a beautiful cream-and-gold gown—the sort that would be set off perfectly by a pearl necklace, yet worn at the Christmas ball with no jewels at the neck.

As the guests fluttered and stomped about the room, pushing roughly past each other and exchanging sharp words, Lily caught Peter Coleridge's arm and pulled him toward a small alcove set near the door.

"What is it?" he asked, frowning, as she drew him aside.

"Peter, has your mother, by chance, mislaid a string of pearls recently?"

"What? No, indeed not, she does not have . . ." Peter hesitated. "That is to say, she has not mislaid . . ." He cleared his throat uncomfortably. "Why do you ask?"

Lily's brows had climbed higher the more he stammered. "Caroline Taylor mentioned to me that your mother had a pearl necklace go missing after a party some weeks ago. And it seems she is not the only one in the neighborhood to have had such an experience. Nor, indeed, the only one in this house."

"Oh. Oh." Peter looked away from her, his shoulders slumping. "Oh heavens. I feel like the worst sort of bounder. Mother insisted she could not find them after a party—she thought one of the servants must have taken them. And I told her it was nonsense, that she must have misplaced them and forgotten about it. It is the sort of thing that has happened before." He grimaced, and Lily felt a pang of sympathy. A woman as fierce as Mrs. Coleridge would be unlikely to accept the indignities of aging with grace. "I suppose I owe her an apology, then." Looking back at Lily, wary once more, he added, "So is there a thief among us? Good God. Does Sir John believe it is connected to . . . That is, does he suspect the captain has also—"

"I do not think anyone here could suspect Captain Hartley of sneaking about, stealing people's jewels," Lily said, not bothering to keep the heat from her voice.

Peter had the decency to look embarrassed. "No, indeed not," he said quickly. "So what does that mean for . . ."

"I could not say," Lily replied, turning away. "But I hope we shall all know soon. Thank you, Peter. I shall tell the magistrate you've been most helpful."

"But, Lily," Peter called. "Are we not supposed to stay with the others?"

"I shall join you in a moment," Lily called over her shoulder. "Do excuse me, please."

It was a blatant lie, and as Peter had already seen her helping Sir John, he likely could guess as much. But she did not care. She had a thief and a murderer to catch. And she was running out of time.

CHAPTER 21

"All right," Mrs. Adler said quietly, surveying her helpers. "Sir John is going to handle the servants' quarters, just to be certain. Mr. Spencer, you will search the rooms in the east hall. Amelia, you and I will take the west."

Amelia nodded. She had barely slept the past two nights, too worried first for herself and then for her brother. At the moment, though, her nerves were enough to keep her focused and alert. She was grateful to have been asked to help and eager to do what she could to assist her brother. But she had never done anything like what Mrs. Adler was suggesting.

"What sort of things are we to look for?" she asked, glancing up and down the halls. She kept her voice low, just as Mrs. Adler had.

"Think about the sorts of places you used to hide things when you were a child," Mrs. Adler suggested with a brief, tense smile. "In the slats under the bed, tucked into drawers, under mattresses . . . wherever you think someone could hide small, valuable objects. Our thief will have been unprepared to hide anything for an extended number of days, which is to our benefit." She too looked around. "And if you hear anyone coming, leave the room at once. Everyone is tense enough as it is. We do not need any more confrontations."

Matthew Spencer gave them a nod, and Amelia saw him clasp Mrs. Adler's hand briefly before he turned to go to his side of the hall.

"Mr. Spencer—" She hesitated, but he had heard her anyway and turned.

"Yes, Miss Hartley?" he asked gravely.

She bit her lip. "Thank you for your help," she said quietly. "I know you've no reason to believe in my brother, given everything that has happened. It means a great deal that you would help us in this matter."

"I . . . Of course, Miss Hartley," he said, giving her a small bow. He glanced past her toward Mrs. Adler, a wry smile on his lips. "I only know the captain a little. But if Mrs. Adler trusts and esteems him, that is enough for me."

It was the third day they had all been trapped together, and they had all grown accustomed to each other's comings and goings. There was no need for a list or map to let them know whose room was whose.

"We would go faster if we split up and searched different rooms," Amelia pointed out quietly.

"We would," Mrs. Adler agreed. "But—"

Amelia sighed. "But it is my brother whose guilt is in question," she said, knowing the reality of the situation. "And if I discover something on my own, there are those who will say I was involved in covering up that guilt."

"We will still go faster with two of us per room than one," Mrs. Adler said encouragingly. "We will see him free, Amelia. Never fear."

"How can you be sure?" she asked, her voice sounding very small to her ears.

Mrs. Adler lifted her chin. "Because I will not allow for anything else. Quickly now. We do not know how much time we have."

Several of the rooms at the end of the hall were empty. At first Amelia thought it useless to search them. But Mrs. Adler pointed out that an empty room could be an excellent hiding place, with no one coming and going from it. Amelia stood in the doorway of the first one, looking about as she tried to think through all the possible hiding spaces.

"You'll take the beds, carpets, and windowsills," Mrs. Adler suggested. "I shall look through furniture and fireplaces. Shall we?"

They got to work, silently and quickly, occasionally helping each other to move a heavy piece of furniture or shift the bed-clothes back into place once they had been searched.

Three empty rooms first, then the Taylors'. They made a good pair, Amelia was pleased to discover, and her spirits rose with each approving nod that Mrs. Adler gave her. She was still all too aware of what the stakes of their task were. But it was a relief to be *doing* something at last, not merely sitting around, scared and waiting.

Mrs. Crewe's room was next. Mrs. Adler paused in the door-way, surveying the room. It was as empty as the other rooms, Mrs. Crewe's evening clothes and borrowed nightdress laid neatly over a chair, an assortment of pins and a hairbrush tidy on a dressing table, a wardrobe in one corner.

Amelia caught herself yawning and shook her head. She needed to stay focused. *Raffi* needed her to stay focused.

Mrs. Adler crossed to the small pile of folded clothing and began to go through it, even taking the elegant little evening slip-pers and shaking them upside down. "You told me she has marvel-ous hats. Do you know anything else about her?"

"Almost nothing," Amelia admitted, "though she has lived in the neighborhood for over a year." She stayed where she was, still looking around. After searching so many rooms, something about this one struck her as out of place. But what was it? "She does not keep her own horses, I think, which has given her less of a chance to socialize with those of us who live farther out of town."

It was the carpeting that had caught her eye. It was bunched up near the head of the bed, the corner flipped up as though someone had disturbed it and forgotten to set it to rights. It could be nothing. But then again, it could be something. "She seems kind. Very helpful to Mrs. Coleridge, who has certainly been out of sorts these past few days. She is sometimes friendly with Mrs. Taylor."

"Well, that is not much of a point in her favor, but everyone can be forgiven a lapse or two in judgment," Mrs. Adler said dryly as she moved to the dressing table.

Amelia huffed in agreement as she knelt next to the bed where the corner of the rug had been disturbed.

The frame was low, and she was forced to lie down on her back and slide underneath to look up at the underside. It was too dark to see anything clearly, but she ran her hand along the surface, examining it mostly by touch. The shape of the frame created a lip, just barely a few inches wide, but enough to form a small platform. She coughed, blinking rapidly against the dust that her search disturbed.

"Are you all right?" she heard Mrs. Adler ask.

"Just the dust," Amelia replied, coughing again. "The edge of the rug—"

She broke off as her searching fingers encountered something. It felt like embroidered fabric, soft and gently ridged, but covering a hard object, which she could hear clicking gently as she wrapped her hand around it. "There's something here. A bag of some sort . . ."

Amelia slid back out with no small difficulty, glad that only Mrs. Adler was there to see her undignified exit and the large portion of her legs exposed by all her wiggling. Coughing once more, she stood, hoping she wasn't too much of a mess but more concerned with what she had found than with her appearance.

It was a lady's evening reticule, embroidered with gold thread and beaded in fanciful shapes. Amelia glanced over to where Mrs. Crewe's evening clothes were neatly laid out on the chair. Mrs. Adler had laid everything back how it was, with Mrs. Crewe's shoes set as a neat pair and her gloves once again resting across her skirt. But there was no sign of a bag.

Amelia pulled the drawstring to open the reticule and spilled its contents into her hand. The garnets in the necklace, earrings, and brooch caught the light, as though sparkling with pinprick dots of flame.

Amelia met Mrs. Adler's stony gaze and let out a slow, shaky breath. "Oh my," she whispered.

Mrs. Adler hesitated, then reached out to pluck the brooch from her hand. She turned it over between her fingers.

"Well," she said at last. "I think some lapses in judgment are not so easy to forgive." She looked up at Amelia. "We must find Sir John. I think it is time that he become better acquainted with Mrs. Crewe."

Amelia slumped against the bedframe. Sarah Crewe. She could hardly believe it.

"Come," Mrs. Adler said, tumbling the jewelry back into the reticule and tucking the whole thing under her shawl. "We must hurry."

Amelia followed as quickly as she could. But the nervous energy that had kept her focused had suddenly fled now that they had found their jewel thief. She felt her steps slowing, every one of her sleepless hours catching up with her.

"Can you go without me?" she asked. When Mrs. Adler turned back to her sharply, her concern evident, Amelia smiled weakly. "I've not been sleeping well, and I just . . . I think I need to lie down. Just for a moment. It's all so much," she said a little help-lessly, knowing it was an inadequate explanation.

But Mrs. Adler seemed to understand. She nodded. "Of course. Will you be all right?"

"Oh yes," Amelia said, pulling herself more upright and trying to sound brisk. She didn't think she had succeeded, though.

But Mrs. Adler did not press. "Mr. Spencer is searching the rooms near yours," she said. "Will you tell him what we discov-ered and send him down? Sir John may need his assistance."

"I shall," Amelia said. "And—" Mrs. Adler, who had been about to go down the stairs, turned back. "Thank you," Amelia added. "For believing me. For letting me help."

Mrs. Adler nodded. "Go lie down," she said, a small smile pulling at the corners of her mouth. "You look dreadful."

It was the sort of thing Raffi would have said. Amelia smiled back and went to do as she was told.

★   ★   ★

Lily waited for Matthew at the top of the stairs to tell him what they had found. He looked as grim as she felt. "But at least we found them," he said quietly. "That is something. That is evidence your brother-in-law can use."

They had finished just in time. The luncheon gong was sounding as they came down the stairs, guests spilling out of the drawing rooms, looking eager for a change of scenery. Lily and Matthew held back, looking for whether Sir John had come upstairs yet.

When the Hartleys walked past with Lady Adler, Lily caught Mrs. Hartley's attention.

"You might want to look in on Amelia," she murmured. "She went to lie down, and I think she is feeling a little overwhelmed by . . ."

"By everything?" Mrs. Hartley replied, sighing. "Of course she is. Thank you. I shall do so immediately."

Lily watched her head up the stairs, then nearly jumped out of her skin as someone caught her arm.

"Only me," John murmured, pulling her to the side of the hall. Matthew followed. The remainder of the guests going past gave them wide berth and several suspicious looks. "Any luck upstairs? There was nothing to be found in the servants' rooms except a few hidden letters and some lewd illustrations. Quite the relief, I must say, to find such banal vices after . . ." He trailed off as Lily opened the reticule and showed him what was inside.

"Good God," he whispered. He stared at the jewels for several silent breaths, then lifted his eyes. "Who . . . ?"

"Mrs. Crewe," Lily murmured, pulling the bag closed again and handing it to him. "Do you want to pull her aside to ask—"

Before she could finish, a scream echoed down the stairs.

Without stopping to think or to see if the others were following, Lily ran in the direction of the cry, racing up the staircase and
toward the east wing of the hall.

The screams were coming from inside Amelia's room. Lily
could hear shouts from downstairs and more footsteps pounding
up the steps. Matthew caught up to her, and without hesitating, he
shoved the door open with his shoulder.

Inside the room, Amelia was curled up on the floor, shaking
and crying, while her mother clung to her, the two of them in a
huddle by the connecting door between their rooms. It was Mrs.
Hartley who was screaming her daughter's name.

"Miss Hartley!" Matthew knelt beside her just as Amelia rolled
over onto her hands and knees. Eyes wide, she vomited before collapsing to the ground once more.

"What happened?" John demanded from the doorway as
Matthew lifted Amelia's head into her mother's lap, both of them
cradling her while she trembled and gasped for air.

"I don't know," Saba Hartley sobbed. "I heard her calling for
help. When I opened the door, she was just standing there, looking
so confused, hardly awake even. And then she just . . . she col-
lapsed, right in front of me . . . I think she was in pain . . . I don't
know."

"Pillow," Amelia muttered, her face pale and her eyes closed,
her forehead creased. She had curled into a protective ball, her
arms wrapped around her abdomen. "Pillow."

"Get a pillow to put under her head," John ordered. Lily could
hear voices outside the room raised in shock and speculation, but
she didn't pay them any mind as she ran to the bed to grab one of
the pillows. Then she froze with her hand outstretched, hovering
inches above the counterpane.

"Take her out of the room," Lily said. Her voice rose as she
added, "Right now."

"What? Why?" John asked. When Lily turned back toward
the group, they were all still clustered around Amelia, their entire

focus on her. Mrs. Grantham had joined them and was chafing Amelia's hands and wrists.

"Not until she is comfortable," Mrs. Grantham insisted. "Miss Hartley, dear, are you in pain? Can you speak?"

"What's wrong with her?" her mother begged. "Amelia, talk to me."

Matthew was the only one who turned to Lily. "What's wrong?" he asked sharply.

"Take her out of the room, immediately. In fact, we should all leave," Lily said, backing away from the bed. "There is something on her pillows. Some kind of powder."

"What?" Mrs. Hartley cried, pulling her daughter protectively toward herself, while John and Matthew both started to their feet.

Lily had forgotten the open door until their cries were echoed by half a dozen shocked and scared voices. In horror, she realized more than half the other guests were hovering in the hallway, their worried faces pressing in at the doorway as they tried to get a glimpse of what had happened. And all of them had heard her pronouncement.

"Someone tried to poison her!" Mrs. Taylor cried.

"I thought we were done with this business," Mr. Hounslow exclaimed gruffly. "Sir John, what has happened? Explain this!"

There was a sudden thump in the hallway; Kitty Hounslow had fainted dead away, and her mother shrieked her name. Lady Adler was trying to rush to her son's side while Matthew struggled to keep her out of the room.

Lily silently cursed herself in half a dozen different ways for her carelessness.

"Quiet, everyone!" John thundered. "Mrs. Grantham, may we take Miss Hartley to your room? Excellent. Mr. Hartley, if you would carry your daughter? Mrs. Hartley, you should of course accompany them. The rest of you—some space, if you please. If you wish for answers, you must remove yourselves at once while I look around. Mr. Spencer, Mr. Coleridge, will you both get them clear—thank you, yes, downstairs—Mother, really, this is not the time for hysterics . . .”

Half ordering, half cajoling, he managed to clear the room. But when Lily would have gone with the others to tend to Amelia, he caught her arm.

“Don’t you dare leave me to figure this out on my own,” he muttered.

Lily, surprised but gratified, nodded. As soon as the room was cleared and the door closed, he pulled out two handkerchiefs and handed one to her. “Cover your mouth and nose, please. I do not want you to breathe in whatever it is.”

He followed his own advice as well, but even with the handkerchiefs held over their faces, both of them hesitated.

“On the count of three?” Lily asked.

John nodded. “One, two . . .” He steeled himself. “Three.”

They both stepped toward the bed, one to each side, and Lily held her breath as they bent over the pillows. Caught in the folds of the bed linens, they could both see traces of whatever the white powder was.

“Have you seen anything like it before?” John asked.

“I have,” Lily replied slowly. “And likely you have as well.”

She didn’t say anything more for the moment, too focused on looking around the room, a worried frown on her face. Amelia said she had slept in her parents’ room so they could keep an eye on her. Her nap that morning might have been the first time she had lain down in her own bed in more than a day. If that was the case, there was no knowing when the powdered poison had been sprinkled on it.

But there was also a good chance that the servants, already saddled with a dozen guests for whom they had not expected to be responsible, might have been less than thorough about cleaning the room if they realized no one had slept there. Which meant that anything left behind by the poisoner could still be . . .

"There," Lily said, pointing toward the unused chamber pot that sat under the edge of the bed. In it, she could glimpse something white. Lily used her handkerchief to pull it out.

It turned out to be half of a torn packet of paper, utterly unremarkable, printed with the typical warnings that the powder inside was intended for vermin. It was empty, all of its contents having been used.

"Rat poison?" John took the paper carefully from her. "But how would that get on a guest's bed by accident?"

"I do not think it would," Lily said, meeting his eyes. "Unless someone was being very careless indeed."

She could see him swallow. "We should not linger here," he said, gesturing toward Mr. and Mrs. Hartley's room. "Not until those linens can be dealt with."

Lily couldn't argue with that; she followed him into the connecting room, breathing a sigh of relief when the door was shut behind them. The Hartleys were still with their daughter; for a moment more, at least, she and her brother-in-law could talk in private.

"Well, Lily, I suppose this is when you have the satisfaction of being told you were right," he said, his voice shaking as he paced around the room, his nervousness once again evident in the way he touched half the things he passed. "There is more to this than whatever revenge Jack may have wanted to exact against Mr. Edison. But why come after Miss Hartley?"

"I can think of only one reason that makes sense," Lily said slowly. "She must know something. Something that could reveal who our murderer is. And whoever it is wanted to make sure she would have no chance to share it with you."

"Jewel thefts, an attempted poisoning . . . It is too much," John muttered, raking his hands through his hair. "God, how I long to be home with Charlotte and the children. I swear, I will never complain about boredom again after this." Lily laid a comforting hand on his back, and he shuddered. They were silent for a moment. Then he straightened. "All right, I am done. Let us go find Mrs. Crewe and see what she has to say for herself."

CHAPTER 22

No one had returned to the dining room for luncheon. Instead, they were all in the drawing room once more, glancing nervously at each other, pacing around or sunk into corners and family groups. Mrs. Grantham looked up as Lily entered, falling silent in the middle of a comment to Mrs. Coleridge, her eyes wide and worried.

Lily glanced around the room, taking in all the guests and their occupations but looking for one in particular. Mrs. Crewe sat quietly in a seat near the fire. She had claimed a basket of embroidery things, and she was quietly working, her head bent over her stitches and her fingers moving with ease and skill that spoke of years of practice. Lily watched her needle moving in and out, something fluttering at the corner of her thoughts.

Whatever she might have put together, though, was interrupted as Mrs. Coleridge let out a loud harrumph. "Returned at last, young lady?" she asked imperiously, banging her walking stick on the carpet. "What has happened? Is our magistrate coming?"

"He is seeing to Miss Hartley," Lily said, hoping her face gave away nothing. "He has asked that we all remain here until he returns."

"Are you all right?"

The quiet murmur caught her off guard, and she started a little as she turned to find Matthew by her elbow. She let out a breath of relief at seeing him, wishing she could wrap her arms around him and press her face against his chest. Instead, she gave him a serious nod and took the arm he offered her.

"As well as can be," she replied as she allowed him to lead her toward the window. Outside, the wind had picked up, scattering eddies of snow across the ground. But the sun was shining, and she could hear the steady drip of melting ice falling from the eaves. It would be possible to leave tomorrow. The cold seeped in through the glass, and Lily shivered.

"We should not stand here long," Lily continued in an undertone. "Everyone is on edge and watching each other, and I've no wish to raise anyone's suspicions any further than they are already."

Matthew nodded. "What do you need me to do?"

"Be prepared, for now," Lily replied, her voice still a whisper. "Sir John will arrive soon to speak with . . ." She flicked a glance toward Mrs. Crewe, and Matthew nodded. "And there is no way to know what the reaction will be. From her, or from anyone else."

Matthew nodded. "I stand ready."

She laid a hand on his arm, giving him a tense nod before going to join Lady Adler.

Matthew stayed near the window, watchful, as John entered and all eyes in the room turned toward him. There was a sudden rise in sound as half a dozen people whispered something to their companions, and then the room fell eerily silent.

John, clearly feeling the weight of that silence, cleared his throat. But he did not get a chance to speak.

"What have you discovered, sir?" Mr. Hounslow demanded, standing. "I insist you share with us what you know."

"I am afraid I cannot do that," John said, looking more resolute than Lily could ever recall seeing him before.

"But what happened to Miss Hartley?" Kitty Hounslow demanded. "You must tell us that at least. Did someone try to poison her?"

"A terrible accident, I am sure," John said firmly. "A cleaning solution—something that was spilled. Miss Hartley already seems a little better." A murmur went through the room at his words, an equal mix, as far as she could tell, of surprise, distress, and relief. "Now, Mrs. Crewe, would you be so good as to accompany me to the library? I have a few questions for you."

She had gone pale, and Lily could see her hands trembling as she laid aside her embroidery. But she did not argue. "Of course, sir," she said politely, standing as she spoke. All eyes in the room were on her, and she swallowed as she glanced from side to side out of the corners of her eyes. "I am happy to tell you whatever I can, little help though I expect it will be."

Lily let out the breath she had been holding. She had worried that Mrs. Crewe would make a scene or refuse the magistrate's request. But it seemed that—

"Was it she?"

Peter Coleridge's question, unwontedly strident from a normally calm-spoken man, cut through the quiet of the room.

"Is she a killer? Is she the thief?"

There was deep silence in the room at his words. Then everyone began speaking at once.

"What does he mean, *thief*?"

"Are you sure she didn't poison Miss Hartley?"

"Did she kill Mr. Edison too?"

"I demand you allow us to leave—"

"Someone explain what is happening!"

Lily had risen at Peter's first shout, though what she might do, she had no idea. Matthew had drifted closer to Mrs. Crewe; whether to stop her from trying to escape or to protect her from the other guests still remained to be seen. Peter and the other gentlemen were standing, still shouting, while Mrs. Hounslow shrieked for someone to explain and her daughter sobbed into her hands.

Mrs. Crewe, terror in her eyes, was standing, pressed back against the wall, her embroidery still clutched in one hand—and the embroidery scissors in the other. They were small, but they were sharp, and Lily felt a swell of panic start to rise in her chest.

"Mr. Coleridge!" John's voice cut through the increasingly panicked babble. Most of the guests, to Lily's relief, fell silent, though they did not sit back down, and a worrisome number of them had moved a step or two closer to John and Mrs. Crewe. "I must insist that you all resume your seats—"

"Sarah could never have poisoned someone," Mrs. Taylor insisted. "Tell them!"

"Peter, what are you saying?" his mother demanded.

"You were right about your missing pearls, Mother," Peter bit off, taking another step forward. "There has been a thief among us for some time. One who struck again last night."

"Mr. Coleridge—"

"I've no idea what you are *talking* about," Mrs. Crewe insisted, her voice hoarse. Lily met Matthew's eyes, her own flicking back and forth toward the scissors clutched in the other woman's hand, hoping he would understand her silent warning.

Peter kept going, sounding increasingly angry and frantic. It was a side of him Lily hadn't seen before, and it was inflaming the others, nearly all of whom were now on their feet.

"The magistrate and Mrs. Adler were asking me not three hours ago about the theft of my mother's pearls. There is a thief in our midst. What chance do you think there is that thief and murderer are separate people?" Gasps of outrage and panic rose through the room as Peter barreled recklessly on. "And why would they want to speak to Mrs. Crewe, all of a sudden?"

"Peter," Lily insisted, trying to cut him off. "We must allow Sir John to explain—"

"By all means!" Peter shouted, his voice growing even louder, while the murmurs grew once more. There was sweat standing on his forehead, in spite of the chill. "Explain, sir. Is Mrs. Crewe— whom, I may remind you, none of us truly know—our thief? Is she responsible for Miss Hartley's accident, if an accident it was? And what does it all have to do with Mr. Edison's death?"

"You cannot leave us in the dark any longer," Mrs. Taylor said shrilly, clutching at her husband's arm. "We deserve to know what is happening. We are all *trapped* here, for the love of God. Tell us what you know!"

The others around the room echoed the demand, many of them pressing toward Mrs. Crewe once more.

"Very well, if you will all simply calm down," John insisted, his voice rising and cracking a little. He was trying to regain control of the room, but Lily could tell he did not know how, not when everyone was so anxious and angry and on edge. Not when Peter had already revealed so much that should have been left unspoken. "Mr. Coleridge is correct."

Lily hissed in a breath, wanting to shout a warning that disclosing what had happened wouldn't calm anyone down. But it was too late.

"I have discovered that at least two ladies here had their jewels taken in the night," Sir John continued. "Perhaps more of you have as well; I do not know."

There was dead silence, as though everyone was holding their breath. Lily wanted to look, to see how everyone was reacting to what the magistrate was sharing. But she couldn't bring herself to take her eyes from Mrs. Crewe.

"Some of the items that were missing were found in Mrs. Crewe's room."

"It's a lie!" Mrs. Crewe gasped, her gaze darting frantically around the room. "I would never . . . I *could* never—"

"Thief!" Mrs. Taylor shrieked. "All this time you spent getting to know us, just so you could—"

"Quiet, madam!" her husband snapped. "Can you not control yourself?"

"But what does that have to do with Mr. Edison?" Mrs. Hounslow demanded.

"I had nothing to do with Mr. Edison," Mrs. Crewe declared.

"And what about Miss Hartley?" Mr. Hounslow continued, ignoring her as he turned to Sir John.

"I do not know," John admitted stiffly, looking tense and miserable. "All I wish at the moment is to ask Mrs. Crewe a few questions. And the rest of you will need to *remain here* while I do. So, madam, if you would—"

"Not damned likely!" William Edison snapped as he stepped forward to join Peter. "If she is guilty of one crime, what are the odds she isn't guilty of the other? Who's to say she did not kill my brother? I say we solve this whole business here and now!"

"What do you mean, solve it?" Lady Adler demanded, rising from her seat.

"Mr. Edison, if you will just—" John began, but the senior Mr. Hounslow cut him off.

"He's right," Mr. Hounslow snapped, stepping forward as well. "It's time to stop asking questions, sir, and take action instead."

"Gentlemen, please," Mrs. Grantham begged, but they were already moving toward Mrs. Crewe, who still stood with her back pressed against the wall. Mrs. Grantham looked about the room for help. But Mrs. Hounslow was bare steps behind her husband, eyes glinting with fury, and the Taylors were exclaiming in agreement. Mrs. Crewe raised her hands defensively, the light glinting on the sharp scissor edges.

But before anyone could move further, Matthew stepped forward, putting his body between her and the men looming toward her. Lily clenched her fists so tightly that her nails dug into her palms, terrified that the cornered woman would lash out, not realizing that Matthew was attempting to protect her.

"Gentlemen, you will step back from the lady at once," he said, his voice cutting through the confusion like a bugle on a battlefield. "We do not take the law into our own hands. We are not brutes. *Step. Back.*"

Everyone in the room seemed to hold their breath. And then William dropped his hands, blinking as though he were emerging from a trance as he obeyed Matthew's order.

Mrs. Crewe let out a sob of relief, the scissors falling from her hand as she clutched at Matthew's arm.

"Dear God," Mr. Hounslow muttered, reaching out to grab William by the shoulder when it seemed as though the younger man would waver on his feet. "Hartley . . . Mrs. Crewe . . ." He looked around at his neighbors. "I apologize, to everyone. It's this damnable snow . . . being trapped here and not knowing . . . I feel as though I am going mad."

"I think we are all feeling that way," Peter said, taking a step backward himself. Lily could see him shaking. He glanced around the room, as though suddenly realizing what a frenzy he had whipped everyone into. "I must . . . excuse me." He pushed through the crowd toward the door before he remembered that they were not to leave. With a short, pained laugh, Peter headed for the windows, turning his back on the rest of the guests.

Sir John let out a shaking breath. "As I was saying. I will need you all to remain here until I say otherwise."

"John," Lady Adler said, drawing herself up with an air of dignity and command, learned from decades of being the woman of highest rank and greatest visibility in a neighborhood. "While I cannot approve of my neighbors' style of comporting themselves"— she cast a critical eye over the still-shaken group—"I am in sympathy with their desires."

"We are all concerned in this," Peter said without turning around, while the others murmured in agreement. "We all have a right to know."

John glanced at Lily. All she could do was lift her shoulders helplessly. They were well outnumbered. And she did not like to think what the other guests might do if they felt the magistrate was keeping secrets from them once more.

"Very well," John said at last. "But I must warn you—" Both his gaze and his voice grew sharp enough that the others exchanged uneasy looks. "If anyone causes a disturbance or hinders my work, I shan't hesitate to summon a footman and have that person locked in the stillroom. Do I make myself clear?" There was a murmur of agreement, and he nodded, satisfied. "Mrs. Crewe, will you please take a seat? No one will come any closer to you, you have my word."

She still looked uneasy, glancing around the room. She looked pale and anxious, and Lily could not blame her for that, but at last she sat. Matthew stepped aside, coming to stand near Lily. She met his eyes, unwilling to say anything in front of their neighbors but hoping he could feel how grateful she was for his presence. When she reached out briefly to touch his fingers, she could feel them shaking, and she kept her hand pressed against his as she turned back to Mrs. Crewe.

John clasped his hands behind his back and cleared his throat. "Mrs. Crewe, you have denied you had anything to do with the death of Mr. Edison. And I wish to believe you. But you also denied having anything to do with the thefts that occurred the night of his death, even though some of your neighbors' jewels were found in your room. I hope you see, then, why it is difficult for me to believe any of your assertions."

He paused, but she said nothing, her back still pressed against the wall as she stared at him. John's jaw tightened.

"I can choose to treat you with every courtesy and keep you in a good deal of comfort until we leave, madam," he said, his voice growing sterner. "Or I can offer you the stillroom as well. I suggest you answer my questions honestly."

Mrs. Crewe took a breath, looking for a moment as though she was about to speak, but at the last moment she hesitated.

"What trade did you used to practice, Mrs. Crewe?" Lily asked, stepping away from Matthew. She didn't speak loudly, but her voice carried through the silence. Mrs. Crewe's head snapped toward her, her eyes wide with surprise, and she was not the only one.

"Lily!" Lady Adler hissed in a dramatic whisper. "We agreed—"

But she broke off when her son held up a hand to forestall her. "Continue, Mrs. Adler."

Lily stepped toward Mrs. Crewe so she stood slightly apart from the other observers. "The maids in this house, as in any other, have hands that are red and rough from their work. Yours do not have that look, of course . . . except for the tips of your fingers.

Mrs. Taylor"—she nodded in that lady's direction, while Caroline Taylor started in surprise at being addressed—"mentioned to me recently that you have, on occasion, given her excellent advice on trimmings and other questions of fashion. And the first thing I heard about you when I saw you at Mrs. Grantham's ball was that you always wear the most magnificent hats."

There was silence in the room. Then Mrs. Crewe sighed. "I was a milliner," she said, sinking back into her seat. "In London."

A shocked murmur went through the room.

"And why are you in Hertfordshire?" John asked darkly.

She shrugged. "I hated the dirt and drudgery of London. Wouldn't you? And I'd been watching ladies long enough. I decided to move where no one knew me and try my hand at living as one."

The murmurs were swiftly becoming angry exclamations. "I let you pour tea in my house!" Mrs. Taylor hissed, looking appalled.

"And you didn't notice a damn thing, did you?" Mrs. Crewe asked, leaning forward. Her accent had altered as she spoke, her words running together and consonants dropping a little. Her fearfulness and shrinking posture had altered as well. The expression on her face was impatient, almost taunting as she stared at them each in turn. "Not so hard to pretend to be a lady, after all. Because—you might be shocked to know—there's nothing different between us except who your parents happened to be. And you lot didn't have any more control over *that* than I did."

"Damned impertinence!" William Edison exclaimed.

Lily raised her voice to be heard above the murmurs, which were growing steadily outraged. "True enough," she said firmly. "But you may notice that none of us became thieves."

"That's because your lot starts out with plenty of money, unlike the rest of us," Mrs. Crewe said scornfully. "And anyway—" she added, glancing at William—"your brother was happy to take his own turn at theft as soon as the chance presented itself."

"He did not." William looked indignant, but there was an uneasiness to his protest. Lily didn't blame him. A man who did not scruple at blackmail might be willing to do a great many other illegal things.

"He did," Mrs. Crewe said firmly. "Always spent more money than he had, didn't he? How do you think he was making up the difference? So don't you go acting all high and mighty, sir, because you're not fooling nobody except yourself."

"And you killed him for it!" William exclaimed.

"Why would I do a daft thing like that?" Mrs. Crewe demanded. "We had a good partnership, me and Gregory. Brought both of us a tidy little income, and far less risky for me than things had been before he found me out."

"Explain yourself," John ordered, glowering down at her. But Lily could see a hint of panic in his expression; he was out of his depth and trying hard to find his footing again. "What was the nature of your relationship with the elder Mr. Edison?"

"Strictly business," Mrs. Crewe said promptly. "I wasn't pretty enough for him to bother with otherwise."

"And is Crewe your real name? Or should we call you something else?"

She shrugged. "My name's Sarah Crewe, true enough. I'm maybe still married, I don't know. I wouldn't be surprised if Dickie Crewe already drank himself to death, but he wasn't worth giving a second thought once I escaped London. And it's easier to come and go as you please if you're a widow, as *some* in this room have reason to know."

"In that case, Mrs. Crewe," John said loudly, over another flutter of murmurs, "how did you and Mr. Gregory Edison come to this *business* relationship?"

She sighed. "I have to get creative when I'm taking a light-fingered turn at a party, and he once saw that I'd stuck Mr. Taylor's diamond cravat pin in my hair to hide it."

"What?" that gentleman's wife screeched before Lady Adler ordered her to be quiet.

"If Gregory'd had any sort of moral compass, the game would have been up then and there. But he decided to pay me a visit the next day and ask me what I planned to do with it. He was more curious, like, than anything else. And since he had me red-handed, and I couldn't risk him exposing me—especially not to yourself, Sir John—I told him."

"That you regularly steal from your neighbors?" Mr. Hounslow thundered.

John glared at him. "One more outburst, sir, and I shall have every one of you escorted out and locked in your rooms."

"And I don't steal *regularly*," Mrs. Crewe insisted. "Only when I need a little extra in the bank. And not always from folks here. There's house parties, aren't there? And visitors." She shrugged again, smiling a little. "I like most folks here, so I'd rather steal from people I'll never see again if I can."

"And what do you do with things once you steal them?"

"Send them to a friend in London who knows how to sell them. He sends me a cut, and everyone does well from it." She glanced at William again. "Including your brother. Once I confessed to him, he wanted in on the game."

"And so you wanted him gone?" William demanded.

"Mr. Edison—" John fairly growled, but William ignored him.

"You were in danger of him revealing your secret at any moment. You had to get rid of him. Didn't you?" he shouted.

But Mrs. Crewe only gave him a pitying look. "Why would I want to get rid of Gregory? His fingers were even lighter than mine. And he was always visiting friends or heading to town or having guests come to him. Even more opportunities to sneak a little something here and there, and with far less risk for me. He'd bring me what he took, and I'd send it to London. Everyone did well from it. Why would I want to get rid of him?"

John frowned. "So you mean to say—"

"It weren't me that did him in," Mrs. Crewe said, her jaw clenched but her voice firm. She turned a cold eye on the others in the room. "Whoever your murderer is, Sir John, it's someone else in this house. That handsome captain, I shouldn't wonder. Gentleman were always getting aggrieved with Gregory."

Lily clenched her hands but said nothing, determined not to draw any more attention to herself.

Mrs. Crewe's expression grew more serious. "And if not him, then . . . well, I suppose it was someone in this very room."

CHAPTER 23

It took some doing, after Mrs. Crewe's confession, but at last John managed to extract her from the continuing questions and accusations and escort her up to the house's former nursery. Mrs. Grantham's children were grown and gone, and the rooms were not much used. But they were out of the way, with sturdy locks, and would do well enough to keep Mrs. Crewe away from the outrage of her neighbors.

Before he left, John raised his voice to request that Lily come with him "to assist with a modest search of Mrs. Crewe's person."

Lily, who'd had no intention of being left with the others, was glad to go.

They were both taken aback, however, when Mrs. Grantham insisted on coming as well. As soon as they were in the nursery, she crossed her arms and glared at all three of them. "I want my mother's jewels back," she insisted. "Now. Which of you has them?"

John sighed and removed the pouch with the gems from his waistcoat. "We were able to recover your property, ma'am," he said, narrowing his eyes at Mrs. Crewe. "But we are still missing my mother's bracelet. And perhaps other things," he added, carefully not mentioning the necklace string that Mr. Edison had been holding, "Which were not to be found in your room."

Mrs. Crewe looked outraged. "Not with a man here," she said, sounding indignant. "Light-fingered and light-skirt are not the same thing, I'll thank you to keep in mind."

John didn't protest. "Shall I turn my back, or must I leave the room?"

"Turn around," Mrs. Crewe sighed. Once his back was turned, she tugged up her skirts, revealing two pretty, lace-edged garters at the top of her stockings. Lady Adler's gold bracelet was tucked into one. She plucked it out and passed it to Lily. Once she had her dress settled modestly again, Lily tapped John on the shoulder to let him know he could turn back around.

"And what made you choose the rooms that you did the night of the storm?" John asked, taking his mother's bracelet gratefully from Lily. "Was it the jewelry you saw those women wearing?"

"No, Mrs. Hounslow's gems were the flashiest," Mrs. Crewe said with a short laugh. "But older folks are less likely to wake up if someone sneaks into their room. Mr. Edison picked your mother for his target that night."

"Well, *I* am hardly elderly," Mrs. Grantham said, sounding irritated. "It is impossible that . . . You could not have come into my room without my noticing. It simply is not possible."

"No more I did," said Mrs. Crewe reluctantly.

"You robbed her in the morning, did you not?" Lily said shrewdly. "When all the commotion was happening. You'd no way of knowing it was because Mr. Edison's body had just been discovered. I imagine you simply thought it a good opportunity to duck into her room while no one was paying any heed. Which would explain why we did not find the jewels during our first search of your room," she added, glancing at her brother-in-law. It was no small satisfaction to be proved right. "You still had them on your person when you went down to breakfast."

"That's about the way of it," Mrs. Crewe muttered.

"So neither of you attempted to come into my room that night," Mrs. Grantham said, sounding relieved. She looked at the jewelry in her hands, then sighed. "I must find a safer place for these, I suppose. And see that all is well downstairs, or as well as it can be." She shot a glare at Mrs. Crewe. "You've upset everyone greatly, you know."

"I didn't say anything that wasn't true, or that anyone with half a brain didn't already know," Mrs. Crewe retorted. Her expression softened, and she added, sounding more like the quiet widow they had all come to know, "I'm sorry for you, ma'am, that this all had to happen in your home. You're a good sort, even if you were born one of this silver-spoon lot."

Mrs. Grantham pursed her lips. "I wasn't, actually," she said. "My father was a merchant who happened to do well for himself. And Mr. Grantham needed to marry money."

Mrs. Crewe laughed shortly. "Well, that explains it, then. I'll hope for your sake, ma'am, that Sir John here gets it all figured out quick and safe as can be."

Mrs. Grantham inclined her head. "And I'll hope for your sake that he takes a lenient attitude toward your thefts," she said, glancing at the magistrate. "You've been a good neighbor, Sarah Crewe, even if you are a thief."

When Mrs. Grantham had left, Mrs. Crewe fixed an eagle eye on John. "Will you?"

"Be lenient?" he asked. At her quick nod, he scowled. "That all depends on what you can convince me of. We have reason to believe that Mrs. Coleridge's pearl necklace, which you had already stolen, was in this house last night. And you have not returned it."

"I certainly don't have that," Mrs. Crewe said defensively.

"You mean to say you did not steal it?" Lily asked.

Mrs. Crewe looked as though she wanted to deny it. Then she sighed. "Gregory did, not long ago. It's been an expensive year. I needed extra funds."

"So why did you bring it here?"

"I tell you, I didn't," Mrs. Crewe insisted, looking nervously at John. She had initially seemed more comfortable when they left the rest of the guests and came upstairs. But Lily suspected the jewel thief was only just remembering, after Mrs. Grantham's parting words, how serious a crime she had confessed to in front of a magistrate. "Even if I'd had reason to—which I didn't—Mr. Edison kept the pearls himself."

"Was that typical?" Lily asked, exchanging a look with John. If Mr. Edison had taken the pearls with him to his meeting, what had been his reason? And who had them in their possession now? "I thought you said you were in charge of sending things to London."

"It wasn't typical," Mrs. Crewe admitted. "Usually, he did the thieving while I kept my eyes open for danger. And then I took whatever baubles he filched and got us paid for them. But the pearls . . ." She shrugged. "He asked for a few days with them; he wouldn't say why. I didn't argue, like, but I still needed money. So he said he'd pick up something that night. Then we met up at the staircase and went to his room to look over what he'd found. I took the bracelet, and that was that."

"And did he have the pearls with him?"

Mrs. Crewe was starting to look exasperated. "If he did, he didn't show them to me. And I can't think of any reason why he'd have brought them here, anyway. Too risky."

John pressed his lips together into a tight line. "I am sure you understand why I cannot take such a claim at face value," he said at last. "We know the pearls are not in your room, at least, but I shall have to insist on a search of your person."

"You'll do no such thing!" Mrs. Crewe exclaimed in horror, drawing back. Her eyes were wide with genuine fear. "I mightn't have been born one of your fine ladies, but I have morals, and I have modesty, same as any other woman. I'll not be handled by any man."

John looked affronted. "And I have my morals and modesty, thank you very much, Mrs. Crewe. You have lived here for over a year; I would hope you know at least my reputation well enough by now that you'd not jump to any such improper conclusions. I shall step out of the room, and Mrs. Adler will conduct the search."

Mrs. Crewe sighed. "Can I at least use the washroom first?"

Lily couldn't help laughing at that. "Do you think we have the wits of babies, ma'am?"

"Well," Mrs. Crewe grumbled, "you can't blame me for trying. But you won't find any pearls, I'll tell you that much now, and you might as well believe me."

"We shall see," John said, clearing his throat. "Mrs. Adler, I will be just outside the door, should you need my assistance."

"Thank you, brother, but I am sure Mrs. Crewe will be entirely cooperative. Will you not?" she added, turning to that lady.

"I might as well be," she said with a sigh. "I've got nothing against you, sir, or you, ma'am, in the general way of things. And I suppose you do have to see the job done properly."

"All right," Lily said briskly, once the door had closed behind her brother-in-law. "Turn around, and I will assist with your buttons and laces. And I warn you, I will be thorough."

"You seem like the type," the jewel thief agreed. "No nonsense. Do you have little ones?" she asked as Lily began undoing the tiny buttons running down her back.

"No," Lily replied, surprised at the question. "Nor likely to, with no husband," she added, before suddenly remembering Matthew's proposal. Would he wish for more children if they were to marry? Did *she* wish for children? She had become accustomed to the prospect of a life without them, content to enjoy both the children of her friends and the independence she had without any of her own. But before Freddy's illness and death, she had always looked forward to the prospect of becoming a mother.

"Well, if you had, I warrant they wouldn't be able to get anything past you," Mrs. Crewe said, jolting Lily out of her tumbling thoughts. She stepped out of her gown, which was made of a stiff brocade in a style nearly twenty years out of fashion, then handed it to Lily, who began going through the folds and seams of fabric. Mrs. Crewe dropped her petticoats to the floor, then stepped out of her shoes, sighing with relief as she freed her toes. "I'm grateful for the loan of them, but they're a mite too small. Though perhaps you already guessed that, sharp as you seem. I don't wonder the magistrate is having you assist him."

"He merely needed a woman to deal with delicate tasks such as these," Lily demurred, glancing at Mrs. Crewe out of the corner of her eye. "And a sister-in-law is as trustworthy as one's mother but easier to order about."

Mrs. Crewe pursed her lips. "I might believe that, ma'am, if I'd seen him doing any ordering." She bent to roll down her stockings. "But I think we both know who has a hand on whose reins here," she added, passing them over as well.

Lily ran them through her fingers. They were pretty, silk things, of excellent quality—likely the ones Mrs. Crewe had worn to the ball. "Let down your hair, if you please," she said, eyeing the other woman's elaborately dressed curls. "I need to make sure you've nothing hidden there either. You've done well for yourself through your thefts," she added, picking up the petticoat to shake it out and make sure nothing was concealed in its folds as Mrs. Crewe obeyed her request. "Was it hard to pass yourself off as a gentleman's widow when you first arrived here?"

Mrs. Crewe, now wearing only her stays and chemise, sat down near the fire, shivering a little and drawing a blanket over herself. "Chilly, it is, without all that fabric on. It made me nervous, but it wasn't hard. I'd been around ladies plenty in my line of work. Easy enough to learn how to talk and walk and sip your tea. Besides which," she added, smiling wryly, "I arrived with a good bit of money, and no one questions a woman with plenty to spend, even if she is a stranger. Saved it up, I did, from all the hats I made and trimmed—I was good at my work—and my useless husband none the wiser. Never fall for a pretty face, my mother always said." She sighed, staring into the distance as she shook her head. "I should have listened to her."

"Are you trying to get me to like you?" Lily asked shrewdly.

Mrs. Crewe glanced back at her. "Is it working?"

Lily laughed in spite of herself. "A little. But that shan't make me careless." She gestured. "On your feet again, if you please, and unlace your stays."

Mrs. Crewe looked for a moment as though she wanted to refuse. But at last she sighed and stood. Her stays were slightly old-fashioned, reaching down to her hips, and Lily—who had once had occasion to hide contraband in her own short stays and found it terribly difficult—suspected they might provide ample space for concealment.

And sure enough, as Mrs. Crewe unlaced her stays, a small felt envelope dropped to the floor. When Lily picked it up and unhooked the button that held it closed, a number of thin metal rods tumbled out.

Lily gathered the lock picks up in one hand, brows rising in an unspoken question as she turned to Mrs. Crewe.

Who sighed again. "I kept them on me, just in case. As you pointed out, I was able to snatch Mrs. Grantham's garnets with barely a moment's notice. It's good to be prepared."

"But surely, when you arrived at the ball, you and Mr. Edison could have had no plans for theft," Lily pointed out, frowning a little. "You could not have known both of you would be here for the night. Why bring them at all?"

"We always keep our eyes open at parties," Mrs. Crewe said reluctantly, while Lily folded the lock picks up once more and tucked them inside the tight wristband of her own sleeve. "Mr. Edison was good at slipping a gem off a lady while they were dancing, that sort of thing, if the opportunity came up. And as you know, a widow might step away during a ball and no one make a protest so long as she doesn't draw too much attention to herself. I came prepared, but nothing happened until everyone was asleep." She frowned. "When we parted that night, Gregory did say he had one more thing to do. I assumed he wanted to try his hand at another room. I told him not to push his luck, but he just laughed, and I let him go his own way. He was the sort that always would."

"And you returned to your room?" Lily asked. Mrs. Crewe nodded. "What time was that?"

"Must have been near two in the morning?" Mrs. Crewe pursed her lips. "I think that's what I heard the clock downstairs striking."

"And you expect me to believe you simply left him, then?" Lily asked, not bothering to keep the skeptical note from her voice. "That you returned to your room, went to sleep, and woke up the next morning as baffled by his death as anyone else? You've no proof, so far as you have shared. In fact, you haven't even any proof that Mr. Edison was indeed involved in these thefts. Who is to say you've not made up your story out of whole cloth?"

"Well, as to that," Mrs. Crewe exclaimed, "ask that housekeeper who she saw sneaking about that night. She was out and about herself, in the middle of the night, mind you, and no good to come of something like *that*. Talk to her if you want to see someone acting suspicious, not me."

Lily paused, considering. Mrs. Reynaud had been uncomfortable and reticent when they spoke—insistent that the servants could not have gone abovestairs in the night but clearly able to have done so herself. Lily had thought briefly that the housekeeper might have been concealing something. But as for what it could have been . . .

"She could have been attending to a guest who rang for assistance," Lily pointed out.

"And why would she have gone herself instead of sending a maid?" Mrs. Crewe demanded, grabbing the blanket from the window seat to wrap around her shoulders once more. She clutched it tightly in both hands and scowled at Lily. "No, I think she was there for some little rendezvous, and I can tell you why. She wasn't wearing her spectacles, see? She'd have had them on if she was there to work, so clearly she wanted to look nice for someone. One of the younger gentlemen might have been interested, like. I'll admit she's pretty enough."

"And you claim she saw you and Mr. Edison together?"

"Caught us on the stairs. And she overheard us talking, which is why we decided to hightail it back to his room to look things over."

"I hope you know Sir John will be speaking to her to confirm your story."

"I hope he does," Mrs. Crewe replied, equally emphatic. "She'll tell him Gregory was a thief right enough, and there wasn't anything but business between us, and good business at that. I may be a thief, but I'm no killer."

She spoke firmly, with no shiftiness or fidgeting. There was nothing in her manner or voice to make Lily think she was being untruthful—but a woman who had spent so long pretending to be someone she was not had to be an excellent liar. There was no possibility of taking her words at face value without speaking to Mrs. Reynaud.

"Very well," Lily said. "Do you need assistance dressing once more?"

Mrs. Crewe shook her head. "Just you get out there and tell Sir John to speak to the housekeeper. And tell him to lock the door," she added.

Lily raised a brow. "I am sure he was going to anyway. But why do you want him to?"

Mrs. Crewe shivered. "He'll have the only key, won't he? And I don't trust the rest of this jumpy lot not to come after me."

Lily nodded. It was impossible not to feel some sympathy for the woman, under the circumstances. "We'll keep them from you. And I shall have the footman bring your luncheon."

Mrs. Crewe's expression softened. "Thank you, Mrs. Adler. You're a good sort. I'm glad I never stole anything from you."

"High praise," Lily said dryly. "I hope you still think as well of me when all is said and done."

★   ★   ★

John, as promised, locked the door as soon as Lily emerged, declining to reinterview Mrs. Crewe and hear for himself what Lily had learned.

"I trust both your memory and your judgment," he said as he pocketed the key. "Did you find anything when you searched her?"

Lily handed over the lock picks. "But no pearls. She seemed to be telling the truth about that much."

He examined them, a thoughtful frown on his face, before nodding and tucking them inside his jacket. "A rather professional-looking set. Makes me wonder what that husband of hers did for a trade."

"I makes *me* wonder what the devil Gregory Edison was doing in that yard," Lily said, smacking her hand against the wall in frustration. "He had to have been meeting someone. But who better than his . . . his *business* partner?"

"Do you believe her?" John asked as they headed for the staircase.

Lily was about to reply when she glanced over the banister and realized they were not alone. Kitty Hounslow stood at the bottom of the stairs, pacing back and forth, before seeming to suddenly make up her mind and begin climbing. But as soon as she spotted them at the top of the staircase, she froze in place. She looked for a moment as though she was going to speak. Then she abruptly turned and began heading back down.

"Miss Hounslow!" John called, striding briskly down the steps toward her while Lily followed at a more cautious pace. "Were you looking for me?"

The girl had stopped at the bottom step and turned back toward him. Her eyes were wide in her peaked face, giving her an almost ghostly appearance, only emphasized by the too-big cut of her borrowed gown. "No, of course I—That is, I *was*, but I don't think . . ." Kitty's hands plucked nervously at her shawl as John came even with her. Lily, not wanting to crowd her, stayed a few steps above.

"Do you have something you wish to tell me?" John asked gently.

Kitty looked up at him with panicked eyes. "No! No, nothing. I just got lost for a moment. I could not remember which . . ." She glanced up and down the halls a little frantically, as though hoping someone would appear and put an end to the conversation. "Excuse me."

Without waiting for a reply, she hurried back down the stairs. For a moment, Lily and John stared after her, both of them too surprised to say anything or to call her back. Lily looked at her brother-in-law. Below they could hear the guests in the drawing rooms—rather like sheep being contained, Lily thought. Or dangerous animals who needed to be caged.

"What do you think that was about?" John asked at last.

"Well, she was not lost, that much is certain. Unless she meant she had lost her nerve," Lily said quietly. "She wanted to speak with you. But as to what she meant to say, or why she became too afraid to say it . . ."

"Do you think she knows something?" John asked. "She sought me out when she thought no one else would be around."

"And you think my presence scared her off?" Lily nodded slowly. "Perhaps. She might have seen something but not known whether to mention it." Lily hesitated. "Or there might be something about her family that she wants you to know."

John puffed out his cheeks and let out the breath slowly. "Do you think it best if you speak with her? Or I?"

"You," Lily suggested. "That way, you can take a turn with the rest of the family as well and see if there might be anything they have not yet revealed. I doubt Mr. Hounslow, either the elder or the younger, will have much to the purpose to say to me."

"And what will you do?" Sir John asked.

"I believe I shall pay a visit belowstairs," Lily said thoughtfully. "Surely someone will be there who can direct me to the house-keeper's room."

"Be careful," John warned as she was about to walk off. When she looked back, his round, cheerful face was creased with worry. "I would never forgive myself if anything happened to you." He grimaced. "Nor would my mother."

CHAPTER 24

"Haven't you and the magistrate kept me from my work enough?" Mrs. Reynaud asked, not looking up from the linen she was counting as she made tiny check marks in the ledger book lying open on her table.

The housekeeper's room, which attached to her bedroom, was almost painfully tidy, scrubbed clean and without a single item out of place. But two cheerful, colorful prints hung in frames on the wall, and a pretty piece of sprigged muslin had been hung up as a curtain.

Mrs. Reynaud, her spectacles perched on her nose, continued working, a gesture that was almost rude. *This is my domain*, she was clearly saying, *surrounded by my people and my things. You are the intruder here.*

Lily couldn't argue with such a sentiment. But she wouldn't be dissuaded either.

"We have discovered some new information," she said, taking a seat without being invited.

Mrs. Reynaud's shoulders stiffened, and she looked up at last, setting her pen down in the inkwell tray. "Do you mean the captain locked up in the attics? Or that jewel thief who stole Mrs. Grantham's gems? I would think you wouldn't need to speak with me after catching your murderer."

"It is related to Mrs. Crewe's thefts," Lily said calmly. "Certainly it is an easy conclusion to draw, that a person who committed one crime committed the other as well. But I've no wish to assign blame wrongly just because it is easy. I'm certain you would agree—especially for something as serious as murder."

A muscle jumped in Mrs. Reynaud's jaw. "What's it got to do with me, then?"

"I was speaking with Mrs. Crewe, who insists that she had nothing but a cordial business relationship with Mr. Edison. That he, in fact, was a thief alongside her. And when it was pointed out to her that she had no proof of such an outrageous claim, can you guess who she said could corroborate her story?"

The housekeeper said nothing, but that muscle leaped once again as her jaw clenched.

"No guesses?" Lily asked. "That surprises me, from such a perceptive woman."

"Say what you mean and be done, if you please," Mrs. Reynaud snapped. "I've neither time nor patience for such games. Some of us have work to do."

"You are right, it is not a game," Lily said softly. "A man was killed. At any moment, someone else could be harmed as well. I am trying to stop that from happening. So please, if you know anything that could shed light on what Mr. Edison was up to that night—or who he might have been meeting with—I ask you to tell me. Did you indeed see Mr. Edison and Mrs. Crewe in the hall?"

Mrs. Reynaud picked up her pen, tapping it against the table and not meeting Lily's eyes. Then she nodded tersely. "I did."

"So you were also up and about that night." Another terse nod. "And I suppose that, given your reticence to discuss the matter, you were not there to respond to a guest who had rung for assistance."

Mrs. Reynaud gritted her teeth. "I was not," she said, her words clipped and her unhappiness plain. "I promised them my silence in exchange for their own. Mrs. Crewe, it seems, has not kept her word."

"Murder changes the bargain somewhat, I believe," Lily replied. "What can you tell me? Did it seem that Mr. Edison was involved in the thefts?"

Mrs. Reynaud let out a sigh. "Aye, he was. I went up the main stairs, which maybe was unwise. I didn't have my spectacles on, and they were in the dark at the top of the stairs, so I didn't see them until I was nearly to the top. They made some . . . insinuations, but I'd overheard a bit of what they were saying, so I was able to make a few insinuations of my own. We all agreed to go our separate ways and keep our mouths shut. I waited until they were inside Mr. Edison's room before continuing," she added. "I didn't want them to see where I was going."

"And where was that?" Lily asked, but she was unsurprised when she received only an irritated look in reply. "So you said nothing when the theft of your employer's jewels came to light?" she continued. She understood why—even an upper servant would not want to be seen having a liaison with a guest. But she wanted to know what the housekeeper would say.

Mrs. Reynaud looked, to her credit, unhappy at the reminder. "I couldn't risk the exposure," she said quietly.

"And what were they saying when you overheard them?"

"I didn't hear much," the housekeeper admitted. "I was trying to keep my distance so they wouldn't see me. Something about selling what they had pinched. But they were thick as thieves, the pair of them—" She broke off, laughing shortly. "Now there's an apt turn of phrase. I mean to say that whatever was happening, it was clear they were in it together."

"And did there seem to be any anger or conflict between them?"

Mrs. Reynaud shrugged a little. "I only saw them briefly. Mr. Edison seemed agitated—far more agitated than Mrs. Crewe—but I don't wonder at that, him creeping around the house as he was. But I am, as you've guessed, good at reading and observing people. I wouldn't think there was any animosity between them, from what I saw. And certainly nothing romantic or affectionate. All business, they seemed."

Lily nodded slowly, thinking that through. "Was there anything else you noticed about them? Anything that stood out?"

"No," the housekeeper said slowly, but she hesitated as she said it. "No, nothing else I noticed about them."

Lily's brows rose. "And what did you notice about someone else?"

The housekeeper wrinkled her nose unhappily. "I saw . . . Well, perhaps nothing. I don't know what, or who, you see, and I don't want to—"

"Mrs. Reynaud," Lily broke in. "Tell me what you saw."

The housekeeper chewed on her lower lip, hesitating again, as though trying to decide exactly what to say. "I saw someone else in the hall. When I was leaving."

Lily, already perched on the edge of her chair, sat up even straighter. "You mean later, when you were leaving your rendezvous?"

Mrs. Reynaud nodded. "I was just looking out the door, making sure the coast was clear, as it were. But it wasn't. Clear, I mean," she said, stumbling over her words a little. She took a deep breath. "I saw someone coming out of a nearby room. They went down the stairs. I waited a little while, to make sure I wouldn't run into them. And then I went back down by the servants' stair, just in case."

"Who was it?" Lily asked eagerly.

The housekeeper looked a little embarrassed. "I couldn't see their face."

Lily frowned. "Well, was it a man or a woman? Which room did they come out of?"

"I truly don't know." Mrs. Reynaud sounded apologetic. "It was a vanity to go up without my spectacles. I really can't see any far distance without them. It was just . . ." She shrugged. "A figure. Going down the stairs."

Lily blew out an impatient breath. "Very well, then. Which side of the hall were you on? That could narrow things down, at least."

"I can't tell you that either," the housekeeper said softly.

Lily gave her a hard look. "You *won't* tell me, you mean," she said, her voice growing a little cold. "Because you do not wish me to guess what room you were coming out of."

The housekeeper said nothing, a small, humorless smile on her lips.

"That is a choice you may make. But here is the thing you must consider, Mrs. Reynaud: by your own admission, you were also up and wandering that night. You claim you were visiting a lover. Very well. But unless you are willing to admit who that lover was, I've no means of confirming your story. For all I know, you were meeting with Mr. Edison. For all I know, he caught you, rather than the other way around, and you killed him to keep him silent about your affair."

Mrs. Reynaud drew in a sharp breath. When she let it out, it shook. "I suppose you could assume so," she said, beginning to sound a little less cool and composed.

"A great many people could assume so," Lily said relentlessly. "An assumption which could even see you forced to make an appearance in court. Unless you tell me who you were visiting that night."

The housekeeper picked up her pen once more, refusing to look at Lily as she adjusted her spectacles. Her hands were clearly shaking. "I've work to do, Mrs. Adler."

There was clearly no point in pressing any further. Not yet. Lily stood. "I hope you will change your mind," she said.

Mrs. Reynaud glanced up, a mere flick of her eyelashes, but Lily caught the glance. There was fear in it, but also determination. "Not likely, ma'am," the housekeeper said softly, turning back to her work. "Not likely at all."

★　★　★

Lily closed the door to the housekeeper's room behind her. But she made it only halfway down the hall toward the kitchen before she slumped back against the wall, closing her eyes. She was exhausted from worry and from being awake half the night. And she felt no closer to the truth than she had been when she was staring down at Mr. Edison's body in the snow.

Very well, he had been a thief. He had been amoral and reckless in his dealings with Amelia, and even his brother had not denied that theft was the sort of thing he would do. But why had he been in the yard at all? It was easy enough to get to, but why go outside in the storm?

And why have the pearls with him, as it seemed he had?

The sound of footsteps made Lily straighten abruptly and open her eyes just as the housemaid she had met the day before—Jane, she recalled—came around the corner. Jane, who was lugging a heavy basket of cleaning tools, stopped in surprise.

"Do you need assistance?" she asked, looking uncertain.

"No, I—" Lily broke off, giving the maid a considering look. "Jane, I am going to ask you to do something I know you're told not to do. But I hope you will help me anyway."

The girl stared at her, plainly nervous. "And what's that, ma'am?"

"Gossip."

Jane let out a relieved breath. "Oh, well, that's no hardship, Mrs. Adler, we hear everything belowstairs," she said with cheerful willingness that made Lily half smile. "What is it you're wishing to know?"

"Was there anyone belowstairs who ever talked of Mr. Edison? Who knew much about him or seemed particularly interested in him?"

"Mr. Edison? The elder, you mean?" When Lily replied in the affirmative, Jane shook her head. "I don't honestly know if he'd ever been here before. He's never come to any of Mrs. Grantham's dinners, I know that for sure. But she casts a wider net for a ball, like. Needs to have plenty of young men for dancing."

"Of course," Lily said, nodding slowly. That fit with what Mrs. Reynaud had said. "My next question is . . . well, less polite. But equally important." She dropped her voice. "Do you know of anyone in service here with any sort of . . . criminal background? Or anyone who might have a skill at picking locks?"

The shrewd look that Jane gave her was unexpected. "You're thinking of that door what Mrs. Reynaud locks, ain't ye?" she asked. Lily considered lying but nodded. "Well, I can't say as I blame you for wanting to know. But I never heard of anyone here who's at all handy with locks. And I think it would have come up, like, because Mrs. Bee, the cook, locked herself in the stillroom by accident just last month, and it were a dreadful furor to get her out. Took us half the day to find the spare keys that Mr. Lambton was supposed to have."

"I see." Lily nodded again.

"And even if anyone could pick locks, they'd be a fool to cross Mrs. Reynaud like that," Jane said, shuddering a little at the thought.

Lily could well believe that; the housekeeper clearly ruled the staff with a will of iron. "Thank you. I hope, if you hear or see anything out of the ordinary, you will tell me. I want to help the magistrate find out what happened as quickly as possible so that everyone—including you—can return to their normal lives."

"Of course," Jane said, nodding. But there was something careful in her expression, as though she wanted to speak but couldn't decide whether to say what she was thinking or not.

Lily raised her brows. "What is it?"

The maid bit her lip. "It's only . . . I found something, ma'am. But I'm not rightly sure what it is. So I don't know if it's important or if it's just trash."

Lily gave her a puzzled look. "Trash?"

"Perhaps? Or . . ." Jane bent down to fish in her cleaning basket and emerged with a much-folded piece of paper. "I found it in the paper basket in the kitchen, with the scraps and kindling that we use for the fires."

It had been crushed and smoothed back out, and Lily could see the faint mark of a dirty shoeprint on one side. But the hot-pressed paper was thick and elegant, in spite of that—the sort that someone like Mrs. Grantham would keep for her own use, not that of her servants.

Lily turned it over to see what was written. It was only a few lines, but it made her stomach flutter with nervous excitement, as one piece in a vast puzzle fell neatly into place.

"Did you read it?" she asked, looking up. "What did you make of it?"

Jane blushed and looked down. "I can't read so well," she mumbled.

When she glanced up, hesitating, Lily nodded encouragingly. "That's all right, Jane. There is no shame in that. And you saw it was out of the ordinary, even without reading it."

The maid nodded, looking a little relieved. "I could tell it was someone's letter, and I've never seen a letter that nice end up in the scrap basket. I was afraid to use it, in case it was important, so I pulled it out." She scuffed the toe of one shoe back and forth. "I was going to show it to Mrs. Reynaud and see whether she thought it had ended up there by accident."

Lily folded the letter carefully, trying not to betray just how important it might be. She didn't think it had ended up there by accident at all. Someone had intended that it be burned. "Well, I thank you for showing it to me. I shall be sure to tell Mrs. Grantham that you have good instincts and a keen eye for detail. You must be very good at your work."

That made Jane smile, though she still looked nervous. "Thank you, ma'am. I do try. Will you . . . That is, I don't want to get in trouble, if someone thinks I'm reading their private letters."

"Not to worry." Lily smiled grimly. "I'm afraid the person who wrote this one is no longer here to object."

CHAPTER 25

"If he did not write it, it was done by an excellent forger," Amelia said, handing the letter back to Lily. Though still cocooned in blankets, she was sitting up in bed and eager to be of use. "I received a few memorable notes from him, as you know, so I remember his writing well."

"I was hoping as much," Lily said, looking over the girl critically. They both spoke quietly; though the door was closed, there was a footman stationed just outside for Amelia's safety, and they did not want to be overheard. "You are looking better than I expected."

Amelia gave her a wan smile. "Apparently, it was only a mild case of arsenic poisoning. Mrs. Grantham says she hopes I will feel better in a day or two, though I should still avoid exerting myself."

Sir John, who had been checking on Amelia when Lily arrived to verify the letter's signature, was pacing around the room, a thunderous frown on his face.

"Does no one sleep in this house?" he demanded, interrupting them as he strode toward the fireplace. His voice snapped with frustration, and the ornaments on the mantelpiece of the little bedroom—opened for Amelia's use while her former chamber was being cleaned and aired—shivered with each pounding step. "Was everyone roaming the halls for some nefarious purpose?"

Lily wanted to be pacing like her brother-in-law, but she could tell he needed a calming presence in the room. So she folded her hands in her lap, hoping he didn't see the tense way her fingers twisted together. Her conversation with the housekeeper had not gone at all as she'd hoped. They were so close to finding out who Mr. Edison might have been meeting with. But unless someone could convince Mrs. Reynaud to speak, they were still stuck. And the longer they stayed that way, the more likely it was that Mr. Edison's killer would escape.

Or kill again, she thought, shivering. Walls and conversations in a house like this could be porous, flimsy things. If the murderer learned there were people out there who could point a finger in their direction, there was no telling what they might do.

John turned to Amelia once more. "Are you certain you cannot remember anything?" he asked, for at least the fifth time, though he also kept his voice down. "Whoever put that poison in your room had a reason. Was there something you saw—something you heard—something you *didn't* hear? Think, Amelia."

"I *have* thought," she insisted, dropping back onto the pillows. "I have thought and thought, and there is nothing. Whatever our killer thinks I know, they were mistaken."

"Then we are no closer to discovering them." John dropped into a chair by the fireplace, limbs sprawling and face turned up toward the ceiling. He looked exhausted, Lily noticed, his eyes bloodshot, with dark circles beneath them. "Do you think Charlotte and the children are well?" he muttered.

"I know they are," Lily said firmly. "They've plenty of food and firewood and everything else they need. And to children, a storm like this is nothing but adventure. No doubt they and Mr. Spencer's young ones have been having a grand time."

John chuckled; it sounded a little forced, but his smile was genuine. "One has to admire children's ability to find excitement in the strangest of circumstances. I cannot decide whether they've far less sense than their parents, or far more." He sat up abruptly. "Very well, I've done with histrionics. Hand me that letter again."

Lily passed him the scrap of hot-pressed paper Jane had found. It was a simple enough note.

I hope you will be so good as to meet me in the passage to the poultry yard at three o'clock this morning. And if you think to refuse, perhaps you will be persuaded when I tell you that I wish to discuss a rather well-kept secret that you do not want your neighbors to discover.

It was signed with a flourish: *Edison.*

"The housekeeper says Mr. Edison seemed agitated?" John asked as he reread the note.

"And according to Mrs. Crewe, he was planning something else after their meeting. She thought he wanted to try his hand at more pilfering."

"So, Mr. Edison was agitated because he was planning a clandestine meeting. None of us knew before the storm that we would stay the night, so he would have delivered this note in some fashion when we were all heading upstairs, or shortly after. Presumably—" John glanced up. "Well, not presumably. But perhaps to whomever Mrs. Reynaud saw going downstairs."

"The timing seems to match," Lily agreed. "And then that person, after receiving this note, retrieved a gun from the gun case, met with him, drove him out into the yard where a gunshot would not be overheard, and . . ." She grimaced. There was no need to finish that sentence. "And then left the note in the scrap basket to be burned. But we've no idea who that was, as Mrs. Reynaud will give no indication which wing she was in. And short of threatening her employment, I do not think we can constrain her to reveal it."

"Well, why not talk to Mrs. Grantham?" Amelia suggested. "Surely she can make her housekeeper tell us the truth."

"Unless Mrs. Reynaud thinks, not unreasonably, that either way she will lose her position," Lily pointed out. "And so chooses to keep silent. Or . . ." She hesitated. "Or unless Mrs. Grantham herself has something to hide."

John blew out a frustrated breath. "So what could this meeting have been about? Whose secret? It seems like half the damned people in this house are concealing something."

"And where have those pearls got to?" Lily added. "Were they important? And if so, why? Mrs. Coleridge and her son insisted there was nothing special about them, nothing out of the ordinary by way of value."

"They are with Gregory's murderer, are they not?" Amelia said, her voice shaking a little as she leaned forward. "Whoever has the pearls has to be the person who killed him."

Lily and John exchanged an uncomfortable look. "But where are they?" John asked.

No one had an answer. In the silence, the dinner gong echoed through the house.

Lily glanced at Amelia. "Will you be all right while we are at dinner?"

"Of course," the girl said stoutly. "Go find us some new information from our horrid neighbors. There has to be something we've missed. There simply has to be."

★ ★ ★

Amelia stared at the ceiling as she waited for her own dinner to be delivered, then lifted her hands, holding them before her face. They were still shaking, no matter how she tried to hold them still, and her stomach still cramped with unpredictable shocks of pain.

She had not told anyone how poorly she was feeling, though. After all that had happened, she did not want them to think her weak. And if someone had indeed tried to poison her, to silence her . . .

Amelia shivered. She did not want word to get back to them that she was yet an easy target.

A knock at the door made her sit up with a start, then swallow hard against a wave of nausea. There was a footman still outside, as far as she knew, but she still hesitated before she called out, "Come in."

Mrs. Grantham poked her head around the door, smiling gently. "Only me," she said as she entered with a dinner tray. Steam wafted from the bowl of what smelled like clear broth, and Amelia could see a small pot of tea and a little bread. It was an invalid's tray, but neither she nor her stomach objected to the prospect. "How are you feeling, my dear?"

Amelia attended to the small talk, the plumping of pillows, and the settling of the tray with half a mind. Inside, she was working up the courage to do what she had suggested to Mrs. Adler and Sir John.

"Mrs. Grantham," she began at last, a little hesitantly, when her hostess was clearly about to excuse herself. Mrs. Grantham paused expectantly, and Amelia took a deep breath. "I have something particular to ask you, for which the magistrate needs your assistance."

"I am at Sir John's disposal, of course," Mrs. Grantham said, a wary note in her voice. "Though I would expect him to ask me himself."

"No doubt he would," Amelia said, plucking at the bedclothes. "But I thought . . . that is, it occurred to me . . ."

Still hesitating, she described Mrs. Adler's conversation with the housekeeper. She could not recall most of the details of what had been said, but she remembered enough to make clear how the woman had refused to help them. Mrs. Grantham's face grew shuttered as she spoke, and Amelia thought she looked displeased. There was no wonder in that—to discover such behavior in a trusted upper servant had to be a blow, especially to a woman who lived on her own and had her own reputation to preserve.

"And so," Amelia concluded hopefully, "I thought perhaps, as her employer, you could compel her to . . ."

"To reveal who she was visiting?" Mrs. Grantham said, a little coldly. Amelia squirmed with discomfort but nodded. Mrs. Grantham pursed her lips. "I will speak with her," she said slowly. "Thank you for bringing the discovery to my attention."

"Of course. Thank you, ma'am," Amelia said, hoping the housekeeper would not lose her position. But finding whoever had harmed Gregory—whoever had tried to poison her—had to be worth the risk.

It wasn't until the door had closed behind Mrs. Grantham that she remembered Mrs. Adler's other comment.

If Mrs. Grantham herself had something to hide . . . it might not be only the housekeeper's employment that was at risk.

Amelia stared at the bowl of soup in front of her, what little appetite she had congealing in her stomach, and hoped she had done the right thing.

★   ★   ★

Dinner was tense and miserable from the beginning, with Mrs. Grantham arriving late and distracted to take her place at the head of the table. Matthew gallantly tried to direct the conversation to lighter matters until William Edison snapped at him to shut up.

"No one wants to hear your damned talk of London amusements or whatever other nonsense you come up with," he snapped.

"No one wants to hear your whining either," Mr. Taylor snorted, already on his second glass of wine. "Shame the captain or Mrs. Crewe or whoever it was shot your brother instead of you."

Gasps echoed around the table, and William bounded to his feet, red with fury, his mouth open as though he would yell. But his face crumpled, and Lily felt an unexpected pang of sympathy for him. Unlikable and immoral he might be, but he was also grieving his brother.

She was about to say something to him, but she did not have a chance. William threw his napkin down and stormed out of the room, pushing past a footman who was just entering. Had the man been carrying a tray, its contents would have toppled to the floor, but he came bearing only a piece of folded paper. After staring after William in a very unfootmanlike manner—Lily wondered how on edge the servants must be, to be losing their studied composure so obviously—the young man recalled himself with a little start and hurried over to Sir John at the head of the table.

A day before, any number of guests would have insisted that William be immediately retrieved so he could stay under the watchful eye of the group. But Jack and Mrs. Crewe were both locked up still. And no one was so eager to spend more time with William that they wanted to go after him.

John, frowning, took the note as the footman bent down to whisper in his ear. Lily was not surprised that everyone at the table watched as he unfolded the paper to read.

"That is Sarah's handwriting," Mrs. Taylor said sharply.

John glanced up long enough to frown at her. "Worry not, Mrs. Taylor, it need not concern you."

"I beg your pardon, sir, but it does concern us," Mr. Hounslow said hotly. "We are all—and have been from the beginning—in this together. Every blessed thing that has happened concerns every one of us. You will be so good as to share what is in that note." His tone made clear that he was issuing an order, not making a request.

John sighed, shaking his head. But he was too genial a man, and too uncomfortable with how much he had been required to set himself in opposition to his neighbors, to refuse. "It is nothing of serious import, I assure you. Mrs. Crewe merely asks to speak with me. Apparently, she has recalled something that she thinks I will wish to know."

"No doubt hoping to ingratiate herself and improve her own outlook," Mr. Taylor snorted.

"Perhaps." John tucked the note into his waistcoat and lifted his own silverware once more. "I shall oblige her once we all go through, but I doubt it is urgent. Now." He tried to smile, looking hopeful that they could return to a discussion of something other than crime and murder. "Has anyone plans to travel to London this winter?"

Lady Adler and a few others joined in the attempt at normal conversation, which was valiant if not entirely successful, until everyone began to stand at the end of the meal. At a typical dinner party, the men would remain for brandy or other spirits, joining the women later for tea and coffee. But they had been skipping such divisions, all going through to the drawing room together and retiring early so as not to waste firewood or candles. This time, there was some confusion about which set of rituals was being followed, most of the guests beginning to rise just as a footman carried in a bottle of brandy. There were suddenly too many chairs pushed back, too many people attempting to move through the same space at once.

It was no surprise, then, when the younger Mr. Hounslow tripped and, flailing as he tried to find his balance, tumbled into the footman, sending both of them crashing into the table and the open brandy bottle flying through the air.

"Damn!" exclaimed Mr. Hounslow as he scrambled to right himself and haul the footman up as well. He glanced around the room, blushing beet red. "Sorry, so sorry, please do excuse . . . I think I tripped on . . . Oh, it was your cane, Mrs. Coleridge—my apologies . . . Yes, here it is—Mr. Coleridge, allow me to help you up . . . Oh, Sir John, your coat—oh dear . . ."

He trailed off, still fumbling awkwardly to set things to rights. John looked as though someone had flung a wash bucket on him, and he was not the only one. Peter, who had been walking behind the magistrate at the time of the accident, was speckled with brandy blotches, and Lady Adler and Mrs. Hounslow were both dabbing at their clothing and muttering unhappily to themselves.

Mrs. Grantham stepped forward. "Oh dear. Perhaps everyone else can go through, while I accompany the four of you upstairs and we sort out some more clothes? And Hugo"—this to the footman, who was trying to look stoic while brandy dripped from his chin—"Go find Mrs. Reynaud, tell her I'll need her assistance upstairs, and get yourself cleaned up. Stop fussing, Mr. Hounslow; these things happen. Yes, you escort Mrs. Coleridge . . ." Efficiently, she ushered the unbrandied guests toward the drawing room and gathered the others to follow her upstairs.

With their hostess gone and the housekeeper pressed into the task of tracking down more spare clothing for the guests, it took some time for tea and coffee to arrive in the drawing room. In the meantime, Mr. Hounslow urged his daughter toward the piano-forte, and Kitty complied reluctantly.

Matthew had offered Lily his arm as soon as they rose from the table, and now he paused at the threshold, glancing around the room. "Shall we sit in the window seat, where you may observe everyone at your leisure?" he asked in an undertone. "Or would you prefer to sit with the Hartleys?"

She ought to sit with the Hartleys. But she was no use to Jack if her mind was occupied with distracting his family. And unlike when Amelia had been the one under suspicion, this time, at least, they had the sympathy of the crowd on their side. It was unfair to poor Amelia, but there was no help for that. And she needed to keep an eye on the rest of the guests. There was still something she was missing.

"The window," Lily said quietly, turning them both in that direction. "Look, Mrs. Coleridge has already gone to join them. I wonder if she is taking the opportunity to urge her son's case?"

"Her son?" Matthew frowned a little as they settled in the window seat, light from the window spilling over the snowy courtyard just outside. "Does Mr. Coleridge's mother promote his investment concerns as well? Or . . ." His eyes grew wide. "Don't tell me he wishes to wed Miss Hartley?"

"I cannot blame you for your surprise," Lily murmured, not taking her eyes from the room. "I've no wish to breech their privacy, but . . ." Keeping her voice low, she provided a few details of Mr. Coleridge's surprising proposal. But her mind was not on the conversation.

Instead, she watched Kitty Hounslow. The girl played through the simple piece as though by rote while she stared into the distance, half a dozen unhappy emotions moving across her face. She had wanted to tell Sir John something, Lily remembered. But for whatever reason, she had lost her nerve, and he had not been able to get her away from her parents long enough to find out what it might have been.

When Kitty's eyes drifted back down to earth long enough for her to notice that she was being watched, Lily didn't look away.

She expected to be on the receiving end of one of the girl's frequent scowls. Instead, Kitty stared at her like a cornered animal, her cheeks growing pale and her eyes wide. She quickly looked away, fixing her eyes on the sheet music, and she didn't look up again.

"What do you make of Kitty Hounslow?" Lily asked.

Matthew turned to give the girl a considering look. "She reminds me very much of a girl that my Eloisa has had difficulty with. Envious, certainly. Longs for attention. Impulsive but not brave. And terrified of anyone disliking her."

"That is rather a thorough analysis," Lily said approvingly.

He flashed a quick smile at her. "Fatherhood has made me wise," he quipped. Then he shook his head, looking sympathetic. "I've always suspected that Julia—she is the girl I know—would be easier in herself if she had less self-absorbed parents. I expect Miss Hounslow is much the same."

"You mentioned envious," Lily mused. "And impulsive. I wonder what sort of thing Miss Hounslow might impulsively do if, for example, she felt that a young man had wronged her."

The tea and coffee arrived at the same time as Lady Adler, who glanced about the subdued gathering with surprise. "Dear me, am I the first one to return? Kitty, that tune is dreadfully melancholy. Perhaps your fingers are tired? Mrs. Taylor, take the poor girl's place. And no Mrs. Grantham to pour? Well, if no one objects, I shall do the honors . . ."

"Miss Hounslow has made no secret of her fondness for Mr. Edison," Matthew said quietly, while Lady Adler settled at the tea cart and the other guests began to gather around.

"But I have a hard time imagining her brave enough to meet a man in private," Lily said, watching Miss Hounslow's expression of relief as she surrendered her place at the pianoforte to Mrs. Taylor. "On the other hand . . ." She stood. "The only way to know for certain is to speak with her."

"You think she will tell you?" Matthew asked with some amusement.

Lily smiled, watching her quarry fidgeting near the tea cart. "I think the ways people try to lie can reveal a good deal more than they realize."

She took Matthew's arm once more, intending to lead him toward the small cluster of people in the middle of the room. But as soon as they stepped away from the window seat, there was a shriek—was it from outside or inside?—and an odd noise, almost like a rush of air. The sound of something heavy hitting the ground in the courtyard made her freeze.

Someone screamed. More voices called in confusion. Lady Adler started to her feet, overturning the tea cart with a jangle of silver and shattering china. Kitty Hounslow stared at the window in slack-jawed horror before collapsing to the ground.

Lily didn't want to turn around. She didn't want to see what was waiting in the snowy courtyard, just at the edge of the window's light.

She took a deep breath and counted to three in her head, forcing herself to turn when she reached the final number.

Mrs. Crewe lay on the flagstones of the courtyard, the light from the window spilling across her. Her head was twisted at an unnatural angle, her eyes wide and sightless. Beneath her, the icy snow was slowly turning red.

CHAPTER 26

"She must have leapt to her death, rather than face prosecution for what she did," John said, his voice quiet and grave as he stared around the nursery–turned–sitting room that had been Mrs. Crewe's prison. He swallowed before turning back to Lily, who had found him there after a restless night, his face ashen in the early-morning light that straggled through the window. "Perhaps that is why she wanted to speak with me. To confess in full, before . . . I thought she had withheld some piece of information. I thought if she grew nervous waiting for me, she would be more honest."

"You'd no way of knowing this might happen," Lily insisted, laying a hand on his arm as she turned them both away from the window. It was hard enough to stand in the room, knowing what had happened there. She couldn't bear to look at that window anymore, and she didn't want her brother-in-law to have to see it either. "I know you, John. You would not have been too harsh, even if she was a thief. And you would have told her so, had she given you the chance."

"Well . . ." John met her eyes, his voice hoarse, his normally cheerful face drawn with misery. "I would have had to be much harsher than I wished, had I seen this."

He held out his hand, and Lily could only stare. It did not make sense.

Draped over his palm was a string of pearls, broken off at one end where the clasp should have been.

"Once I realized she was guilty of murder as well as theft, I'd have had no choice," John said quietly. He glanced at the window again, then looked quickly away. "She must have realized that. I suppose this seemed like the better option."

"But . . ." Lily couldn't gather her thoughts well enough to frame her protest. "But how . . . where did you get those?"

He nodded to the desk, which was not far from the window. "It was laid out there, along with a few other of her things. Apparently, she had it with her the whole time. Which tells us all we need to know."

"Does it?" Lily asked, still staring at the pearls in his hand.

"Does it not?" he asked, a little impatiently, scowling at the broken necklace before dropping it carefully into his waistcoat pocket. It seemed to slither, the pearls striking each other with sharp, ominous clicks. "They must have quarreled—perhaps he threatened to reveal her deception, or she was tired of sharing her profits—and she clearly grabbed it from Mr. Edison's hand, either before or after she shot him." He shook his head. "She seemed so engaging and honest when we spoke to her. Did you have any thought that she was lying to us the whole time?"

"None at all," Lily said, shuddering a little as, turning her head, she caught a glimpse of the window out of the corner of her eye. She quickly looked away, fixing her eyes on her brother-in-law instead. "In fact, I still have trouble believing it. Especially since I searched her, John. Those pearls were nowhere to be found, I am certain of it."

"Lily." He stared at her impatiently. "Are you trying to claim it is impossible for you to have made a mistake?"

She felt her cheeks grow hot. "Of course it is not impossible," she said, working hard to keep her voice even. There was no point in losing her temper with John. And he did not deserve it when he was already feeling so miserable. "But in this case, it strikes me as highly improbable. There was nowhere else on her person for the necklace to be concealed."

He gestured impatiently around them. "There are any number of places—"

"And we were with her up until the point when she was searched," Lily continued over him, in a slightly louder voice. "She was never alone to hide them somewhere in here. So where did they come from?"

"Lily, please don't," John said, one hand rubbing his temples. "You missed them somehow; that is clearly all there is to it. And in this case, her suicide is as good as a confession."

"But—"

"And I should think you would be glad about that!" he snapped at last. "If she was our murderer, then Jack cannot be."

Lily shut her mouth abruptly. Dear God, Jack. She did not want to argue him into a prison sentence, or worse. She closed her eyes while she let out a slow breath. "Of course." She opened them and nodded. "Of course I am glad of that, John."

He sighed, glancing around the room once more. "Terrible business," he muttered, looking relieved as he headed toward the door. "Are you coming?"

Lily hesitated. "You go ahead, if you please. I just need to . . ."

"Look around?" he finished for her, exasperated once more.

She said nothing. Any protest would be a lie, and she did not want to lie to him.

John sighed again. "Suit yourself. But Mrs. Crewe had both reason and opportunity to kill Mr. Edison. And she would have had no reason to leap from that window were she not guilty."

"I know." But still Lily did not move to join him.

He shook his head. "Suit yourself," he said again, striding from the room as though he could not wait to leave it.

Lily could not blame him for that. More than anything, she wanted to be gone as well. Her gaze kept straying toward the window, and every time it did, a sick feeling settled in the pit of her stomach and she quickly looked away again. She didn't want to think of Mrs. Crewe teasing her, shrugging away her concerns and making pointed comments about the class of people she had pretended to be part of so well.

But that was exactly why Lily couldn't force herself to leave. Not yet.

It didn't make sense.

Lily took a deep breath, steeling herself to look around. And she almost leapt out of her own skin when a quiet voice asked, "Mrs. Adler?"

Lily spun around to find Amelia peering nervously around the door. Lily took a shuddering breath. "Dear God, you gave me a fright," she muttered. "Come in, quickly, before someone sees you. Should you be up and about?"

"I am feeling well enough for short walks," Amelia said, closing the door behind her. "Did you hear? They're saying Sir John will have to release my brother because Mrs. Crewe was . . ." She trailed off, glancing toward the window as well, then looked back at Lily. "You don't look pleased, ma'am."

Lily hesitated. "I am glad about your brother, to be sure. But I am not entirely satisfied with the situation."

"Why?"

Lily let her eyes drift slowly over the furniture, trying to decide if anything was different, anything out of place, since she had last been there. "To begin, there are the pearls," she said, telling Amelia about her previous search of Mrs. Crewe's person, almost absent-mindedly, while she moved slowly about the room, touching a chair here, the mantelpiece there. "And what's more, Mrs. Crewe didn't act like someone with a . . . a murderous secret that could be discovered at any moment. And yet she jumped to her death, rather than face judgment, so soon after?" Lily shook her head. "It does not make any sense."

"Then what do we need to look for?" Amelia asked.

Lily looked over her shoulder, not bothering to hide her surprise. "We?"

"Of course," Amelia said, swallowing nervously but nodding nonetheless. "You said I was to help you catch a murderer, did you not?"

"That was when your brother was in danger," Lily pointed out.

"Well, if you are correct, then we are all in danger still. So." Amelia squared her shoulders in a gesture that was endearingly reminiscent of Jack. Was it something one of their parents did? Or had Amelia learned it from him during his too-few visits home? "What should I look for?"

Lily thought about objecting, but two sets of eyes were better than one. Or at least, they were better than the time and effort it would take to send Amelia back to her room to rest. "Anything that strikes you as out of the ordinary." Jack would have words to say, none of them polite, when he found out Lily had involved his sister. But that was a problem for another time. "Anything that seems odd or out of place."

Amelia nodded and began to walk slowly around the perimeter of the room, her eyes on the floor and carpeting. Lily glanced toward the door, wishing once more that she could make herself leave, before turning to walk toward the awful window. She didn't let her steps slow as she got close, not stopping until she was standing right in front of it.

But there was nothing to see. The casement was closed. Lily let out a slow breath, then, before she could talk herself out of it, pushed sharply against the panes with both hands. There was no give; the latch was firm and would not have come open unexpectedly if someone fell against it. Lily knelt below the window, scanning the floor and nearby furnishings. There was nothing odd or suspicious, nothing to indicate that there had been any violence or foul play inside the room.

But of course there wouldn't have been. Lily stood up slowly, her eyes fixed on the window without really seeing it. The door had been locked—she had seen with her own eyes that John had locked it after their interview with Mrs. Crewe, and she had raced up the stairs in time to see him unlock it after Mrs. Crewe fell. How would someone else have gotten in?

"Mrs. Adler, does this count as something odd?"

Amelia's question recalled her to where she was, and Lily shook her head to clear it as she turned away from the window. "What did you find?"

Amelia was kneeling near the door, picking up several small things from the floor one by one. When Lily appeared at her shoulder, she held them out. "Hairpins. They were scattered about here."

Lily took one, then another, between her fingers, turning them over and frowning. They were hairpins indeed, but curiously shaped—some of them straightened, some of them bent at odd angles. Seeing them, she remembered the masses of coils and curls that Mrs. Crewe had let down at her request, to ensure that no pearls were hidden within her coiffure. Easy enough for her to have dropped some as she put her hair back up once she was alone. But why were they all bent out of shape? And wasn't it odd for her to have stood next to the door as she put her hair back up?

"What do you think?" Amelia asked, dusting off her gown as she stood up.

"What I think is that neither of you ladies ought to be in here."

Amelia, less accustomed to being caught where she shouldn't be, yelped in surprise before Lily caught her arm and gave it a quick tug to silence her. Lily herself, though equally startled, managed to keep her composure as she turned toward the door.

"Mrs. Reynaud," she said politely, meeting the housekeeper's narrow-eyed gaze with her own calm one. "Was there something you needed?"

"I might ask you the same thing," Mrs. Reynaud said, eyeing them uneasily. Jane the housemaid stood behind her, clutching a basket of cleaning things and staring between the two women as they faced off. Amelia, beside Lily, looked equally worried. "Mrs. Grantham sent us to see that the room is set to rights once more. She didn't say a word about any guests poking their noses around."

"Then we shall be out of your way immediately," Lily said, her hand closed around the hairpins. She didn't think Mrs. Reynaud had noticed that she was holding them, but she folded her hands carefully in front of her, just to be safe. Out of the corner of her eye, she saw Amelia, who had been holding the other hairpins, tuck her hands behind her back. "Once you answer a question for me. I am sure you can guess what it is."

The housekeeper frowned, but she seemed resigned to the fact that Lily was not going to budge until she was ready. Mrs. Reynaud glanced at the maid. "Jane, step off down the hall, there's a good girl. The ladies and I need to have a quick chat."

"Yes, Mrs. Reynaud," Jane said, still wide-eyed as she looked back toward Lily and Amelia. She placed her basket carefully next to the doorframe, then bobbed a brief curtsy and scampered off down the hall.

Mrs. Reynaud faced the two women, her arms crossed. "I already said I'm not going to tell you," she said, glancing uneasily toward Amelia.

An upper servant she might be, but she was still nervous about being accused of impropriety, and rightly so. Lily hesitated over her words for a moment; she wanted to gain the woman's trust, not squander it.

"Mrs. Reynaud, I beg you to reconsider," she said at last. "You must see how important it is for us to know which room you were exiting. It might be our only way to discover who Mr. Edison was meeting with that night. And whoever it was—"

"You don't need to know where I was anymore," Mrs. Reynaud interrupted, not bothering to hide her impatience. She gestured broadly toward the room behind them. "Everyone in this house knows why Mrs. Crewe—" She broke off, looking a little ashamed of what she had been about to say. "What Mrs. Crewe did. Magistrate has his murderer now, and all of you are to go home. Isn't that the end of it?"

"It is only the end of it if you believe Mrs. Crewe's death makes sense," Lily said. She could feel Amelia's fascinated attention volleying back and forth between the two of them. "Which, in many ways, it does not. Please. All I want is to ensure that whoever is truly guilty here is found."

"Well, if it wasn't that fraud, maybe it was that navy captain all along," Mrs. Reynaud suggested, glancing at Amelia. "Wasn't everyone saying just a day ago how justified he would have been to defend his sister's honor?"

"My brother would *never* do such a thing," Amelia said hotly, stepping a little too close to the housekeeper before Lily could stop her.

Mrs. Reynaud shifted back, looking unnerved. "Then maybe it was you? You certainly seem to have a temper on you, and worse, so we've heard downstairs."

"How *dare* you—"

"Enough," Lily said sharply. To her relief, Amelia subsided. "Mrs. Reynaud, I ask you one more time to reconsider. I promise, whatever you tell me will be kept in the strictest confidence."

For a moment, the housekeeper hesitated, and Lily felt a surge of hope. Then—

"Jane!" Mrs. Reynaud called down the hall, before turning back to the two women. "We need to be about our work, ma'am, if you've quite finished in here?"

The clock downstairs was chiming nine o'clock. Lily sighed. "I suppose we have, then. Come along, Amelia. You need to rest before the journey home."

They made their way back to the second floor, which was in a bustle of preparing for the guests to leave—a stranger bustle than Lily was used to in such situations. No one had clothing to pack or servants to muster. Instead, several footmen and gardeners had been sent out to break up the remaining snow and ice on the road and see if any carriages could be summoned from their neighbors. The guests, waiting in their chambers or in the breakfast room, were jittery and excited, some of them still casting nervous glances at each other, others behaving as though nothing out of the ordinary had happened at all in the past few days.

Lily left Amelia in front of the fire in her room, both of them tense and thoughtful, before heading back to her own room. She felt as though she were walking in a dream. After all that, were they simply to go home?

"Damnation!"

The sudden curse made Lily jump. Mrs. Coleridge's door was ajar, and she could see the elderly woman at the dressing table, fussing with something and muttering to herself. Worried, recalling what Peter had said about his mother growing more frail and sometimes even disoriented, she tapped on the door.

"Are you all right, ma'am?" she asked, poking her head inside the room.

Mrs. Coleridge darted to her feet, quick and agile as a snake that had been frightened and was ready to strike. She stared at Lily, a hairbrush held in her hand like a weapon, her eyes wide and startled under a half-pinned riot of silver curls.

"Oh, Mrs. Adler." She sat back down, seeming to sink into herself in relief, her head and shoulders bowed as though under a heavy weight. "I apologize, I thought it was—" She shook her head, smiling tremulously. "I do not know what I thought it was. All this terrible business with Mr. Edison and Mrs. Crewe has left me so flustered. I can't seem to manage properly without a servant, and . . . oh dear . . ."

Her cane had been leaning against the table, but she had knocked it over as she started to turn. Lily managed to catch it before it hit the ground.

"Thank you." Mrs. Coleridge sighed. "I shan't be a mite sad to go home, believe you me."

"I think you'll hardly find any argument on that score," Lily replied, trying to sound as soothing as possible. She wondered if she should go fetch Peter. But Mrs. Coleridge seemed to be recovering from her distress. And perhaps all she needed was a little help. "Shall I assist you, so you can go down for breakfast?"

"Thank you, my dear." Mrs. Coleridge seemed to gather herself with some effort, sitting up straight and turning toward the mirror. When she spoke, she began to sound a little more like her familiar, commanding self again. "None of these fanciful modern styles, if you please. They do not suit a woman my age. I prefer something elegant."

She proved as exacting about hair as everything else, and Lily had begun to regret her offer of help when Mrs. Coleridge finally announced, "It will do, I suppose." She turned her head from side to side, nodding in satisfaction. Catching Lily's eye in the mirror, some of her imperiousness flickered, and she gave another tremulous smile. "It makes everything else feel more manageable, do you not think, to at least feel good about one's appearance? Particularly as one grows older and, well . . ." She laid a hand on her cane.

"Of course," Lily said quickly, feeling a little ashamed of herself. "Is there anything else I can assist you with?"

She was saved from having her offer accepted by a timid tap at the door. When they turned, Jane the housemaid was peeking her head inside.

"Mrs. Coleridge, ma'am? I have your necklace for you. Mr. Lambton and I were able to repair it with the tools Mrs. Reynaud keeps for her spectacles." Jane laid it across Mrs. Coleridge's hands, hovering a little anxiously. "It isn't properly done, not like a jeweler would do," she said quickly, blushing. "But it'll hold together for now, until you can get someone to fix it for good."

Mrs. Coleridge's sigh was full of unfeigned relief. "You've no idea how worried I was to see it gone. Lily, be a dear and help me fasten it."

"Thank you, Jane," Lily said quietly as she took the necklace and did as requested.

Mrs. Coleridge sighed again once it was in place, her satisfaction evident as she ran her fingers along the smooth, pale beads. Catching Lily's eye in the mirror, she wiped at her eye and sniffed a little. "My husband gave them to me the first year we were married, the dear man. How I miss him. Having them gone was like losing a piece of his memory." She gave Lily a little smile. "I am sure you can understand."

Lily swallowed down the lump that wanted to rise into her throat. "Of course. I am truly glad they have been returned to you. Shall I assist you to the breakfast room?"

Mrs. Coleridge sniffed again, searching for a handkerchief. "No, thank you, I believe I would like a moment to myself. If you see Peter, though, send him to me."

"What a dear thing," Jane exclaimed quietly, once she and Lily were in the hall together and the door was closed to give Mrs. Coleridge her privacy. "Her treasuring something so common, in memory of her husband." The housemaid shook her head. "That's real love, that is. How grand. If you'll excuse me, ma'am? Mrs. Reynaud warned me not to dawdle upstairs; we've ever so much to do to get everyone sent off."

Lily laid a hand on Jane's arm to stop her from leaving. "A moment. What do you mean, something common?" she asked, urging the maid away from the door so they wouldn't be overheard. "I believe they are quite valuable."

To her surprise, Jane laughed. "Not hardly. Though you can't really blame the fellow, the former Mr. Coleridge I mean, can you? If he gave them to her when they was young and first married, like as not he couldn't afford anything better."

"Do you mean . . . Are they not real?"

"False as hen's teeth," Jane said, looking surprised that Lily had to ask. "Every single one, as far as I could tell."

Lily stared at her. "How do you know?"

"My brother works for a jeweler in London," Jane said. "That's how I knew something of how to fix them. They're pretty baubles, right enough. But it wouldn't cost more than a few shillings to buy them." A thought occurring to her, Jane suddenly looked worried. "Do you think she doesn't know?"

Chapter 27

When Lily finally made it back to her room, it was not empty. Mrs. Grantham was pacing from one wall to the other, her hands fluttering and clasping at each other.

"Oh, Mrs. Adler!" she exclaimed. "You startled me. That is—I apologize for intruding. But I need to speak with you. In private."

"Certainly," Lily agreed cautiously. "Is there something I can assist you with?"

"No. That is . . ." Mrs. Grantham hesitated, shifting from one foot to the other and casting anxious looks toward the door.

"If you are hoping I will be the one to begin, Mrs. Grantham, I am afraid I cannot," Lily said quietly. "Except to ask you what it is that has you so distressed."

Mrs. Grantham nodded, folding her hands in front of her. She fixed her eyes on a point over Lily's shoulder and took a deep breath. "I think, Mrs. Adler, that you had some suspicion on your first day here that I had not spent the night entirely in my room. That I was one of those—one among many, as it seems—creeping about the halls at night."

"I did suspect so, at least at first," Lily admitted. Like Mrs. Grantham, her voice was low. "Your distress at Sir John's questioning seemed . . . particular. But that was before you told me about the theft of your mother's jewelry."

"Yes. Well . . ." Mrs. Grantham swallowed nervously. "You were not entirely mistaken. I did not leave my room that night. But I also did not spend the night alone."

Lily's mind whirred through the possibilities, but there was only one that made sense. And it went a long way toward explaining her hostess's nervousness. She let out a breath at the realization. "You were the one Mrs. Reynaud was visiting that night."

Mrs. Grantham nodded, her cheeks pale. "She and I have been . . . close for nearly five years now. That is why she did not want to answer your questions. She didn't . . . Well. I am sure you understand." She glanced quickly at Lily to gauge her expression, then just as quickly away. Lily nodded slowly. Mrs. Grantham and her housekeeper were certainly not the first women to have such a relationship—nor indeed the first ones that Lily herself had known. But such intimacies could be dangerous if discussed too publicly.

"But we just spoke, after she saw you upstairs, and we decided that, after what happened to Miss Hartley and . . . well . . ." Mrs. Grantham floundered a little, unsure of what to say or how to say it. "I know you will have to tell the magistrate. I hope that we may rely on your, and his, discretion. But that is what you wished to know. It was my room she was leaving that night when she spotted the figure going downstairs."

★ ★ ★

"Her room is at the end the wing west of the stairs," Lily said, watching her brother-in-law pace around the library. He had listened in incredulous silence as she shared Mrs. Grantham's admission, then launched into motion, as though he could not process such information while remaining still. "Which narrows down the list of guests considerably."

"Yes, but she . . . and the housekeeper?" John demanded for the third time. He stopped at the mantel as he said it, but as soon as he met Lily's eyes, his face flushed with embarrassment, and he looked away.

"Surely you have heard of such things," Lily said impatiently. The carriages would be leaving soon. They were running out of time.

"Of course I have. I just never expected . . . A close neighbor, you know! And a woman of her years—how am I to meet her eye when next I see her?" His face had gone from red to deep scarlet as he spoke.

"*John*," Lily snapped. "Dear God, brother, *focus*. If I can handle such a revelation with equanimity, surely your worldly self can manage?"

"I've never claimed to be worldly," he muttered.

"Well, now is your chance," Lily said. "Which matters more right now, the amorous interests of one neighbor or the possibility that another is a murderer? Because if Mrs. Reynaud saw someone leaving their room from the west hall, that means there is someone whose movement in the night we have not accounted for. Someone who, unlike the others, *went downstairs*. Someone who was not Mrs. Crewe."

John rubbed his hands across his face. "All right, then. So that means what? That she was not our murderer? Then why did she leap to her death?"

"I do not think she would have. And I think someone put those pearls in her room to make her seem guilty."

"But—"

"Indulge me, John," Lily begged. "Treat it as a thought experiment, if you must. But you must consider it before everyone here departs. If Mrs. Crewe was indeed murdered herself, the person Mrs. Reynaud saw in the hall could be our killer."

John let out a sigh that was nearly a growl. "Very well. Whose rooms were in that wing?"

"The Hartleys," Lily said, consulting the much-folded map that Mrs. Reynaud had drawn for them what seemed weeks ago. "William Edison, the Coleridges, and the younger Hounslows."

They were both silent for a tense moment, considering the possibilities.

"What if Mrs. Crewe's murder was not only to make her seem guilty?" Lily said suddenly, sitting bolt upright. "There could have been another reason."

"Are you merely suggesting the possibility, or do you have some idea what that reason might be?" John asked.

"We think our murderer came after Amelia because she knows something about who it is, something incriminating," Lily pointed out. "What if she was not the only one? Recall what happened just before Mrs. Crewe's fall."

John frowned in confusion, clearly searching his memory. "We had recently finished dinner, had we not? And . . . the letter," he said with a grimace. He clearly had followed her thinking and did not like where it was going. "Mrs. Crewe sent me that note, asking to speak with me."

"Someone could have already been plotting to do away with her," Lily continued, nodding. "But what if it was an impulse? The murderer realized she had something to tell you, something too revealing to permit being shared, and so went to silence her."

"But how?" John insisted. "I had the keys with me the whole time. Unless Mrs. Grantham was lying about there being no other set." His eyes widened in dismay. "Are you suggesting that Mrs. Grantham—"

"No." Lily shook her head. "I think the culprit was hairpins."

Her brother-in-law was plainly confused. "You mean the ones you found by the door?"

"The lock-picking tools I took from her were well used," Lily said, standing and beginning to pace around the room. She could feel John following her with his eyes, but her own vision was elsewhere, picturing the room where Mrs. Crewe had been held, the good-humored resignation on the woman's face when she was forced to hand over her tools. "She clearly had plans to use them, and what for but to escape? If she had been able to get one of Mrs. Grantham's horses that night, likely no one would have been able to follow until she was well away. No wonder she was so unworried. And when we took away her lock picks, she turned to the next best thing she had on hand. Hairpins."

"Dear God. She unlocked her own door," John said, looking horrified. "But instead of letting herself out, she permitted a murderer to come in. Who then took advantage of the fact that we were all occupied with dinner some floors away."

"And in a great deal of confusion," Lily added. "Remember, that was after Mr. Hounslow knocked over the brandy bottle."

John frowned. "Do you think that was deliberate?"

"He did not leave the company afterwards," Lily said slowly. "But there was one person who was gone longer than anyone else. Who left first and who did not, in fact, return to the group until well after Mrs. Crewe had fallen to her death."

"William Edison," John said, rising slowly to his feet. The look on his face was dreadful, hard and resigned and relentless all at once. Lily shivered a little, suddenly seeing her brother-in-law in a new light. "He was ruthless enough to continue his brother's blackmail scheme, and even to expand it. He might have been ruthless enough to do a great deal else besides. And whatever secret he was keeping, his brother found it out."

"Or William may have found out what his brother was up to, with the thefts," Lily pointed out. "If their handwriting was similar, perhaps that note the housemaid found was actually written *by* William, *to* his brother."

"Whatever the case, I must find him instantly, before he leaves the house," John said, striding toward the door. "If he departs, there is every chance he will take the opportunity to flee the county, and then who knows if anyone will be able to track him down again."

"I am coming as well," Lily insisted, only to have John hold up his hand to stop her.

"I cannot permit it," he said, shaking his head.

"Why on earth not?" Lily demanded. "I have done far worse, and far more dangerous."

"No, I think it better that we split up," he said, heading toward the door. "I believe he is up in his room. But if he has slipped away . . . I can only hope one of us will spot him in time."

"Very well," Lily said impatiently. She didn't like being set aside at the last moment, and she fully intended to berate her brother-in-law later. But she did not want to waste time arguing, not while William was likely preparing to leave at that very moment. "But we must be quick."

★　★　★

Lily paced through the house, watching the anxious clusters of guests drifting through the halls or settling in the front parlors. William Edison was nowhere to be seen, but she did spot Matthew in conversation with Mr. Hounslow and Peter Coleridge. Matthew had a polite smile fixed firmly in place, but she could see his eyes darting from side to side, as though looking for a chance to escape, and she was not surprised when he beckoned her to join them.

Lily hesitated. But the parlor door was open; she could keep an eye on the hall from there, and it would look odd if she ignored him. Making up her mind quickly, she stepped up to his side just in time to catch the end of Mr. Hounslow's comments.

"Surely you cannot be talking about investments, of all things?" Lily asked. "Not at a time like this?"

Mr. Hounslow smiled, a suave, insincere expression that was second cousin to a leer. "You know how gentlemen are, my dear. We cannot help ourselves. Coleridge, Spencer." He bowed. "Do excuse me."

Lily raised her eyebrows at Matthew in an unspoken question, and his quick, flickering smile was a little embarrassed. "Mr. Hounslow was extolling the merits of Mr. Coleridge's Irish bank fund to me," he said. "I thought it behooved me to listen."

"Well, by all means." Lily glanced toward the stairway, impatient for news from John and trying to hide it. "Do not let me deter you. It is a new venture, is it not, since I last saw you?"

"Indeed," Peter said, glancing at Mr. Spencer and shifting in his seat before giving her a friendly smile. "It is very technical, though, and I've no wish to bore you. We can certainly talk of something else."

Lily knew she wasn't imagining the hint of condescension in his voice, and she bit the inside of her cheek to keep her temper in check. "Oh you couldn't possibly," she said, smiling across gritted teeth. "I've heard so many of your neighbors speak of its profits in glowing terms. And if Mr. Spencer is considering investing, then I am certainly curious to know all about it. It is a consolidated fund, is it not? Could you explain what that means for the structure of it?"

Peter looked taken aback by the question, and his eyes darted around the room, settling on Mr. Spencer once more with a look of mild panic before returning to her. "Well, it is all a bit complicated, but in simple terms—oh dear."

He broke off as a bout of violent coughing interrupted all the conversation in the room. Mrs. Coleridge, seated across the room with the Hartleys, seemed to be in some distress; her coughing shook her so much that her cup tumbled from its saucer and landed on the carpet, sending tea spiraling through the air as it fell.

"Excuse me a moment." Peter sprang from his seat to go assist his mother. "I think Mother and I will be departing soon, in any case. Mrs. Grantham said the carriages are almost ready."

Matthew gave Lily a curious glance once they were alone again. "Are investment structures another hobby of yours?"

"Hardly," she said, shaking her head, still irritated with Peter. "I can think of few things more dull to discuss. But I consider it of great importance that I understand what is happening with my money. So I take an interest when I must."

Matthew shook his head. "Ah, but this time it was my money we were talking about," he said with a small chuckle. "Not yours."

Lily stared at him, her brows climbing, waiting for him to see the connection. But he was smiling at her with a look that was . . .

almost indulgent. "Which you have proposed would become one and the same," she said. "Which would indeed make how you invest it my concern."

The chuckle died on his lips, and he blinked at her in surprise, as though the thought had genuinely not occurred to him before that moment. Lily watched him, her stomach fluttering with anxiety, waiting to see how he would respond.

"Well," he said slowly, a thoughtful frown gathering between his handsome eyes. "I suppose I can see—"

"My apologies."

Lily clamped her jaw shut on a frustrated curse at Mr. Hounslow's poorly timed return. She wanted so terribly to know what Matthew might have said. "I believe I dropped my watch here . . . ah, yes, there it is." He chuckled a little. "For a moment, I was worried someone stole it," he added, bowing as he departed once more.

Lily frowned after him. "I shall be happy not to see him again, at least," she grumbled as she watched him head for the doorway. "Unpleasant man."

"Why do you keep watching the door?" Matthew asked quietly. "Are you waiting for someone."

"Yes," she whispered. "Sir John went to find William Edison, and . . ." She trailed off suddenly, her eyes still on Mr. Hounslow. He had said something about William. What was it?

"Why?" Matthew asked, frowning.

He had complained about William's behavior at the ball, tracking down everyone who owed him money and demanding that they pay.

And she had overheard William talking with Peter Coleridge that night.

It could have been nothing. But . . .

Lily sprang to her feet. "Excuse me a moment. I must find my brother-in-law."

"Why—" Matthew frowned, following after her. "What happened? Lily, what is it?"

She whispered a quick explanation, leaving out the specifics of Mrs. Grantham and Mrs. Reynaud's admission, as he followed her to the library. She had hoped she would find John returned, with William in tow, but there was no one there.

"The music room, or the drawing room, perhaps?" Matthew suggested. "They are just down the hall from here."

There were voices coming from the music room as they approached, but neither of them was Sir John. Lily would have hurried past when she heard the housekeeper speaking. "Wait," she said, gesturing to Matthew as she rapped on the half-open door to announce her presence. "Mrs. Reynaud?"

The housekeeper was just setting a tea tray next to Amelia Hartley, who was wrapped in a blanket once more and settled in front of a blazing fire. At the sound of her name, she straightened quickly, her expression stricken as she saw Lily.

"Mrs. Adler!" Amelia exclaimed as they entered. She looked very young and tired as she sat there, and Lily felt a pang of regret that she had allowed the girl to assist her that morning, so soon after her near-poisoning. Clearly, the exertion had been too much for her. "What is it?"

"I am hoping Mrs. Reynaud can assist me."

The housekeeper had smoothed her expression back to its usual polite mask, but her fingers were plucking anxiously at the edge of her apron. "Mrs. Adler. I am happy to be of assistance, of course. But I hope . . . That is, I know Mrs. Grantham . . . You've been described to me as a lady of great discretion—"

"Mrs. Reynaud, I would be happy to reassure you to your heart's content, were my errand now not absolutely urgent," Lily said. "Have you seen Sir John Adler? He went in search of William Edison."

"Mr. Edison?" The housekeeper frowned. "But . . . it certainly wasn't him that I saw going down the stairs. His room was closest to . . ." She hesitated, glancing at the other two. "That is, I'd have been able to tell if it was him."

"I know," Lily said impatiently. "But do you know where he is now? Or where the magistrate might have gone?"

Her instinct had not been wrong; the housekeeper, as always, had noted where everyone was as she moved through the house. "I saw them heading to Mr. William's room. Why—"

"I must go." Lily didn't stop to explain, but before she could take a step, she felt a hand on her arm.

"I'm coming with you," Matthew said. It was not a question, but Lily nodded anyway.

"All right. Amelia!" she called. "Lock the door. Do not let anyone in until Sir John or I return."

The girl frowned at them. "What—"

Lily turned to Matthew. "We've no time to lose."

"I am coming too!" Amelia cried, struggling out of her cocoon of blankets.

Lily let out a frustrated growl. She did not want to waste time in either arguing or in forcing the girl to stay put. "Stay close, then. We must hurry."

★ ★ ★

They rushed through the back halls, which had grown emptier as the guests gathered in the front sitting rooms to await their turn to be escorted home, and up the stairs toward William's room. When they arrived, Matthew raised his fist to knock, but Lily did not wait. She stepped under his arm and shoved the door open.

The response to her entrance was instant. William Edison bolted to his feet, while John spun around, his hands raised in a defensive gesture.

"Good God, what do you mean by barging in here like that?" he exclaimed, one hand going to his heart instead once he realized who had startled him.

"It could not wait, John," Lily panted. "We—"

"What the devil is *she* doing here?" William demanded, staring not at Lily but at Amelia, who had pushed into the room as well. Matthew, with great circumspection, closed the door behind them.

"Lily, we are in the middle of a *sensitive* conversation," John insisted, pushing William back into his chair.

"Sensitive, is that what you call it?" William demanded hotly. "You've accused me of killing my own brother! That isn't sensitive, sir, that is slander."

"William did it?" Amelia demanded incredulously, swaying a little on her feet. Matthew took her arm to steady her. "And did he poison me as well?"

"John, we were wrong—" Lily tried to explain, but William interrupted once more.

"I did no such thing," he insisted, struggling to his feet only to have John push him easily down again. "And I will have you know—"

"William, shut up," Amelia snapped, and he was startled enough that he obeyed, staring at her with his mouth agape. "Mrs. Adler, what is it?"

"Do you recall what Mr. Hounslow's complaint was about Mr. Edison here?" Lily asked, still struggling a little to catch her breath. "That he spent the entirety of Mrs. Grantham's ball cornering people who owed him money and demanding payment. Which, Mr. Hounslow says, was unbecoming of a gentleman."

"What is unbecoming of a gentleman is not paying his debts," William interrupted. "They owed me money, and I was within my rights to insist on payment."

"William," Lily said, walking toward him. "Matthew and I overheard you speaking to Mr. Coleridge at the ball. I thought you were telling him you could not pay a debt you owed to him because you had need of the funds yourself. But that was not it, was it?" She took a step closer. "He owed you money, and you were telling him you required *payment* because you had need of the funds."

"Well, I had!" William exclaimed, flushing with embarrassment. "And it was damned awkward to admit, too. No man likes to say out loud that he is strapped for cash. But Coleridge was so stupid about the whole thing, going on about a gentleman's word of honor and asking for more time to pay. I could almost believe he had no intention of ever paying me, the old miser."

"It would be miserly of him, indeed," Lily agreed. "If he had the money to pay you."

"Of course he has it!" William snapped. "His Irish properties make him near five thousand a year; everyone knows that. That's why we all invested in them as soon as he let us. Well, not you," he added, giving John a withering look. "But you'll regret that, this time next year."

"No," Lily said softly. "I do not think he will. And we know your brother wanted to speak to Mr. Coleridge at the ball."

"What are you saying, Lily?" John demanded. "Why worry about what Mr. Coleridge was doing? We have all known Peter for years. He is a shrewd man and a devoted son. What connection had he to Mr. Edison?"

"He clearly had one, or why else would Mr. Edison have been seeking him out at the ball?" Lily insisted.

"He wanted to discuss his brother's—" John froze, his lips half-parted, the words dying even as he spoke them.

"His brother's debt," Lily said, nodding. "But it was Peter who owed a debt to William, not the other way around. And he would not pay William. Why do you think that was?"

"But he could not have been the one to harm my brother," William pointed out. "How could he, when . . ." He glanced around at them, as though to gauge what they already knew. "Surely you know he spent the night with Mrs. Taylor?"

"He what?" Amelia demanded, swaying again before Matthew steadied her once more. Lily eyed her worriedly; the girl was still weak from her ordeal, and who knew what further shocks or excitement she could endure.

"How do you know that?" John asked.

William shrugged. "There has been a good deal of gossip."

"*I* have not heard any such rumors," Amelia insisted.

William rolled his eyes. "Well, of course not; no one would repeat such things in front of an unmarried girl. But in any case, I am sure Mrs. Taylor would have noticed had he slipped away for any part of the night."

"And yet he still offered to marry me? How churlish," Amelia said, looking offended.

"Well, as William is right, does that not settle it?" John pointed out.

"But I am certain that is not all there is to it," Lily insisted, taking a step forward. "Peter is concealing something. If nothing else, he lied to us. Should you not ask him why?"

When John hesitated, William chimed in again. "If you want to speak to him, you will need to hurry."

"What?" Lily turned to him, her surprise mirrored by the others only an instant later.

William shrugged again. "He and Mrs. Coleridge were preparing to depart when the magistrate dragged me here," he said resentfully.

"John." Lily met her brother-in-law's eyes. "If something does not make sense, we must pursue it."

"Yes," he agreed, nodding. "We haven't much time . . . but I cannot leave Mr. Edison here."

"Give me the keys," Lily suggested. "You go ahead; I shall lock him in. He won't be going anywhere."

"You'll do what?" William demanded, his voice rising and breaking.

But John was already nodding, pulling the ring of housekeeper's keys he had carried for the past few days from his waistcoat pocket and tossing it to Lily. She caught it neatly in two hands. "The rest of you wait in Miss Hartley's room for me. And you—" He fixed William with a narrow look. "I do not like you," he said at last. "And I never have."

There was a stunned silence as he left the room, then Amelia giggled nervously. "I have never heard Sir John say something so rude," she said.

"Poor John," Lily said, shaking her head. "This has all been too much for him. All right. Let us go."

"Wait!" William insisted shrilly, following them to the door. "You cannot just leave me here!"

"We can," Amelia said with undisguised satisfaction, hanging back just long enough to smile at him. "And we shall." She pulled the door firmly shut behind her, stepping aside so that Lily could lock it.

But instead of heading down the hall to Amelia's room, Lily began to climb the stairs.

"Where are you going?" Matthew demanded as both he and Amelia followed her.

Lily passed the third floor and continued upward. "To put these keys to use and set the captain free."

"Raffi?" Amelia exclaimed, a little breathlessly. "Did Sir John say you might?"

"No," Lily said, not looking back. "But we shall need his assistance when we get there."

"Where?" Matthew demanded.

"To the Coleridges' home, of course," Lily said as they reached the attic floor. "John wants to talk to Peter, but we already did that once, and he lied to us. We need to see his private papers. And then we'll know."

"His private papers?" Matthew repeated. "You mean while Sir John keeps him here?"

"How devilish," Amelia panted.

"But hardly honorable," Matthew insisted, following her down the hall.

"It is not," Lily admitted as she unlocked the first door. "But as I told my brother-in-law once before: People lie. Their things do not." They reached the sixth door, and she rapped on it firmly. "Captain, are you there? It is jailbreak time."

It took her a few attempts to find the correct key. When she unlocked the door at last, Jack stood there, grinning at her. "I hope you are not about to get arrested for this," he said, shrugging on his coat.

"If I do, it will be for far worse than releasing you," Lily said, smiling in return. In spite of everything, she felt as though a knot in her chest had unclenched. It was so good to see him once again.

"We are heading to the Coleridges' house while Sir John keeps them occupied downstairs. He does not know we are going. Are you ready?"

"For any particular reason, if I may ask?"

"To find out whether a liar is also a murderer."

"I trust you will explain on the way?"

"Of course. Shall we, Captain?"

"Certainly," Jack said, striding into the hall. "I am, as ever, at your service. Will we have to commandeer horses?"

"And I," Matthew said, following them as they headed toward the servants' stair. "If you are going, Lily, I am as well."

"But what about me?" Amelia cried. "What should I do?"

Jack paused his stride long enough to turn and wrap his arms tightly around her, pressing his cheek against her dark hair. "You must stay here, Noor. This will be no place for you."

"But—" Amelia stared at Lily. "Mrs. Adler!"

"You are in no condition to go charging off after anyone," Lily said, pausing on the threshold. "Please, Amelia, take care of yourself and do as your brother said. We would never forgive ourselves if anything happened to you. Here." She handed Amelia the ring of keys. "When you give these back to Sir John, you can tell him where we have gone." She turned to Jack and Matthew. "Come, we must hurry."

★   ★   ★

Amelia trailed slowly down the stairs, feeling despondent and trembling with what she told herself was emotion, not weakness. While she knew that she was still recovering from the arsenic, she couldn't help feeling . . . She grimaced. Furious. Or perhaps just hurt.

Her brother had offered her an embrace and then left her behind, like a child. And all she had wanted to do was help.

"The carriage that the Lincolns sent will do for Mrs. Coleridge and her son. We want her to be comfortable for the journey home. Luckily, theirs is one of the shorter drives."

Amelia froze, then ran to the banister, peering over the railing to see who was speaking. It was Mrs. Grantham, talking with her elderly butler as they walked down the hall toward the front door. "Have it brought around, please. They are already waiting outside and are more than eager to depart."

Amelia stared around frantically. Where was Sir John? Had he not found Peter in time?

She dashed down the steps, trying to decide what to do. It would be safer, certainly, to find Sir John and tell him where Peter was. But the carriage could be brought around at any moment. If she didn't find him before the Coleridges left, they would come upon Raffi and the others unawares.

Making up her mind in an instant, Amelia dashed toward the kitchen stairs. She could grab one of the servants' cloaks on her way to the stables. A horse was faster than a carriage, especially if the roads were not quite clear. If she saddled one quickly, she could beat them there.

CHAPTER 28

The front hall of the Coleridges' house was bitterly cold and echoed oddly. It took Lily a moment to realize that both effects were due to the lack of carpeting on the floor. Indeed, there were very few furnishings at all. Lily had to blink against the dimness, after the blinding glare of the sun on the snow outside. But once her vision cleared, she could see spots on the walls where she thought paintings had been removed.

"I am sorry, sirs, ma'am," said the nervous maid who answered the door. "But Mr. Coleridge isn't here. Nor Mrs. Coleridge. They've been detained—"

"We know," Jack said, striding past her as Matthew closed the door against the wind. "We are not here to see them. Where is Mr. Coleridge's study?"

"His study?" the girl stammered, glancing between the four of them with terrified eyes. "I can't . . . I'm afraid . . . I'm not allowed in there!"

"No need to fret," Matthew said kindly. "You do not have to go in."

"If I recall, it used to be in the back of the house, by his mother's favorite sitting room," Lily said, striding in that direction. "I've not been here in years, but that's as good a place to begin as any."

"I'm not allowed to let folks inside without Mrs. Coleridge's say-so neither," the girl insisted loudly as they walked past her.

"Well, then, when they return home, you may tell them we forced our way past you," Lily called over her shoulder.

Jack caught up with her as they walked. "They have let go all their servants," he murmured, glancing around. When Lily met his eyes, he added, "You are not surprised to find it so. What do you suspect?"

"I suspect the servants have gone the same way as the art on the walls and Mrs. Coleridge's real pearls. And likely many of her other jewels as well," she said, glancing at the cold, empty rooms they were passing. They had ridden over, as Mrs. Grantham's carriages were all being pressed into service, and she had been able to tell the men only the bare outline of what she expected to find. "And I think, when we look through Peter's papers, we shall find that the condition of his Irish properties is not quite what he has proclaimed it to be." She took a deep breath as they arrived at Peter's study. "Shall we begin our search? We likely only have as long as Sir John keeps them busy. If they can get away, they'll return straight here."

"I shall keep watch, in case any of the servants who are still in residence try to interrupt," Matthew said, lingering on the threshold of the room. "Call me if you find anything."

They didn't waste time. Jack went to the cabinets below the bookshelves, while Lily began to search the desk. Its drawers were remarkably tidy—which didn't surprise her at all, given what she knew of Peter—but they were also remarkably free of papers. No reports from tenants, nothing from his Irish banks. Lily's heart began to race. The absence was enough to convince her. But John, she knew, would require something more.

One drawer held a stack of letters. Lily sifted through them, scanning each opening and signature to see whether it touched on business concerns, but all were old correspondence from friends and relatives.

"Anything?" Matthew called from the doorway.

"Nothing," Jack replied, his frustration plain. "Books, maps, about five years' worth of letters from his aunt Constance. There is a box full of bills, from local tradesmen and the like. Some paid, some unpaid. But nothing out of the ordinary way."

"I've had no luck either . . . Wait." Lily broke off as she pulled at the last drawer and found it locked. "Jack, have you seen any keys tucked about?" Even as she spoke, she was searching the desk's other drawers again, hoping Peter kept his keys close to hand.

"No keys," Jack said, coming to stand next to her. He picked up the silver letter opener from the desk. "But I think I can manage. If you would stand aside?"

Lily watched in amazement as he slid the slim, sharp blade into the lock, pressing one ear very close to it as he wiggled the blade left and right with tiny, careful movements.

"What—" Lily gaped at him as there was a pop of metal on metal. Looking very proud of himself, Jack gave the handle a tug, and the drawer slid open. "Where did you learn to do that?"

He grinned at her, tossing the letter opener in the air with a small flourish and catching it once more. "Where do you think? Jem taught me." He chuckled at the expression on her face. "At the risk of dimming some of that awe, Lily, I have to admit that a lock like this one isn't much at all to get past. It's the sort to foil prying wives and sons, not criminals. Perfect for an amateur like me."

"Well, I am still duly impressed," she said, shaking her head. "Do you mean to say you could have left that attic room at any time, had you wished to?"

"If they had left me something to pick the lock with, yes," Jack said, winking at her. "But no one did that. And even if they had, I had no wish to leave, remember? I made that confession for a very particular reason."

"One I am still angry at you for," Lily muttered, bumping him out of the way so she could look inside the drawer. "But we will deal with that later."

"As you like," he said with a shrug, still fidgeting with the letter opener, until the edge caught his thumb and he grimaced. "Sharp, that. What did we find?"

Lily was pulling out a sheaf of letters, all written in the same hand. "Matthew, I think we found them," she called quietly.

She laid all of the letters on the desk, flipping through the signatures at the bottom. "These are from properties in Ireland," she said slowly, skimming the contents as she spoke. "They . . . it looks as though all of them have been sold, over the last seven years or so."

"All of them?" Jack demanded.

"Well, there is no master list here, but . . ." There had been a ledger in the drawer; when she pulled it out, she discovered it was for household accounts. Flipping back several years, she scanned the income columns. "It looks as though the incomes began dropping . . . there were significant debts . . . They had to sell some of the properties to pay off the debts of others. As well as other things, it seems, to economize. There was no income anymore . . ." She broke off, frowning. "Until about twelve months ago."

"But everyone has been talking of this consolidated fund of his, that he has allowed people to invest in his banking properties," Matthew said, frowning as he took some of the letters from her. "I've grown heartily sick of hearing it mentioned, and it has been only four days."

"If his Irish properties aren't supplying his four thousand a year, or whatever it is, what has he been persuading people to invest in?" Jack asked, taking the account book and stepping aside so that he had more space to flip through its pages.

"In him, it seems," Lily said quietly. "He has begun to repay their debts from their neighbors' pocketbooks. And I've no doubt that Mr. Edison died because he discovered the scheme and sought to profit from his discovery." She lifted her head to look at Jack. "The same way he did with your—"

She broke off as Peter Coleridge strode into the room. "Hello, Lily," he said, almost pleasantly.

Lily heard the sharp, shocked inhales from the men standing next to her. But she didn't turn to look at them. Her attention was fixed on the two figures coming through the doorway.

Mrs. Coleridge stared at them haughtily as she strode across the threshold. Instead of her cane, she was holding a pistol. And its muzzle was tucked just under Amelia Hartley's chin.

CHAPTER 29

"Good afternoon, Mrs. Coleridge," Lily said. The sight of the gun pointed at Amelia was twisting her stomach into panicked knots, but she refused to let her fear show. She needed Amelia—and everyone else in the room—to stay calm. And she needed Mrs. Coleridge to wonder whether she truly had the upper hand. Lily glanced at Jack, the briefest flicker of her eyes, and received only a hint of a nod in response. It would have to do. She shifted toward Matthew, away from Jack, as though seeking his comfort and protection. And she kept talking. "I would say it is a surprise to see you here, but of course it is your house."

"And you are trespassing," Mrs. Coleridge agreed, lifting her chin regally. "You oughtn't to have done that, you know."

"I thought to warn you," Amelia said hoarsely. "But they caught me outside. I am so—" She broke off with a gasp as the muzzle of the gun pressed more tightly against her chin.

"We needed to confirm a few things. I am certain you understand." Lily could feel Matthew shifting his weight next to her and laid a quelling hand on his arm. They couldn't do anything—not yet, not without putting Amelia in more danger. "And hello to you as well, Peter," she said, her eyes narrowing, her smile a mockery of a polite greeting. "Still cowering in your mother's shadow, I see."

"I beg your pardon," he said, pulling himself upright with a great deal of offended dignity. "I never cower."

"You do precious little else," Lily said. She wanted to look at Jack, but she didn't dare. "What is a lie like yours but a man cowering from the truth? You could not bear to admit that you had lost your income or deal with the consequences of your own poor management. So you built a lie, and you hid behind it like a coward while you stole from everyone who believed you."

"How *dare* you—" Peter stepped forward, one hand raised as though he would strike her.

"Peter, do not be a fool," his mother snapped.

He subsided, but not without giving Lily a scornful look. "You always were too mouthy for your own good. You were insufferable when Freddy married you, and you're insufferable now."

"Perhaps," Lily said, undaunted. "But I am not the one here who is guilty of fraud and murder." If Peter thought to put her off balance with insults, he was sorely mistaken in how much she cared for his opinion. And it was clear that he was not the most dangerous person in the room. "So it was you who killed Gregory Edison, ma'am, was it not? After all, Mr. Coleridge was occupied for most of the night. It could hardly have been he."

"Mrs. Coleridge?" Matthew demanded, turning to stare at that lady in shock before looking back to Lily. "Surely not. What . . . how would she . . . and why?"

"Peter has never defied his mother in anything," Lily said, a hint of a taunt in her voice. "She stood to lose as much as he by admitting to their poverty. And she had as much to gain by his fraud. In fact, I would not be surprised if it was her idea. Was it, ma'am?" she asked, a small smile on her lips as she attempted to play to the old woman's vanity.

But Mrs. Coleridge regarded her coldly. "Peter is right," she said. "You talk too much."

"But . . . but why?" Amelia demanded in a strangled voice. She swallowed against the muzzle of the gun, and Lily felt her stomach knot even further. "I still do not understand. Gregory was an ass, to be sure. But most people seemed to like him in spite of that."

Mrs. Coleridge snorted. "Because he was stupid and greedy."

"Rich words, ma'am," Matthew said stiffly.

But she only sneered at him. "I'm no more greedy than most, and I am far from stupid."

"He died because he realized the pearls were fake," Lily said, watching Mrs. Coleridge as she spoke. Amelia was trying to breathe shallowly, staring down toward the gun tucked under her chin. "He found you after the ball, did he not, Peter?" she added. Peter jumped a little at being addressed. "He had concluded that you were in financial difficulties. Selling off paintings, dismissing servants . . . and replacing real gems with fake. And just as he did with Amelia, he attempted to blackmail you. And yet," she added, a hint of a taunt coming into her voice, "it was your mother who dealt with the situation, not you. It was she who was spotted going downstairs. It was she who retrieved the gun from Mrs. Grantham's gun case. And it was she who forced Mr. Edison into the poultry yard and shot him while he was expecting you to join him. Was that because she did not trust you to do it?"

Peter scowled at her. "I did not know what she intended until it was already done," he said, a hint of a whine in his voice. "As soon as I heard he was dead the next morning, I knew what must have happened."

"Peter," his mother snapped.

But he only turned his glare on her. "And then it was *I* who had to help her deal with the mess, which I had never agreed to in the first place!"

"Yes, starting with that promissory note from Gregory," Lily said, nodding. "You had to get rid of that, of course, so Sir John would have no reason to connect the two of you. A simple thing, to spill tea on your shirt and excuse yourself for a brief time. A shame that we found it before it burned completely."

She took a step to the left as she spoke, so that she crossed to Matthew's opposite side.

"Be still!" Mrs. Coleridge snapped, shaking Amelia so hard that the girl gasped.

Lily stayed where she was, but it had been enough. The Coleridges had both turned to keep their eyes on her.

"And you must have been so nervous when we began asking about your mother's pearls. Though, once you understood why, it presented you with an opportunity," she continued. "Discover who Sir John suspected. Then find a way to put the pearls, which your mother had already recovered, with them. Our magistrate would have to conclude that person was guilty of murder. How fortunate for you that so many accusations were being thrown about. You practically had your pick of victims. And then . . ." She shook her head. "Better and better, Mrs. Crewe was caught and confessed to theft. You were more than happy to get everyone else worked up and angry to try to pin as much blame as possible on Mrs. Crewe. Had you any idea before that moment that Mr. Edison had a partner in his crimes?"

"You talk as if we wanted any of this to happen!" Peter exclaimed. His mother tried to hush him, but he continued heedlessly. "All we wanted was to live our lives in comfort. And then Gregory comes along with his *blackmail*—surely you can understand our fury!" he added, turning toward Amelia.

She managed to give him a scornful look, in spite of the deadly position in which his mother held her. "Seeing as I was not moved to embark on a festive round of murders, no, I cannot say that I—" She broke off as Peter took a sudden step toward her.

"I already told you, I did not kill him," Peter yelled.

"Peter, stop *shouting*," his mother ordered. Scowling, he fell silent.

"But you did kill Mrs. Crewe," Matthew said, his voice heavy with quiet fury. "It had to be him, did it not?" he added, glancing at Lily. "Mr. Hounslow tripped over Mrs. Coleridge's cane. Deliberate on her part, I assume? And then Peter had the excuse he needed to go upstairs, slip away from the group under the pretext of changing his clothes, and . . ."

"One almost has to admire the smoothness of how they accommodated and covered for each other over these past few days," Lily said coldly, with no admiration at all in her voice. "Consider what happened when I asked Peter about the structure of his fund. I thought you didn't want to answer because you disliked being questioned by a woman." Lily stared at the man in front of her, who she had so long considered a friend. "And I am so accustomed to such dismissiveness that it surprised me not at all. But that was not the reason, was it?" She watched Peter's jaw tighten as she spoke, and she pressed on relentlessly. "You did not want *anyone* questioning you too closely, because you were terrified of revealing that it was all a sham. You were looking anywhere in the room that you could, not because I made you uncomfortable, but because you were trying to signal to your mother to save you."

"And she did," Matthew recalled, not hiding his astonishment. "By feigning some difficulty that he had to assist her with right away."

"Indeed," Lily said coldly. "Mrs. Coleridge did a great deal of feigning over the past few days, acting progressively more feeble and distressed. All so no one would think her physically or mentally capable of such an act as murder. And none of us questioned it, of course, because who would not be distressed? It seemed the most natural thing in the world for an older woman, whom her own son described as *losing her touch*, to be overcome, to be aged, by such tragedies."

"You think you are underestimated because of your sex, Mrs. Adler?" Mrs. Coleridge snapped. "Ha. Try spending a day as a woman past her prime. They applaud you if you manage to keep your head on your shoulders, never mind have a coherent thought in it."

"You let the facade slip, though," Lily said quietly. "When I startled you this morning, you jumped to your feet quite like your old self. You even forgot about your cane for a moment. I was a fool enough at the time to think surprise alone could account for it. But I got there eventually."

"You've more brains than some," Mrs. Coleridge said grudgingly.

"And more spine than your son," Lily said, not bothering to hide her disdain as she turned toward Peter once more. "I thought you a better man than this."

"She is my *mother*," he said, looking affronted. "And what was I supposed to do? Admit to everyone I know that I had been stealing their money? We were already barely keeping up appearances as it was. Besides, if I had been able to attract more investors this spring, I could have paid the first ones back."

"And on and on, without ceasing?" Lily said. "Tell me, Peter, did you have a plan for how to end it?"

"I did not need one. People are stupid," he snapped. "Where one fellow puts his money, another is bound to follow. And anyway," he added with a sniff, "Gregory had already created a fine opportunity to refresh my accounts. The circumstances of his death only made that easier."

"Ah yes, of course," Lily said, nodding. "Your proposal to Amelia. Couched with such a gentle reminder to her parents that they had promised her a substantial dowry." She frowned. "Then why the arsenic? It is the only thing that does not make sense. You could not get her dowry if she was dead."

"I would never resort to poison," Mrs. Coleridge said, looking disgusted. "Dirty, sneaky way to solve a problem. No, my girl," she said, giving Amelia a shake. "Someone else must hold quite a grudge against you."

Lily frowned. "Then what—"

"We were glad they did not succeed," Peter interrupted earnestly. "My proposal was real, Amelia, and I had every intention of upholding it honorably." For a moment, Lily could see her husband's old friend in his concern, his attempt at a genuine smile. It was chilling. She shuddered, drawing back toward Matthew in search of some comfort.

"I would never have married you," Amelia bit off, trying to yank away from Mrs. Coleridge's grip. "You selfish, deceitful . . . You would have been happy to see me blamed in your place!"

"Don't be a fool," Mrs. Coleridge snapped, tightening her pincerlike grip with a shake. "You would never have been charged without more evidence. And no one else would have wanted to marry you. We were doing you and your family a favor, stupid girl."

Their attention, for the moment, was fixed on Amelia. Lily sneaked a glance at Jack, whom she had so carefully stepped away from while she spoke. His jaw was clenched with the effort to remain silent, but he still had not said a word. And just as Lily had hoped, no one had been watching him.

Lily took a deep breath. She had to keep talking and keep their attention on her. But Amelia was not done.

"And what about my brother? Were you doing him a favor as well?" she demanded.

"We never asked him to confess to anything," Peter said petulantly. "In fact—" He turned toward Jack as he spoke.

And that was when everyone else in the room saw what Lily had known the whole time. In slow, careful, almost imperceptible inches, Jack had been moving closer to his sister. And he was now only steps away.

Lily's feet and lungs both felt frozen, and for a moment she was unable to breathe or move or know what to do. Then—

"Peter!" she called.

Instinctively, his head snapped toward her. That was when Jack charged.

Amelia, realizing in an instant what her brother was about to do, drove her elbow back into Mrs. Coleridge's stomach. The old woman gasped for breath, and the muzzle of the gun wavered, pointing, for just a moment, away from Amelia.

Jack grabbed his sister, yanking her from Mrs. Coleridge's grip and turning to tuck her behind his own body. With a shout, Matthew charged toward Peter, knocking him off-balance and upsetting a table ornamented with paperweights and globes. Peter, who was no fighter, yelped as Matthew's weight drove him to the floor. Jack tried to wrestle the gun from Mrs. Coleridge while keeping it pointed away from both him and Amelia.

The sound of a pistol shot exploded through the room.

For a moment that seemed to last forever, no one moved. Then Jack yanked the gun from Mrs. Coleridge's grip, sending her stumbling to her knees. Matthew managed to grab one of the paperweights and backhanded Peter across the temple with it. He dropped to the floor and did not rise.

That was when Lily saw Jack's left arm hanging limply by his side. He took a step backward, the pistol falling from his grip, as his hand rose slowly toward his left shoulder. He fumbled at his coat, and when his hand came away, it was streaked with blood.

Amelia screamed, catching her brother as he fell, his weight bearing them both to the ground.

Before anyone else could move, Lily had snatched the pistol from the floor. She felt as though she was going to be sick, but her hand was steady as she pointed the gun at Mrs. Coleridge, who was just trying to rise. "I suggest you stay where you are, ma'am. Because if you have killed him, I will shoot you dead, you and your son both."

"You'll be hanged," Mrs. Coleridge snarled, regal no more in her rage and fear.

Lily stared at her, feeling numb. She took a step closer, the gun still held unwaveringly in her hand. "Do you think I care?"

Whatever the other woman saw in her expression seemed to frighten her. She looked down and did not try to stand again. Out of the corner of her eye, Lily could see Amelia, sobbing, yanking off her cloak and pressing it against her brother's shoulder with both hands.

Lily looked to Matthew. "Can you find something to bind them with?" When he nodded and strode from the room, she glanced at Amelia. "Did you ride?"

"Yes," the girl whispered.

"Go for the doctor. Tell him to send a servant for Sir John and anyone who can come help. But the doctor must come here, as fast as he can."

"But Raffi—" Amelia gasped through her tears.

"He needs a doctor now, Amelia. *Now*." Lily took a deep breath, willing the numbness to stay just a little longer. She couldn't afford to be afraid. Not yet. "I won't leave him, I promise."

With another sob, Amelia dashed from the room, just as Matthew returned with a bundle of rope. Outside the door, Lily could hear the little maid crying, but she didn't have time to care. With Peter unconscious and Mrs. Coleridge unresisting, Lily and Matthew were easily able to tie their hands and feet together.

Finally, Lily could lay the gun aside. Her hands were shaking at last as she knelt by Jack and lifted his head into her lap.

"I'll be well," he grunted. "Took off a chunk of me is all." His skin was ashen, and he breathed in deep, shuddering gasps, but he still managed to smile weakly at her. "Got 'em, Lily."

She swallowed. "Once again," she whispered, trying and failing to return his smile. She pressed down on his wound, praying that the shot had indeed gone wide in the scuffle, that the bleeding would stop, that there would be no infection. Her other hand fumbled for his and squeezed tightly. "You're going to be all right."

"'Course I am," Jack gasped, his eyes closing in pain. "Hurts like the devil, though."

"Hold on just a little longer, my friend," Lily whispered. He would be all right, she told herself, her heart knotted with fear. He had to be.

Jack nodded. His whole body was shaking now, and his hand was growing colder in hers. Matthew, who had seen plenty of battlefield wounds, knelt on Jack's other side. He pressed his hand on top of hers, holding the wadded fabric in place with a steady grip. She could feel him watching her, but she couldn't bring herself to look at him, too scared to see what silent message he might be trying to give her.

Beneath her hand, she could feel the frantic beat of Jack's heart—too fast, too much blood pumped too quickly. She closed her eyes against the tears that wanted to come, bending her head until her brow was pressed against his.

"Just a little longer."

CHAPTER 30

"As soon as I confronted her, she started sobbing and admitted to everything," Amelia said, taking a careful sip of her tea. She looked fully recovered, Lily was relieved to see, the weakness that had plagued her after the arsenic poisoning faded at last. "It took me days to recall that I had found her coming out of my room. At the time, I thought she just wanted to say nasty things, since that was what she proceeded to do."

"How did you convince her to come?" Lily asked, glancing toward the second floor, where Kitty Hounslow was currently ensconced with her mother in Sir John's study, her sobs and muffled protests echoing down the stairs.

Amelia added a splash more milk to her tea. "I told her that if she did not accompany me, I would go by myself, so if she wanted the magistrate to hear her side of the story, she had best fetch her coat and be quick about it."

Lily found herself smiling for the first time in days. "A straightforward and simple strategy. I like it very much."

"And a successful one," Amelia added. She shook her head. "She claims she regretted it as soon as she was back in her own room and wanted to tell Sir John what she had done. But she was too scared to admit it." Amelia shrugged. "I do not know if I believe *that*. But I've known her nearly my whole life. I can believe that she did not intend any lasting harm. She was just angry and impulsive and cruel."

"She did come to tell him something and lose her nerve," Lily said slowly, remembering the way the girl had sought out the magistrate and then changed her mind so abruptly. "Still. Most people's impulses, even when they are angry, do not run to poison."

"No," Amelia said with a short, humorless laugh. "But apparently unrequited love can make one do all kinds of stupid things. I am glad I seem inclined to avoid such entanglements." She stared into the fire, clearly not seeing it, and swallowed. "It is hard enough loving one's family and friends, without adding the pain of romance into the mix."

Lily wanted to speak but could not quite bring herself to. They were both thinking of Jack, she knew, though neither one wanted to say his name.

Amelia sniffed, setting down her teacup so she could wipe the tears from her eyes with deliberate briskness. "The Hounslows have never been the sort to consider others as important as themselves. Perhaps this will teach her to think more on the humanity of others, and not simply her judgments of them." She shrugged. "Or at least to keep her uglier impulses in check."

It reminded Lily of what Matthew had said about Kitty and her parents. As though summoned by the thought, he appeared in the doorway of the sitting room, knocking softly.

"Miss Hartley? Sir John has sent word that he would like you to join them once more." He grimaced. "Not to be indelicate, but the shrieking was rather loud, so I think I've gathered what is happening up there. I think he wished for your opinion on any . . ." He hesitated. "Pronouncements he might be considering for Miss Hounslow's future."

"Well, that seems only fair," Amelia said as she stood. "Will you still be here, Mrs. Adler, when I return?"

"I have no other engagements today," Lily replied, glancing out the window. A second snowstorm had swept through the county after they had all left Mrs. Grantham's house, lasting as many days as the first, but it had finally passed. The sun was shining, while the wind whipped gusts of snow and ice across the ground. She shivered and pulled her shawl more tightly around her shoulders, glad for the warmth of the fire and, even more, for the comfort of being somewhere safe. She had no intention of venturing from the house for any great length of time until she was ready to leave Hertfordshire entirely. "I shall see you when you emerge."

Silence settled over the room once Amelia was gone. Matthew strode to the window, looking out at the glittering, icy beauty of the grounds. Lily poured him a cup of tea and carried it to him, putting the saucer on the windowsill for when he wanted to set it down.

"Thank you," he said, taking the cup from her. He took a sip, but he was distracted, and set it aside to take her hand in his. "How are you today?"

"Well," she said, considering the question. "Better, I think. It has not been easy, certainly. As you know." She gave his hand a squeeze. "And you, Matthew? Have you told your children what happened?"

"Enough of it," he said, nodding. "At their ages, it does no good to keep such things from them entirely. They hear whispers, however much I might try to shelter them. Better that they hear the truth from me, so they might ask questions and be comforted, than draw their own conclusions and remain afraid."

"What an excellent father you are," Lily said quietly. "They are fortunate to have you."

"And I them," he said, smiling. "But as you know, they are not the only ones I wish to have in my life." He took a deep breath. "I know the past week has been difficult, to say the least. I can continue to be patient, Lily, but I must ask at least whether I can hold out some hope? If you are still considering—"

"Matthew." Lily cut him off gently. He fell silent, waiting and still, and she knew he could guess what her answer would be. "You are one of the best men I know, and I am more honored by your proposal than I could ever say."

"But?" Matthew asked. He did not look angry, but his mouth had tightened, as though he were holding back his own impulse to argue or persuade her to change her mind.

"But I cannot accept," Lily said. Her voice was quieter than she expected it to be, but it was firm. She knew her answer was the right one.

He slowly released her hand, taking a step toward the window and looking away, his expression unreadable for the moment. Lily held her breath, wondering how he would react. It was impossible, under such circumstances, for their friendship to continue as it had. But her heart twisted at the thought that she might have forfeited his goodwill and good opinion as well.

He turned back at last. "Forgive me for asking," he said, his voice catching a little. "But I must. Do you answer this way because . . . is it the children?"

"No!" Lily's answer came out louder than she intended, so shocked was she by the question. "No, of course not," she continued, more gently. "Matthew, I hope you know me better than that. As honored as I am that you would wish me to be your wife, I am even more honored that you would wish me to be a mother to your children. Little though I think I am suited to such a role," she added, shaking her head. "Knowing that you, who care more for them than you do for yourself, would think me capable of it is the greatest compliment I have ever been paid."

"Then why?" His voice caught on the words, and he cleared his throat. "I will not attempt to change your mind, because I do know you." His smile was sad. "And you would not give your answer if you were not firmly decided. But after our time together . . . I care for you, very much, Lily. I do not think I am wrong in believing that you have grown to care for me. And perhaps even for Eloisa and Matthew."

"You are not wrong," Lily said.

"Is there . . ." He hesitated. "Is it because of what happened to the captain?"

Lily shook her head. He had been there when Jack was shot. She could not blame him for asking. "No."

"Then am I competing with someone else?" He cleared his throat again. "Perhaps with the memory of someone else?"

"No more than I am competing with the memory of your Harriet," Lily replied. "Our first loves stay with us, you know that as well as I. But that should not keep us from living our lives."

"Then why?" he repeated, even more softly. "Please."

She hesitated, then took a deep breath. "Matthew, for all that you have complimented and admired me, for all that you have said you care for me—and I believe you do, because I care for you as well—you have never yet said you love me. And I know you well enough," she continued, watching his eyes slide away from hers almost guiltily, "to know that if you did, you would not hesitate to declare it."

"I ought to have remembered that you notice everything," he said, an edge of bitter humor to his words. "But Lily . . ." He took her hand once more. "Even without it, would a marriage between us truly be so difficult? Many are built on a foundation that is far less solid than care and respect and . . ." His gaze grew heavier. "A great deal of enjoyment."

"It would not be difficult, no," she said quietly. She did not know if she could make him understand, but she owed it to him to try. "But for a woman in my circumstances . . . Had I been given the choice when Freddy was still alive, I never would have chosen this life. But now that it is mine . . . You grew up with the expectation that you would own yourself, Matthew, and since you came of age, you have. So perhaps you take it for granted. But I grew up knowing that I would pass from the ownership of my father to the ownership of a husband. I never expected such a thing, so I did not know to miss it. But now that my life is my own—my time, my property, my very body belong to me and no other—to give that up is an extraordinary thing. And so there must be an extraordinary reason to persuade me to do so."

Matthew had been watching her silently as she spoke, his face a mask of tightly held emotions. Lily squeezed his fingers gently.

"I hope you will tell me if I am wrong," she said. "Do you think a marriage would be something extraordinary for us? Or would it simply be . . ." She glanced around, searching for the right word, before her gaze settled back on his. "Enough?"

He was silent, and Lily was almost afraid to know what he would say when he spoke again. But in spite of the ache in her chest, she did not want to take her words back.

At last, he lifted her hand to his lips. "Lily Adler," he said softly. "The time we have spent together has truly been a privilege. I thank you for it."

"And I you, Matthew. I hope you know that if you ever need anything—you or your children—my door is always open."

He nodded, his fingers sliding from hers as he stepped back. He looked for a moment as though he would say something more. But Lily was left wondering what it might have been as Amelia returned.

"Well, that was unpleasant, to say the least," she said, grimacing. "Oh, Mr. Spencer, my apologies. I hope I did not interrupt you?"

"Not at all," he said smoothly. "I hope you were not too unsettled by your conversation with Miss Hounslow?"

"Not unsettled, no. But I would not be sad to never see her again."

"What have you got there?" Lily asked curiously, gesturing toward the sheets of paper than Amelia had returned with.

Amelia looked down at the papers in her hand as though reading through them one last time. "My letters to Gregory. Sir John still had them." She looked at Lily, a wry smile on her face. "He suggested I burn them."

Matthew gestured her forward. "Then by all means."

Amelia took a deep breath as she stepped up to the fireplace and tossed the papers onto the flames. For a moment their edges crackled, then the fire swept over them in a sudden rush. When it died back down, the letters were blackened ash and nothing more.

"Poor Gregory," Amelia said quietly. "He was hardly a model of virtue. But he did not deserve what happened to him." She sniffed a little, then wiggled her shoulders, as if shaking away a feeling she disliked. "I only hope his brother has learned a lesson from all this, weasely little fellow that he is."

"Even weasels have their place in the world," Matthew said, his laughter sounding forced. He bowed. "Forgive me for leaving so abruptly, Miss Hartley, but I must return to my children. We are to depart tomorrow."

"Matthew—" Lily began, then stopped. She did not know what she wanted to say.

He paused in the doorway, turning to meet her eyes. "It's all right," he said softly. "Please do not worry about us."

Lily caught her lower lip in her teeth to stop it from trembling and nodded. She hated feeling so wrung out by her emotions, but the sensation had been impossible to escape these past days.

Matthew hesitated, then drew himself up. "Good afternoon," he said, bowing politely, before vanishing into the hall.

Lily turned away quickly, crossing back to the tea table and retrieving her cup so she would have something to do with her hands. The tea had gone cold, but she took a long gulp anyway. She needed the sweetness.

"Did something happen, Mrs. Adler?"

The quiet question caught her off guard. She started, setting her teacup down with more of a clatter than she intended. "No, why do you ask?"

"I thought . . ." Amelia shook her head. "Never mind."

"How are your parents?" Lily asked, to change the subject.

Amelia sighed, crossing to the window and staring out at the snow. "It has been hard. To have their neighbors turn on us—on me—so suddenly, and then Raffi . . ." Her mouth trembled, and she sniffed again, fidgeting with the fringe on her shawl. "They think it would be best for me to be absent from the neighborhood for some time."

"And what do you think?" Lily asked gently. As hard as the past week had been for her, she could only imagine how much worse it had been for Amelia. And that was after weeks of rumors and gossip from neighbors she had known her whole life.

Amelia sighed. "I want to get away too," she said quietly. "*Ammi* has been talking of renting a house, in Bath or Lyme Regis. But that would not be possible until the spring at the earliest, perhaps even summer. Which means I have a whole winter yet to survive. And Kitty is not the only one I would be glad to never see again." The look on her face was bleak. "I shall manage, I suppose. It is only a few months."

"I have another idea," Lily said. She waited until Amelia turned to look at her before continuing. "Do you think your parents would allow you to come to London with me?"

"To London?" Amelia stared at her blankly. "With you?"

"If they would feel comfortable with you going away without them, after. . . . after all that has happened. If they would trust me to be your chaperone. If you wanted to, of course," Lily added, starting to feel a little disconcerted by the way Amelia was staring at her.

"Oh, Mrs. Adler," the girl breathed. Her eyes were alight as she seized Lily's hand. "Yes, oh yes, I want to! How soon could we get away?"

"As soon as we like," Lily said, overwhelmed by Amelia's response. "As soon as your parents give their permission."

"They will, they certainly will," Amelia declared. "Oh, I cannot wait. To be one unknown, unremarkable girl among hundreds—thousands, even! How heavenly it sounds. Is that . . . ?" The sound of carriage wheels clattering in the drive made her turn back to the window. "It's my father come to fetch me. We can go ask for his permission now. Come on!"

She dashed from the room, Lily following at a more sedate pace. Amelia's enthusiasm was almost desperate, but she could not blame the girl for that. After all that had happened, Lily would be feeling desperate in her place. She hoped Mr. Hartley would give his permission.

Surely he would. He had to know that it would do his daughter good. And London was not so far away. It would be easy for them to return, if . . . Lily swallowed. If anything changed.

Amelia had run out the front door, leaving it open for Lily to come after. As soon as the carriage stopped, she hurried toward it, jittery and impatient in the cold as she waited for the groom to let down the step.

But when the door swung open, it was not Mr. Hartley who emerged. Lily caught her breath, grabbing at the frame of the door for support.

Jack ducked out from the door of the carriage and straightened, his eyes going directly to her. A smile spread across his face, even as he wobbled a little and had to take the groom's hand to be helped down. His other arm was in a sling, his coat hanging over the heavy white bandage wrapped around his shoulder.

It was the first time Lily had seen him since he was taken from the Coleridges' house, unconscious from the shock of the injury and from losing so much blood. The bullet had gone wide in the struggle, clipping his shoulder and taking a chunk of flesh with it but missing the bones and arteries. But it had been two days before he woke, longer still before they knew whether an infection would set in. And in that time, the snow had kept anyone but his family from seeing him, or even hearing word of how he was. Lily had nearly cried with relief that morning when Amelia told her the doctor believed Jack was at last out of danger.

Amelia had also told her that no one knew yet how the muscles in his arm would recover. But he was there, standing in front of her, while Amelia clasped his uninjured hand, exclaiming with delight to see him walking about and telling him of Mrs. Adler's plan.

Lily smiled at her friend, the expression trembling across her face like a wobbly child just learning to stand and unsure what would happen next. She felt as though someone had clamped a fist around her heart and squeezed, and she could not tell whether the sensation was pain or happiness. "Hello, Jack," she said, the greeting coming out as more of a whisper than she meant.

She had not known, until that morning, whether she would ever have the chance to say those words again.

He smiled back at her, his usual, playful expression mellowed into something gentler, more serious. "Hello, Lily," he replied.

They stared at each other for a long moment, neither of them needing to speak.

"Well?" Amelia asked. She glanced between the two of them, nearly bouncing on her toes, eager and impatient. "When do we leave for London?"

AUTHOR'S NOTE

In April 1815, the volcano Mount Tambora, located in what is today known as Indonesia, erupted. It was a massive event, the largest eruption the world had experienced in at least 1,300 years. Scientists believe it led to a volcanic winter that lowered global temperatures in 1816 by up to a full degree Fahrenheit. The impact was seen across the Northern Hemisphere. Monsoon season was delayed in China and India, while ice dams formed in the middle of summer in Switzerland. Central England experienced frosts as early as August.

It was known as The Year Without a Summer. And if you're a writer who needs an uncommon December snowfall in the middle of England that's severe enough to strand a houseful of people for several days, that makes 1816 a convenient time to set a book.

In the early nineteenth century, Anglo-Indian families like the Hartleys had become less common than they were in the eighteenth century, but they were not surprising either. Many English men who married Indian wives stayed in India; some returned to England with their families. For an upper-class couple like the Hartleys, their wealth and preexisting social status would have gone a long way toward ensuring that their children were accepted into English society. But that acceptance could be precarious. A young woman involved in a scandal like Amelia's risked being ostracized from her community no matter who she was. But, as Lily reflects, being a woman of mixed race made Amelia even more vulnerable to suspicion and social punishment than many of her contemporaries would have been.

To learn more about Anglo-Indian families in the eighteenth and nineteenth centuries, I recommend *White Mughals* by William Dalrymple.

ACKNOWLEDGMENTS

To Whitney Ross, for helping me take this book apart and put the pieces back together in the correct order when I was worried I'd have to start over from scratch.

To Faith Black Ross, for your always-insightful edits, for making sure I had my timeline right once all those pieces were back together, and for your patience when I asked for a new deadline on this one.

To Sarosh Arif, for generously making the time in your schedule to read through Amelia and Jack's story, even with the New Year just around the corner.

To Madeline Rathle, Rebecca Nelson, Dulce Botello, Rachel Keith, Thai Fantauzzi Perez, and everyone else at Crooked Lane books for all the hard and unglamorous work that goes into making these books real. It's a privilege to work with each of you. And you have my deepest thanks for your flexibility during an unexpectedly challenging summer.

To Reagan, Courtney, Kimmie, Alida, Isabel, and all the teachers who make up our village. Our children's lives are richer and brighter with you in them. Mine is too.

To Shannon, Thomas, and Amy, who read some of the earliest chapters and gave such thoughtful notes.

To the Beach Crew, the Behelders, Gemma, Laura, Ryan, Neena, Jim, Andrea, and all the Paljugs. To Oliver and Hazel, who are no help at all, and Brian, who is more help than I could ever ask for. You keep me laughing, keep me working, keep me loved.

And to you, reading this today. I am so grateful for you.